GW00750404

Poppy's Choice

Dilly Court is a No.1 *Sunday Times* bestselling author of fifty-one novels. She grew up in North East London and began her career in television, writing scripts for commercials. She is married with two grown-up children, four grandchildren and three beautiful great-grandchildren. Dilly now lives in Dorset on the Jurassic Coast with her husband.

To find out more about Dilly, please visit her website and her Facebook page:

www.dillycourt.com
/DillyCourtAuthor

Also by Dilly Court

Mermaids Singing
The Dollmaker's Daughters
Tilly True
The Best of Sisters
The Cockney Sparrow
A Mother's Courage
The Constant Heart
A Mother's Promise
The Cockney Angel
A Mother's Wish
The Ragged Heiress
A Mother's Secret
Cinderella Sister
A Mother's Trust
The Lady's Maid
The Best of Daughters
The Workhouse Girl
A Loving Family
The Beggar Maid
A Place Called Home
The Orphan's Dream
Ragged Rose
The Swan Maid
The Christmas Card
The Button Box
The Mistletoe Seller
Nettie's Secret
Rag-and-Bone Christmas
The Reluctant Heiress
A Thimble for Christmas
The Snow Angel

AS LILY BAXTER

Poppy's War
We'll Meet Again
Spitfire Girl
The Girls in Blue
The Shopkeeper's
Daughter
In Love and War

THE RIVER MAID SERIES

The River Maid
The Summer Maiden
The Christmas Rose

THE VILLAGE SECRETS SERIES

The Christmas Wedding
A Village Scandal
The Country Bride

THE ROCKWOOD CHRONICLES

Fortune's Daughter
Winter Wedding
Runaway Widow
Sunday's Child
Snow Bride
Dolly's Dream
The Lucky Penny

Dilly Court

Poppy's Choice

HarperCollins*Publishers*

HarperCollins*Publishers* Ltd
1 London Bridge Street
London SE1 9GF

www.harpercollins.co.uk

HarperCollinsPublishers
Macken House, 39/40 Mayor Street Upper
Dublin 1, D01 C9W8, Ireland

First published by HarperCollins*Publishers* 2025
1

Copyright © Dilly Court 2025

Dilly Court asserts the moral right to
be identified as the author of this work

A catalogue record for this book is available from the British Library

ISBN: 978-0-00-858081-0 (HB)
ISBN: 978-0-00-858091-9 (PB)

This novel is entirely a work of fiction.
The names, characters and incidents portrayed in it are
the work of the author's imagination. Any resemblance to
actual persons, living or dead, events or localities is
entirely coincidental.

Typeset in Sabon Lt Std by HarperCollins*Publishers* India

Printed and bound in the UK using
100% renewable electricity at CPI Group (UK) Ltd

All rights reserved. No part of this publication may be
reproduced, stored in a retrieval system, or transmitted,
in any form or by any means, electronic, mechanical,
photocopying, recording or otherwise, without the prior
permission of the publishers.

MIX
Paper | Supporting
responsible forestry
FSC™ C007454

This book contains FSC™ certified paper and other controlled
sources to ensure responsible forest management.

For more information visit: www.harpercollins.co.uk/green

*For Janet Bird, my neighbour for nearly
thirty years, and always first to have my new book.*

Chapter One

Nine Oaks, Essex, 1899

The walled garden at Nine Oaks held a special place in Poppy Robbins' heart. It was here that Ma and Pa first met, or were literally thrown together by a naughty pony. Poppy had grown up listening to the story of how young Flora Lee, a ward of the wealthy Stewart family, who owned Nine Oaks, had been flung over the animal's head and landed in a vegetable patch where gardener Daniel Robbins was weeding. Flora had come from a troubled background, but had grown up with the daughter of the house, Arabella Stewart. They were as close as real sisters, even after Arabella wed Frederick, the Earl of Dorrington, and Flora married Daniel, the head gardener's son and the love of her life.

Poppy sniffed the bunch of fragrant herbs and laid

them carefully in the trug she was carrying. It was early morning, and dew diamonds sparkled on the fronds of fennel and the spikes of rosemary in the well-stocked bed of herbs. The sun was warm on her back as she walked slowly out of the walled garden. She crossed the ha-ha, that was a notional boundary between Nine Oaks and the grounds of Rainbow's End, the fashionable restaurant owned and run by Poppy's parents. The eighteenth-century manor house, where Poppy had been born and raised, had once been the property of Freddie Ashton's great-aunt, but had been lovingly restored and tastefully modernised by Flora and Daniel. They now ran a very successful business, but Poppy knew that it had not always been so. Her mother had worked tirelessly to create the perfect ambience for those who could afford to dine in an elegant, out-of-town restaurant, surrounded by beautiful gardens that Pa had brought back to life and turned into an oasis away from the crowded city.

'Good morning, Miss Poppy. You're up and about early.' Ted Carlton tipped his cap as he looked up from hoeing the weeds in one of the many rose beds.

'I love the early morning,' Poppy said, smiling. 'I find I can get so much more done before the day gets too busy with deliveries and all the other things that happen by the time we open at noon.' She was about to walk on but she hesitated. 'By the way, did you remember that I asked for pink and white roses for table decorations?'

'Aye, miss. I picked them first thing and put them in buckets of water in the flower room.'

'Thank you, Ted. I knew I could rely on you.' Poppy quickened her pace and headed for the yard, which was surrounded by the stables and various outbuildings. She entered through the back door, which led into a passageway with the various utility rooms leading off it, including the large kitchen and scullery.

The head housekeeper, Mattie Briggs, was standing in the doorway, issuing instructions to Ivy, the new chambermaid, who was looking very unsure of herself. Poppy gave her an encouraging smile.

'How are you getting along, Ivy?'

'Quite well, thank you, Miss Poppy.'

'Off you go, Ivy.' Mattie shooed her away with a wave of her hand. 'You have to watch these young girls, Miss Poppy. They aren't raised as strictly as I was. When I started here, more than twenty years ago, we knew how to carry out orders, but today they are a lazy lot.'

Poppy smiled. 'I'm sure you are more than capable of managing the staff, Mattie.'

'I've had enough experience, to be sure.' Mattie eyed her curiously. 'Can I help you with something, miss?'

'No, thank you. I went out to collect the herbs I need for the dish I intend to make. At least, I will if Ma lets me. I try to relieve her of some of the daily tasks, but she likes things done her way.'

Mattie sniffed. 'They all said it would never work. We was too far out of town, for a start, and no one would travel east of the River Lea for luncheon or dinner. Your ma and pa have proved them wrong. Now, if you'll excuse me, I have work to do before Mrs Robbins comes down to breakfast.'

'Yes, of course.' Poppy was eager to get away and begin her morning routine. Once started, Mattie could go on for hours.

'In the old days, when Lord Dorrington's great-aunt was alive, it was proper for the lady of the house to take breakfast in bed.' Seemingly satisfied that she had had the last word, Mattie walked away with a twitch of her shoulders, as if to demonstrate her contempt for modern ways.

Poppy sighed. Her parents had inherited Mattie Briggs with the house, although she must have been a young girl then and quite far down in the servants' pecking order. Now she had risen to the top in her profession Mattie seemed intent on trying to reverse the march of time.

Poppy was about to enter the flower room when a noise outside in the cobbled yard made her hurry to the back door. Mattie, however, was there before her.

'It's one of those devil's machines,' Mattie cried in panic. 'Horseless carriages are the curse of Satan. Who has the nerve to drive one onto our property? Shall I send them packing, Miss Poppy?'

Poppy laughed. 'No, it's all right, Mattie. Go about your business. I'll deal with this.'

She stepped outside, closing the back door so that Mattie had little choice other than to do as she was told. Poppy hurried out to greet the young man who leaped out of the motor car, taking off his goggles and hat and flinging them onto the seat as he walked towards her.

'Poppy, you look as fresh as a summer morning and yet you work hard to earn your living. I am full of admiration for you.' He picked her up and swung her round, setting her feet on the ground as he kissed her on the cheek.

'Adam Ashton, you scared our housekeeper to death. She thinks you brought the devil's machine to Rainbow's End.'

'There don't seem to be many motor cars in this part of the world.' Adam held her at arm's length. Warm honey-coloured flecks gleamed in his smiling dark eyes, and his generous lips curved in a mischievous grin. 'You are prettier than ever. Are you still slaving away in the kitchen and waiting on ungrateful gluttons?'

'I wouldn't put it like that. You love teasing me, but I refuse to rise to the bait.'

He slipped his arm around her waist. 'Since you are the daughter of a famous restaurateur, could you throw a couple of eggs and some bacon in a pan, and maybe a slice or two of toast? I'm absolutely starving.'

Poppy wriggled free from his grasp and opened the door. 'I thought your papa always brought his favourite chef to Nine Oaks when he and your mama are visiting.'

'Not this time.'

'Why not?' Poppy led the way into the large kitchen, set up to work on a professional scale, with rows of copper pans hanging from a beam over the vast black-leaded range, and an array of chef's knives set in wooden blocks.

'Mama chose to remain in Dorrington Place, for a while at least. Young Afterthought has chicken pox or some such thing, so he has to be cosseted and pampered because he's the youngest.'

Poppy laughed. 'You are cruel, Adam. You know you love little Arthur. He can't help being ten years younger than you and Charlotte.'

'I know and I love him dearly, when he isn't being an utter nuisance. Poor chap was covered in a red rash and miserable as sin when Lottie and I left home. Papa has business in London so we opted to stay at Nine Oaks instead of the house in Piccadilly.'

'I haven't seen Lottie for ages, or you, come to that.' Poppy unhooked a frying pan and set it on the hob. 'Be a dear and fetch a bowl of eggs from the larder.'

Adam did as she asked. 'I wasn't expecting to be a sous chef.'

'I hope you aren't too grand to help a little, Viscount Ashton.'

'You know better than that. Anyway, I've passed out of Sandhurst so I'm now Second Lieutenant Ashton.'

'Really? Congratulations. Why didn't you send me an invitation to your passing-out parade?'

Adam's smile was replaced by a frown. 'I did. Of course, I did. You know I wouldn't forget you.'

'I didn't receive it.' Poppy sliced several rashers from a joint of smoked bacon and tossed them into the hot pan. 'Oh, well. It doesn't matter, I would probably have been too busy here anyway.'

'I promise I did send you an invitation, or rather I told my batman to include you as well as my family. I'll have severe words with Watkins when I go back to the barracks.'

Poppy stopped what she was doing to give him a searching look. 'You really are a serving soldier, then?'

'Of course. Didn't you think I would last the course?'

Poppy laughed and turned back to the sizzling pan. 'To be honest, yes, that's exactly what I thought. You've never stuck at anything in your life. Admit it, Adam.' She cracked three eggs into the pan.

'You're right, but that was before. Now I'm a soldier of the Queen and proud to be so.'

'I'm sorry I misjudged you.' Poppy lifted the pan off the heat and set it down on a trivet. 'Pass me a plate, please, Lieutenant Ashton. If it's not beneath you.'

Adam reached for a plate from the dresser, which took up a whole wall. He rounded the table and put it down, but before Poppy could move he slipped his arms around her waist.

'You do still love me, though?'

'Of course I do. We pledged our troth when we were eleven and twelve years old, and you wound a stem of grass round my ring finger.'

Adam caught hold of her left hand. 'You're not wearing it now. I'm heartbroken.'

'You are nothing of the sort.' Poppy wriggled free in order to serve the bacon and eggs. 'Now eat this up and let me get on with my jobs. This is a busy establishment. We have to earn our living and Mama will be down at any moment.'

Adam picked up the plate and, without the need to ask, went straight to the cutlery drawer. 'Your mama loves me, too. You know she does. I am the eldest of our little gang of friends, or rather I should say that Lottie and I share that distinction. However, I came first and she entered the world some fifteen minutes later, or so I've been told.'

'Where is she now? I've really missed her.'

Adam pulled up a chair and sat down to start on his meal. 'She's probably in bed or being pampered by her maid. I don't know what takes you ladies so long to get dressed and make yourselves presentable.'

Poppy took a seat opposite him. 'I don't have time for all that fussing. I get up early and start work straight away.' She held up her hand as he was about to speak. 'And I love what I do, Adam. I'm not complaining.'

'I believe you, but it seems a dashed dull life for a young woman like you.' Adam applied himself to enjoying his breakfast.

'I don't know anything else,' Poppy said thoughtfully. 'I grew up here at Rainbow's End and I started helping out as soon as I could walk. In fact, I much preferred working in the kitchen or in the garden to attending lessons at the village school.'

Adam pushed his plate away and sat back in his chair. 'All I remember are the long summer days roaming round the flat Essex countryside with you, Lottie and that tall, gangly boy – the doctor's son from that old house on the edge of Hackney marshes.'

'You mean Gideon Taylor?'

'I suppose so.' Adam shrugged. 'Something like that. He was always hanging around.'

'Gideon is my friend,' Poppy said firmly. 'His father is a doctor and his mother is a couturier of some note. All the fashionable ladies in London go to her for their elegant clothes, your mama included.'

Adam laughed. 'And is Gideon going to follow in his mama's footsteps? Does he design gowns for rich women?'

'No, Adam. Gideon is at medical school. He's going to be a famous surgeon one day, so there's no need to be nasty about him.'

'There, there, Poppy. Don't get on your high horse. I was joking, of course.'

'I know you only too well, Adam Ashton. It wasn't funny.'

He held up his hands in a gesture of submission. 'I'm sorry. What more can I say?'

His expression was so comical that it made Poppy laugh. 'You are ridiculous.'

'That's a nice thing to say to an old friend.'

Poppy turned her head to see her mother standing in the doorway. Sunlight streamed in from a window in the corridor, creating dazzling copper highlights on her carefully coiffed red hair. The passing of the years had been kind to Flora Robbins, adding just a few laughter lines to her lovely face, and her green eyes had lost none of their sparkle or intensity. At the age of forty she was a handsome woman with a sharp sense of humour and a successful business. Poppy adored her mother, and although people told her that she was a younger version of Flora, with similar hair and eye colouring and a complexion of peaches and cream, she never quite believed them. Mama was her idol and her role model, and Poppy was proud of Mama's achievements. However, Poppy dreaded the day when she would have to admit that her heart was not as involved with Rainbow's End as those of her parents. She did not want to disappoint them, but sometime soon she would have to break free and find her own way in the world. This, though, was not the moment. She rose to her feet.

'Adam is a fully fledged second lieutenant in the army, Mama. He's come to show off and scare the life out of people with his horseless carriage, starting with Mattie.'

Adam was already on his feet and he enveloped

Flora in an affectionate hug. 'Good morning, Aunt Flora. I may still call you that, mayn't I?'

Flora returned the embrace. 'Of course you can, Adam. I wouldn't have it any other way.'

'Even though we are not related,' Poppy said with a wry smile. 'We have to grow up sometime, Adam.'

'Of course, but allow me to wallow in nostalgia for a few moments. I'm expecting to receive my posting at any time now, and I want to remember all this when I'm away from home.'

'Are you being sent away soon?' Poppy demanded sharply. Although it might seem obvious that a serving officer would be posted abroad, she had not imagined that it would happen so quickly.

'To be honest, I don't know, but there's more trouble brewing in the Cape Colony, and it's quite possible I might be among the next contingent to be sent there.'

Flora laid her hand on his sleeve. 'Oh, my dear boy. That's awful. I mean to say, it's so far away, and I remember hearing about the atrocities that happened during the last war with the Boers. What do your parents think about it?'

Adam pulled a face. 'Well, you can imagine that Mama is not too thrilled, but Papa says if the call comes then I must do my patriotic duty, and of course I agree with him.'

'Naturally,' Flora said, smiling. 'I always knew you were bound for greatness, Adam. No doubt we

11

will be reading about you in the newspapers and you'll be a hero.'

'Don't encourage him, Mama. He's very full of himself as it is.' Poppy rolled her eyes.

'I was going to take you for a spin in my motor car,' Adam said with mock severity. 'But as you are being disrespectful to an officer and a gentleman, I think I will withdraw that offer.'

'Stop bickering, children.' Flora gave Adam a gentle push towards the doorway. 'Take her for a drive, Adam. It will blow the cobwebs away and she'll come home refreshed and with renewed enthusiasm.'

Poppy was suddenly alarmed. Had Mama read her thoughts? That would be dreadful. She wanted to pick the right moment to admit her feelings and that was definitely not now.

'But, Mama, we have a large luncheon party arriving at midday.'

'My dear girl, I could manage that with my hands tied behind my back, metaphorically speaking. I have plenty of help in the kitchen today and they'll be arriving at any moment. Now, do as Adam suggests. Take the morning off and enjoy yourself.'

'There, Poppy. You have your mama's permission,' Adam said, grinning. 'Or are you afraid to go for a drive in my horseless carriage?'

Poppy tossed her head. 'Of course not. Although I dare say you are a terrible driver, just as you were when handling a carriage and pair.'

12

'I'm an officer in the British Army, not a coachman, but driving a motor car is another matter. Come with me and I'll show you.'

It was good to feel the wind in her hair, although Poppy knew that Mama would disapprove if she knew that her daughter was being driven at a reckless speed along the country lanes and, even worse, that she had taken off her bonnet and gloves and was clinging to the side of the car for dear life. She was enjoying the exhilaration of discovering automotive speed, even though she shouted at Adam when he sent a flock of hens scattering in all directions and startled an old man who was pushing a barrow laden with early potatoes.

'Don't go so fast,' Poppy cried, trying not to laugh as she looked back to see the man shaking his fist at them. 'He nearly lost his crop of potatoes, thanks to you tooting that wretched horn at him.'

Adam laughed. 'Would you rather that I ran him over?'

'Heaven help the Boers, that's all I can say. I hope they don't allow you to drive a motor vehicle in the army.'

'No, we have plenty of soldiers to take on that responsibility.'

'Just as well, if you ask me. You would kill more of the enemy on the road than with your gun.' Poppy turned her head to study his profile. 'I suppose you do have a gun?'

'Not on me at the moment. The powers that be are a bit fussy about who goes round armed, especially in peacetime.'

'Do you ever take anything seriously, Adam?'

'Life is too short. I want to enjoy every last minute I have on this earth.'

Poppy's smile faded. 'Don't say things like that. It sounds as if you expect to be killed.'

'It's a possibility. But don't let us get morbid. I have you all to myself for a change. I intend to enjoy every minute.'

'I'd like to see Lottie. Shall we call for her and make a threesome?'

'That wasn't my intention, but if that's what you want, that is what we will do.' Adam turned the wheel sharply and swerved into a lane that led directly to Nine Oaks, the estate that his mother had inherited from her parents.

'I'd like to arrive there in one piece,' Poppy said breathlessly.

Adam's response was to laugh and toot the horn, terrifying a curious cow so that it bellowed loudly and raced away to the other side of the field.

'You are a frightful show-off, Adam Ashton.' Poppy patted her hair in place. 'I'll look as if I've been dragged through a hedge backwards, and with you driving that's a distinct possibility.'

'You've hurt my feelings now.' Adam braked hard, bringing the motor car to a sudden halt. 'You're so clever, Miss Robbins. Let's see you drive.'

He leaped out of the car and strode round to open the passenger's door. 'Out you get. Let's see what you can do.'

'Now you're being silly. I don't know how to work this contraption.' Poppy glared at him, refusing to budge, but with a sudden swoop he lifted her bodily and marched around the vehicle to dump her down in the driver's seat.

'I'm deadly serious.' Adam slammed the door. 'This is your first lesson,' he said as he settled himself in the passenger seat. 'You'll need to drive when I am not around to act as your chauffeur.'

She turned her head, expecting to see him smiling, but she realised with a shock that he was serious. 'This is madness, Adam,' she said nervously.

'Don't tell me that you're scared. You were always the first to accept a challenge when we were younger.'

'That's right – when we were younger. I'm older and wiser now. Please get back into the driver's seat, Adam.'

He shook his head. 'Oh, no. You don't get out of it that easily. Sit facing the front, take the wheel in both hands and I'll go through it one step at a time.'

Poppy met his dogged expression with a sigh. 'You think I can't do it – well, I'll show you, Adam.' She grasped the wheel. 'Now what?'

Chapter Two

Lottie gazed at Poppy in amazement. 'You didn't really drive that terrifying machine, did you, Poppy?'

Poppy laughed. 'Indeed I did. Although I have to admit I was a bit nervous to start with, but I persevered.'

'And she only killed two chickens and maimed one of the under-gardeners,' Adam added, grinning.

'Liar.' Poppy smiled and shook her head. 'He's teasing you, Lottie. But I did drive the horseless carriage, as Mattie would have it. She was so terrified when Adam drove it into the back yard that she fled. Anyway, I brought it to a stop in front of your house. I thought poor old Pickering was going to have a heart attack when he saw me alight from the vehicle.'

'He's an antique,' Adam said before his sister had a chance to speak. 'The old fellow should have been pensioned off years ago.'

16

'He's not used to modern ways.' Lottie frowned at him. 'Don't be unkind, Adam. You know that Pickering was Grandpapa's butler in the London house for years before he came here. He's devoted his life to this family.'

'I was only saying . . .'

Poppy held up her hand. 'Stop arguing, you two. I came here because I wanted to see you, Lottie. How are you, anyway? Did you meet an eligible gentleman during the Season?'

Adam had been sitting in a chair by the window in the morning parlour but now he jumped to his feet. 'I don't want to listen to a lot of chitchat about the wretched Season. Let's go out for a drive in the motor car. You, too, Lottie.'

'I don't think I want to go in that contraption, Adam,' Lottie said nervously. She brushed a strand of dark hair back from her flushed cheek, her brown eyes troubled. 'Let's send for the carriage.'

Adam eyed her warily. 'I'll wager you wouldn't say no if Gideon Taylor was driving.'

Poppy gasped. 'That's not fair, Adam. Don't tease her.' She had always known that Lottie had a soft spot for handsome Gideon Taylor, but Poppy also knew that Lottie was sensitive and easily hurt by her brother's careless remarks.

'Lottie knows I don't mean it,' Adam said carelessly. 'Come with us, please, Lottie. I promise not to embarrass you again, and I will drive as if you were a very old lady on her way to matins.'

Lottie picked up a needlepoint cushion and threw it at him, narrowly missing his head. 'I just don't want to die in a road accident.'

'Where shall we go?' Poppy said, hoping to change the subject. 'What were you planning, Adam?'

'I wasn't thinking of anything in particular. It's a lovely day and I'm feeling benevolent. You ladies may choose.'

Poppy and Lottie exchanged amused glances.

'Well, there happens to be a fair on Wanstead Flats.' Poppy had heard about it from diners at Rainbow's End, although at the time she had little hope of going there. Now it seemed like a wonderful opportunity. 'What do you think, Lottie? I know I would love to go.'

'It does sound exciting.' Lottie glanced anxiously at her brother. 'It's quite a long drive, Adam. Would your motor car make it that far?'

Poppy tried not to smile. The brother and sister might argue, but Lottie knew exactly how to get the better of Adam without so much as a harsh word or the need to resort to bargaining.

Having agreed to the outing, Lottie made them wait while she searched for a suitable bonnet with a veil to protect her skin from road dust, as well as a pair of goggles. Adam said that they made her look like a frog, which started another argument. Poppy mediated, and when peace was restored they were ready to leave Nine Oaks. However, once settled in the automobile,

18

Lottie insisted that Adam should keep strictly to the speed limit of fourteen miles an hour. Poppy had to agree, if only for the sake of stray animals and unwary pedestrians. Adam complied with a set jaw, and thankfully the journey was uneventful.

It was midday by the time they arrived at the fairground on the wide green expanse of Wanstead Flats, which abutted Epping Forest. They were immediately surrounded by a crowd of adults and children, all eager to look at and touch the new-fangled machine.

'Anybody would think we'd arrived from outer space,' Lottie said nervously as she moved closer to Poppy in order to avoid a young boy's grubby fingers as he ran them over the bodywork.

Poppy laughed. 'Is this the first horseless carriage you've seen?'

The tousle-haired urchin gave her a gap-toothed grin. 'Nah, miss. Me dad has three of 'em parked outside our mansion.'

'You cheeky little brat. Go away,' Lottie said crossly.

Poppy ruffled the boy's hair. 'Best get back to the mansion then, old chap.'

'Spare a copper for some hokey-pokey, miss?'

Adam put his hand in his pocket and tossed some small change onto the grass, which had the desired effect of diverting the children's attention. He sprang from the driver's seat and helped Lottie to alight, but Poppy, always independent, climbed down from the other side of the vehicle.

19

'What shall we do first?'

Adam frowned thoughtfully. 'I don't like to leave the motor unattended.' He beckoned to the boy who had spoken to Poppy. 'Here, sonny. Do you feel like earning sixpence?'

'Who do I have to kill, sir?'

'Less of your cheek. If I leave you in charge of my motor car, will you make sure that no one touches it? Threepence for you now and the rest when I return, providing there is no damage. What do you say?'

'Saul Martin's the name, guv. I'm your man.'

Adam pressed a coin into the boy's hand. 'It's a deal, Saul. I expect you to keep your side of the bargain.'

Saul saluted and leaned nonchalantly against the side of the car. 'You hear that?' he called out to the other children. 'I'm in charge. Touch the horseless carriage and you're in for it.' He fisted his hands.

Poppy linked arms with Lottie. 'Come on, let's see what the fair has to offer.'

'Best keep close to me,' Adam said firmly. 'There are some dodgy characters hanging around.'

'One look at you and they'll run a mile.' Poppy linked her free hand in the crook of his arm. 'Let's just enjoy ourselves, Adam. I'm sure we are safe enough. There are plenty of families here and it is broad daylight.'

'I can hear a Dutch organ,' Lottie said excitedly. 'Look, there's the merry-go-round. I really would love to have a ride.'

'Me, too.' Poppy tugged at Adam's arm. 'You may stand and watch if it's beneath your dignity, Lieutenant.'

'You girls go ahead. I fancy my hand at the coconut shy.' Adam walked with them to the merry-go-round, but he strolled away when they were settled on the horses' backs.

Lottie uttered a cry of delight as the ride began, but Poppy was amused to see that she was holding on for dear life, as if she half expected the painted wooden horse to break into a gallop and carry her off across the sweep of flat ground. When the ride was finished the fairground attendant had to help Lottie to alight and she swayed a little, holding her hand to her forehead.

'I feel as though I'm still going round.'

'You'll be all right in a minute.' Poppy glanced over her shoulder. 'I can't see Adam. Shall we go and look for him, or shall we be very daring and explore by ourselves?'

'I think I would like to sit down for a moment, Poppy. I feel a bit sick.'

'I can't see any seats, but we could find a sunny spot and sit on the grass for a while.'

'I don't want to get my gown dirty.'

Poppy was beginning to lose patience, but she could see that Lottie was very pale and close to tears. 'There's a refreshment tent. Perhaps you'll feel better if you have a drink or maybe something to eat.'

'Yes, maybe.'

'Come on then. Hold on to my arm and we'll walk slowly until you get your land legs again.'

They made their way towards the refreshment tent, weaving in and out of the throng of people out for the day and enjoying themselves. Just as they reached the tent Poppy spotted a familiar figure striding towards them. She dragged Lottie to a halt and waved.

'Look who's here, Lottie.'

Lottie shaded her eyes and was suddenly alert. 'Gideon. What a surprise.'

The tall young man doffed his hat and his fair hair gleamed in the sunlight. 'Lady Charlotte. I'm delighted to see you, and Miss Robbins, too.'

'It's just Lottie.' A rosy blush banished the pallor from Lottie's cheeks.

Poppy held out her hand. 'It's good to see you, Gideon. But why so formal? We used to be good friends.'

'I'm sorry, I didn't mean to sound pompous, it's just that I've been away at medical school for so long I thought my old friends would have forgotten me.' Gideon glanced around. 'Is Adam here? The last I heard he was at Sandhurst, but that was some time ago.'

'He's a fully fledged second lieutenant now,' Lottie said proudly.

'And he's here somewhere,' Poppy added. 'We should go and find him. He'll be pleased to see you, Gideon.' She shot a sideways glance at Lottie.

'Although we were going to go into the refreshment tent and get something to eat and drink. Lottie felt a bit faint just now.'

Gideon's blue eyes narrowed with concern. 'Do you want to sit down, Lottie? I'm sure I can find you a seat in the shade.'

She shook her head. 'It's passed now. I think it was just the motion and speed of the merry-go-round. I really do feel much better.'

'All right, but just tell me if you feel unwell.' Gideon gave her a sympathetic smile. 'Perhaps some light refreshment is called for.'

'Just what I thought.' Poppy made for the tent entrance, leaving them to follow her. It was a fortunate coincidence that led them to cross paths with Gideon, and she was sure that Adam would find them easily enough.

The inside of the marquee smelled of warm grass, crushed underfoot, and hot tea. Most of the tables and chairs were occupied, but Poppy spotted one at the back of the tent and she threaded her way between the diners, catching snatches of conversation as she went. It was important to get Lottie fed before she collapsed, although of course Gideon was there to catch her if necessary.

Gideon gallantly fetched a tray of tea and cakes. 'They had sold out of pies and sausage rolls,' he said apologetically.

'The cakes look delicious,' Lottie lied politely.

Poppy thought they looked dry and tasteless but

she merely smiled and nodded as she poured the tea into thick china cups. 'Have you finished medical school now, Gideon? We seem to have lost contact during the past year.'

He offered the plate of rock cakes to Lottie. 'Yes, I'm fully qualified now, although I intend to keep up my studies while working. I want to specialise in paediatrics: treating sick children. In the meantime, I am assisting my father in his practice, which has grown considerably over the years.'

'Does that mean you will continue to live in Marsh House?' Lottie selected the smallest cake and placed it on her plate. 'I have fond memories of playing in the gardens when we were children.'

Poppy laughed. 'I remember you falling out of the dead tree, Gideon. You said it had been struck by lightning but no one had the heart to chop it down.'

'It's still there, but my tree-climbing days are over. I seem to remember that I broke my arm and had to have it in a plaster cast for weeks.'

'I always thought that Adam had pushed you,' Lottie said, sighing. 'He was a rough boy when we were younger.'

'Well, here he comes now.' Poppy stood up and waved. 'You can put it to him, Gideon. Maybe he'll admit it after all these years.'

Adam made his way towards them, stopping twice to acknowledge people who recognised him.

'Gideon. I wasn't expecting to see our illustrious medical friend here today.' Adam pulled up a chair and sat down. 'Is there any more tea in the pot, Poppy? I'm parched.'

'I'll get a refill.' Gideon was about to rise to his feet but Adam shook his head.

'I think they've closed the counter. Probably run out of everything, judging by the crowds. I'll finish off what Lottie has left.'

'You might ask first.' Lottie pouted as he picked up her cup and drank the last drop of tea. 'Your manners haven't improved during your time at Sandhurst.'

'There is more tea in the pot.' Poppy refilled the cup and offered it to Lottie, who shook her head.

'I don't want it now.'

'Contrary as ever.' Adam grinned and took another mouthful of tea. He eyed the remaining cake on the plate. 'Will I upset anyone if I eat the last one?' He waited for a second and then seized the cake, taking a large bite. 'I've had better, but it fills a gap. Now, Gideon, old chap. It's good to see you. We must go out for a few drinks this evening and we can have a proper chat.'

Gideon nodded. 'I'd like that. Luckily I'm not on duty until tomorrow morning.' He turned his attention to Lottie and Poppy. 'But for now I suggest we do what the ladies choose.'

'You are a gentleman,' Poppy said, looking pointedly at Adam. 'Some people only think of themselves.'

'I'd like to visit the stalls and see what they have to offer,' Lottie added without giving Adam a chance to respond to Poppy's veiled criticism.

Gideon stood up and proffered his arm to Lottie. 'May I escort you, Lady— I mean Lottie?'

She rose quickly to her feet and laid her hand on his sleeve. 'Thank you, Dr Taylor.' A mischievous dimple and a flutter of her eyelashes added to a sweet smile.

Poppy rolled her eyes. She could see how the rest of the day was going, and that meant she would be thrown together with Adam whether she liked it or not. The fact that she was perfectly happy to be in his company was irrelevant. She loved Lottie like a sister, but like an older sibling she could be irritating at times.

'Come on, then, Poppy.' Adam took her by the hand. 'It looks as if it's you and me.'

'I suppose I can put up with you for half a day.' Poppy allowed him to help her up, and she tucked her hand in the crook of his arm as they made their way between the tables and out into the fresh air once again.

Lottie and Gideon had strolled on ahead, stopping at each stall to study the array of objects on show, from china fairings to brightly painted dolls and assorted bric-a-brac. There was a stall selling candy floss, which the man made by heating sugar in a large metal pot over a brazier. People gathered around watching him spin the molten sugar on forks until it resembled sparkling strands of thread. Gideon purchased some for Lottie, but Poppy shook her head when he offered to treat her, too.

'I haven't got a sweet tooth, thank you, anyway, Gideon.' She glanced up at Adam. 'And if you say I'm sweet enough already I will hit you with my reticule.'

He pulled a face. 'I wouldn't dare. You are many things, Poppy, and I admire them all, but you are not sickly sweet.'

She laughed. 'I'm not sure how to take that. But, look.' She pointed to a showman waving a large hammer and challenging gentlemen to prove their strength. 'Show me how strong you are, Lieutenant.'

'You'll be amazed,' Adam said confidently. 'Come and watch.'

'I must see this.' Lottie tugged at Gideon's hand. 'Adam is always boasting. Let's see what he can do.'

They all converged on the high striker stand and Adam paid for three attempts. The first two failed but, after shouts of encouragement from Poppy, he succeeded at last in ringing the bell. Then Gideon had to have a turn to see if he could beat Adam, which he did on the second attempt. The competitiveness was becoming serious and Poppy defused the situation by encouraging them to move on to the stall where, for a penny, they could try to hook wooden ducks from a barrel filled with water. They all had a go at this and Lottie surprised everyone by winning. Good humour was restored and they strolled on, stopping to buy paper pokes filled with boiled sweets.

They walked slowly round the perimeter of the fairground, laughing and talking, but were brought to a sudden halt by a blood-curdling scream. A young woman emerged from the forest and ran towards them, her gown torn and her hair dishevelled. She was sobbing uncontrollably as she collapsed at Gideon's feet.

He kneeled down at her side. 'Are you hurt, miss?'

Poppy dropped to the warm grass. She put her arms around the girl and held her. 'She's obviously had a terrible fright. Fetch some water or something for her to drink from the refreshment tent, Adam.'

'Poor thing,' Lottie said tearfully. 'What can have upset her so?'

Gideon prised the girl gently from Poppy's arms. He ran his hands gently over her limbs. 'She doesn't seem to have broken bones, and I can't see any traces of blood.' He brushed the girl's tumbled golden locks back from her face. 'You're safe now, miss. Can you tell us what happened? Did someone hurt you?'

'What's your name?' Poppy asked gently.

'Miranda. Don't let him get me.' The girl attempted to rise to her feet, but Gideon restrained her.

'Take a moment, Miranda. No one is going to harm you. Who is this person? Did he hurt you?'

Miranda shook her head. 'I fought him off.' She glanced towards the forest. 'I was minding my own business when he jumped out at me. He stole my things.'

Adam came hurrying towards them with a glass of water and a smaller spirit glass. 'How is she?'

Poppy took the water from him and bent down to hold it to Miranda's lips. 'I don't think she needs the brandy or whatever it is, Adam. A sip of water should suffice.'

'This is for me. It's for shock.' Adam downed the brandy in one gulp.

'You are horrible,' Lottie said angrily. 'The poor girl was attacked and robbed and you're drinking alcohol.'

'You should go after the attacker, Adam. He should be brought to justice.' Poppy frowned. 'You might be able to get back what was stolen.'

'He'll be far away by now,' Adam said firmly. 'We'd never find him in the forest anyway.'

Gideon rose to his feet. 'Can you stand, Miranda? We'll take you to the nearest police station and you can report the crime.'

'I'm all right now.' Miranda stood up with his help. 'It's no use telling the cops. They'll think I'm lying.' She adjusted her torn bodice. 'He took all me clothes. I got nothing else but what I stand up in.'

'You poor thing.' Lottie wiped tears from her eyes with a hanky embroidered with her initials.

'Where were you going?' Adam asked gently. 'Can I take you somewhere in my motor car?'

'I was looking for work.' Miranda's voice broke on a sob. 'I can't go knocking on doors looking like this.'

'That settles it.' Poppy slipped her arm around Miranda's shoulders. 'You must come home with us and we'll find you something to wear. You've had a terrible fright and you should rest. Isn't that so, Gideon?'

He nodded. 'Yes, you should rest, Miranda. But where is your home? Maybe you should return there until you are better?'

'No. I can't never go back there. I don't really have a proper home. I was raised in the workhouse. I don't know who my parents were.'

Poppy gave her a hug. 'That settles it. You must come home with me. We have a huge house with plenty of rooms. I'm sure my mama will allow you to stay until you feel well enough to continue your journey.'

'Ta, miss. You are all very kind.' Miranda wiped her streaming eyes on her sleeve.

They returned to Rainbow's End, having parted with Gideon, who promised to call on Adam later on in the day. Adam dropped the girls off at the front entrance before driving round to park in the stable yard. Miranda was still in a tearful state and obviously suffering from the shock of what had happened to her. She leaned heavily on Poppy as they entered the front hall where they were met by Flora, who looked up from checking the restaurant bookings. She closed the large, leather-bound diary and laid it neatly on the reception desk.

'Who is this?' Flora asked suspiciously.

Poppy stared at her mother in surprise. She had expected a warmer welcome for the unfortunate stranger.

'Her name is Miranda, Mama,' Poppy said in

a low voice. 'She has suffered a dreadful attack in the forest. You can see the state she's in, and all her possessions were stolen.'

'That's terrible.' Flora lowered her voice. 'Shouldn't you have taken her to her own home, Poppy?'

'She said she has no home. She was looking for work, Mama.'

'Miranda grew up in the workhouse,' Lottie added. 'That must have been awful.'

Flora drew Poppy aside. 'What was she doing all alone in the forest? That seems odd in itself.'

'She hasn't been in a fit state to be cross-examined,' Poppy said stiffly. 'I thought you would be more sympathetic, Mama.'

'Normally I would, although you can't be too careful these days. However, it's obvious that she needs help.' Flora turned to Miranda with a genuine smile. 'I'm sure Poppy can find you something to wear and you may rest here for a while. Where were you headed?'

'I was looking for work wherever I could find it, missis.' Miranda sniffed and wiped her eyes on her sleeve.

'I'll find her a change of clothing,' Poppy said firmly. 'Perhaps she could stay here for a little while, until she's recovered from the shock of being brutally set upon.'

Flora's green eyes darkened. 'We know nothing of this person, Poppy. We could be harbouring a criminal or a runaway.'

'Look at her, Mama. Does she seem like a bad person? She was attacked.'

'You can't tell just by appearances, Poppy. Did you see her assailant?'

'No,' Poppy said reluctantly. 'But she was very upset.'

'You may take her to your room and find her something to wear, but she should go on her way when she feels fit enough. She must have been heading somewhere. I'm sure that Adam will give her a lift there in his motor car.'

Poppy could see that her mother was adamant and she chose not to argue. 'Very well, Mama.'

'You probably think I'm being hard,' Flora said, frowning. 'But I've had more experience of the world than you have, Poppy. I spent my first six years living in an East End slum. I know that people are not always what they seem.'

'Yes, Mama. I will be careful.' Poppy turned to Miranda. 'Come upstairs to my room. Lottie and I will help you to clean up and tend to your cuts and bruises.'

'I'll send Ivy to your room with some hot water.' Flora walked away, turning her back on them.

'Thank you, Mama.' Poppy was quick to note the slightly grudging tone in her mother's voice and she was even more puzzled. Normally Flora Robbins was the soul of generosity and hospitality, which made her suspicious attitude to Miranda seem very strange. However, Poppy put all such thoughts out of her mind as she led the way upstairs, intent on helping her new friend.

As Poppy and Lottie helped Miranda to undress it seemed very odd to discover that her gown, although torn and dirty, was of good quality, as were her underclothes. They were not the sort of garments that Mattie hung out on the line when she did her personal laundry. Poppy was eager to question Miranda, but she was still very upset and there were bruises on her breast and neck, as well as scrapes on her hands and knees. Poppy could see that Lottie was thinking along similar lines. There really did seem to be a hint of mystery attached to the beautiful young stranger and Poppy was determined to discover the truth of what lay behind Miranda's seemingly tragic past.

Chapter Three

Poppy and Lottie spent the next hour tending to Miranda's injuries. It was a relief to discover that, although they might be painful, they were superficial and would clear up within a few days. A clean chemise and petticoats were found as well as a pale grey cotton gown that was both practical and flattering. Miranda's soiled clothing was bundled up ready to be sent down to the laundry room.

'You look lovely, Miranda,' Lottie said, smiling. 'That gown fits as if it were made for you.'

'I don't know how to thank you.' Miranda gazed at her reflection in the cheval mirror. 'I will return the dress as soon as mine is fit to wear. But I can't impose on your family, especially as they are obviously very busy.'

'Yes, the restaurant is very popular, thanks to my

parents' efforts over the years, although I believe it was very difficult when they started out.'

'But they've been very successful.' Miranda smiled sweetly. 'How wonderful.'

Poppy was suddenly wary. It seemed that Miranda was a little too interested in the family business. 'It has its drawbacks,' she said casually. 'I will have to work this evening as there is a large party booked.'

'It must be a very profitable business.' Miranda eyed Poppy's reflection in the mirror. 'Of course, you would think it vulgar to speak of such things.'

'Why would you say that?' Lottie demanded. 'I don't think it's any of your business, Miss Miranda . . .'

'Flyte,' Miranda replied casually. 'My name is Miranda Flyte. I'm sorry if I spoke out of turn.'

Poppy met Lottie's glance with a frown. 'That's not like you, Lottie. Where are your manners?'

Lottie's normally pale cheeks were suffused in a blush. 'I didn't mean to be sharp. I apologise, Miranda.'

'At least now I am able to help wherever I'm needed,' Poppy said hastily. 'I am quite a competent cook when I'm given the chance and I do most of the bookkeeping and ordering supplies. My grandfather was a famous restaurateur. Sadly he passed away a couple of years ago.'

'It's such a romantic story of how Poppy's mama discovered her true identity,' Lottie added eagerly. 'She was rescued from the Thames as a tiny baby, having been found floating in a doctor's bag. Isn't that so, Poppy?'

'It sounds like a fairy tale, but it's true.'

'What happened?' Miranda looked from one to the other. 'Can you speak of it?'

'There was a terrible accident on the river,' Poppy said, sighing. 'Two vessels collided with a tragic loss of life.'

Miranda clasped her hands to her cheeks, her eyes wide with dismay. 'Oh, no. How dreadful.'

'My uncle Amos was also saved from a watery grave. He is now our head chef.' Poppy had a feeling that Miranda was a little too interested in her family's history. She picked up the bundle of soiled clothing and backed towards the door. 'I really haven't time to go into details now. Lottie will show you to our private parlour, and I'll ask Cook to make some sandwiches for us, since we missed luncheon.'

Lottie pulled a face. 'I dare say Adam has already pestered the kitchen staff for food. He is always hungry.'

'I could help,' Miranda said casually. 'I would be more than happy to assist in the kitchen this evening. I would like to repay your kindness, Poppy.'

'Wouldn't it be better if you returned to wherever it is you came from?' Lottie plucked a silver-backed mirror from the dressing table and patted a stray hair in place. 'I mean, you need somewhere to sleep tonight.'

Poppy hesitated in the doorway. 'I don't know

what's got into you, Lottie. I'm sure we can put Miranda up in one of the guest bedrooms until she feels well enough to continue her search for work.' She left the room but Lottie followed her, catching her by the sleeve.

'I'm not sure about that person. She seems to infer that she's a servant of some sort but her clothes are of good quality, and did you notice her hands?'

Poppy put her finger to her lips. 'Not so loud, Lottie. She'll hear you.'

'I'm just saying that she hasn't done a day's hard work in her life. That is all.' Lottie glanced over her shoulder. 'Come along, Miranda. I'll take you to the parlour. We must allow Poppy to get on with her work.'

'Give her a chance,' Poppy said in a low voice. 'That's the least we can do.' She walked off without waiting for an answer. Lottie's comment only added to her own feeling of disquiet. It was unlike her to take against someone she barely knew. Adam was the one who always suspected an ulterior motive in others.

Poppy found him, as she had thought, in the kitchen, using all his considerable charm on Cook, who was plying him with sandwiches and cake.

'I knew I'd find you here,' Poppy said, smiling. 'You seem to have a lot of food there, even for you, Adam.'

He swallowed a mouthful and grinned. 'Cook spoils me.'

'I'm sorry, Miss Poppy. I understood you wanted me to provide food for you and your friends.'

'I most certainly did. Thank you, Mrs Burden.' Poppy took a sandwich and bit into it, savouring the tasty freshly baked bread, ham and a hint of mustard. 'Excellent as always.' She gave Adam a meaningful look. 'Perhaps you'd like to take the rest to the parlour so that Lottie and Miranda can have something before you scoff the lot.'

'As if I would.' Adam picked up the plate and headed for the doorway. 'I want to see how Miranda looks without the coating of dust and mud.'

Mrs Burden gave Poppy an enquiring glance. 'I gather we have another guest to feed.'

'It's a long story, but I think she will be staying tonight. I'll make sure she's looked after.'

'We'll be very busy, Miss Poppy. Chef Amos will be here soon to start on the meal for tonight. We've done all the preparations needed, but of course he will be in charge of the dinner itself. Although I'm sorry to say we're one short this evening. Meg was poorly so I sent her home.'

'I could help out.'

Poppy turned to see Miranda standing behind her. 'I didn't hear you come in,' Poppy said sharply.

'I passed Adam in the hall. He told me that one of the kitchen staff had been sent home. As I said before, I would like to repay your kindness, Poppy.'

Mrs Burden smiled approvingly. 'You must be the young lady from the fairground. What a terrible experience you've had. Did you know the brute who attacked you?'

'No, he was a complete stranger.' Miranda clasped her hands to her breast. 'It was so frightening, ma'am. I just want to forget all about it.'

'We could do with another pair of hands.' Mrs Burden turned to Poppy. 'What do you say, Miss Poppy?'

It would look churlish to refuse such an apparently genuine offer. Poppy was not entirely convinced, but they were expecting a large party of diners celebrating a birthday that evening and would need all the help they could get. She stifled a sigh.

'Very well. Thank you, Miranda. I'll leave you in Cook's capable hands. She'll explain what is needed. Take your instructions from her.'

'I always pay my debts,' Miranda said smugly. 'Is there an apron I could borrow, Cook?'

Poppy left them chatting and made her way to the large, airy dining room where the waitresses were stripping the cloths from the tables at the end of the lunchtime session. She had a brief word with the head waiter, who was about to take his afternoon break. Everything seemed to be in order and the wines for the main party had been brought up from the cellar: the white wine duly placed in an ice box to cool and the red brought to room temperature. It was all routine, but Poppy liked to keep an eye on all aspects of the proceedings. There was no excuse for sloppiness or a casual approach when it came to providing the guests with a pleasurable experience they would remember for years to come. She went next to the flower room and inhaled the delightful scent of freshly cut blooms from the gardens so lovingly nurtured by her father. Huge buckets of pink and white roses, white lilies, stately gladioli and deep blue delphiniums greeted her. It was her favourite task to arrange them in vases to decorate the dining room, and make up smaller posies for each of the tables, including a grand centrepiece for the top table.

She was concentrating on the largest arrangement when her mother walked into the room.

'This was my favourite room in the house before you took over the floral arrangements, Poppy. I've always loved flowers, hence your name.'

Poppy smiled. 'You could have called me Dandelion. I'm lucky to have escaped with the flower you chose.'

'As if I would burden my daughter with such a silly name.' Flora selected a deep pink rose and sniffed it, closing her eyes. 'That is quite intoxicating. You have a definite talent for floral arrangements, darling girl.'

'Thank you, Mama.'

'Actually, I wanted to ask you something, Poppy. I went into the kitchen just now and found your new friend helping Cook.'

'I know, Mama. Mrs Burden said that she had to send Meg home and so we were one short.'

'And you thought of Miranda Flyte.'

'Actually I didn't. Apparently, Miranda heard that Meg had gone home and she volunteered to help, making it almost impossible for me to refuse.'

Flora frowned. 'There is something odd about that young woman. I can't put my finger on it, Poppy, but I want you to keep a close eye on her.'

'Do you think she might steal the family jewels, Mama?'

Flora laughed. 'Put it this way, dear. If we had any valuables I think I would lock them up until Miss Flyte has flown. If you'll excuse the dreadful pun.'

'You could simply ask her to leave tonight, Mama. It's not my place to send her on her way, but you could.'

'On what grounds? I can't find anything to complain about. It's just a feeling I have, but I do hope I am wrong.'

'I'll make sure her gown is laundered and mended. We found her in Wanstead – perhaps Papa could drive her back there tomorrow morning and she can continue on her way.'

'An excellent idea. There is something disquieting about her presence and I'll feel happier when she's gone. Anyway, I'll leave you to get on, Poppy. Begg will arrive shortly with your uncle Amos. I need to go over the menu for tonight with them both so that Amos understands exactly what is wanted.' Flora left the room, closing the door softly behind her.

Uncle Amos. The mere mention of her mother's

younger brother made Poppy smile affectionately. The trauma he had experienced as a young baby, left unattended in a basket caught among the weeds on the river's edge, had left him slightly different from everyone else. He might not have had much education, but the couple who had saved him and raised him like a son had done their best by him. Ted Tulliver, the owner and patron of the Playhouse Inn, had taught young Amos how to work in the pub kitchen, and the talent for creating delicious dishes had come naturally to him. However, sometimes Amos had difficulty in expressing himself fully and that could lead to explosive outbursts in the kitchen. It was left to his right-hand man, Silas Begg, to diffuse such situations and calm down the temperamental chef as well as the upset staff.

Poppy finished off the arrangement she had been creating and placed it on the work bench, ready to be place in situ when she had completed her task. She had just inserted the last single rosebud into a cut-glass vase when the door opened and Adam strolled into the flower room.

'So this is where you've been hiding, Poppy?'

'I've been working, as you can see. Although sometimes it is nice to shut myself away in here with all the beautiful flowers and allow everyone else to get on with running the restaurant.'

He leaned against the table in the centre of the room where she had laid out the arrangements. 'I thought you were happy living and working here.'

'I am, of course, but occasionally I get itchy feet. Sometimes I long to get away, although of course I could never let my parents down. They rely on my help.'

'You'll marry one day, Poppy. They'll have to do without you then.'

'I don't think that will happen very soon.'

'Is there no one you have in mind?' Adam was suddenly serious.

Poppy eyed him curiously. 'Why are you so interested in my personal affairs? It's not like you to think of anything other than what affects you.'

'Perhaps this does.' Adam gave her a boyish grin. 'Maybe I'm in love with you, and have been since we were small children climbing that wretched tree in Gideon's garden.'

'This isn't like you at all, Adam. I think you're allowing yourself to wallow in sentiment.' Poppy laid her hand on his arm. 'Are you worried about joining your regiment and being sent to the Cape?'

'That is what they trained me for. Thanks to an accident of birth I could have settled for taking over the management of our estates from Papa, but I chose the army, even though Mama begged me to reconsider.'

'It's only natural for a loving mother to want to protect her children.'

'I agree, but I'm no longer a child. I want to prove myself as a man before I take up my onerous duties and a seat in Parliament, which, I might add, my papa has managed to avoid.'

'So you think the trouble with the Boers might escalate?'

'That's in the lap of the gods at the moment, or perhaps I should say in the hands of the War Office. I'll go wherever I'm sent and that's that.' Adam laughed and reached out to stroke her cheek with the tip of his forefinger. 'But I would like to think there was someone at home praying for my deliverance and looking forward to my return.'

Poppy caught his hand in hers. 'You know I will do all those things, Adam. I really care about you and Lottie. You're like my own family.'

'You think of me as a brother?' Adam forced a smile. 'We are a family, all four of us.'

Poppy released his hand. 'Aren't you forgetting little Arthur?'

'The Afterthought? He's just a child.'

'He's ten years old, but he'll be a man one day,' Poppy said lightly. 'No doubt he's very proud of his dashing brother.'

'Do you think I'm dashing?'

Poppy picked up a tray containing the smaller flower arrangements. 'I don't want to inflate your ego any more than it is already. Besides which, some of us have work to do. So if you'll excuse me I'll take these to the dining room.'

'Wait. There was something I want to ask you.'

Poppy hesitated, clutching the tray tightly with both hands. 'All right. But please be quick. I have rather a lot to do.'

'Would you like to accompany me to the Derby next Wednesday? It's quite an occasion.'

'I don't know, Adam.' Poppy stared open-mouthed. The sudden turn in the tone of the conversation had taken her by surprise. 'I'll have to find out what bookings we have and then I need to ask Mama if she can manage without me.'

'But you would like to come?'

Poppy smiled at his eagerness, so unlike his normal casual indifference. 'I've only ever been to a point-to-point in the past, but I would love to go to Epsom with you. What did Lottie say when you suggested it?'

'I haven't asked her. I thought it might be nice if it was just you and me.'

'I'm not sure Pa would approve of that.' Poppy eyed him warily. 'Besides which, I know I'm not the sort of young lady you might usually ask out. My parents are quite strict when it comes to accepted social mores.'

'They never seemed to mind in the past.'

'We were just children then. It's different now, and you have a reputation to keep up as well. Anyway, perhaps you should ask Lottie. She'd be so disappointed if you left her out.'

'I suppose so,' Adam said grudgingly.

'You could invite Gideon, too. We would be such a jolly party.'

'I'm sure you're right,' Adam said stiffly. He moved quickly to open the door and held it while she

45

left the flower room, carrying the tray. 'I'll do what you suggest, Poppy. You will come, won't you?'

She gave him a bright smile. 'Of course. But I still have to check that we won't be too busy that day. Anyway, it will give me something to look forward to.'

'Excuse me, Miss Poppy.'

Startled, Poppy turned to see Miranda standing behind her.

'Yes, what is it?'

'Mrs Burden asked me to find you, miss. I was to tell you that Mr Amos has arrived and he's not happy.'

Poppy thrust the tray into Miranda's hands. 'Take this to the dining room, please. Just leave it on the nearest table.'

'That sounds like trouble,' Adam said in a low voice as Miranda sashayed away carrying the table decorations.

'Uncle Amos might be in one of his moods.' Poppy sighed. 'That's all I need on such a busy evening.'

'Do you want me to come with you?'

Poppy laid her hand on his arm. 'Thank you, Adam, but I'm not afraid of Uncle Amos, and anyway, Begg will calm him down. I just need to pacify Mrs Burden and the kitchen staff. I'll see you tomorrow unless you're otherwise engaged.'

'I am at your disposal. Perhaps you would like me to drive you and Miranda to Wanstead Flats, where we found her.'

'Yes, indeed. That is even better than my idea. She can stay for the night but tomorrow she must go.'

Despite a busy and highly successful night, Poppy was up early next morning. Her first task every day was to check the bookings, if any. There was nothing at lunchtime, although with the increasing number of travellers on the roads they often had unexpected visitors requesting a meal or perhaps just morning coffee. Once they discovered the peaceful ambience of Rainbow's End and enjoyed the delights of Mrs Burden's cakes or biscuits, they would almost certainly come again. All this was good for business, but Poppy realised that Rainbow's End was likely to be surrounded in the ever-encroaching suburban housing boom. The modern railway system encouraged office workers to move out of dismal, dirty, soot-covered London, into neat new rows of terraced houses with the benefit of gas lighting and water at the turn of a kitchen tap. It seemed that quite soon Rainbow's End and Nine Oaks would become islands of greenery in a sea of red brick and shiny slate tiles.

Poppy hurried to the kitchen and found Mrs Burden purple in the face, standing arms akimbo while Chef Amos Calvert waved his arms and bellowed at her in a torrent of words that meant nothing to anyone but himself.

'What's going on, Begg?' Poppy eyed her uncle warily. 'What has upset him?'

Begg sniffed and stroked his grey beard, his shaggy brows lowered in a frown. 'Leave it to me, Miss Poppy. I can deal with Amos if you'll deal with the cook.'

'Deal with me?' Mrs Burden puffed out her cheeks and exhaled heavily. 'The cheek of the man. I put up with a lot but this is my kitchen in the daytime. I run things and always have. I won't be told how to do my job.'

Poppy placed herself between the irate cook and Chef Amos. 'Come to our parlour with me, Mrs Burden. We'll leave Begg to sort things out here. I'm sure a glass of sherry wine would help to calm your nerves. Purely for medicinal purposes, you understand.'

Mrs Burden glared at Ivy, who was cowering in the scullery doorway with two kitchen maids who came in for the evening service. 'Get on with your work, Ivy Morris. That goes for you two as well.'

Somewhat reluctantly Mrs Burden allowed Poppy to lead her to the family's private parlour. Poppy filled a glass with sherry from a decanter on the sideboard and handed it to Mrs Burden.

'Sit down for a while,' Poppy said firmly. 'How did Chef Amos upset you this time?'

Mrs Burden swallowed a mouthful of wine. 'He came storming in. I knew by the look on his face that we were in for trouble. Anyway, he insulted my béchamel sauce. He threw the pan into the sink and turned on the tap. It's a miracle he didn't scald Miranda. She was the nearest to him.'

'That is unacceptable behaviour.' Poppy sighed. 'I am so sorry. We can't allow that, but I need to find out what has happened to put him in such a bad mood. Did anyone speak out of turn? I hope the new maids didn't make fun of his appearance?'

'I didn't hear anything, but I was busy stirring my sauce. It was absolutely perfect, too. Now I'll have to start all over again, although I've a mind to hand in my notice. I don't see why I should work with that man.'

'You have the patience of a saint. Sit there and sip your sherry. I'll go to the kitchen and make sure such a thing doesn't happen again. We have a very busy evening ahead of us.' Poppy did not wait for an answer. She returned to the kitchen to find Miranda, Ivy and the rest of the staff clustered in the scullery while Begg helped Amos into his chef's white jacket. Begg talked slowly and calmly, as if speaking to a recalcitrant toddler, but his soothing voice seemed to have the desired effect. Amos began breathing normally and the deep red flush on his cheeks slowly faded.

'I'm sorry if someone upset you, Uncle Amos,' Poppy said cautiously.

'I have to get on.' Amos nodded vigorously. 'Must start work. Much to do. Where's the list, Begg?'

'Hold your horses, sir.' Begg buttoned the double-breasted white jacket. 'You have to be smart always. Didn't your pa teach you that?'

Amos nodded enthusiastically. 'Yes, Pa was the finest chef in London. I am like him and Ted. He's a good chef, too.'

'Of course he is, and people had the greatest respect for Mr Calvert in his lifetime. Now, sir, here's the list. Shall I read it to you?'

Amos shot a mischievous look at Poppy. 'I never learned how, Pansy. But you're clever like Begg. You can make those squiggles into words.'

'I'm Poppy, not Pansy, Uncle Amos. Yes, I can read, but I can't make delicious dishes like you.'

'I am a good chef.'

'And I hope you will be polite to Mrs Burden when she comes back,' Poppy said cautiously. 'She is very upset because you shouted and threw her béchamel sauce in the sink.'

'Did I? That was wrong, wasn't it, Begg?'

Begg nodded. 'Yes, sir. But you won't do it again, will you?'

'I can't think about that now. I have work to do.' Amos rammed his chef's hat on his head and picked up a knife, causing the women who were huddled together in the scullery to mutter anxiously. Poppy turned to them and laid her finger on her lips, shaking her head. She caught sight of Miranda, who was openly smirking, as if amused by the situation.

'You may all go about your tasks now,' Poppy said hastily. 'I'm sure Mrs Burden has told each of you where to start. What about you, Miranda? Have you been given orders?'

Miranda sidled up to Begg. 'I'm sure Mr Begg will put me right if I don't do what's required of me.'

Begg glowered at her. 'You need to ask Mrs Burden.

50

I ain't in charge of the women in this kitchen. That's her province.'

Miranda giggled. 'Oh, pardon me, sir. I thought you looked like a man who is used to command.' She fluttered her eyelashes at him, but Begg merely turned away.

'I have things to do, but I'll send Mrs Burden back to work, if she's recovered.' Poppy shot a warning glance in Miranda's direction. She had a feeling that Miranda might have been the person who made fun of Uncle Amos. That settled it as far as Poppy was concerned. Miranda was a disruptive influence and what was more worrying, she appeared to enjoy creating dramas wherever she could. Miranda would very definitely have to be taken back to Wanstead Flats where they had found her.

The sherry seemed to have calmed Mrs Burden's delicate nerves and she returned to the kitchen. Poppy waited until her uncle had apologised for his rudeness, prompted by Begg, and peace was restored. After that, Poppy had too much to occupy her to worry about what mischief Miranda might get up to, and fortunately the rest of the evening went well. The birthday celebration was a huge success and, as always, the food was excellent, receiving the highest of praise from the guests. Poppy's main task was to liaise with the kitchen staff and make sure that the different courses were served on time. In the meantime Flora always took care of the guests, greeting them warmly and making sure they had everything they wanted. Daniel and Ted Carlton were in charge of the guests' vehicles, whether horse-drawn or horseless carriages. Motor cars were parked in the forecourt and the horses were led to the stables to wait until their owners were ready to leave. It was a well-organised routine that they had executed and polished over the years and it ran mostly without a hitch.

When the last guest had departed and the kitchen staff had finished their work and gone home, Poppy did her last rounds, ensuring that all the doors were locked. She had shown Miranda to her room on the top floor and the old house was quiet, except for the odd creak and sigh of old timbers contracting in the cool of the night. Poppy went to her room satisfied by the success of the evening. She was too tired to think of anything other than enjoying a good night's sleep. She made herself ready for bed and lay down, putting aside all thoughts of the strange young woman who had come into their lives in such a dramatic fashion, and she fell asleep anticipating a day at the races with three of her best and dearest friends.

Next morning, refreshed and eager to start another day, Poppy was up early as usual. Washed, dressed and with her burnished copper hair confined to a neat chignon, she went downstairs to go about her usual routine. Ivy was already in the kitchen, supervising young Meg as she riddled the ashes in the range in order to encourage the embers of the fire into life. Beasley, who had been the butler to the former owner and kept on by Flora and Daniel despite his advanced years, had already brought in a hod of coke and a bundle of kindling. It was a well-practised routine. Poppy went over the bookings they had for the day, making notes as she went. She would go over them again with her mother when Flora came downstairs for breakfast.

Mattie Briggs was the next person to join them. She made tea, and Ivy took a cup to Mrs Burden's room. It was only then that Poppy realised that someone was missing. She could not help feeling annoyed that Miranda had chosen to sleep in when everyone else was up and about. She made her way to the top floor and knocked on the door. When there was no answer she opened it and walked into the room. There was no sign of Miranda and the bed had not been slept in. The clothes she had borrowed were laid out neatly on the bed and her newly washed and mended gown was nowhere to be seen. Poppy rushed downstairs to check if anything had been stolen.

Chapter Four

There seemed to be no logical explanation for Miranda's sudden flight. Although it was obvious that she had left in the middle of the night, nothing appeared to have been stolen. Flora and Daniel shook their heads but neither of them placed much importance on her disappearance. If Poppy were to be honest, she felt a certain amount of relief that the mysterious Miranda had saved them the trouble of taking her back to Wanstead Flats. Besides which, the good early summer weather was bringing more and more customers out of the city, eager for refreshment. This kept everyone busy and left little opportunity to brood on past happenings. Poppy was sorry not to have more time to spend with Adam and Lottie, but she was looking forward to their trip to the races at Epsom.

Derby day dawned bright and sunny, promising

to be hotter as the morning progressed. Poppy dressed carefully, having spent a good hour the previous evening deciding what to wear. In the end she opted for a simple gown in cream shantung with the fashionable leg-of-mutton sleeves and a demure high neck. She borrowed a large straw hat trimmed with silk roses from her mother and a pair of lace mittens. The pretty young woman who gazed back at her from the mirror looked so different from her in her usual plain, serviceable outfits that Poppy laughed out loud. She could not wait for Adam to see her transformed into a lady of fashion, and she was not disappointed. His eyes widened when he saw her and a slow smile spread across his handsome features.

He held her at arm's length. 'My goodness, Poppy. You look absolutely spiffing.'

She smiled. 'I'm not sure if that's actually a compliment, Adam. Does it mean that I don't normally look good?'

'You're putting words into my mouth.' Adam leaned forward and brushed her cheek with a kiss. 'You are always lovely but today you look incredible.'

Poppy looked to Lottie, who was laughing. 'Your brother has a wonderful way with words.'

'Don't tease him, Poppy. He's telling the truth – you look beautiful. I feel quite in the shade.'

'Oh, no! I hate that,' Poppy said hastily. 'That is impossible.'

Adam smiled. 'Let's settle for the fact that I am

a lucky fellow to have two glorious creatures to accompany me to the races.'

'Gideon is coming, too.' Lottie shot him a challenging glance. 'Did you arrange to meet him there?'

'I'm sorry, dear girl. I had a message before we left that he's been called out on an emergency and he wouldn't make it. I meant to tell you earlier.'

Lottie's pretty lips formed a sad pout. 'Yes, you should have, Adam. You are so thoughtless sometimes.'

'You'll be able to tell him all about it when you next see him,' Poppy said with a sympathetic smile. She knew that Lottie had been pinning her hopes on having a day out with Gideon. 'He must be terribly disappointed.'

'That's right,' Adam added cheerfully. 'You'd have to put up with that if you married a medical man, Lottie.'

'Don't be horrid, Adam. I wouldn't have come if I'd known.' Lottie turned her back on him but Poppy was quick to see the tears of disappointment sparkling on the tip of Lottie's thick eyelashes.

'Anyway, I think we'd best leave now,' Adam said, apparently oblivious to his sister's genuine distress. 'I don't want to miss the first race.'

'What about luncheon?' Poppy asked, ever practical. 'I could get the kitchen staff to make us up a picnic basket.'

'No need. I thought of that. I have a hamper from

56

Fortnum's attached to the rear of the motor car. I think of everything,' Adam said smugly.

Lottie rolled her eyes. 'I think we'd better leave before his head gets any bigger or my dear brother won't be able to get through the doorway.'

'Very funny,' Adam said with a good-natured grin. 'Come along, ladies. Your carriage awaits, although you might consider a duster coat and some goggles, Poppy. They will make you look like a beautiful frog, but much better than getting grit in your eyes.'

'I've thought of that already. I remember my first ride in your horseless carriage, so I'm prepared. You two go out to the motor car and I'll join you in a minute. I need to let Mama know that I'm going now.'

It took almost three hours to get to Epsom Downs. Lottie complained that it would have been quicker to travel in the barouche with a pair of well-matched horses, but Adam merely laughed and demanded to know what had happened to her sense of adventure. This was the modern way to travel and soon the roads would be crammed with motor vehicles with the power to go even faster. Lottie appealed to Poppy, but Poppy knew better than to take sides in a family argument and she skilfully steered the conversation to a safer topic. However, all differences of opinion were forgotten once they arrived at the racecourse. Poppy had never seen so many people crowded together. They were a colourful gathering from all walks of life. Buskers went through their acts, adding to the noise and general air of festivity. In the midst of all this, the ticktack men stood on chairs, stools and even barrels, waving their arms and using their hands to express the bookmakers' odds across the heads of the eager punters.

The scent of warm, trampled grass mingled with the smell of sweaty humanity, cheap perfume and wafts of vanilla ice cream as the hokey-pokey man peddled his rapidly melting confection. Somewhere a brass band was playing, although it had to contend with fiddlers entertaining the spectators, and a barrel organ where a monkey in a bright red jacket held out a collection cup.

Poppy was quite dizzy with excitement, and she managed to persuade Adam to put a couple of small bets on for herself. Lottie refused, tossing her head and pursing her lips at the likely prospect of losing to the tote. However, Poppy won a couple of shillings, which she saved to put on to the favourite in the big race. Finally, persuaded by Adam, Lottie agreed to part with sixpence each way on Damocles, while both Poppy and Adam opted for the Duke of Westminster's horse, Flying Fox.

They crowded round the railings at the start of the race and Poppy found herself shouting and cheering with the rest of the onlookers. She could hardly believe her luck when Flying Fox won and Lottie was mildly excited when Damocles came second.

Adam went off to join the queue to collect their winnings, having given Poppy and Lottie strict instructions to stay where they were or they might never find each other. Lottie was flushed and complaining of the heat while she fanned her face with her hand, but Poppy had just caught sight of a familiar figure. She grasped Lottie's arm.

'Look, Lottie. I'm certain that's Miranda.' Poppy pointed to a well-dressed young woman wearing a large hat decorated with ostrich feathers.

Lottie shielded her eyes from the sun. 'It can't be. That outfit didn't come from a department store, nor the hat.'

'I'm sure it's Miranda, and she's spotted us. She's coming this way.'

Lottie grasped Poppy's arm so tightly that it made her wince. 'Who is she with? He looks very well-to-do, and rather handsome.'

'I don't know, but it seems that we're going to find out.' Poppy stood very still, eyeing Mirada suspiciously as she sauntered towards them on the arm of her good-looking escort.

'Poppy! I thought it was you.' Miranda smiled sweetly. 'Did you back the favourite? I'm afraid I put all my money on Innocence, who came third.'

'You should have listened to me, my dear.'

'Where are my manners?' Miranda said with a trill of laughter. 'Poppy Robbins and Lady Charlotte Ashton, may I introduce my dear cousin, Sir Gervase Mulliner?'

Poppy bobbed a curtsey. 'How do you do, sir?'

Gervase took her hand and raised it to his lips.

'How do you do, Miss Robbins?' He turned to Lottie with an ingratiating smile. 'How do you do, Lady Charlotte?'

'I think you have some explaining to do, Miranda,' Poppy said coldly.

'What's this, my pet?' Gervase raised an eyebrow. 'What have you been doing now, Miranda?'

'It's too silly for words.' Miranda smiled coyly. 'I went out on one of my adventures and almost came off the worst for it, Gerry. These people saved me from disaster.'

Poppy and Lottie exchanged outraged glances.

'Do you mean you were play-acting all along?' Poppy stared at her in horror. 'You were not attacked in the forest?'

'Not again, my love.' Gervase shook his head. 'I am so sorry, Miss Robbins. I must apologise for my wayward cousin. Miranda is a spoiled brat and she enjoys creating dramas wherever she goes.'

'But why would you do that, Miranda?' Lottie demanded angrily.

'It was fun at the time,' Miranda said with a careless shrug. 'And I paid for my supper by working in your kitchen, Poppy. I quite enjoyed the experience but I'm afraid the bed wasn't up to my standard so I had to leave rather than wake up crippled.'

'You dreadful creature.' Lottie turned away and beckoned to Adam, who was strolling towards them with their winnings clasped in his hands. 'Adam, I want you to hear this. I am quite shocked.'

'You have obviously led a very cloistered life, my dear Lottie.' Miranda gave Adam a brilliant smile. 'Adam, we meet again, only under more pleasant circumstances. How lovely to see you.'

Adam looked from one to the other. 'I seem to have missed something. Are you the same Miranda Flyte we saved from an attacker at the fair?'

Gervase proffered his hand. 'How do you do, sir? Gervase Mulliner at your service. I apologise again for my headstrong cousin, but I gather I should thank you for saving her from her imagined assault.'

'Imagined?' Adam shook hands with Gervase before turning to give Miranda a searching look. 'Is this true?'

'I'm afraid so,' Miranda said airily. 'I do enjoy these little diversions, but this one turned out well. I met you and your delightful sister and Miss Robbins.'

'Perhaps it's time for us to leave.' A sharp intake of breath from Lottie made Poppy intervene. She knew the signs when the normally placid Lottie had been pushed to the limits and was about to lose her temper. 'We have a long drive ahead of us, Adam,' she added pointedly.

'Yes, of course, but I would like to hear more of this little diversion that so amused Miss Flyte,' Adam said firmly. 'I'm rather bewildered by the whole thing.'

'I'd love to visit you at home, and explain further.' Miranda smiled coquettishly. 'You're staying at Nine Oaks, I believe?'

'We really should leave now, Adam.' Poppy laid her hand on his arm. 'It's going to be so late by the time we get home.'

'Don't spoil my fun, Poppy, dear.' Miranda's smile did not reach her eyes.

'Now, Adam.' Lottie tugged at his coat-tails. 'I want to go home.'

'All right, Lottie. Don't get yourself in a state.' Adam turned to Mulliner with an apologetic smile. 'We should be on our way, Mulliner. It was nice to meet you.' Adam acknowledged Miranda with a curt bow.

'So soon, and we've just been reacquainted.' Miranda clutched her cousin's arm. 'If we are not invited to Nine Oaks I think we should visit Rainbow's End as guests, Gerry. I can't wait for you to see it. Maybe we will even meet your papa, Adam. I've heard so much about him.'

Poppy was even more suspicious. The sooner they were far away from here, the better, as far as she was concerned, but good manners prevailed and she managed a tight little smile.

'Goodbye, Miranda. It was nice to meet you, Sir Gervase.' Poppy started walking at a brisk pace, leaving Adam little choice other than to follow, Lottie clinging to his arm.

'Hold on, Poppy.' Adam came to a halt when they reached the place where the motor car was parked. 'Why the sudden haste? I mean, it's a rather bizarre story that Miranda told us, and patently ridiculous, but you seem very upset.'

'I can't put my finger on it exactly, but I simply don't trust her, especially since she admitted that that drama at the fair was all an act. Why did she pick on us, and what is her interest in your papa?'

'It does seem a little strange,' Lottie said, frowning. 'I don't like her at all and I do not want her to visit us at home.'

Adam opened the car door. 'I think both of you are making too much of the whole thing. Gervase seems like a decent fellow, and Miranda is obviously a bit of a handful, but I don't imagine there's any real harm in her.'

Poppy climbed into the car and sat down. 'I hope you're right.' She settled herself for the long drive home, but privately she was still concerned. There was something about Miranda Flyte that did not add up.

The sun was beginning to set by the time they reached Rainbow's End, having stopped on the way to enjoy light refreshment at a roadside inn. Poppy was tired and hungry and still feeling annoyed with Miranda. She did not believe her feeble excuse that she had fallen in with them by accident, but try as she might, she could not think of a plausible reason for the deception.

Adam drew the motor car to a halt in the courtyard next to a chaise that Poppy recognised as belonging to Lord Dorrington. Freddie was one of her most favourite men in the world, second only to her father.

'Your papa is here, Lottie.' Poppy gave her a shake. 'Wake up, we're home.'

Lottie opened her eyes and yawned. 'I am so stiff. I don't think I can move.'

'Of course you can.' Poppy alighted from the vehicle and helped Lottie to her feet. 'It's only a few steps into the house.'

'That's Papa's chaise.' Lottie shot a sideways glance at her brother. 'I'm going home with him. I've had enough of horseless carriages for one day.'

Adam had already climbed out of the car and he took off his goggles, leaving them on the driver's seat. He patted the metalwork as if it were a much-loved pet. 'Do as you please, Lottie. I'll admit it was a long drive, but you would grumble if you were taking a ride on a magic carpet.'

'That's untrue and you know it. Stop teasing me, Adam.'

'I suggest we go indoors and have something to eat,' Poppy said hastily.

'I'm starving.' Adam set off towards the back door. 'I wonder if Mrs Burden is still on duty. I hope she is, because I don't fancy my chances of persuading your uncle Amos to whip up a quick meal.'

'Don't be mean, Adam. You just have to know how to handle Uncle Amos. He's a dear when you get to know him.' Poppy linked arms with Lottie. If she were to tell the truth she too was stiff and aching after hours on the road. She could not help comparing the suspension of the motor car with the well-sprung comfort of the barouche, or perhaps, as Adam had claimed, it was the state of the road surfaces that were more culpable. Whichever it was, she was relieved to be on firm ground.

Lottie, however, was looking very pale. 'Are you all right?' Poppy asked anxiously. 'You haven't got one of your heads coming on, have you?'

'I'll be fine if I have something to eat and drink, but I'm still furious with that dreadful woman. How dare she put on such an act and take us in? Not only that, but she thinks it was amusing.'

'The best thing to do is to forget all about it, Lottie. Put her out of your mind. We don't have to see her again, especially you. I can't imagine that she would turn up uninvited at Nine Oaks, although she could come here as a customer.'

'And what if she does?'

Poppy laughed. 'I'll make sure we charge Sir Gervase double. I am going to put her out of my mind and I'd advise you to do the same. Come on, let's get these dusty garments off and wash our faces before we eat. I'll have a quick word with Uncle Amos and he'll feed us royally.'

'All right. I'll do as you say, Poppy. You are always more sensible than I am.' Lottie fell into step beside Poppy as they followed Adam into the house.

Poppy had a few words with Begg, who passed

the message on to Amos as he was totally absorbed in finishing off one of his famous classic dishes.

'Don't worry, miss. There'll be something tasty for you and the young lady and gentleman,' Begg assured her, and she left the kitchen, aware that her uncle was so intent on his culinary art that he would not even have noticed her.

Lottie was waiting in the passage outside the kitchen but Adam had gone on ahead to the drawing room.

'We'll make ourselves presentable,' Poppy said, smiling. 'I refuse to enter the dining room with untidy hair and a dirty face.

Lottie laughed. 'You do look like a scarecrow.'

'That makes two of us.' Poppy took her by the hand. 'Come on, we can work miracles in ten minutes.'

It was more like a quarter of an hour before Poppy and Lottie entered the drawing room, where Adam was already ensconced in a chair by the fireplace. Seated opposite him was Daniel, and Freddie Dorrington was standing with his back to the empty grate. His charming smile reminded Poppy how Aunt Bella must have felt when she first met the earl, who was almost twenty years her senior. He was simply an older version of Adam, and Poppy cared deeply for both of them.

'Here they are at last,' Adam said, grinning. 'You took your time, ladies.'

'Leave them alone, Adam,' Freddie said mildly. 'You can't put a time limit on perfection.' He hugged Lottie and then Poppy.

'That machine takes even longer than a carriage and pair.' Lottie tossed her head. 'And it's not as comfortable, but Adam won't have it. I'm sure we could have been back much earlier had we taken the barouche.'

'I was beginning to worry when I arrived here and found you had not returned,' Freddie admitted with a twinkle in his blue eyes. 'I'm not sure I trust the horseless carriage a hundred per cent on a long journey.' He turned to Adam, holding up his hands. 'I'm not here for an argument about motor cars versus horse-drawn vehicles. I merely came here to see if you had returned from the races.'

'I'm glad to hear it, Papa,' Adam said solemnly. 'The motor car is the future of road travel.'

Daniel Robbins rose to his feet. 'I'll be relying on horse power for now. I'll wait and see what happens in the next ten years. I reckon motor vehicles will be consigned to the history books. They're a fad for rich young gentlemen like you, Adam.'

Adam laughed. 'I expect you said that of the steam engine, sir.'

Poppy cleared her throat. 'Ahem! Before you gentlemen get involved in an argument, I have checked with Uncle Amos and we are just in time for a meal if we go to the dining room now, even though the other diners will have finished eating.'

'You'd better check with your mother, Poppy,' Daniel said, frowning. 'Just in case she has taken any more bookings. You know how people like to turn up on a lovely summer evening and expect to be served.'

'Only too well, Papa. I spoke to her as we came past the dining room. She was just working out someone's bill.'

'Then of course it's all right,' Daniel nodded his assent. 'Are you going to join them, Freddie, or will you take a glass of port wine with me and perhaps a cigar?'

Freddie smiled. 'That is an admirable suggestion, Dan. But first I need to know who won the Derby. I've contained my curiosity for long enough.'

'Flying Fox won by two lengths, and I backed the winner.' Adam proffered his arm to Poppy. 'Shall we go into the dining room? I think I should order a bottle of Veuve Clicquot to celebrate my winnings.'

'You are not to get your sister drunk, Adam,' Freddie said with mock severity. 'You know champagne makes her giggle.'

'Oh, Papa! How can you say such things?' Lottie turned to Poppy. 'He is just teasing me, really.'

'Don't worry, Lottie.' Poppy walked to the door and opened it. 'Champagne makes me sneeze and everyone laughs at me. We are quite a pair. Anyway, I am hungry, so let's go and see what Uncle Amos has provided for us.' She turned to give her father a mischievous smile. 'I also backed Flying Fox, Papa.

68

I think I should treat you and Mama to a bottle of champagne.'

Daniel shook his head. 'Buy yourself a new bonnet or something pretty and frivolous, my love. And please don't tell your mother that I condone gambling in any shape or form.'

'I promise, Pa.' Poppy left the room with Lottie, Adam following close on their heels.

Flora met them in the dining room and Poppy could not help but be amazed by her mother's seemingly indestructible beauty and poise. Even after a long day working hard, as was required of someone running such a high-class establishment, Flora was impeccably dressed in a watered silk gown, with a modest neckline, leg-of-mutton sleeves and a draped skirt drawn in at the back in a neat bustle. Flora's friendship with Gideon Taylor's famous couturier mother, Amelia, enabled her to buy designer gowns at a fraction of their normal price. Poppy had heard Amelia say that Flora Robbins was a better advertisement for her gowns than any high-born lady with a title. Although of course she did not include Arabella Dorrington in that group. Freddie's lovely wife was a favourite with everyone.

Flora held out her arms and embraced Poppy, giving her a gentle hug. 'I was beginning to worry, darling.' She turned her gaze to Lottie and she frowned. 'You look very pale, my dear. Are you feeling unwell?'

'I was feeling poorly in the motor car, Aunt Flora, but I'm glad to say that I feel much better now.'

'I expect you need something to eat. Amos has made a special dish for you three. I think he wants to impress you in particular, Lottie.' Flora laughed and led them to a table by the open French doors. A warm breeze rippled the heavy Regency stripe curtains in delicate shades of blue and gold, and potted palms swayed as if on a beach in an exotic location far away from the Essex countryside.

Adam pulled out a chair for Poppy and one for Lottie.

'May we have a bottle of Veuve Clicquot, Aunt Flora? I picked the winner of the big race.'

'Of course you may,' Flora said, smiling. 'Although I'm not sure if the girls are allowed to imbibe.'

'You know that I am, Mama,' Poppy protested, shaking out a white linen napkin and laying it on her lap.

'But what about you, Lottie, dear? I don't want to offend your papa.'

'I can have one glass,' Lottie said boldly. 'Papa said so, but I am not to giggle.'

Flora laughed. 'How like Freddie to say such a thing. Beasley has gone off duty, bless him, so you'll have to wait while I go down to the cellar and fetch a bottle of champagne.'

Adam jumped to his feet. 'I can't allow you to do that, Aunt. If you give me the key I'll do it.'

Flora hesitated and then she handed him a bunch

70

of keys from the chatelaine at her waist. 'It's the largest one, Adam. You can't mistake it. Thank you, anyway. It's very thoughtful of you, but do you know where to look?'

'We used to play hide and seek in the cellars when we were children,' Adam said, grinning. 'I always won.'

Lottie rolled her eyes. 'That's not true. Poppy and I usually had the advantage over you.'

'Just fetch the champagne,' Poppy said hastily, heading off another argument. 'It's supposed to be a celebration, although after the shock we had today I think we need a glass of something bubbly.'

Adam hurried off with the keys, leaving Flora staring at Poppy with a questioning look. 'What happened today?'

'You'll never guess, Mama. That person we rescued at the fair turned up on the arm of someone called Sir Gervase Mulliner, whom she introduced as her cousin. She was dressed to the nines and greeted us like old friends.'

'Do you mean Miranda Flyte? Surely not.'

'It was an act, Aunt Flora,' Lottie said firmly. 'She fooled us all and she thought it funny. I must say I don't think it amusing or clever.'

'How extraordinary.' Flora frowned. 'Why on earth would anyone do such a thing?'

'She wanted to meet Uncle Freddie,' Poppy said thoughtfully. 'She talked about visiting Nine Oaks, but I don't recall mentioning the name of your estate, Lottie.'

'I'm sure you didn't.' Lottie shook her head. 'It was all very strange. I felt very uncomfortable in her presence.'

'Why are you frowning, Mama?' Poppy eyed her mother curiously. 'What is it?'

'Sir Gervase Mulliner. Was that his name?'

'Yes, Mama.'

'I can't put my finger on it but the name Mulliner is vaguely familiar. I seem to have heard of it a long time ago. It's going to bother me now until I can remember why.'

Chapter Five

Amos had excelled himself and in a short time had created filet mignon with a rich Madeira sauce, asparagus, fresh from the garden, and new potatoes tossed in butter and chopped parsley. The diners were all very hungry and did justice to his delicious food. Lottie drank two glasses of champagne, even though Adam warned her of the consequences, which occurred when she almost fell asleep over a dish of strawberries and cream. Poppy was more used to drinking wine with meals, although she felt a little light-headed as she helped Lottie to the drawing room.

Freddie stubbed out his cigar and leaped to his feet.

'Lottie! What did I tell you?'

'One glass of champagne, Papa,' Lottie said giggling. 'I only had one, or maybe one and a half. I am quite sober.'

Freddie laughed. 'Really? Well, whatever the case I think I should take you home.' He glanced towards Adam, who was standing in the doorway. 'I'll have words with you later, sir.'

Poppy knew that was very unlikely. Freddie was an indulgent father and clearly doted on all his children.

'Shall I take her home in the motor car, Papa?' Adam asked casually.

'I don't want to get into that rattletrap,' Lottie said, covering her mouth to disguise a hiccup.

'I'll take you in the chaise.' Freddie slipped his arm around his daughter's waist. 'Lean on me if you feel dizzy.'

'I am perfectly sober, Papa.' Lottie lifted her hand to her brow. 'But I do feel a little odd. It must have been the Madeira sauce.'

'Thank goodness your mama is still at Dorrington Place,' Freddie said with a sigh. 'Where are your bonnet and shawl? It gets a little cold when the sun goes down.'

'I'll fetch them.' Poppy was about to leave the room when Adam caught her by the wrist.

'I fancy a walk in the gardens. There's a glorious sunset and I need to wear off some of that delicious but very rich dinner.'

Poppy smiled. 'That sounds delightful. I love this time of the year. I'll fetch my shawl as well as Lottie's.'

* * *

74

The sun had plummeted in a fireball, leaving the darkening sky streaked with scarlet, purple and flaming orange. As Poppy and Adam walked side by side through the fragrant rose garden, bats zoomed crazily overhead and a robin trilled his evening song, warning rivals to keep clear of his territory. Adam curled his fingers around Poppy's hand.

'We did well today at the races.'

She laughed. 'You mean you did well. I only put a couple of shillings on Flying Fox. I hate to think how much you gambled.'

He came to a halt. 'But I won. I'm a gambling man, Poppy. However, I always study the odds. I doubt if I would be so lucky in the romance stakes.'

'Why do you say that? Your father is an earl and one day you'll inherit everything, including the title. Débutantes must be desperate to attract your attention.'

'I'm a soldier first and foremost. I didn't ask to be born into the nobility with all the responsibilities that go with a title and a grand estate. Have you any idea how many servants are employed at Dorrington Place, both indoors and outdoors?'

'Some people might say you are very fortunate. Your family are wealthy landowners. Isn't that enough?'

'Could you face being a countess with all the dull duties and obligations?'

Poppy met his intense gaze with a smile. 'I take it that wasn't a proposal of marriage?'

'Not at this moment, but you haven't answered my question.'

'Adam, if I truly loved a man it wouldn't matter if he were a duke or a dustman. That's your answer.'

He nodded and released her hand. 'What about you? Are you happy to be a general factotum for the rest of your life?'

'I might marry a wealthy landowner and be a lady of leisure.' Poppy stood on tiptoe to brush his cheek with a kiss. 'We've been friends for most of our lives, Adam. You have your place in society and I have mine. My family will expect me to marry someone suitable and give them grandchildren to coo over. You at least have a choice and you've chosen the military.'

'You're right, as always.' He tucked her hand in the crook of his arm. 'Let's enjoy this evening. Tomorrow will take care of itself.'

'How long have you got before your posting, Adam?' The glory had gone from the sunset and now the garden was being consumed by dark shadows. Poppy felt a shiver run down her back and she tightened her grip on his arm.

'Four days. I'm not sure where I will be sent, but you will be the first to know.' Adam squeezed her fingers. 'You know that I care deeply for you, Poppy.'

She shot a sideways glance at him as his strong profile was outlined by the fading light. 'Yes, I do, and I have feelings for you, too.'

Once again he came to a halt and drew her into

a close embrace. Their lips met in a tentative kiss, which deepened into something much more intense on both sides. Poppy was the first to draw away, shivering with a mixture of emotion and a sudden feeling akin to fear.

'What's wrong? Have I offended you, Poppy?'

She shook her head. 'No, of course not. I wanted you to kiss me. But it's getting rather cold. Perhaps we should return to the house.'

'Of course. I'm sorry.' Adam slipped off his jacket and wrapped it around her shoulders. 'Will I see you tomorrow?'

The warmth from his body still lingered in the expensive suiting material, as did the familiar scent of sandalwood soap, which Adam had always favoured. Poppy nodded.

'Yes, of course, although I'm going to be very busy. We have several bookings for luncheon, and we will be packed in the evening.'

'I'll be round at some point with Lottie.' Adam bent down to kiss her briefly on the lips. 'I'll see you safely into the house and then I'd better be off.'

They walked slowly and parted in the courtyard where Adam climbed into his motor car and drove off with a final wave.

Poppy went into the scullery and was thankful to find everything closed down for the night. The range in the kitchen was still hot enough to boil a kettle and she made herself a cup of tea. With the tea brewing in the pot, she sat down at the freshly scrubbed table and attempted to gather her scattered thoughts. She had always been fond of Adam but she had never questioned her feelings for him, until now. His kisses had been sweet and more exciting than she could have imagined. Several young men had attempted to court her and she had gone out with a couple of them, but the nearest either of them had come to passion was holding hands during a walk and parting with a shy peck on the cheek. Poppy had not been attracted to either of them physically, although she had liked them well enough. Tonight had been different on all counts. In fact the whole time since Adam had arrived in the motor car, and scared Mattie Briggs out of her mind, had been a series of unusual events.

The kitchen door opened and Poppy turned with a start to see her mother enter the room. Her luxuriant hair was concealed in a lace-trimmed nightcap and she wore a flowing white robe.

'What are you doing up at this hour, Poppy? You should be in bed asleep by now.'

Poppy smiled. 'I could say the same about you, Mama. You of all people need to get a good night's rest.'

Flora took another cup and saucer from the dresser and placed it on the table in front of Poppy. 'I do sometimes find it difficult to drop off, which is why I often creep downstairs in the middle of the night for exactly what you are doing. I find a cup of tea is very relaxing after a busy day.'

Poppy filled two cups with tea and added milk,

passing one to her mother. 'You work too hard, Mama. I do try to take some of the tasks from you.'

Flora spooned sugar into her cup and stirred the tea, gazing thoughtfully at Poppy.

'I know you do, my love. You are a wonderful help, but I sometimes worry that your heart isn't really in it. Your pa and I love this place and we built up the business together, but I do understand if it's not the same for you.'

Poppy stared at her mother in amazement. 'I've always done my best, Mama. I do love Rainbow's End; it's my home.'

'But not your life, Poppy. I appreciate that, and I want more than anything for you to be happy.'

'I would never let you down, you know that.'

'But something has disturbed you recently and I think it has to do with that Flyte woman.' Flora sipped her tea, replacing the cup gently on its saucer. 'What has she said or done to upset you?'

'Nothing really, Mama. But there is something odd about her, and not just the fact that she acted out that charade, pretending to be a servant girl in distress, although that was bad enough.'

'I think you're right to be suspicious. I am, too. I've been racking my brains trying to place the name Mulliner, and it came to me just as I was about to fall asleep. I had to get up and come down to the kitchen for a cup of tea in order to clear my thoughts.'

'It must have been something serious. What was it?'

'You know that I was taken in by the Stewart family and brought up as if I were Arabella's sister.'

'Yes, of course, and I love that story.'

'Well, there were two men who were cousins. One was Gabriel Cutler, a sea captain, and the other was Ralph Pettigrew, a ne'er-do-well who wanted to inherit their uncle's castle on the coast of North Devon and the title Baron Pettigrew.'

Poppy frowned. 'I've heard bits and pieces of the story. Didn't the evil Ralph kidnap Aunt Bella and try to force her into marriage so that he could claim his inheritance?'

'Yes, that's exactly what happened, but Freddie and I got there in time to save her. It was all very romantic, although quite frightening at the time. Anyway, neither Ralph nor Gabriel inherited the title and castle because their uncle had disowned them and everything went to Sir Phillip de Crecy.'

'That seems fair, but I don't see what it has to do with Miranda Flyte or Sir Gervase Mulliner.'

'I don't move in those exalted circles now, but I remembered that Ralph Pettigrew had a sister, although I believe they were estranged many years ago after she married a man called Charles Mulliner.'

'And you think there could be a connection to the man I met at the races?'

'It seemed strange that Miranda picked on you and Adam. Perhaps it was the Ashton family she wanted to meet? I don't know, Poppy. Maybe it's my imagination leading me astray.'

'But it does seem like a strange coincidence, and she was asking questions about Nine Oaks. I didn't put too much importance on it at the time.'

Flora smiled. 'Perhaps she has her eyes set on Adam. He must be the catch of the century for all the eager young women on the hunt for a husband.'

'I told him that earlier,' Poppy said, turning her head away to hide her blushes as the memory of Adam's kiss came flooding back. Her hand shook as she raised the cup to her lips. 'But I think Adam is quite capable of looking after himself, Mama.'

'My thoughts entirely, but what about you, my love? Are you really content to work here for us?'

'Of course I am,' Poppy said hastily. 'I enjoy working with you and Papa. I don't even mind when Uncle Amos shouts at me.'

'You know he doesn't mean it, but if you should change your mind I need you to understand that your papa and I would support you in anything you wished to do.'

'What else could I do?' Poppy pulled a face. 'I'm not talented in any way that might earn me a living.'

'You are a very clever young lady.' Flora gazed at her, frowning. 'I don't want you to remain here out of a sense of duty.'

'That isn't so, Mama. I told you that I love Rainbow's End. I was born here and it's been my home all my life.'

'Freddie told me that he's sending Lottie to stay with a distant relative in Paris for a few weeks so that she can visit the Louvre and museums, and attend the theatre. Perhaps you would like to accompany her?'

'Mama, how can I? June and July are almost fully booked. We have wedding parties as well as other family occasions. Lottie may well need to know about art, music and the theatre, but that isn't necessarily for me.'

Flora yawned. 'It was just an idea. I think Miranda Flyte's little escapade has unsettled us all. Anyway, thank you for the tea. I am just about ready for bed.' She rose from the table, blowing a kiss to Poppy. 'Good night, my darling. Don't stay up too late.'

'I won't. I'll just clear away these things so that Mattie doesn't have a fit in the morning and then I'm off to bed, too.'

Poppy set about tidying the kitchen before making her way to her bedroom. She went about her nightly routine, which helped to soothe away the tension that had built up during the day, but her mother's words weighed heavily on her conscience. She had not been entirely honest with her much-loved mama. It was hard to admit that she was suddenly restless and longed to have a life outside the walls and beautiful gardens of Rainbow's End, especially when she knew how much her parents loved the place they had built from scratch. Poppy had been tempted to tell her mama exactly how she felt, but now she was left with a dilemma. It was a long time before she finally dropped off to sleep.

* * *

Next day Poppy threw herself into her normal duties with forced enthusiasm. She decided that she was just going through a restless phase, which would soon pass, although she also decided that Miranda Flyte had a lot to answer for and she hoped that they had seen the last of that particular person. However, Adam and Lottie arrived just before midday when the restaurant was getting busy, and minutes later a smart chaise came to a halt at the kerb outside Rainbow's End and Miranda alighted, leaving the coachman to walk the horses. She waved to Poppy, who had just opened the door to welcome Adam and Lottie.

'Good heavens!' Lottie said sharply. 'Does that woman follow us around, Adam?'

He glanced over his shoulder. 'What now? I thought we had shaken her off at the races.'

Poppy was tempted to turn Miranda away but she could not justify such rudeness. Instead she waited until Adam and Lottie had stepped into the entrance hall.

'Miranda, this is an unexpected pleasure,' Poppy said, stretching her lips into a smile. After all, it could simply be that Miranda was just another customer, although it was almost unheard of for single ladies to dine alone in a restaurant.

'I suspected that you were less than pleased to see me yesterday,' Miranda said, glancing over Poppy's shoulder. 'Adam and his sister didn't wait to greet me.'

'Is there a reason for this visit?' Poppy gave up the attempt to be gracious. 'What do you want, Miranda?'

'My dear, that is not very friendly,' Miranda slipped past Poppy and strolled into the entrance hall. 'Good day, Lottie, and the same to you, Adam. I'm delighted to see you, but you look a little wary.'

Adam eyed her suspiciously. 'Is there any reason why we should welcome you, Miranda? You tricked us all with your play-acting. What do you want from us?'

'That is very unkind.' Miranda pouted. 'I came to make my peace with you all. I do sometimes do things to liven up my rather dull life, and my little drama at the fair was one of them. I thought I had made peace with you yesterday, but it seems I was mistaken.'

'You can't blame us for being suspicious,' Poppy said firmly. 'Why have you suddenly come into our lives? You weren't introduced formally and we know nothing about you.'

'Do you make all your customers go through such a cross-examination?' Miranda laughed. 'I would like a table for luncheon. You are all invited to join me, although of course you are working, Poppy, but that doesn't mean I can't treat Adam and Lottie.'

Poppy turned to Adam. 'Is it a table for three?'

'No, it is not.' Lottie tugged at her brother's arm. 'We have already had a light luncheon at home. We came to see you, Poppy.'

'Adam? Can't I tempt you to join me?' Miranda fluttered her eyelashes at him.

'I'm sorry, but as my sister said, we have already eaten,' Adam said, unsmiling.

'And there are no free tables,' Poppy added hastily. 'We are fully booked for luncheon.'

'Are you going to turn me away without so much as a glass of wine or a tasty nuncheon?' Miranda looked from one to the other, but Adam turned and followed Lottie towards the family parlour, leaving Poppy to deal with a sulky Miranda.

'I am very sorry,' Poppy said with more conviction than she was feeling. 'We are very busy all year, but particularly in fine weather such as we have today. Where are you staying? If it's a considerable journey I'm sure I can get Cook to make you up a snack to take with you.'

'There's no need, but thank you for the offer.' Miranda tossed her head. 'I just want us to be friends, Poppy. Is there anything so wrong with that?'

'No, of course not, but I don't understand why you wish to get closer to me and my family. We have virtually nothing in common and you did trick us into bringing you here. I can't think what you hope to gain by such behaviour.'

Miranda's smile faded and her lips trembled. 'It is a sad story. I didn't want to tell you straight off and appear to be asking for sympathy, but I thought perhaps you, Adam and Lottie might be sympathetic to my plight.'

Poppy glanced out of the window as a motor vehicle drew up outside. 'I would stop and listen, but I'm afraid I have to ask you to leave. The first guests of a rather large luncheon party have arrived. Perhaps another time, Miranda.'

'Yes, of course. I'll book a table next time and we can sit down over a glass of wine while I tell all. You will be fascinated by my story, of that I am certain.'

'Yes, perhaps.' Poppy hustled Miranda towards the door. 'Send your servant to arrange a mutually convenient time and date.'

Miranda stepped outside into the sunlight. The expression in her grey eyes was stormy, which did not match her wide smile. 'Indeed I will. I am sorry to have bothered you.'

'Not at all,' Poppy said out of politeness, although she had her fingers crossed behind her back. She managed a more sincere smile as some of the party approached the door and Miranda walked away, swinging her hips as she went. Poppy had the uncomfortable feeling that this was not the last she might see of the enigmatic Miranda Flyte. She sighed, shaking her head as she recalled what her mother had told her about Captain Cutler and Ralph Pettigrew. That was all a very long time ago, before she was born, and the story seemed highly far-fetched. Poppy pushed Miranda Flyte to the back of her mind as she launched into well-practised words of welcome to the new arrivals.

The guests had just been seated when the next party

arrived and soon the restaurant was filled with people who were bent on enjoying themselves. As always it was a pleasure to deal with appreciative diners, but there were always those for whom nothing would ever be perfect. Poppy had learned to deal with them politely but firmly, although some belligerent people tested her patience to the limit. It was not her job to wait on tables, although she often did so if they were short-staffed. Her main task was to liaise between the dining room and the kitchen. However, today her heart was not in her work and she was glad when the luncheon session ended and the dining room emptied. She left the staff to clear the tables and set them up for dinner that evening. As Poppy made her way to the parlour, she found herself wondering if her mother had been right. Perhaps she needed a temporary change of scene, although that would definitely have to wait until the summer season was over and done with.

There was no one in the parlour, which was disappointing. Poppy had been looking forward to a chat with Adam, especially as his time at home was almost over and she had no idea where he might be posted. Poppy went next to the kitchen where she found her mother talking earnestly to Cook.

'I'm sorry to interrupt, Mama, but have you seen Adam and Lottie? They were going to wait until we'd finished service but they are not in the parlour.'

Mrs Burden straightened her white cap, which only partially covered her head of springy grey curls. 'They went for a walk in the grounds, Miss Poppy.'

'Thank you, Cook. I'll go and look for them.'

'Have you eaten, Poppy?' Flora asked anxiously. 'You really should have something before you go out.'

But Poppy was heading for the scullery door and she did not stop. 'I'll get something when I've seen them. Don't worry about me, Mama.'

'All right, but if you see your papa will you please remind him to come in for luncheon? He gets carried away with one task or another and forgets to eat. You two are so alike in some ways.'

'Yes, I'll remind him.' Poppy escaped through the back door into the courtyard where Adam's car was still parked. At least she knew now that he and Lottie had not gone back to Nine Oaks, and she made her way past the stables and coach house, through the parterre garden and the rose garden to a copse. As children they had made hidey-holes there in the roots of some of the ancient trees, and had paddled in the brook that gurgled over a bed of shiny stones on its way to join a tributary of the River Lea. It had been their favourite place and, sure enough, as she approached the trees Poppy caught a glimpse of frilled pink seersucker and Lottie's straw bonnet lavishly trimmed with satin ribbon.

Poppy called out to them as she quickened her pace to a run. She arrived in the dell breathless but triumphant.

'I knew I'd find you both here.'

Adam was sitting on a tree stump but he rose to

his feet as she approached. 'That was a long session. I hope the till is full after all that work.'

Lottie frowned at him. 'Don't be vulgar, Adam. You know Mama would not approve. We don't mention money.'

Adam laughed. 'That's because we have plenty. It's different for the poor and needy.' He smiled apologetically. 'I didn't mean your parents by that, Poppy. You know what I was trying to say.'

'Yes, of course. The difference between our families, Lottie, is that you have inherited wealth and we have to make ours.'

'I'm sorry,' Lottie said, blushing so that her cheeks matched her summer gown. 'I didn't mean to boast.'

'Of course you didn't. I know that. Anyway, let's forget about commonplace things like money and enjoy our time together.' Poppy turned to Adam. 'Have you received your posting yet?'

'Even though I have to report to the barracks in three days' time, I still don't know where I'll be after that.'

Poppy swallowed hard as tears burned her eyes, but she managed to force a smile. 'Then we must make the most of today and tomorrow.' Her lips trembled and she looked down, pretending to brush a tiny insect from her serviceable calico skirt. She should be used to saying goodbye to Adam by now, but this time it seemed suddenly very final and frightening. He was a soldier and could be killed in action, which was a possibility she had not admitted to herself until now.

'Well, at least I get some peace when Adam is away,' Lottie said cheerfully.

'And I get a rest from your constant prattle.' Adam picked up a last-season's acorn and tossed it at her.

'Gideon isn't rude to me like you are, Adam,' Lottie said crossly.

Poppy could see a quarrel brewing and she stepped in between them. 'I suggest that whatever we decide to do, we should invite Gideon to come. It's a pity he missed the races.'

'Oh, yes, that would be lovely.' Lottie's expression changed instantly and she smiled, clapping her hands. 'May we drive over to Marsh House and ask him, Adam?'

'I don't see why not.' Adam winked at Poppy. 'I don't suppose you are free this evening?'

'No, I'm sorry. But perhaps I could get tomorrow off, if I ask nicely. We have a few parties booked but they are quite small and easy to manage. We could all do something special.'

'That's settled then. I'll drive to Marsh House and see if Gideon is free to join us. You may come, too, Lottie, but only if you promise not to complain about my motor car.'

'I promise, Adam. Cross my heart and hope to die.' Lottie made the sign of the cross on her frilled bodice.

'I have an idea,' Poppy said eagerly. 'I've never been on a train and I've never seen the sea. I would really love to go to Southend. I've heard people talk about it and there's a pier you can walk on and get all that lovely sea air. Wouldn't that be wonderful? What do you say, Adam? Could we do that tomorrow?'

'Oh, do say yes, Adam,' Lottie added eagerly. 'Maybe Gideon can come too.'

'I don't see why not,' Adam said thoughtfully. 'I could drive to Fenchurch Street Station and we could go from there. A day at the seaside might be fun, and we would be safe from Miranda Flyte.'

Poppy glanced over her shoulder. 'Don't say that, Adam. I have a feeling she is going to turn up everywhere we go, like a bad penny.'

'I think we will be safe in Southend,' Adam said with a wry smile. 'It will be my last outing before I join my regiment.'

Poppy sighed. 'I had hoped you might have a little longer.'

'Will you miss me?' Adam met her troubled gaze with a searching look.

'Don't fish for compliments, Adam.' Lottie rolled her eyes. 'He has to be the centre of attention, Poppy. Take no notice.'

'Of course I will miss him,' Poppy said firmly. 'You will be gone soon, too, Lottie. No doubt you will return to Dorrington Place before long.'

'I don't know about that. Perhaps Mama will decide to bring Arthur to Nine Oaks for a while if all his spots have cleared up. I hope so, anyway.'

'The Afterthought is a brat,' Adam said casually. 'He should be sent away to boarding school as I was, but he's always ailing. Mama coddles him.'

'He's only ten,' Lottie protested. 'You're just jealous.'

'No I am not. He is so spoiled that he only has to cough and it sends Mama into a frenzy.'

'He was a very sickly baby.' Lottie turned to Poppy. 'You remember that, don't you? Arthur nearly died when he suffered from whooping cough.'

Poppy nodded. 'I did hear something of the sort, although I don't remember much about it other than the fact that Mama was very concerned. I believe that Gideon's pa cared for Arthur. He saved the baby's life, so I was told.'

'Precisely so,' Lottie said triumphantly. 'So you see, Adam, your comments about Arthur are very unkind.'

'All right, I apologise. He's not a bad fellow, but he needs to toughen up or when he does go out into the world he will find it very difficult to survive.'

'I think he's a delightful boy,' Poppy said hastily. 'He's very artistic, Adam. He loves books and music. He's never going to be a soldier like you, but he'll do well in life nevertheless.'

'Why are we arguing about Arthur?' Lottie demanded. 'We should be enjoying ourselves. Anyway, I need to go home and sort out what I will wear for a day at the seaside. Also, I need to change into something more suitable if we're to visit Marsh House.'

Poppy laughed. 'I'm sure that Gideon will think you look lovely no matter what you're wearing.'

'But his mama is one of the most highly thought of fashion designers in London.'

'She is the most down-to-earth person I've ever met,' Poppy said firmly. 'I love Aunt Amelia. I only wish I saw her more often, but we are all working hard to give our families the best lives possible. I'm sure she would tell you that herself.'

Lottie pulled a face. 'I know I am shallow and justifiably vain because I inherited Mama's beauty, but I do want Gideon to think well of me.'

'Go with Adam and charm Gideon into accompanying us tomorrow. I must admit I'm looking forward to a day at the seaside. I'll ask Cook to make us up a picnic and if it's fine we can eat it on the beach. It will be lovely.'

Chapter Six

For once Adam was in agreement that to leave the motor car parked outside the railway station was not a good idea, and the excited party of four travelled instead in the comfortable Dorrington barouche, driven by Freddie's coachman. They set off in high spirits, but as they ventured into the poorest parts of the East End, which were unfamiliar to Poppy, she was shocked to see just how many barefoot, ragged children were running wild in the streets when they should have been attending school. Many of the smaller waifs had obviously been left in charge of even tinier children, some of them babes in arms, and they were clad in filthy rags, often nothing but a tattered vest.

'How awful,' Poppy said with a heartfelt sigh. 'Those poor little mites, how can anyone allow such poverty to go unchecked?'

Gideon followed her gaze, shaking his head. 'There are organisations and charities who try to deal with the problem, but it's almost impossible to stamp out such want and need.'

'Adam, tell your coachman to stop. I must give those little girls some money for food,' Poppy said urgently.

'If you do that, they will be robbed by older children before you get back into the carriage.' Adam laid his hand on her arm. 'It's sweet of you to be so concerned and I agree with you that more should be done, but Papa donates handsomely to the relevant charities.'

Poppy subsided back onto the luxuriously padded squabs. 'We have a picnic basket filled with delicious food and yet they look as if they haven't eaten for weeks.'

'Our luncheon would feed a few of them but they would be in the same predicament tomorrow and the next day.' Lottie yawned, covering her mouth with her gloved hand. 'We must be nearing the station now, are we not, Gideon?'

'Not far, I think.' Gideon gazed out of the window, frowning. 'I wish I could do more for those in want, particularly the children and the elderly, but if I give my services free to those who are desperate, I would never be in a financial position to marry and have a family of my own. It is a terrible dilemma, and I admire those who can give themselves so selflessly for the good of others.'

95

'Have you a prospective bride in mind, Gideon?' Lottie leaned forward, treating him to a wide smile.

'Maybe, or maybe not. In my position I rarely meet young ladies who might wish to marry an impecunious doctor.' Gideon shook his head. 'But let's not dwell upon matters about which we can do nothing, at least for the moment. I think we should concentrate on enjoying our day out together.'

Adam slapped him on the back. 'Absolutely, my friend. I couldn't agree more. Who knows when we might all be together again?'

'Don't say things like that, Adam.' Poppy shuddered. 'You make it sound as if you are going to be away for ever and a day.'

Adam glanced out of the window. 'At last. There's the station. Leave all your worries behind, Poppy. This is going to be a day to remember for all of us. I'll get the tickets, Gideon, if you will see the ladies towards the right platform. I'll join you there.'

'Of course.' Gideon proffered an arm to Lottie and the other to Poppy. 'Let's forget everything other than enjoying a day out together.'

'Poppy has never seen the sea,' Lottie said smugly. 'My parents have friends who own a castle on the coast of Devonshire. We visit them quite often.'

Poppy could not compete with this and she remained silent, although her thoughts kept straying to the poor children she had seen that morning. She knew she would be unable to rest unless she did something to help, although she had no idea what that might be. The plight of the young ones had registered more due to stories told to her by her mother, whose early life had been one of privation and ill-treatment by people who claimed to be her close relatives. However, it would be selfish to spoil everyone's fun today by brooding.

She put all such thoughts aside as Adam came striding towards them, waving the tickets in his hand. He showed them at the barrier and they were allowed onto the platform just in time to see the huge iron giant wheezing towards them, billowing smoke and letting off steam. The high-pitched sound made both Lottie and Poppy cover their ears, and that made them all laugh, setting the tone for the day.

When they were comfortably settled in a first-class carriage, Poppy was too fascinated by watching the neat fields bordered with lush hedgerows, and the small towns, villages and hamlets flash past the windows to join in the general conversation. The train stopped at every station, to drop off and take on passengers. The guard took two calves from the luggage van, but the young animals seemed to have other ideas than being delivered to the burly farmer who waited for them. They tugged at the ropes looped around their necks and, having reached a lamppost, they somehow managed to go different ways, tangling their leashes and tripping up the unfortunate guard. The train left the station before he had managed to sort out the muddle, leaving Poppy wishing she had witnessed the eventual outcome.

The journey was relatively quick and when they alighted from the train at Southend-on-Sea station, Poppy had put all her worries behind her to concentrate on enjoying a lovely sunny day by the sea.

After an exhilarating walk to the end of the pier, they took the train that ran the whole length of the structure and dropped them off where they had started on the seafront. By now the sun was high in the sky and it was too hot to do anything other than to find a little shade so that they could sit down on the damp sand and enjoy their picnic. However, despite her good intentions, each mouthful Poppy took served to remind her of the unfortunate children she had seen earlier that day. She toyed with her lunch, swallowing the delicious food with difficulty. No one seemed to notice and the others were obviously enjoying their meal. Gulls circled overhead, seeming to offer their services in clearing up anything that was left, but a cheeky herring gull swooped down and snatched a ham sandwich from Gideon's hand. This act of bravado made everyone laugh, including Poppy, and she forced herself to join in the conversation.

When the meal was finished and everything packed back into the wicker basket, which Adam had carried without so much as a quibble, they decided to go for one last walk along the promenade before returning to the station. Poppy was amused to see Gideon and

Lottie strolling ahead, arm in arm. Lottie invariably managed to get her own way and she had always shown a marked preference for Gideon. Poppy was not sure whether it was mutual, but she knew Gideon well enough to worry. He had been the most sensible one in their group when they were children, and he had grown into a strong, stalwart man like his father. However, the difference in station between himself and Lady Charlotte Ashton would be enough to prevent him from ever acknowledging whatever feelings he might have for her. Poppy wished that she could wave a magic wand and take away the barriers of class and social status, but she had been brought up in the world of commerce, whereas Lottie had been pampered and cosseted all her life. Poppy could not imagine delicate, beautiful Lottie living in a small house without an army of servants to attend her every need. Even on a consultant's salary it would be impossible for Gideon to achieve the standard of living that Lottie had grown up expecting.

'A penny for your thoughts.' Adam slipped Poppy's hand through the crook of his arm. 'Are you still worrying about the poor children?'

Poppy was about to answer when she spotted a now-familiar figure approaching them, followed by a neatly dressed maidservant. Even though the lady's face was half hidden by a fashionable straw hat trimmed with huge silk roses in eye-catching scarlet, and shaded by a fringed parasol, there was no mistaking Miranda Flyte. She advanced quickly, flashing a smile at Lottie and Gideon before coming to a halt in front of Poppy and Adam. She fluttered her eyelashes, giving him a seductive smile.

'What a coincidence. Poppy and Lord Ashton, how delightful.' Miranda shot a casual glance over her shoulder. 'And Lady Charlotte with a gentleman whose name I cannot quite recall.'

'Then might I introduce you to Dr Gideon Taylor?' Poppy said icily. 'Are you following us, Miranda? How did you know we were coming to Southend?'

'Goodness me, how suspicious you are, Poppy, my dear.' Miranda shrugged, shaking her head. 'It's pure coincidence. I have been visiting my uncle, who lives in Eastwood, a few miles away. I had a sudden urge to see the sea, as I imagine is true in your case. Unless, of course, you have been following me.'

'We seem fated to keep on meeting in out-of-the-way places,' Adam said calmly. 'But if you will excuse us, Miss Flyte, we should be walking back to the railway station.'

'You came by public transport?' Miranda raised a delicate eyebrow. 'I admire your egalitarian attitude, although I'm surprised that you didn't drive down in your motor car. However, I chose to travel in my barouche.'

Gideon cleared his throat. 'I think we should head for the station, Adam.'

'Yes, so do I.' Poppy tightened her grasp on Adam's arm. 'It was nice, although rather surprising, to see you again, Miranda.'

'Life is full of surprises, my dear.' Miranda turned to her maid, who was hovering awkwardly behind her. 'Where did you see that tea shop, Jones? I have a fancy for a cup of tea and some dainty pastries.' Miranda smiled graciously and walked past them, heading for the centre of the town with her maid hurrying after her.

Lottie stared at Poppy open-mouthed. 'Well, I never did!'

Poppy laughed. 'You've been spending too much time with us commoners, Lottie. But I agree with the sentiment. I swear that Miranda Flyte would turn up if we were at the top of the Eiffel Tower in Paris.'

Lottie's eyes widened. 'Have you been to Paris, Poppy?'

'No, of course not. It was a figure of speech. But seriously, how did she know we were going to be here today?'

'Maybe it is just another odd coincidence,' Gideon suggested, frowning.

Adam shook his head. 'Unlikely, I'd say. That woman is stalking us as if we were prime game, for what reason only she knows.'

'But how does she know where we will be?' Poppy said thoughtfully. 'And what does she want from us?'

'Who knew we were coming to the seaside today?' Adam looked from one to the other.

Gideon shook his head. 'I told my mother, and she was delighted to think that we were all going out together, but she wouldn't have reason to tell anyone else.'

'I let Papa know what we were planning,' Lottie added. 'He said he would have liked to accompany us but he had to go into town on estate business.'

'Mrs Burden made up the picnic for us.' Poppy thought hard, trying to recall which of the servants were in the kitchen at the time. 'The only other person who knew was that young maid we took on recently: Ivy Morris from the village.'

Adam nodded. 'Perhaps a conversation with young Ivy might reveal the spy in the camp.'

Poppy laughed. 'You make it sound like the plot from a penny dreadful or a gothic novel, Adam.'

'It's beginning to feel that way.' Adam glanced up at the sky where ominous dark clouds were gathering. 'I agree with Gideon: we should set off for the station at a brisk pace. It looks like rain.'

'Oh dear,' Lottie said anxiously. 'I didn't bring an umbrella. My new straw hat will be ruined if it gets wet.'

Gideon patted her hand as it rested on his sleeve. 'If the worst happens I'll be a gentleman and take off my jacket and use it to keep you and your bonnet from harm.'

Lottie shot a sideways glance at her brother. 'You see, Adam. That's what a real gentleman would do. I doubt if you would be so gallant.'

'Adam would simply say, "Run for it, girls," and

that would be that,' Poppy said, laughing. 'Don't look at me like that, Adam. You know it's true.'

'When have I not behaved well towards you, Poppy?' Adam demanded, quickening his pace.

'I could give you a list. What about the time when I was only seven and you convinced me that the river was shallow enough to wade across? I nearly drowned.'

'I pulled you out, didn't I?'

'No, it was Gideon who rescued me. You thought it was funny.'

Lottie poked Adam in the back. 'Stop goading her, Adam. You two squabble like a pair of five-year-olds. I think you should grow up.'

Poppy and Adam exchanged amused glances.

'I prefer to remain as we are,' Poppy said, suppressing a giggle. 'It's more fun this way, isn't it, Adam?'

He nodded. 'Poppy understands me, Lottie, which is more than you do.'

Gideon glanced up at the sky. 'We'd better hurry up. It's going to pour down at any minute.'

Poppy slipped her hand free. 'I'll beat you to the station, Adam.' She picked up her skirts and ran.

The journey home was enjoyable but uneventful. When they reached Rainbow's End, Lottie was eager to return to Nine Oaks in order to change ready for dinner, and Gideon was keen to get home in case he was called out that evening. They took their seats in the car, but Adam followed Poppy to the front door.

'I'll call in and see you tomorrow,' he said gravely. 'I'll be leaving the following day for the barracks.'

'Have you any idea where you might be posted?' Poppy had not meant to sound anxious but she could not keep up the pretence of being casual about Adam joining his new regiment.

'None at all.' Adam tweaked a copper curl that had escaped from beneath Poppy's bonnet. 'Will you miss me?'

She tossed her head. 'I shan't even notice you're gone. I dare say you'll be back on leave soon enough.'

He laughed and leaned forward to plant a kiss on her lips. 'You won't get rid of me easily, Poppy. You and I are a pair and always have been.' He gave her a mock salute and returned to the motor car, climbing in without bothering to open the door.

Poppy stood on the front step as Adam expertly reversed the car and drove off at an impressive and illegal turn of speed. Poppy watched until the motor car was out of sight. Despite the threat of rain earlier, it was a fine evening and she could imagine driving into the sunset with Adam at the wheel. However, real life was not so romantic and, somewhat reluctantly, she opened the front door and stepped inside.

The delicious aroma of her uncle's culinary expertise mingled with the scent of French wine, and judging by the hum of voices emanating from the dining room, evening service was already in full swing. Poppy was supposed to have the whole day off, but she felt restless and in the need of something to take her mind off the inevitable parting with Adam. They had met often during his time at Sandhurst and it was comforting to know that, while there, he was safe, but the life of a serving officer might be all too short. Adam claimed to lead a charmed life, but that was so typical of him. Bravado might as well have been his middle name. A wry smile curved her lips as she hurried upstairs to her room, where she changed into a serviceable navy-blue skirt and a neat white cotton blouse. There was always something that needed doing in the busy restaurant kitchen even if the main courses had been served.

Poppy made her way downstairs, ready to make herself useful. However, she had not expected to walk into the kitchen in the middle of a full-blown row. Mrs Burden was standing arms akimbo, facing Amos, who had flung his chef's hat across the room. There was no sign of Silas Begg.

'What is the matter?' Poppy demanded.

Mrs Burden turned to her, red in the face and clearly distressed. 'It was my béchamel sauce all over again. Chef Amos said that my custard was curdled. He tipped a whole jugful into the sink. A waste of good cream and eggs, I say.'

'This woman is a cook,' Amos said angrily. 'I am a chef, Poppy. Tell her that I am right. I refuse to work with her again.'

'Where is Begg?' Poppy asked in a low voice. 'He should be here, Mrs Burden.'

'I need more eggs, Miss Poppy. I asked him to

fetch some from the dairy. I'm a good cook. I won't be spoken to in such a rude way, not by Mr Amos or anyone.'

'Of course not.' Poppy glanced at Mattie, who was standing by, saying nothing. 'How many orders are there to go through to the dining room?'

'I only came down for a cup of tea,' Mattie said crossly. 'They was going at it hammer and tongs, Miss Poppy.'

'Don't speak, woman.' Amos glared at her. 'I don't like women, except for Poppy and my sister, Flora.'

Poppy took him by the arm. 'No one means to upset you, Uncle Amos. But you must not be rude to Mrs Burden. She is, like the rest of us, doing her best.'

'But I am the chef, Poppy.'

'Yes, of course you are, and there are paying customers in the dining room waiting to enjoy the delicious food that you create.'

He nodded. 'That is true. But I am upset now. I cannot do any more today.'

At that moment Begg hurried in through the scullery. He set a basket of eggs down on the table. 'What's happened?'

Mrs Burden opened her mouth to speak but Poppy sent her a warning frown.

'I think my uncle has had enough for one evening, Mr Begg,' Poppy said firmly. 'Perhaps you would be kind enough to take him home. He has treated the guests to delicious food and now he deserves a rest.'

Begg winked and tapped the side of his bulbous nose. 'Understood, Miss Poppy.' He stepped forward and laid his hand on Amos's shoulder.

'Come now, boss. You've done your share of the work. Let the underlings finish off what you began.'

'Underlings! Bah!' Mrs Burden muttered, covering her mouth with her hand.

'I'm relying on your expertise, Mrs B,' Poppy said in a low voice. 'You know that my uncle didn't mean a slur on your cooking.'

'I can't leave my kitchen to that creature,' Amos protested, shaking off Begg's restraining hand.

'There he goes again.' Mrs Burden puffed out her cheeks, exhaling loudly. 'I was never so insulted.'

'I doubt that.' Amos pulled a face, giving him the appearance of an angry pug.

'Mr Begg?' Poppy sent him a pleading look.

'Don't worry, miss.' Begg ushered a protesting Amos from the kitchen, pausing in the doorway. 'I'll see Mr Amos safely to his cottage.'

Poppy sighed with relief. 'I never worry about my uncle when you are in charge, Mr Begg.' She turned to Mrs Burden. 'Now, what next? Are the diners waiting for desserts? If so, how can I help?'

'My custard never curdles. That man should wear spectacles.' Mrs Burden handed Poppy a sheaf of orders.

'I can help with these. If you make another batch of custard, I'll do two jam omelettes as these are needed first. We'll go on from there.' Poppy seized an apron and tied it round her waist before starting to prepare eggs.

'I can help,' Mattie said, sighing. 'Tell me what you need, Mrs B. I'll do the fetching and carrying. I can weigh things out on the scales, too.'

'Thank you, Mattie.' Mrs Burden rolled her eyes. 'Mr Amos is a wonderful chef, but he's the most difficult person I've ever had to work with.'

There was no arguing with that statement. Poppy set about making the omelettes and, as neither of the two waitresses had made an appearance, she took the plated desserts to the dining room. Flora was standing by the door as she stared at her daughter in surprise.

'I thought you had the day off, Poppy.'

'We returned early enough for me to make myself useful. Uncle Amos was on one of his rampages and he upset Mrs Burden, so I'm helping with the desserts.'

Flora beckoned to Gertie, one of the waitresses. 'Take these to table two, please.'

'Yes, ma'am.' Gertie hurried off to deliver the omelettes to eager diners.

'Where is your uncle now, Poppy?'

'Begg took Uncle Amos to his cottage. We won't see him until tomorrow.'

'Oh, well, it happens. Amos is a brilliant artist in the kitchen, but he's temperamental. However, it should have been your night off, my love.'

'Really, I don't mind, Mama. I'll get back to

the kitchen if you'll send Gertie to collect the next orders.'

'Of course, darling. I'll do my bit. I can't allow everyone else to bear the brunt of my brother's ill temper.'

The rest of the evening passed smoothly enough. When the last diner had left and the kitchen had been cleaned and tidied, Poppy and her mother sat down at the table to enjoy a cup of tea. They were joined by Daniel, who had been doing the rounds and locking up outside as well as checking windows and doors.

'Will you have a cup of tea, darling?' Flora asked, smiling up at her ruggedly handsome husband.

'No, thank you. I had one earlier with the Carltons. I've got an early start tomorrow so I'm turning in now.'

'Yes, of course. You're going to Smithfield to get the meat and poultry I ordered.' Flora blew him a kiss. 'I won't be long. I'm just hearing about Poppy's day at the seaside.'

'Of course. I hope it went well, Poppy. You can tell me all about it in the morning.' Daniel leaned over to kiss his wife on the cheek. He left the room, closing the door behind him.

Poppy sighed. 'You and Pa were so lucky you found each other. I can't imagine a happier couple.'

'Indeed, yes. Although there were times when we didn't get along so well. However, we found our

Rainbow's End together, I'm happy to say.' Flora leaned her elbows on the table, giving Poppy a searching look. 'But what about you? Adam will be leaving soon.'

'Yes, and I'll miss him, but there is no real romance between us, Mama. You can put all thoughts of a wedding out of your head. Adam is not for me.'

'You can't possibly know that for certain. Unless you dislike him, of course.'

'I know that's a subtle way of making me confess that I'm madly in love with him, but that isn't so either. I am very fond of Adam and I will miss him terribly, but there are other things on my mind at present.'

'Are you able to tell me about them?' Flora sipped her tea, replacing the cup on its saucer. 'I don't wish to pry, Poppy.'

'You suffered terrible privation as a small child, didn't you, Mama?'

'The couple who plucked me from the river after the ships collided and sank were a pair of unscrupulous rogues. They raised me after a fashion, intending to sell me to the highest bidder when I was old enough, but I was kept in truly awful conditions.'

Poppy shuddered. 'I can't bear to think of you going through that at such a tender age.'

'You know the story so well, darling. It was a lucky penny that changed my life forever and I was taken in by your aunt Bella's parents, but it all happened a long time ago. So why the interest now?'

'It seems that nothing has changed. We drove through the East End and I was shocked by the state of the poor children I saw on the way to the station. I know there are institutions that try to care for such youngsters, but the little ones I saw today were ragged, filthy and starving.'

'We give to charity when we can, Poppy.'

'Yes, I know, and so does Uncle Freddie, but I would like to do something practical.'

'You want to feed the poor and hungry?'

'I would like to help at least some of the children who roam the streets.'

'How would you do that? I mean, in practical terms, you can hardly fill a basket with food and take it to the poorest areas without being set upon and having everything stolen by those who are bigger and stronger. There are soup kitchens set up to feed the poor. I suppose you could offer to help in one.'

Poppy shook her head. 'I don't know, Mama. It does seem impossible when you put it like that.'

'Perhaps something will come to you, but just be aware of the difficulties. I know because I lived in those conditions for far too long.'

'I promise not to do anything rash, Mama. But there is something else. That woman Miranda Flyte was in Southend today. We met her on the promenade.'

'That is one coincidence too many. What on earth can she want with you? And how does she find out where you will be from one day to the next?'

'Adam and I think she is getting the information she wants from someone working here. I suspect young Ivy, the girl from the village. She hasn't been with us long.'

'It's possible.' Flora frowned thoughtfully. 'But what is Miranda's aim? Is it you she wants to be near or – and I think this more likely – would it be Adam and Lottie? Although what she can hope to gain by insinuating herself into their company is beyond me.'

'We don't know where she lives or even who she really is, come to that. She told us a pack of lies in the beginning, and now she appears to be wealthy. Today she was with her own personal maid. I intend to find out, although where to start is beyond me at the moment.'

Flora rose to her feet. 'If she is so persistent I imagine you won't have to wait long before she turns up again. If I were you I would ask her to explain herself. Don't take no for an answer.'

'You're right, as always, Mama. That's what I will do.'

'I'm off to bed, darling,' Flora said, yawning. She kissed Poppy on the forehead. 'Don't stay up too long. We have a busy day tomorrow.'

Chapter Seven

Poppy was too occupied the next day to worry about when Miranda Flyte might choose to descend upon them. The restaurant was particularly busy with large parties and Amos had been called in to manage the kitchen, although as a rule he only performed his culinary magic in the evenings. Poppy had been a little nervous as to how her uncle would treat Mrs Burden after their previous argument, but he seemed to have forgotten all about it and was in a very sunny mood, which was unusual. Begg hovered in the background, making himself useful by helping Beasley to fetch wine and bottles of ale from the cellar. The guests were obviously out to enjoy themselves and a wedding party called for more champagne, having downed several bottles in quick succession.

When the last dish had been served and diners

had gravitated to the lounge or had wandered outside to enjoy the pleasure of the gardens, the task of clearing up had begun in earnest. Poppy found herself helping Begg to crate the empty wine bottles.

'My uncle seems happier today, Mr Begg. You always know how to handle him.'

'The best part of my life on merchant ships prepared me for anything.' His shaggy grey beard moved up and down as he grinned, exposing a row of broken teeth. 'More'n thirty years, Miss Poppy, man and boy.'

'You must have seen a lot during that time.'

He eyed her warily. 'I dare say I have. What in particular interests you, miss? I can tell there's something on your mind.'

'Is it that obvious?' Poppy laughed.

'You seem thoughtful, that's all.'

'Did you see a lot of poverty in the places you visited, Begg?'

'I dare say I did, miss. But I was younger then and I suppose I accepted it as normal. What's troubling you?'

'I was shocked to see such deprivation when we were on our way to the railway station, particularly so many barefoot, ragged children.'

'It is the same story the world over.' Begg sighed and shook his head, his beard flapping as if caught in a sudden breeze. 'There's not much any one person can do to help them, miss.'

'Well, there should be,' Poppy said passionately.

'What could someone do to alleviate the situation, even in a small way?'

Begg put his head on one side, giving her a searching look. 'Would you be that someone, miss?'

'Perhaps. If I could find a way to help poor children I would do so, willingly.'

'You have enough to do here, surely?'

'Not all the time, Mr Begg.'

'I can't help you myself, not being of a charitable nature, nor do I particularly like nippers, but I know someone who does. He might be able to assist you.'

'That would be wonderful. I feel a desperate need to do something useful, other than working here, of course. I couldn't leave Ma and Pa in the lurch.'

'Understood, miss. Let me have a word with the gentleman and I'll see what I can do.' Begg hefted a crate of empty bottles with ease. 'I'll take these outside and come back for the rest.'

'Yes, of course. Thank you, Mr Begg. Can you tell me who this person is?'

'His name is Eddie Taverner. That's all you need to know, for the present. I can't promise anything, but I'll have a word with him.'

'That's all I ask.' Poppy set about filling another crate as Begg left to take the empty bottles to the outside store. She had only just completed her task when Adam strolled into the restaurant.

'It looks as if everyone had a good time today,' he said, smiling.

Poppy glanced at the waitresses clearing the tables

of the debris left by the guests. She acknowledged Adam's remark with a smile.

'It all went very well, and thank goodness we only have a few bookings tonight. I don't imagine Ma feels the same way, but I'll be glad to finish early.'

'I hope she's in a good mood,' Adam said seriously. 'It's my last night at home, Poppy. I'd like to take you to the theatre in the West End and supper afterwards, but I need to persuade your mama, or perhaps I should say your papa. Lottie is coming too, I hasten to add.'

Poppy laughed. 'I think Ma and Pa know you well enough to trust you, Adam. I would love to go to the theatre.'

'Excellent. Well, I'll go and find Aunt Flora first and then I'll have a chat with your papa. I'll let you know what they say.' Adam walked off humming a popular melody.

That evening, dressed in her best gown with her hair put up in an elaborate coiffure, studded with white rosebuds, Poppy walked slowly down the sweeping staircase at Rainbow's End to meet Adam. His obvious admiration was even more pleasing than his compliments on her appearance. Flora stood by the door with Daniel, both parents smiling proudly as Adam escorted Poppy to his motor car.

'Don't keep her out too late, Adam,' Daniel said with mock severity.

Lottie waved to them from the back seat of the car.

'Don't worry, Uncle Daniel. I will make sure we get Poppy home at a reasonable hour. Adam wouldn't dare risk a telling off from Papa if he upset you and Aunt Flora.'

Flora laughed. 'Your dear papa never scolds anyone unless they have done something really dreadful. Just drive carefully, Adam. No heroics, please.'

Adam handed Poppy into the passenger seat. 'Absolutely not, Aunt Flora. I will bring Poppy home after a late supper at Frascati's.'

'Enjoy yourself, my darling,' Flora said, smiling. 'Have a lovely time.'

'I will, Mama.' Poppy had barely spoken the words when Adam leaped into the driver's seat, having cranked the engine with the starting handle. They drove off with the wheels spinning, leaving a cloud of dust in their wake.

'Stop showing off, Adam.' Lottie tapped him on the shoulder. 'We want to get to the theatre in one piece.'

Poppy sat back in her seat. 'It's so nice to have an evening off, and to be going to the theatre, too. Is Gideon going to join us?'

Adam nodded. 'Yes, he's going to meet us at the Shaftesbury Avenue theatre. Apparently he has been doing a day course at the Middlesex Hospital, so it's quite convenient for him.'

'Are we driving all the way in the motor car?' Poppy asked, brushing dust from her coat.

'No, it would take too long. We'll leave the car at the railway station and travel on by train. It's quicker, considering the traffic in the West End.'

'I wonder if that dreadful woman will greet us outside the theatre,' Lottie giggled. 'I think she's a witch and spies on us from her broomstick as she flies overhead.'

'Maybe she could give us a lift,' Adam said, grinning. 'Flying into town would be quicker even than the train.'

Poppy laughed. 'You two do talk nonsense. I will miss you terribly when you go away, Adam. And you, too, Lottie. I suppose you and Uncle Freddie will be returning to Dorrington Place before long.'

'I don't know and that's the truth.' Lottie sighed. 'I love Nine Oaks because it's so much cosier than Dorrington Place, which is huge. I doubt if we've discovered all the rooms there, although we did try as children, didn't we, Adam?'

'We did, and we also got lost on numerous occasions and Mama had to send a servant to look for us.'

'You'll find it so different living in a barracks,' Poppy said thoughtfully. 'Do you think you'll like being in the army, Adam? I mean, there's talk about more trouble with the Boers. How would you feel if they sent you to South Africa?'

Adam swerved to miss a startled rabbit that had wandered into the middle of the road. 'I'm prepared to go wherever the army sends me, Poppy. It's as simple as that.'

'I believe you're looking forward to going into battle.'

He shot her a sideways glance. 'If it didn't mean leaving you behind, I would be excited about travelling and getting into a skirmish with the enemy.'

'What about me?' Lottie demanded. 'You have to miss me, Adam. I'm your twin sister.'

'Of course I will. That goes without saying.'

'Liar.' Lottie subsided onto the seat. 'I think you'll forget about all of us when the fighting begins. You always enjoyed a scrap with the village lads.'

'It's hardly the same thing, old girl,' Adam said, laughing. 'We might have bloodied each other's noses, but no one died. I don't like violence, but sometimes there is no alternative. I'll be fighting for Queen and Country, not to mention protecting my loved ones at home.' He signalled that he was turning left and pulled in outside the station where he climbed out to open the door for Poppy and Lottie. 'Wait inside the ticket office and I'll find somewhere safe to park the motor car. I don't want the local brats jumping all over it.'

Poppy and Lottie walked into the ticket office. The now familiar smell of burning coal, soot and engine oil assailed Poppy's nostrils. Colourful posters depicting exciting destinations hung on the walls, promising holidays of a lifetime or visits to towns of historical interest, but before Poppy had a chance to study them in detail Adam hurried in and purchased tickets.

'Just in time,' he said, smiling. 'The next train is due at any moment.' He ushered them out onto the platform and the train rumbled to a halt, ejecting a cloud of steam and an ear-splitting whistle.

Poppy could hardly contain her excitement at the prospect of an evening in the West End. She could tell by the expression in Adam's eyes that the trouble she had taken over her appearance had not been in vain, and he held her hand as they climbed into the carriage. He was slow to release it as they sat side by side on the upholstered seat, and Lottie sat opposite them, staring out of the window. At a signal from the guard, the train lurched forward and they were off at a breath-taking speed, heading towards an evening devoted to pleasure.

As arranged, Gideon was waiting for them outside the Shaftesbury Avenue theatre. Lottie had been quiet during the train ride, but she brightened up at the sight of him, and she slipped her hand through the crook of his arm as they entered the theatre.

Poppy could hardly wait for the curtain to rise and she was not disappointed by the performance. She found herself spellbound by the tale of love and mistaken identity, put to music with the touching lyrics of the 'Gypsy Love Song' and others just as stirring. After the finale and the fall of the curtain, Poppy was still in the romantic world of handsome hussars, counts and beautiful fortune-tellers. A late supper at Frascati's was a perfect end to the evening, and the euphoria lasted the entire journey home. It was only when she had to part with Adam on the steps of Rainbow's End that the reality of their situation overcame her. She returned his kiss with equal fervour, but then the door opened and Daniel stood there, holding an oil lamp.

'Your mama wanted to stay up to ask how the evening went, but I managed to persuade her to go to bed.'

'I hope we aren't too late, Uncle Daniel,' Adam said hopefully. 'It's my last night at home. I join my regiment in the morning.'

Daniel nodded. 'So Flora told me. I hope you don't get posted too far away. You know you're always welcome here.'

'You must write to me, Adam,' Poppy said firmly. 'I'll be waiting for the postman every day until I know that you are somewhere safe.'

Adam laughed. 'I'm a soldier, Poppy. I'm not a boy on his way to boarding school. I dare say I'll be facing danger at some time in my career.' He held up his hand as she opened her mouth to protest. 'But I will write to you and you must keep me up to date with the goings-on here and at Nine Oaks. I doubt if Lottie will bother.'

'I heard that, Adam Ashton,' Lottie called from the motor car. 'I'm getting cold and I'm tired. For goodness' sake say good night to Poppy and take me home.'

Poppy stood on tiptoe to kiss Adam on the cheek. 'Good night, Adam. I'll miss you.'

He hesitated as if he had something more to say but glanced at Daniel and seemed to think better of it. 'Good night, sir. Good night, Poppy. I won't say goodbye – that's too final.' He left with a cheery wave.

Daniel closed the door. 'He's a fine young fellow, Poppy. But he's an aristocrat and we are just ordinary folk. One day he'll marry into his own class.'

Poppy tossed her head. 'I know that, Pa. We're just friends.'

'I'm glad to hear it, love. I don't want you to get hurt.'

'I hope one day I'll find another man just like you, Pa.' Poppy gave him a hug. 'I'm going to bed. It's been a long day. Good night, Pa. I love you.'

She left him in the entrance hall and made her way to her room, a turbulent maelstrom of emotions threatening to overcome her. What Pa had said was only too true. She had allowed herself to dream of marrying Second Lieutenant Viscount Ashton, but it was just a childhood fantasy. She would love him for ever, but marriage, as Pa had said, was out of the question. Perhaps their enforced separation now would turn out to be a blessing. Poppy sat down at her dressing table and plucked the withered rosebuds from her hair, laying them in a neat line on a cut-glass pin tray. She released her long hair from the pins that had held it in position all evening, and brushed out the curls, tugging at them until the pain made her eyes water. But she would not cry. She would never allow a man to bring her to tears. It was time for bed. Tomorrow was another busy day and her heartache was her own private affair. However, she would have to put a brave face on matters when speaking to Mama, who could spot a lie even before it left the guilty party's lips.

Poppy replaced the hairbrush next to the matching hand mirror, and stood up, allowing her gown to fall to the floor. Her stays and chemise followed before she slipped on her nightgown, doused the oil lamp and climbed into bed. As she laid her head on the pillow the music of Victor Herbert from *The Fortune Teller* rang in her ears and lulled her to sleep.

Keeping busy was the key, and Poppy was fully occupied for the next few days. She did think about Adam, but she chose to remember the good times they had enjoyed together and tried not to dwell on what might occur in the future. Lottie visited almost every day, but only because she was bored and lonely without her brother, and she wanted to talk about Gideon. Poppy usually managed to snatch a break when Lottie arrived after the lunchtime rush of customers had died down.

'I think Papa wants to return to Dorrington Place next week.' Lottie sat in the rose arbour idly plucking the petals off a daisy she had just picked. 'He loves me,' she added, smiling.

'Of course your papa loves you.' Poppy stopped cutting blooms for the dinner tables that evening. She stared at Lottie, perplexed. 'What makes you think he does not?'

Lottie rolled her eyes. 'I was talking about Gideon, you silly-billy. I haven't seen him since we went to the theatre and Frascati's.'

'He's doing a course at the Middlesex Hospital,' Poppy said patiently. 'You know that.'

'Yes, I do. But I'm sure he goes home to Marsh House in the evenings. I was expecting him to call on me by now. Do you think he has a lady friend at the hospital?'

'I really couldn't say. He's a very good-looking fellow and he's clever. I wouldn't be surprised if the nurses rather fancy him. He's quite a good catch.'

Lottie shuddered. 'Don't say that. You make him sound like a codfish.'

'You know I didn't mean it that way. It's obvious that Gideon is very fond of you, Lottie.'

'Is he really? Do you think so?'

'I wouldn't say so if I didn't mean it.' Poppy paused, wondering how much to say on the matter. She took a deep breath and went to sit beside Lottie. 'You know we are both in a similar predicament.'

Lottie's dark eyes widened. 'Really? How so?'

'Well,' Poppy said slowly, measuring every word, 'I care deeply for your brother and I think he's fond of me, but I know it can never amount to anything, and it's the same sort of thing between you and Gideon.'

'Now I really am lost. I'm sorry, Poppy, I don't know what you're talking about.'

Poppy took a deep breath. She laid the flowers down on the bench and took Lottie's small hands in hers. 'I am not the sort of girl that Adam will marry. He will have to choose someone from his own sphere. It's the same for you.'

'But the gentleman chooses his bride. Why can't Gideon pick me?'

'Because Gideon is not from your social class, and it's the same for me. We are from working families, if you like, while you and Adam are aristocrats.'

'But Papa works hard. He is always telling me how much he has to do with running the estate and looking after stocks and bonds and all that sort of thing. I bet he works just as hard as your mama and papa.'

Poppy sighed. 'I'm sure he does. But one day you will marry someone with a title and a lot of money. Adam will find a suitable débutante whose family can be traced back to William the Conqueror.'

Lottie frowned. 'I thought that William the Conqueror was French and he fought the English. I'm not sure he is a good example. Now if you had said King Arthur and the Knights of the Round Table, I might have agreed with you.'

'Yes, well, all of them, too.' Poppy retrieved the rapidly wilting flowers. 'I must get these into water. Would you like to come into the house? It's getting rather hot out here. I think I saw a couple of freckles pop out on the tip of your nose.'

Lottie's hand flew to cover her nose and cheeks. 'Oh, no! Mama will scold me for not carrying a parasol, even though I am wearing a straw bonnet.'

Poppy stood up, staring in disbelief at the woman walking towards them. 'It can't be. I thought she had given up.'

Lottie turned her head to look. 'It's her! The witch who knows exactly where to find us.'

'And she's seen us. There's nowhere to hide.' Poppy drew herself up to her full height. 'I'm going to have it out with her, here and now. Sit tight, Lottie. Leave this to me.'

'Poppy and Lottie.' Miranda approached them with both hands extended. 'What a happy coincidence.'

'Hardly,' Poppy said stiffly. 'This is my garden and Lottie often visits me here. You are the interloper. What do you want, Miranda?'

'Now that's not very friendly, is it? I came to see you and pass the time of day. I thought that we were friends.'

'Friends? What on earth gave you that idea? You simply turn up wherever we happen to be. What is it you hope to gain from shadowing us, Miranda?'

'That's rather harsh. I merely extended the hand of friendship and you seem to think the worst of me. Why is that?' Miranda dropped her hands to her side, gazing at Poppy with tears in her eyes.

'Don't pretend to be upset. I know that you are a consummate actress, Miranda Flyte, if that is your name. You tricked us into bringing you here from the fairground and you told us a pack of lies. How do you explain yourself?'

'I feel a little faint. It is rather hot and I am very thirsty. Might we continue this conversation indoors? I would like some iced water, if that's not asking too much?'

Lottie jumped to her feet. 'You poor thing. We were just about to go inside out of the sun. Take my arm, Miranda. I'm sure that one of the staff will find some ice to cool you down.' Lottie turned to Poppy, frowning. 'You are being very inhospitable. It's not like you, Poppy.' She took Miranda by the arm and set off purposefully towards the house.

It was Poppy's turn to roll her eyes and sigh. What was Miranda Flyte up to now? She had managed to convince Lottie that she was genuine, but then Lottie was an easy touch. She might not be clever intellectually, but she had a good heart and was often brought to tears by the plight of others. Poppy followed them into the house, stopping only to take the roses into the flower room and leave them standing in a jug of water until she had time to arrange them properly. Having done that, she went straight to the parlour where she found Lottie and Miranda waiting for her.

'Do take a seat, Miranda,' Poppy said politely. 'I think it's time we had a proper chat, don't you?'

'I most certainly do,' Lottie added quickly. 'I don't wish to be rude, but why do you turn up wherever we happen to be, Miranda? What possible reason could you have?'

Miranda sank down gracefully on the nearest chair. 'Perhaps it's fate that brings us together.'

Lottie took a seat opposite her. 'That doesn't make sense.'

'No, it doesn't.' Poppy continued to stand, glaring at Miranda. 'You obviously have some ulterior motive for haunting us, so I think you owe us an explanation.'

Miranda smiled calmly. 'My mother's maiden name was Jane Pettigrew. Does that mean anything to either of you?'

'Mama did mention something about the Pettigrew family,' Poppy said cautiously.

Miranda was suddenly serious. 'Ralph Pettigrew was my uncle. He died by his own hand many years ago, leaving his two sisters heartbroken.'

'I'm sorry to hear that, but I heard that he and his cousin abducted my mama and tried to force her to marry Ralph so that he could inherit his uncle's title and castle.' Lottie's pale cheeks flushed scarlet and her voice trembled. 'If my papa and Aunt Flora had not rescued her I hate to think what might have happened.'

Poppy stared at her aghast. 'I didn't know all that until recently, Lottie, and I certainly did not realise that you were aware of the story.'

'It's not the sort of thing one speaks of very often.' Lottie shrugged. 'It's best forgotten, if you ask me.

But what do you want with us, Miranda Flyte? I think your family owes mine an apology.'

Miranda's arched eyebrows snapped together in a frown. 'My uncle killed himself after he lost his inheritance, and it was all because of your mama, Lottie.'

'It seems to me that he brought the disgrace upon himself,' Poppy said angrily. 'What do you want from us, Miranda? Are you blaming Lottie's family for your uncle's death?'

'His life was in ruins after the affair. Cousin Gabriel lost his life at sea a few months later. The blame lies with the Ashton family. I believe that your mama was also involved in their downfall, Poppy.'

Miranda stood up, meeting Poppy's gaze with a menacing glare. 'We want a public apology from both your families. A full and frank written statement to be printed in *The Times*, and monetary reparation for all that our families have lost.'

'Just a minute,' Poppy said angrily. 'Is there someone encouraging you to take this action? Could it be that man who was with you at the races?'

'How clever of you to guess.' Miranda curled her lip. 'My cousin Gervase Mulliner will back me up. His mama is my mother's elder sister. Uncle Ralph was the baby of the family and your families are both responsible for his early demise. How would you feel in similar circumstances?'

Lottie opened her mouth to answer but Poppy held up a warning hand. 'You have just threatened our families and demanded money under what I can only call false pretences. Why should we not report you to the police?'

'I would have thought that was glaringly obvious. Do you really want the world to find out that your mama teased my late uncle into thinking she would marry him, Lottie? And your mama was little better, Poppy. I believe your mama travelled to Devonshire, unchaperoned in the company of Lord Dorrington, and their unfounded accusations were the direct cause of Pettigrew's sudden death. They might as well have plunged a knife into his heart.'

'That's not true. You're telling lies, Miranda.' Lottie covered her face with her hands and her body shook with barely suppressed sobs.

Poppy controlled her voice with difficulty. 'I think you'd better leave now, Miss Flyte.'

'I'm going, but this is just the beginning, Poppy Robbins. You will be hearing from me or my cousin Gervase before too long.' She swept out of the room.

Lottie raised a tear-stained face. 'Will she do as she threatens, Poppy? She could ruin both our families.'

'I think it would take more than that to create the scandal that she obviously wishes to inflict upon us.' Poppy frowned. 'On the other hand, I can't think why they have left it so long to come up with such a story.'

'It must be money. Perhaps they are in financial difficulties and they know that my papa has a large fortune.'

'Blackmail is a crime, Lottie. Besides which, all that happened before either of us were born. I can't believe something that took place more than twenty years ago would be of much interest today.'

'I wish that Adam was still here,' Lottie moaned. 'Adam would have known what to say to Miss Flyte.'

'Well, he has gone to join his regiment, and anyway, he would have lost his temper and might have thrown her out of the house. Physical violence is never the answer, although I was close to slapping her when she made all those accusations against our mothers. How dare she?'

'What will we do now, Poppy? I feel I should tell Papa, but I don't want to upset him.'

Poppy smiled. 'I think your papa has lived through worse times. He will have to be told and so will my parents. This isn't something that we can handle on our own. Anyway, the luncheon parties will be arriving at any moment and I have work to do.'

'I should go home but I'm shaking. I don't think I can walk back to Nine Oaks.'

'I'll get Ted's brother, Joseph, to drive you in the chaise. Just sit there and keep calm while I go and ask him to bring the carriage round to the front. We need to talk about this later. Perhaps you could ask your papa to visit later today in the quiet time between luncheon and the start of the evening service.'

'Yes, of course. Thank you, Poppy. You always know what to do. I'm lost without Adam. He'll be so angry when he finds out what Miranda has been plotting.'

'Quite rightly, too. I'm livid, but it's no use losing one's temper. This needs careful handling. We'll speak to your papa first and see what he has to say, and then I'll tell my parents. I'm not looking forward to that, but it must be done.'

Chapter Eight

Poppy waved goodbye to Lottie as Joseph encouraged the horse to break into a trot and the chaise drove away into the cool green shade of the overhanging trees. Poppy was deep in thought as she stepped back into the house. Miranda's revelations had been shocking, but had left Poppy even more suspicious. How much of the story was true and how much was pure fabrication was something she intended to find out. However, she would have to wait until the end of the dinner service that evening. There was no point in upsetting her parents any more than was absolutely necessary. She retired to the flower room to complete the arrangements for the tables and was immediately lost in the most pleasant of tasks. The atmosphere in the long narrow room was serene and the scent of roses and lavender mingled with the tangy aroma of lemon balm. She put all thoughts of Miranda and her shocking stories to the back of her mind as she arranged the blooms in small glass vases, one for each table. She had just finished when the door opened and, to her surprise, it was Begg who walked into the room.

'I thought I'd catch you in here, Miss Poppy. I didn't want to speak in front of them women in the kitchen. Gossips, the lot of them.'

'What is it you have to tell me, Begg?'

He took a slip of paper from his inside jacket pocket and laid it on the worktop. 'You said you wanted to meet Eddie Taverner. That's where you'll be most likely to find him. He goes to his office there at noon most days.'

Poppy picked up the paper. 'It says Spitalfields Market. Is Eddie Taverner a trader?'

Begg stroked his beard, his shaggy brows drawn together in a thoughtful frown. 'He's a lot of things, miss. I suggest you go there and speak to him. If anyone can help you it's Eddie, but if I were you I wouldn't mention his name in front of your parents.'

'Why not? I don't want to mix with criminals, Begg. I want to help poor children.'

'Best join the Salvation Army then, miss. All I can tell you is that Eddie Taverner operates on many different levels and he has connections in all walks of life.'

'He does? Well, that might come in handy. Thank you for the information, Mr Begg.'

'You're welcome, miss. You know I'd do anything to help your family.'

'I do know that and I'm very grateful.'

Begg nodded and backed out of the flower room, closing the door quietly. Poppy lingered for a minute or two, deep in thought. She had a feeling that Miranda was a professional when it came to blackmailing innocent victims such as herself and her family. Perhaps Eddie Taverner might be able to help with that problem as well. If he mixed with the criminal classes, he might be well acquainted with the Pettigrew family. Begg would not have mentioned Taverner if he had not been confident in the outcome, but there was only one way to find out. Poppy was due some time off, which she usually took on a day when they had fewer bookings, and she went to check the diary. Fortunately for her there was only one party booked for luncheon so far next day, and the evening seemed to be reasonably quiet. She would wait for the right moment before making her request, but she would have to think of a good excuse to account for her absence.

The obvious person to give her an alibi was Lottie, although Poppy knew that Lottie could not keep a secret to save her life. She was probably preparing to tell her papa everything that Miranda had said at this very minute. Poppy experienced a moment of panic. It was too soon to tell either family. If there was the slightest possibility of obtaining help from the mysterious Eddie Taverner, then their parents should be spared the humiliation of being exposed to Miranda's preposterous lies. Poppy glanced at the grandfather clock at the foot of the stairs. If she was quick she had time to get to Nine Oaks and back before she was needed to help in the restaurant.

She left the house without stopping to fetch her bonnet and ran through the gardens, startling Ted, who was weeding the vegetable patch. She shouted an apology and raced on, slowing down only when she reached the ha-ha that divided the land belonging to Rainbow's End from the Nine Oaks estate. She crossed the neatly clipped lawn and found the door to the music room was conveniently open and she was able to enter the house unseen. Taking care not to make a noise, Poppy made her way to Lottie's room. It was more than likely she would be there changing her garments or at least tidying her hair before she went in search of her papa. Lottie was always very conscious of her appearance and rarely had a hair out of place, let alone a muddy hem to her gown or scuffed shoes.

As Poppy had hoped, Lottie was seated on a damask-covered stool at her dressing table. She spun round, clutching her hand to her heart. 'You gave me a start, bursting in like that, Poppy. What's the matter?'

Poppy slumped down on the edge of the bed. 'Don't tell your papa what Miranda said, Lottie. At least not yet. I want to find out if she was telling the truth.'

'He was busy when I arrived home so I haven't spoken to him yet. Why the change of heart?'

'Begg has given me the name of a man who might be of some help, but I really need to meet him and find out if he knows anything about the Pettigrew family before I say anything to my parents. The same goes for you, too.'

Lottie frowned. 'What are you up to now, Poppy? I thought you wanted to do something to help the poor waifs we saw recently.'

'I do, of course, but at the moment I think it's more important to protect our families from that witch Miranda Flyte.'

'So who is this person you wish to meet and how can I help?'

'His name is Eddie Taverner, and Begg says I might find him in Spitalfields Market at around midday. Apparently he has contacts in the city and it occurred to me that he might even have some information regarding Miranda Flyte. I can't believe that this is the first time she and her cousin have tried to extort money from innocent victims.'

'I still don't see what I can do.'

'No one will think it odd if you and I go out together in your family's carriage. I could say I was accompanying you to your dressmaker or milliner, or something.'

Lottie nodded. 'Yes, but what then?'

'All you have to do is to wait for me while I go into the market and look for Eddie Taverner.'

'On your own?' Lottie pursed her lips. 'Really? Wouldn't that be rather risky?'

'Perhaps, but if I can prove that Miranda is lying it will be worth it. As for my ambition to do something useful, that might have to wait awhile.'

'I don't know, Poppy. Mightn't it be better to wait and see what Miranda does next? I mean, she's put her cards on the table, so to speak. If we tell our parents, it will be up to them to decide what to do about her.'

'Do you really want to upset your mama by bringing up the past? I believe Miranda would be capable of creating a scandal just for the sake of seeing us squirm. My mama is involved, too. Something like this could affect the business that she and Pa have worked so hard to build up.'

'I hadn't thought of that.' Lottie sighed. 'I'll do it, Poppy. I'll ask Papa to order the barouche tomorrow morning, if that's what you want. But perhaps we ought to go into the market together. This man might be dangerous.'

Poppy shook her head, stifling the desire to giggle. She could not imagine timid Lottie Ashton standing up to a villain. 'Don't worry about that, Lottie. Begg wouldn't have given me Eddie's name if he thought I would be harmed.'

'I wish that Adam was here. He would have sorted this out immediately.' Lottie rose from the stool. 'Shouldn't you be working now, Poppy?'

Poppy jumped to her feet. 'Heavens, yes. I'll have to run home and hope I haven't been missed. I'll see you tomorrow. We'll go on a mission together as we did when we were children.'

'But we were only playing then,' Lottie said seriously. 'This is a little different.'

Just how different it was became glaringly obvious when Poppy walked into the market unaccompanied. Although she had visited markets before, it had always been in the company of her father, and the atmosphere had been businesslike and respectful. It was not so this time and she realised that a comparatively well-dressed young woman on her own attracted the wrong sort of attention. Poppy almost wished that she had taken up Lottie's offer to accompany her, but looking round at some of the big burly market traders, Poppy decided that Lottie was safest in the barouche in the care of Uncle Freddie's coachman. Disreputable-looking men hung around in doorways, their torn and dirty vests exposing muscular arms and shoulders. Most of them chose to ignore her, but there were others who were leering openly, and some made suggestions that brought a blush to Poppy's cheeks. She had dressed in her plainest and most modest gown, with a straw bonnet adorned only with a dark blue satin bow. Even so, she felt vulnerable and yet conversely overdressed compared to the women who helped out on the stalls, their garments patched and none too clean. Some of them smoked clay pipes and others took surreptitious nips from grimy glass bottles tucked away in their apron pockets. Their glances weren't at all friendly either, and Poppy felt her courage ebbing away. She hesitated, wondering whether to turn and run or to put on a show of bravado, both of which would be difficult as her knees were shaking uncontrollably.

'What are you doing here, lady?' an older trader demanded gruffly. 'Dollymops beware. This ain't the place for the likes of you.'

'I'm not a dollymop,' Poppy said indignantly. She had no idea what the word meant, but the inference was clear. 'I'm looking for Mr Taverner. Eddie Taverner.'

'You don't want to know the likes of him, lady. Take my advice and go back to where you come from.'

'Who's looking for me?'

Poppy spun round to face the owner of the deep, surprisingly well-educated voice. The man standing behind her was a subtly imposing figure. It was neither his stance nor his physique, although well-muscled, that made him different from the rest of the men in the market place, it was more the air of authority that emanated from him. He was well dressed, wearing a dark suit that might have come from Savile Row, a white shirt and a tie held in place with a diamond stick pin. His dark hair waved back from a high forehead, and his neatly trimmed moustache and beard did nothing to disguise a firm chin. His dark gaze rested on Poppy's face as if he were reading her thoughts and it made her nervous.

'I was told I would find Mr Taverner here.'

'And what is your business with him?'

Poppy had the feeling he was teasing her even though his expression was serious. She tossed her head. 'I will discuss that with Mr Taverner. If you are not him, then please stand aside.'

'Best take her out of here, guv.' The trader jerked his head in the direction of the curious male onlookers, who were edging closer. 'This ain't no place for a young lady.'

'You are right, as ever, Bill,' Taverner said with a hint of a smile. He turned to give Poppy a cool appraising look. 'I am Eddie Taverner. Come into my office.' He strode off, leaving Poppy little alternative than to follow him. She could simply have headed for the main road and waited for Freddie's coachman to spot her, but she had come this far and was not about to give up. Taverner opened the door into what appeared to have been the front room of a small terraced house abutting the market square. Crates and boxes were piled high against the walls with only the fireplace left exposed. Four chairs surrounded a small pine table in the centre of the room, which appeared to be the only furniture.

'Take a seat, please.' Taverner pulled up a chair for her. 'You can start by telling me who you are.'

'My name is Poppy Robbins. You don't know me, Mr Taverner, but I was told you might be able to help me.' Poppy sat down on the edge of the hard wooden seat. The front door had been left ajar and

141

that was a relief. She was prepared to make a run for it, should things go wrong, although to be fair to Taverner, he did not seem to pose a threat.

'And what do you want with me, Miss Robbins?'

'Silas Begg gave me your name.' Poppy eyed him curiously. 'May I ask you a question, sir?'

Taverner remained standing. 'I'm a busy man, Miss Robbins. Is this more than a purely social call? I saw you climb out of that barouche with the lozenge on the door. I believe that coat of arms belongs to the Earl of Dorrington.'

Poppy stared at him in amazement. 'How did you know that?'

'It's of no importance. Tell me what you want from me.'

'I don't really know.' Poppy rose to her feet, a feeling of unease making her close to panic. 'I think I made a mistake by coming here today. Perhaps I should leave now.'

A flicker of amusement lit Taverner's dark eyes and his lips curved in a smile. 'I'm sorry, I seem to have caused you some alarm. Please sit down again, and tell me why Silas Begg thought I might be of assistance to you.'

'It sounds rather silly now, but originally I wanted to find a way to help the poor children I have seen roaming the East End streets.' Poppy sank back onto the wooden chair. This was not going to be easy.

'That sounds very laudable, but what has changed, Miss Robbins? There is more, I can tell.'

'My family and the Dorringtons have come under a threat recently.'

'A threat? That sounds ominous.'

Poppy had a feeling he was laughing at her, although his expression was carefully controlled. 'Yes, as I said, a threat. It all started at the fair on Wanstead Flats.'

'I'm a busy man, Miss Robbins. Could you make this brief?'

'Do you know anything about the Pettigrew family who once owned Pettigrew Castle in Devonshire?'

Taverner pulled out a chair and sat down opposite her. 'I have heard of them. A bad lot, so I believe.'

'Exactly so.' Poppy sighed with relief. 'One of their relatives, a woman called Miranda Flyte, is threatening to blackmail the Earl of Dorrington and my parents regarding something that happened more than twenty years ago.'

'Surely that would not be of interest to anyone nowadays?'

'I think it would be a serious embarrassment if Miranda were to go ahead. My parents are in business and Uncle Freddie is a good man. He and Aunt Arabella do not deserve to have the past raked over by a greedy descendant of the Pettigrew family.'

'Is it just this woman who is threatening you?'

'Her cousin Gervase Mulliner is involved in some way.'

Taverner frowned. 'I have come across Mulliner in the past. He is a second-rate crook, more accustomed

143

to preying on vulnerable elderly widows than doing anything that might be a risk to himself. It seems to me that he and Miss Flyte are amateurs.'

'Amateurs or not, they could cause my family some distress. My parents have worked hard to build up their restaurant business. I don't want to see them lose everything because of a twenty-year-old scandal brought to light.'

'Answer me one thing, Miss Robbins. Why are you here, risking your own safety in this part of London? Shouldn't it be your pa or Freddie Dorrington sitting on the other side of the table to myself?'

'Are you refusing to help me because I am a woman, sir?'

'I wouldn't put it like that, but you said in the first place you wanted to help poor children. Now, quite suddenly, you are dealing with a pair of blackmailers, presumably with only the other young lady in the carriage to assist you.'

'Lottie is nervous and a little shy. I am neither, Mr Taverner. Are you able to help me, or not?'

'I like you, Miss Robbins. You aren't afraid to speak your mind, which is refreshing. I deal with all manner of people in my profession, and I can see your predicament. Will you leave Miss Flyte and her puppet to me?'

'I will, but I am not sure if I can afford to hire your services, Mr Taverner. It might take me a while to raise the amount I am sure you will charge.'

'We'll talk about money if and when I deliver a

satisfactory service. As a matter of fact, there is one type of criminality I abhor and that is blackmail. It is the most cowardly form of abuse.'

Poppy could see that he was sincere, which was surprising, but then Eddie Taverner was not what she had expected in the first place. 'What exactly is your business, if you don't mind me asking? I mean, you dress and speak like a gentleman, and yet you have a reputation for dealings that are not strictly above board.'

'Why does that surprise you? Do you think that all gentlemen are scrupulously honest and law-abiding?'

'I suppose I do.'

'You have obviously led a very sheltered existence then, Miss Robbins.' Taverner smiled and shook his head. 'But I will do what I can to help you. I don't like to see honest, hard-working people driven to extreme lengths by the unscrupulous.'

'Thank you, sir.'

'It's Eddie to my friends and associates.'

'In that case, Eddie, you may call me Poppy. So what now? How will you contact me? I really don't want my parents to know.'

'I'll be in touch through Begg. And don't ask how I know him. I never repeat anything told to me in confidence. I suggest you return home now and leave the rest to me.'

Poppy rose to her feet. 'If I had asked you to help me relieve the suffering of the local children, would you really have been able to assist me? How does that fit in with your business activities, whatever they might be?'

'Just because I don't necessarily follow the rules doesn't make me heartless, Poppy. I see the suffering all round me and I try to do something to alleviate it, but it's never enough.'

'When I am certain my family is safe from Miranda Flyte and her cousin I will come to you again, and maybe you can find a way for me to help you in your good works, Eddie.'

A genuine smile curved his lips. 'I don't know about good works, but I appreciate the sentiment. However, I suggest you keep to your own part of the world, Poppy. The underbelly of London society is not for the likes of you.'

'I think you underestimate me. I am tougher than you might think.'

'I think you should go home. If you want to help the poor there are ways of raising money for charities. Make cakes to sell at church garden parties, organise raffles, but steer clear of the people who wish to drag you down to their level.'

'I'm not sure what you mean, but I'll think about what you said. Anyway, I'd better go now, but I would appreciate it if you could let me know if you make any progress with Miranda and her cousin.'

'As I said, I will let Begg know.'

'If I don't hear from you soon I will feel obliged to come here again,' Poppy said firmly. 'Maybe I'll bring Begg with me next time.'

'Begg should have had more sense than to send you here. The people with whom I associate daily are not the sort your parents would wish you to meet, Poppy. Remember that.' Taverner led the way into the street and hailed Freddie's coachman. When the barouche drew up at the kerb, he opened the door and handed Poppy inside.

She was conscious of the aroma of expensive toiletries, with just a hint of Havana cigar smoke. 'Thank you for doing this for us, Eddie. I realise you have more pressing matters to attend to.'

'Your problem is as important as the next person's. You will be hearing from me, so don't do anything before then. I want you to promise that.'

Poppy sank down on the seat beside Lottie. 'I promise. Thank you again, Eddie.'

He closed the door and stood back as the coachman encouraged the horses to walk on.

Lottie grasped Poppy's hand. 'Was that handsome man Eddie Taverner? You seemed to be on very friendly terms. Almost like old friends.'

'I've never set eyes on him until today. I don't know what he does for a living, but it's unlikely to be legal. Aside from all that, he said he would help us.'

'He's a criminal and you are on first-name terms with him?'

'He asked me to call him Eddie, and personally I don't care what he is, Lottie. He knows something about the Pettigrew family, although he really didn't tell me much. The main thing is to get the better of Miranda and that cousin of hers.'

'Do you think you can trust him, Poppy?'

'I have no alternative. I promised not to do anything about Miranda until I hear from him. He could have been fobbing me off, but somehow I don't think so. I will give him a chance. After all, what choice have we?'

'I'm beginning to think we should tell our parents and let them sort things out.'

'Just be patient for a while, Lottie. We'll give Eddie a chance, unless you have any better ideas?'

Lottie shook her head. 'No, I can't think of anything.'

'We'll keep this to ourselves,' Poppy said firmly. 'Eddie is going to contact me through Begg. He didn't even ask where I live.'

'Isn't that rather odd? Perhaps he was just trying to get rid of you.'

'No, for some reason I trust him. I don't know why, but I do.' Poppy settled back on the luxuriously padded seat. She could not explain why, even to herself, but she had a feeling that Eddie Taverner would not let them down. It was a comforting thought.

However, comforting thoughts disappeared when they arrived back at Nine Oaks and found Freddie waiting for them in the main entrance hall. He did not look pleased.

'What's the matter, Papa?' Lottie asked anxiously. 'You look upset.'

'Come into the drawing room, both of you. I think you have some explaining to do.' Freddie marched off towards the drawing room on the ground floor, which overlooked the parterre gardens.

'I can explain,' Poppy said hastily. 'It was my fault we took so long, Uncle Freddie.'

He stared at her, frowning. 'What are you talking about, Poppy? I said you might use the barouche. It isn't that.'

Lottie peeled off her lace gloves and untied her bonnet strings, laying the confection of flowers and feathers on a side table. 'What is it then, Papa? Is it something to do with Arthur or Mama?'

Poppy sent Lottie a warning look. 'Shouldn't you allow your papa to speak, Lottie?'

'Thank you, Poppy. You have always been the sensible one.' Freddie motioned them both to sit. 'I have had a visit from a certain young lady, who I believe is a friend of yours, Poppy? Miranda Flyte.'

'She is not my friend,' Poppy said angrily. 'She had no right to involve you in her Machiavellian scheme, sir. We are dealing with it, Lottie and I.'

A glimmer of a smile made Freddie's blue eyes twinkle. 'In what way, Poppy? Miss Flyte seems a very determined young woman. She hinted that she had some knowledge that would be very embarrassing if it were made public. I sent her packing, of course.'

'She agreed to keep it between us, Papa,' Lottie

protested, tears filling her eyes. 'She is such a mean person.'

'We have made arrangements to silence her and her wretched cousin,' Poppy said hastily. 'It was not supposed to come to you, Uncle Freddie, nor my parents. Miranda is a snake.'

Freddie took a seat in a chair by the fireplace. 'I think you girls ought to tell me exactly what has been going on.'

'You really mustn't worry, sir.' Poppy had sat down but she jumped to her feet. 'Eddie Taverner is going to make it right. We left him not an hour ago, and he promised.'

'Eddie Taverner? You went to see him on your own and you took Lottie with you? What were you thinking of, Poppy?'

'Begg said he would help us, Uncle Freddie.'

'Eddie Taverner comes from a good family, but his business dealings are highly suspect. Who knows how he has made his fortune, because it's well known that his father lost all the money he inherited through gambling and poor investments.' Freddie stood up and walked over to the window. 'This is a serious matter, Poppy. I need to speak to your papa urgently. This must go no further.'

Chapter Nine

Despite their protests that they had only been acting in the best interests of both sets of parents, Poppy and Lottie had no say in the matter, and next day they were put on the train heading for Exeter. Both Freddie and Daniel had been horrified to learn that Poppy had met Eddie Taverner and asked for his help in dealing with Miranda and her cousin Gervase. Although Daniel and Flora were upset and extremely anxious, they were also very sympathetic, but they agreed with Freddie that sending the girls to Devonshire for an extended stay was the safest course of action. Poppy was hurt and humiliated by her parents' refusal to accept that she was able to use her own judgement in the matter. Although they had depicted Taverner as a man who had scant respect for the law, Poppy was not convinced. It was true that she had only just met him, but she was certain that Taverner would have kept his word. Now it seemed that she was the one who had broken a promise by admitting what they considered to be her foolish error, although in truth it had been Lottie who had confessed to being an accomplice. Poppy tried hard not to blame her but she had known all along that Lottie was not a strong character, and Lottie's constant apologies only made things worse.

They were met at the station by the head coachman from Dorrington Place, driving the stately landau, and the under-coachman had brought a wagonette for all their luggage – not that Poppy had very much in the way of bags and valises, but Lottie did not travel light.

It was a good hour's drive to the Dorrington estate, and although Poppy had not wanted to leave Rainbow's End, she was excited to revisit the Ashtons' family home again after an absence of several years. Lottie admitted to suffering from mixed feelings. She said she adored Nine Oaks but Dorrington Place, in all its grandeur, was her home, and she had missed her mother and younger brother. Not having any siblings, Poppy could only imagine how Lottie must be feeling, but she was fond of young Arthur, who might appear to be a golden-haired cherub, a disguise that fooled his doting mama. Poppy, however, had seen Arthur at his impish worst and she knew he was far from angelic.

Lottie became more animated as the carriage entered the grounds of Dorrington Place and she peered out of the window as the barouche drew to a halt in front of the columned portico. The sun was shining and the stunning white stucco façade of the Adams-designed building looked even more stately and impressive than Poppy remembered. The front door opened and a liveried footman hurried out to open the carriage door and put down the step. Lottie alighted first and rushed on ahead, leaving Poppy to follow more slowly. She smiled when she saw the reason for Lottie's dash into the marble-tiled entrance hall. Lottie hugged her ten-year-old brother before throwing her arms around her beautiful mother.

'I've missed you both,' Lottie said emotionally.

'And we've missed you, too. Haven't we, Arthur?' Arabella said pointedly, but Arthur was not paying any attention to her or his sister. He marched up to Poppy and came to a halt, staring up at her.

'D'you want to play cricket?'

Poppy laughed. 'Well, not at this moment, Arthur. Maybe later.'

'Grown-ups always say that, but they never mean it.'

Arabella sent him a warning glance. 'Where are your manners, Arthur Ashton?'

'Sorry,' Arthur said sulkily. 'Adam would have played with me.'

'Adam is in the army, doing his duty.' Lottie gave him a playful cuff round the ear. 'I'll have a game of cricket later, after we've had a chance to settle in, but if you pester us, Arthur, you will have to find someone else to join your team.'

Arthur pulled a face. 'I'm not allowed to play with the village boys in case I catch some dreadful disease. Mama still thinks I'm delicate.'

'Nonsense, Arthur. I mean, I don't encourage you mixing with the boys from the village because some of them come from very rough families, but you are much stronger now than you used to be.' Arabella sighed. 'He really needs to go away to school, but I hate the idea of sending a small boy so far from home.' She lowered her voice. 'I believe that the young ones are very often bullied by the older boys. I don't want that for Arthur.'

Lottie shrugged. 'I think he's capable of standing up for himself, Mama. I think Arthur might be the one who does the bullying.'

'That's ridiculous.' Arabella slipped her arm around Poppy's shoulders. 'Anyway, welcome to Dorrington Place, my dear. I'm afraid I don't know the full story. All I had was a telegram from Freddie telling me to expect both of you, which was a lovely surprise, but how are your parents going to manage without you, Poppy?'

Lottie glanced at Arthur, who was suddenly interested in the conversation. 'You know what they say about little pitchers, Mama. Might we discuss this after we've had time to change out of our travelling costumes?'

'Yes, of course.' Arabella turned to the parlourmaid,

who had been supervising the unpacking of the wagonette. 'Miss Robbins will be in the blue room, next to Miss Lottie's bedchamber, Violet.'

'Very well, my lady.' Violet bobbed a curtsey and continued to issue orders to the under-footman.

'I suggest we take tea in the drawing room while Violet unpacks your bags, and then you may change into something more comfortable. I expect you remember your way round, Poppy?' Arabella said, smiling.

'I'm not sure, but I expect it will all come back to me.'

'Don't worry, I'll make sure you don't get lost,' Lottie said, laughing. 'Anyway, I'm starving, Mama. I hope Cook has made one of her fruit cakes. What about you, Poppy? Are you hungry?'

'A cup of tea and a slice of cake would be most welcome,' Poppy said appreciatively. 'Travelling always gives me an appetite.'

'Nanny has had your tea sent to the schoolroom, Arthur.' Arabella barred his way as Arthur attempted to follow them. 'You may join the girls later, when they have had time to settle in.'

'I'm too old to have a nanny,' Arthur said sulkily. 'You think I'm still a baby, Mama.'

'You will always be my baby, darling.' Arabella dropped a kiss on his golden curls. 'You are so like your papa, Arthur. I wish you could stay like this for ever.'

'Do as Mama says, Arthur.' Lottie pulled a face at him as she walked off, arm in arm with her mother.

Poppy laid her hand on his skinny shoulder. 'If you set the stumps up and get everything ready, I'll have a game with you before dinner. But I warn you, Arthur, I'm very good at running and catching. You'll have a job to beat me.'

'You're on,' Arthur said, grinning. 'I love a challenge. I'll see you in the garden in half an hour. Don't be late.'

'I'm not guaranteeing anything, but I will be there when I'm ready.' Poppy strolled off in the direction of the drawing room where she found Lottie and Arabella seated side by side on the sofa. Poppy was struck by the likeness of mother and daughter, both of them with their abundant dark hair and lustrous brown eyes.

'Come and sit down, Poppy,' Arabella said, smiling. 'I've rung for tea and cakes, which will keep you girls going until dinner. In the meantime you must tell me everything. I must confess I'm curious.'

Poppy took a seat in a chair opposite them. She had a feeling that Aunt Bella was not going to be satisfied with anything other than a full explanation of the circumstances that had brought them to Devonshire.

'I think you are owed an explanation, ma'am,' Poppy began hesitantly.

'Only if you feel up to it, my dear.'

Poppy knew that meant a gentle interrogation would follow if Aunt Bella was not completely satisfied. She took a deep breath and began at the beginning, when Miranda Flyte had come into their lives.

Arabella listened intently, with Lottie adding extra bits of mainly superfluous observations. There was a pause when the parlourmaid entered with a tray of tea, followed by another maid with a magnificent fruit cake, glistening with glacé cherries and plums. In between sips of tea and mouthfuls of cake, Poppy continued the story, but when she mentioned the name Pettigrew, Arabella almost dropped her teacup.

'I haven't heard that name mentioned for almost twenty years. My involvement with that particular family brought about the most horrifying experience of my life.'

'I'm sorry to bring back unpleasant memories,' Poppy said apologetically. 'But that is why Lottie and I tried to avoid telling everyone at home about Miranda's threats.'

'By enlisting the help of a man of ill repute.' Arabella shook her head. 'I know Eddie Taverner, or at least I met his parents on a couple of occasions. They are a Devonshire family, as it happens. Lady Taverner is delightful but I did not take to her husband, who I thought was rather ill-mannered and arrogant. I believe he has all but bankrupted the estate with his excesses. I don't wonder that your fathers sent you here to safety, girls.'

'Mr Taverner didn't seem dangerous,' Poppy said mildly. 'In fact, my parents' most trusted employee, Silas Begg, advised me to seek his help when I wanted to do something for the poor children in the East End. Surely a villain would not be concerned about such things?'

'I didn't speak to him, Mama.' Lottie reached for the knife and cut herself a slice of cake. 'I only went to Spitalfields to keep Poppy company. Not that I mind being sent home, but I didn't do anything wrong.'

'I understand that, darling.' Arabella turned to Poppy with a sympathetic smile. 'And I realise that you were only trying to protect your parents as well as my family, but Eddie Taverner is not the person I would recommend.'

'Even so, I wonder what my pa and Uncle Freddie are going to do about Miranda Flyte and her cousin.' Poppy put her cup and saucer back on the table. 'She threatened to go to the newspapers with the story.'

Arabella sighed. 'Miss Flyte sounds like a horrid person, but that story is more than twenty years old. I can't imagine that anyone would be interested in it now.'

'I'm not sure about that. People are always open to hearing about a scandal, no matter how long ago it happened, and apart from upsetting you and Uncle Freddie, it might harm my parents' business,' Poppy said sadly. 'They have worked so hard for years to make a success of Rainbow's End.'

'I admire them for that,' Arabella said earnestly. 'I, on the other hand, have always been fortunate and have never had to worry about money and status. But if anyone can help your parents it will be Freddie. He is very fond of you and your family, Poppy.'

'I couldn't love him more if he were my real uncle.' Poppy swallowed hard as a lump in her throat brought tears to her eyes. 'He's always been so kind.'

'I know, my dear. You can trust Freddie implicitly so I don't want either of you girls to worry. Just settle in and we will think of interesting things to do while you are here.'

'Thank you, ma'am,' Poppy said politely. She knew that what Arabella said made sense, but it was hard to sit back and do nothing, especially when she was so used to working. It was difficult to imagine the life of a lady of leisure. She cleared her throat. 'Would you both excuse me? I promised Arthur a game of cricket before we had to change for dinner.'

'Of course.' Arabella gave her a sympathetic smile. 'But don't allow Arthur to monopolise you, Poppy. I'm afraid he will if he gets a chance.'

Poppy rose to her feet. 'Don't worry. I think I can remember how to handle young Arthur.' She left the room and made her way to the croquet lawn where she thought she might find Arthur setting up the stumps. She did not imagine he would spend much time in the nursery eating cucumber sandwiches and cake if there was a chance to play bat and ball. It could hardly be called cricket with just the two of them, but Poppy was willing to oblige. She felt sorry for the lonely boy, who would probably benefit from attending boarding school, despite his mother's fears for his wellbeing.

Arthur hailed her with a cry of delight and handed her the cricket bat. 'You go first. I need practice at bowling. When I go to Papa's old school I hope to get into the cricket eleven.'

'Are you looking forward to going away to school, Arthur?'

'I'll say I am. I love Dorrington Place and it's home, but I'm too old to have a governess and a nanny. Mama still thinks I'm sickly, but I'm not.'

'Have you spoken to your papa about this, Arthur?'

'No. I don't want to upset Mama.'

'She will want to do what is best for you. I suggest you tell your pa exactly how you feel. I'm sure he will back you up. In fact, I'll bet he put your name down for his old school the moment you were born.'

'Do you really think so?'

'Assuredly. Now are we going to play or are we going to stand around chatting?'

Arthur tossed the ball up in the air and caught it in one hand. 'Just you wait, Poppy. I'll bowl you out in ten seconds.'

That night, having enjoyed a delicious dinner in the stately dining room, and a pleasant game of backgammon after coffee in the drawing room, Poppy was ready for bed. It had been a long and emotionally trying day, but as she undressed, washed and sat at the dressing table brushing her long hair, she could not get Eddie Taverner from her thoughts. The man she had met seemed to be a figure of authority in the confines of Spitalfields Market, and it was obvious that he was held in respect by the men who knew him, but he had changed subtly when they were alone in his office and she had not felt threatened in the slightest. He had shown a glimmer of compassion when referring to the poor and needy, and it was hard to believe that beneath his well-spoken, public-school-educated exterior there lurked a common criminal. Perhaps that was how he kept himself out of prison, but somehow Poppy did not believe that he was all bad. He had offered his help without any mention of financial gain and so far no one had been able to give her an example of what had so tarnished his reputation.

The next few days passed pleasantly, with Arabella doing her best to keep the girls entertained. However, tea parties with the ladies of Arabella's acquaintance were on the dull side and Poppy had a feeling that, charming and well-mannered though they might be, they were summing her up to determine how the daughter of tradespeople came to be sponsored by the Countess of Dorrington. It was not a comfortable thought, and it made Poppy homesick for Rainbow's End and her hard-working parents. Lottie was totally oblivious to any undercurrents and she accepted the compliments of the well-intentioned ladies without question. However, Arabella did her best to provide other entertainments and they visited local beauty spots, taking a picnic on sunny days. Then there was the church garden party, with stalls raising money to repair the ancient building, and an entertainment laid on in the evening with dancing on the village green. Arabella would not allow the girls to stay on after dark and, as the sun set, they were bundled into the landau and driven back to Dorrington Place.

'Events like that tend to get a little rowdy later on,' Arabella explained seriously. 'The young men and boys get quite drunk on beer and cider and might take liberties. It's best to leave before that happens. It's a pity that most of the families with whom we are friendly have gone away for the summer. I believe Deauville is very popular this season, and of course, Monte Carlo. I love Bath, but it gets very crowded at this time of the year. Maybe we could have a day or two there later on.'

'But, Mama, don't you want to go to Nine Oaks?' Lottie asked plaintively. 'We always spend part of the summer there so that we can go into London and visit the theatre or the opera.'

'I know, dear. I love Nine Oaks – it's my old home – but with this business of Miss Flyte and Eddie Taverner I doubt if your papa would want us to leave Dorrington Place.'

Lottie and Poppy exchanged meaningful glances. The only scrap of encouragement that Poppy could think of was that Lottie was as eager to return to Nine Oaks as she was to go home to Rainbow's End.

'It does seem a little unfair, Mama,' Lottie said, pouting. 'I mean, it's not right that you and Arthur have to stay here, too.'

Arabella laughed. 'Well, darling, I can hardly take Arthur to Nine Oaks and leave you two girls to fend for yourselves here.'

'We would hardly be on our own, Mama.' Lottie smiled mischievously. 'With at least thirty indoor servants, not to mention a small army of estate workers, I think we might survive.'

'Indeed, but that will not happen.' Arabella glanced from one to the other. 'I realise that you are a little bored, but I have arranged for Grundy to drive us to the coast tomorrow. I thought the sea air might blow away some of the cobwebs.'

'That sounds lovely, ma'am,' Poppy said eagerly. 'We visited Southend not too long ago, but it was one of those times when Miranda appeared suddenly.'

'Like a genie from a lamp,' Lottie added, laughing. 'Only she wasn't a good genie.'

'I don't think she'll turn up at Exmouth. There's a lovely hotel on the clifftop where I thought we might have luncheon. I might even allow Arthur to paddle in the sea, if it's warm enough.'

'That sounds lovely,' Poppy said eagerly. 'I might dip my toes in the water myself.'

'That's settled then.' Arabella looked from one to the other with a pleased smile. 'I suggest we all retire to bed and have an early start. I hope it's a fine day tomorrow, but the weather is one thing we cannot control.'

Lottie kissed her mother on the cheek. 'Good night, Mama. I think it's a delightful idea.'

'Good night, ma'am,' Poppy added hastily. 'It will be a lovely day, rain or shine.'

Unfortunately, the weather did not look promising, but they left after an early breakfast, as arranged. Arabella refused to be downcast, despite the drumming of the rain on the roof of the barouche and the spray from the large puddles created by the horses' hoofs and the carriage wheels. They stopped mid-morning to have coffee at a wayside inn and to give the horses a rest. Grundy was not optimistic about the weather but Arabella said they had come this far and it would be a shame to go home too soon, as the sun might come out later on and they would have missed the opportunity to see the sea. Poppy was quick to note that Grundy did not share his employer's opinion, but he went off to the stables to tend to the horses, leaving them to enjoy their coffee.

When Grundy reappeared he was even less optimistic about the weather, predicting a much worse storm to come, but Arabella was determined to see the sea. She chided him for being pessimistic and insisted that they continue their journey.

'I am,' she said firmly, 'looking forward to a

delicious luncheon in Exmouth with a wonderful view of the sea from the restaurant window. Cheer up, Grundy. I'm sure the storm will pass us by.'

Poppy glanced out at the lowering clouds and the hint of sulphur in the air and she was not so sure. Lottie, on the other hand, seemed to share her mother's optimistic spirit and she, too, was convinced that the sun would battle its way through the clouds. Arthur did not seem to care either way and he dashed into the rain and splashed through several puddles before reluctantly obeying his mother's command to get into the carriage. He sat next to Lottie, who complained bitterly.

'Mama, it's like sitting next to a wet dog. Can't you do something about Arthur?'

Poppy could see that Arabella was at a loss and she stood up, which was difficult in a moving vehicle.

'Change seats with me, Lottie. I don't mind sitting next to a wet dog.'

Arthur grinned and growled at his sister as she manoeuvred around Poppy and almost fell into the space beside her mother. Poppy patted Arthur on the head.

'Good dog. Now go to sleep and allow everyone else to enjoy the journey in peace.'

Arthur giggled, but a severe glance from his mother made him subside into the corner and he closed his eyes. Within minutes his regular breathing told Poppy that he had fallen asleep and she was able to relax. However, it was not for long. A sudden flash followed by a rumble of thunder made them all jump, including Arthur, who reached out to clutch Poppy's hand.

'Maybe we should turn back,' Arabella said nervously. She peered out of the rain-spattered window. 'I don't know where we are exactly. It's raining so hard that I can't see any landmarks.'

'We must be more than halfway to Exeter,' Poppy said slowly. 'But we seem to be in the middle of nowhere.' Another flash of lightning confirmed her suspicions, and a loud crash of thunder overhead made the horses rear in fright.

'We should find shelter,' Arabella said anxiously. 'I wish we had remained at the inn until the weather improved.'

'We couldn't have forecast this, Mama.' Lottie held on to the seat as the carriage rattled along at an alarming speed. 'I hope Grundy hasn't lost control of the horses.'

'I've never driven so fast,' Arthur said gleefully. 'I wish I was up there on the box with Grundy.'

'Well, I don't.' Arabella fanned herself with her gloved hand. 'Tap on the roof with my umbrella, please, Poppy. I want Grundy to pull over until the storm passes.'

Poppy glanced out of the window. 'I don't think he can, ma'am. I think the horses have bolted.' She wrapped her arms around Arthur, who had begun to cry. 'We'll be all right. Don't be scared.' But she did not believe that for a moment. She, too, was terrified as the carriage plunged headlong through the narrow lanes, seemingly out of control.

There was nothing any of them could do and it was so dark outside that it might have been late at night instead of close to midday. Lottie was growing hysterical and Arabella's pallor was alarming. She threw her arms around her daughter, burying her face in Lottie's shoulder, the bonnet she had been wearing having slipped off and landed on the floor. The vehicle swayed dangerously from side to side, its wheels dragging through mud and potholes until finally it overturned, throwing everyone into a heap on the floor. Poppy was deafened by the ear-splitting sound of breaking glass and splintering wood.

There was a sudden even more terrifying silence as the damaged vehicle sank into the mud. Poppy was the first to free herself and she dragged Arthur to a sitting position on her knee. A flash of lightning revealed Lottie and Arabella clutched in each other's arms. Arabella appeared to be unconscious and Lottie had a trickle of blood oozing from her forehead. Her eyes were wide with shock and her lips moved silently.

'Are you hurt, Lottie?' Poppy heard her own voice as if it were coming from far away. Her ears were ringing with the combination of thunder and the crash. Lottie did not answer but, apart from the graze on her forehead, there was no obvious sign of injury. As Poppy's eyes grew used to the darkness inside the carriage, she realised that a branch of a tree had shattered the roof, making it difficult to escape, but she knew she must get out of the carriage in order to find help. What had happened to Grundy and the horses was even more worrying than the damage to the barouche. Poppy eased herself free from Arthur, who was sobbing silently.

'Are you hurt, Arthur?'

He shook his head. 'I don't think so.'

Poppy looked up as rain spattered on her head from the hole in the roof. She could see the sky above them and a sudden break in the clouds.

'If I help, do you think you could climb out of the hole in the roof, Arthur?'

'I'll try.'

'Good boy. Maybe you could open the door from the outside.' Poppy manoeuvred herself so that Arthur could climb onto her shoulders. He was small enough to squeeze through the gaping aperture in the soft leather hood. With amazing agility he was up and out onto the roof.

'What can you see, Arthur? Is Grundy there?'

'I think he's dead, Poppy. I can see him lying face down on the road. The horses have bolted.'

Poppy stood up, testing her limbs to make sure there were no broken bones. She stood on part of the seat that had broken away and she managed to get her head and shoulders through the hole. Arthur was sitting on the only part of the roof that was intact. Rain was still pouring down, but the worst of the storm seemed to have passed over.

'I can't get to the door, Poppy,' Arthur said, sniffing. 'There's a tree growing out of it.'

Poppy nodded wordlessly. There was no use sending a small boy onto the road where there might be any number of obstacles. Finding help herself was her only option. With a supreme effort she managed to heave herself out and join him on the roof, but the broken struts had begun to crack and the leather had torn. She found herself slithering to the muddy ground and landed in a deep puddle, but she was past caring about mere discomfort. At least she was unharmed, despite a cut on her cheek and grazes on her hands. She held her arms out to Arthur.

'Jump and I'll catch you.'

'Wheee!' Arthur leaped off the roof with the complete trust and abandon of a ten-year-old and Poppy caught him, although her knees gave way and they ended up in a heap on the wet road.

'That was fun,' Arthur said, grinning. 'But it's not fun for Mama and Lottie,' he added, suddenly serious as the full impact of the disaster struck him. 'Are they dead like Grundy?'

Poppy scrambled to her feet. 'No, they are all right, just shocked and probably bruised. We must get help, Arthur, but first I will take a look at Grundy. You stay there.' Poppy made her way to the place where Grundy lay motionless on the ground. There was a pool of blood around his head, and his left arm was buckled at an alarming angle, as was his left leg. She held her hand in front of his mouth to see if he was breathing. A soft moan escaped his lips, causing Poppy to utter a sob of relief.

'Is he really dead?' Arthur demanded.

'No, but he's badly hurt. I don't know where we are, but you and I will have to walk on and hope we find habitation close by. Can you do that, Arthur?'

Chapter Ten

The storm had passed over, leaving a trail of damage in its wake. Poppy looked round in desperation. They seemed to be in the middle of farming country and there was no sign of the horses.

'Come along, Arthur. Best foot forward. I'm afraid we will have to walk until we find someone to help us.'

'I don't want to leave Mama and Lottie. They might die.'

'They aren't badly hurt, but we can't get them out by ourselves so we'd best walk as fast as we can.'

Arthur nodded wordlessly, although his blue eyes filled with tears. However, he sniffed manfully and grasped Poppy's hand. She let out a sigh of relief as they rounded a bend and saw a small cottage, but when Poppy knocked on the door there did not seem to be anyone at home. There was nothing for it but to trudge on, hoping for better luck next time.

'My right ankle hurts, Poppy,' Arthur said plaintively after they had been walking for a good twenty minutes.

Poppy came to a halt. She bent down to get a better view of the afflicted limb. 'It is a bit swollen, but we have to walk on, Arthur. Lean on me and we'll stop as soon as we find a place where there's someone at home.'

Arthur leaned heavily on her arm, which slowed their progress even more, but he did not complain. Poppy could only hope that they were heading in the right direction to soon find the help they so desperately needed. She was anxious for Arabella and Lottie, but even more worried about Grundy. The storm might have passed but it was still raining and soon they were both soaked. It was obvious that Arthur was in pain from his sprained ankle and Poppy's back ached miserably, as did her left arm. However, this was not the time to think about herself and she plodded on, helping Arthur to keep up with her. Then, just as Poppy was beginning to feel desperate, they rounded a sharp bend where the road divided, and were faced with tall iron gates hanging at odd angles from rusty hinges in a stone wall. On the other side of the gatekeeper's cottage an avenue of beech trees stood like sentinels, although the main property was out of sight.

'Look, Poppy,' Arthur said excitedly, pointing to

a lichen-covered stone half hidden by a privet bush. He moved closer, pulling back a frond of ivy. 'It says Domesday House. I don't like the sound of that.'

'Neither do I,' Poppy said, frowning. 'But we must find someone to help us.' She hurried up to the cottage door and tugged at the bell pull. The jingle-jangle echoed through the house and then there was silence. It seemed that their luck was out yet again, but then there was the sound of footsteps, slow and heavy on a tiled floor. Poppy held her breath as the door opened and she found herself face to face with a man of indeterminate years, whose craggy, weathered features suggested he was more used to working outside than indoors.

'What d'you want?' he growled. 'I got a flood in me scullery, lady.'

'I'm so sorry,' Poppy said hastily. 'We've had an accident further along the road. The coachman is hurt quite badly, I'm afraid.'

'What d'you expect me to do about it? I ain't no doctor. I've got me own problems.'

'This seems to be the gatehouse of a much larger establishment. Could you tell me if there is anyone in residence?'

'That depends upon what you mean by someone. If you mean a person who is likely to worry about an accident away from his estate, then no. The person concerned would not be bothered.'

Poppy was beginning to lose patience with the grumpy old man. 'Is there a male servant who could help us? Perhaps a groom or maybe some of the ground staff.'

'You ain't from these here parts, are you, miss? If you was you wouldn't ask such stupid questions.'

'You are very rude,' Arthur said angrily. 'You shouldn't speak to a lady like that, and I've hurt my ankle. I'm in agony.'

'You are just a nipper. Children should be seen and not heard.' The old man cocked his head on one side. 'Are you handy with a mop, miss? Help me get the water out of the scullery and I'll see if there's anyone left at Domesday House who might oblige you, although I don't hold out much hope. None of us servants have been paid for over a year, and the master is barmy.'

'Again, I'm sorry to hear that, but I must get assistance quickly. I can't help with your flood, but if I find someone in the big house I'll send them to assist you.' Poppy tucked Arthur's hand in the crook of her arm. 'Come along, Arthur. We'll try Domesday House.'

'It sounds creepy,' Arthur said in a small voice.

'Quite right, too, boy. You'd do better to walk to the village.' The old man half closed the door, peering out at them with a beady eye.

'How far is the village?' Poppy asked hopefully.

'About four miles, unless the river has burst its banks, in which case you'll have to take a detour of about ten miles.' He cackled with laughter. 'Good luck, lady. You, too, young master.' He slammed the door without waiting for a response.

174

'I think we'd best try the house,' Poppy said slowly. 'I doubt if anyone could be less helpful than that fellow.'

Arthur clutched her arm tightly. 'You won't leave me on my own, will you, Poppy?'

'Of course not, Arthur. Don't worry. We're sure to find someone who will get your mama and Lottie out of the carriage. I just hope we are not too late for poor Grundy.' She started walking along the tree-lined avenue, wishing she had worn her high-button boots instead of a pair of fashionable leather shoes that had leaked and now rubbed blisters on her heels. The avenue had been planted in a huge curve, which was very attractive, but it made for a long walk, and raindrops dripped from the leaves on the overhanging branches. She was trying desperately to be positive, but her first sight of Domesday House was not encouraging. The Tudor house, built in the shape of a letter E, as was fashionable in the time of Good Queen Bess, must once have been very imposing, but now most of the red brick was covered in ivy, and one of the wings seemed to have been damaged at some time by a great fire. The gravelled carriage sweep was interspersed with a variety of weeds and wildflowers, and the roof had collapsed in the stable block at the far side of the main building.

'Do you think anyone lives here, Poppy?' Arthur's voice shook and she squeezed his hand.

'We'll soon find out.' Making an effort to sound more confident than she was feeling, Poppy marched up to the heavy oak door and hammered on the iron clenched-fist knocker. After what seemed like an eternity, the door creaked open and grim-faced woman, dressed in black from her frilled cap to her scuffed boots, stared at them with a blank expression.

'Tradesmen go round the back of the house,' she said abruptly and made to close the door, but Poppy put her foot over the sill.

'I'm not selling anything. We need help, ma'am. Our carriage overturned a mile or so along the road and there are people trapped inside. The coachman is lying on the road, badly injured.'

'Speak to Coggins, the gatekeeper.' The woman glared pointedly at Poppy's foot. 'Move it now.'

'Your gatekeeper was not helpful. In fact, his cottage is flooded and he needs assistance, too. I'm sorry, ma'am, but I'm asking for your aid. Is there a man about the house who might be able to get my friends out of the carriage? We would need a doctor to take care of the coachman, too.'

'What's going on, Eliza? Can't a man read *Racing Illustrated* in peace?' An elderly man with an unkempt mop of curly grey hair pushed the housekeeper aside. His oriental style dressing gown was stained and hung open to the waist, exposing a vest that could definitely benefit from laundering.

Poppy withdrew her foot instinctively. The body odour from the old gentleman was nauseating, but despite his dishevelled appearance he had an air of authority that made her cautious.

'I'm sorry to bother you, sir, but we really are in desperate need of help,' she said earnestly. 'I was telling this lady that our carriage overturned and there are people trapped inside.'

'Eliza is my housekeeper. Has been for the past thirty years. Don't go spreading rumours about our relationship, young lady,' he said with a wag of a bony finger. 'Ain't that so, Eliza?'

'Yes, to my cost. I could have worked for the Elsenhams for twice the pay and more respect. I don't know why I stick with this madhouse.'

'Be silent, you old harridan.' The old man peered myopically at Poppy. 'Who are you, anyway? We haven't been introduced.'

'My name is Poppy Robbins, sir. Have you any male servants who could help us?'

'You should wait to be introduced properly,' Eliza said primly. 'This gentleman is Baron Taverner of Oakley. You address him as "my lord".'

By this time Poppy was too agitated to pay much attention to names. 'My lord, can you help us?'

'Speak to Masterson, my butler. I am too busy to deal with commoners.' Lord Taverner walked off waving his sporting magazine.

'Don't listen to him,' Eliza said crossly. 'He's mad as a March hare. So is the mistress, only she keeps to her room most of the time. Are you sure you want help from this place, miss?'

'Where will I find Masterson, please?'

'Six foot under in the graveyard, miss.' Eliza

cackled with laughter. 'He passed away ten years ago.'

Arthur slipped past Poppy. He faced Eliza with a pugnacious set to his jaw. 'My mama might die if we don't get help. What's the matter with you, old woman? Don't you care?'

'Come inside, ducky. I'll give you a glass of lemonade and some cake.'

'I don't want lemonade and cake. Are you all mad in this house?'

Poppy reached out to restrain Arthur, who was growing more desperate with each passing minute. 'There's no need to be rude, Arthur. We will get help soon.'

'You are a cheeky boy,' Eliza said, smiling. 'But I like boys. I had a son, once, but that's another story. If you come into the kitchen I'll send the daft girl to get Ned and Bert. They'll know what to do.'

Poppy sighed with relief. She did not want to go to the kitchen in this strange house. Judging by their eccentric employer and his housekeeper she could only wonder what Ned and Bert might be like, but she had very little choice. Arthur was pale and in need of sustenance as well as the comfort of knowing his mother and sister would soon be rescued. She stepped into the entrance hall, blinking as her eyes became accustomed to the dim light. Ghostly holland covers shrouded the furniture, although what lay beneath them was anyone's guess. The only piece to escape was a towering grandfather clock, which seemed to have stopped working at midday or midnight, its silent presence looming over the desolate scene. Dust lay thickly on the ornate carvings on the coffin-like case, and cobwebs hung from the ceiling. Poppy took a deep breath and followed Eliza across the worn flagstone floor and along a narrow, wainscoted passage to the back of the house.

The kitchen was huge, as if in the past it had catered for a large household and a small army of servants, not to mention honoured guests. But the enormous range was covered in rust and a small fire sputtered and spat sparks as if it were disgusted to be seen in such uncared-for company. The flagstone floor was slippery and littered with vegetable peelings, crumbs and empty bottles, jars and leaking sacks of what might have been flour or sugar – it was impossible to tell. A long pine table in the middle of the room was piled high with dirty crockery, stale bread and tattered copies of racing journals. At one end, seen through a haze of pipe smoke, sat two men drinking tea from chipped mugs.

'You two lazy good-for-nothings.' Eliza picked up a potato and tossed it at the nearest man. 'You, Ned Hawke. Stand up when I'm talking to you.'

Reluctantly Ned heaved himself off the wooden bench. 'What now, you old battleaxe?'

'Less of that, mister. There's been an accident up the road. You need to go now and help. You, too, Bert.'

'I haven't finished me tea, Eliza,' Bert said plaintively.

'I'll tip it over your stupid head if you don't do as I say.' Eliza marched up to him but he was up and out of the back door before she could carry out her threat. She caught hold of Ned by the collar as he was about to follow. 'Take the dog cart. There's a man injured on the roadside. You might need more help, but see what you can do.'

'Yes, Eliza.' Ned hunched his shoulders and snatched his jacket off a wall peg before following Bert outside.

'Thank you, Eliza,' Poppy said earnestly.

'It's Mrs Whiddon to you.' Eliza tossed her head. 'I'm a respectable housekeeper, never mind the fact that this place is a lunatic asylum. It weren't always like this.'

Poppy nodded politely. 'I can see that it must have been a grand house at some time.'

'I want to go back to the carriage, Poppy.' Arthur tugged at her sleeve. 'Come on, maybe we can help.'

'Yes, of course. At least we can talk to your mama and she'll know that you are safe.' Poppy turned to Eliza. 'I hope you don't mind if we bring them back here?'

'Same if I do or if I don't, for that matter.' Eliza shrugged. 'You can look after them. It's not my job.'

'He needs proper medical attention. Could you please send someone to fetch the doctor?' Poppy said anxiously. 'The coachman will certainly need treatment if it isn't already too late.'

'Don't want no corpses here, miss. If he's a goner

you can leave him in Coggins's cottage. He can deal
with it.'

'We must hope for the best. Come on, Arthur.
We'll see what we can do.' Poppy had nothing more
to say to the unhelpful Eliza Whiddon. She would
have to bring the casualties back here, since there
was no alternative, but the sooner she could get
them home the better. It would mean finding another
method of transport, but she would worry about that
later.

Despite her sore feet she set off again, Arthur
clutching her hand as he limped along beside her.
They had not gone very far when Poppy came to
a halt and hastily drew Arthur aside as Bert drove
a battered wagonette past them, Ned sitting beside
him. Bert reined in and turned his head to give them
a wide grin.

'Hop on. You can take us to the spot.'

Poppy hoisted Arthur into the vehicle and climbed
in beside him. The planked floor was filthy and the
wooden seat none too clean, but it was better than
walking through muddy puddles and she sat down,
hoisting her skirt above her ankles in an attempt to
keep the hem from trailing in the mixture of straw,
mud and manure. At least the rain had stopped,
although heavy clouds hugged the horizon and a
brisk wind did its best to rip Poppy's bonnet from
her head. Her heart was thudding uncomfortably
against her stays as she recognised different
landmarks, knowing that they were nearing the site

of the accident. A suffocating feeling of dread made her clench her hands in her lap as her imagination ran away with her. They might be too late to save Grundy, and heaven alone knew what state Aunt Bella and Lottie were in after being trapped for so long. Poppy was startled when Arthur leaped to his feet, shouting and pointing.

'There it is – and I see the horses in that field. They haven't gone far.'

Bert drew the wagonette to a halt and climbed off the driver's seat. For a moment Poppy could not see Grundy, but when she stood up to allow Ned to get past her, she could see the coachman's inert body with Bert bending over him.

'Is he breathing?' Poppy asked anxiously.

'Just about, miss. Got a nasty gash on his head and I dare say a few broken bones.'

Ned lowered himself to the ground. 'Best lift him into the wagon, Bert. Then we'll try to right the carriage.' He glanced at Poppy, who was about to alight. 'I should stay there if I was you, miss. The boy, too. I'll check on the occupants first.'

Arthur pushed past Poppy and jumped to the ground. He dodged past Bert's restraining hand and climbed onto the side of the carriage. Unfortunately, the door was jammed but the window glass had shattered. 'Mama, it's me, Arthur. Are you all right?'

Poppy held her breath and released it on a sigh of relief as she heard Arabella's faint but positive response.

'We aren't badly hurt, Arthur. Have you brought help?'

'Yes, Mama. We'll get you and Lottie out very soon. They're just seeing to Grundy. He's in a bad way.'

Poppy managed to alight without help. 'Be very careful when you lift him,' she said sharply. 'You might make his injuries worse.'

'Look, lady, we've got to get the poor fellow into the wagon. You go and calm the ladies in the carriage.' Bert slipped his hands under Grundy's shoulders, signalling to Ned to take his legs.

'Don't worry, miss,' Ned said cheerfully. 'We'll take care of this chap. At least he's unconscious so he won't feel no pain. Right, Bert, ready to lift when you are.'

'Is Poppy there, Arthur?' Arabella's voice from inside the carriage drew Poppy's attention away from the combined efforts of Bert and Ned. She went to stand beside Arthur.

'I'm here, Aunt Bella. Are either of you injured?'

'Fortunately, we are unharmed, apart from a few bruises. But we're wet and cold.'

'Don't worry,' Poppy said firmly. 'We'll have you out very soon. The men are getting poor Grundy into the wagonette and then I'm sure they'll be able to right the carriage and you'll be able to get out.'

'Do hurry, Poppy,' Lottie wailed. 'I've got terrible cramp.'

Arthur slid down to the ground. 'Hurry up, Bert.

My mama and sister are stuck here until you can get them out.'

'Coming soon, young master. Don't fret.' Bert left Ned making Grundy as comfortable as possible and came to join them. He gave the carriage a tentative shove, shaking his head. 'I think it will take more than Ned and me to shift this. Trouble is, the tree has gone through the roof and it's pinning the vehicle down.'

'We need to get them out soon,' Poppy said in a low voice. 'They're wet and cold. They'll come down with a chill if we leave them much longer.'

Bert curled his lip. 'Well, miss, unless you can work miracles we're going to need someone with an axe and a saw to cut down the tree. Then we need more hands to right the carriage. I doubt we can lift the ladies through the window and they can't climb out unaided.'

Arthur began to snivel. 'Mama is going to die from the cold.'

'No, she is not, Arthur.' Poppy gave him a hug. 'Don't worry, my dear. We'll get both of them out as quickly as possible.' She turned to Bert. 'Do you know of anyone who will help us?'

He shrugged. 'I'll bet the local farmers are all dealing with floods and trees fallen down.'

'There must be something we can do,' Poppy said in desperation.

Arthur tugged at her sleeve. 'Poppy, I can hear a motor-car engine. Do you think it's Adam, come to save us?'

'I don't imagine so, Arthur. There are many more people who own motor cars than Adam. But I can hear it too.' Poppy hesitated, listening to the sound of the approaching engine. She could have cried with relief but then she realised the danger. 'Stay here, Arthur. I'll run and flag them down. We don't want a huge crash on our hands.'

'I'll do it. I can run faster than you.' Arthur raced off before she could stop him.

Bert pushed his cap to the back of his head. 'I doubt if a rich gent will be willing to get his hands dirty, but he might be persuaded to take you and the boy to the village.'

Poppy did not stop to argue. She followed Arthur, holding up her skirts to keep them from trailing in the deep puddles. As she rounded the bend in the road she could see the vehicle coming towards them at an alarming speed, but it would have been hard to miss Arthur, who was jumping up and down in the middle of the road, waving his arms and shouting. The motor came to a halt and the man behind the wheel stepped out.

'What's the matter, youngster?'

'Round the bend in the lane,' Arthur said breathlessly. 'Our carriage overturned. Mama and my sister are trapped.'

Poppy hurried up to them but she came to a sudden halt. She had the feeling she had stepped into a weird dream. She stared at the man in disbelief. 'Mr Taverner!'

Eddie Taverner took off his cap and goggles. 'Miss Robbins?' His expression was one of total astonishment. 'What on earth are you doing here in the wilds of Devonshire?'

'More to the point, what are you doing here?' Poppy countered, dazedly. 'I thought you lived in London. You're the last person I expected to see today.'

'I'm not sure whether to be flattered or offended,' Taverner said with a wry smile. 'But I have several homes, Miss Robbins. However, you haven't answered my question. Is it your carriage that has been involved in an accident?'

'No, sir. I was with Lady Dorrington, her daughter, Lottie, and her son Arthur.' Poppy slipped her arm around Arthur's shoulders. 'A tree fell on the carriage and now Arabella and Lottie are trapped. The coachman is badly injured.'

Taverner walked past her, heading for the site of the accident. Poppy followed him and Arthur ran along at his side.

'Mr Edward, sir.' Bert stared at Taverner, eyebrows raised. 'We wasn't expecting you home, sir.'

Poppy stared at him in amazement. 'You are the errant son from Domesday House?'

Taverner shot her a sideways glance, a glint of amusement in his dark eyes. 'I do have a home nearby, Miss Robbins. That is why I am here now. I was on my way to visit my parents.'

'Your father is Lord Taverner of Domesday

House?' Poppy knew she was repeating herself but the coincidence seemed too unlikely to be true.

'Yes, a wry name, isn't it? However, it was not our choice. The name was given to the property several centuries ago. Obviously by a monarch with a sense of humour.' He turned to Bert and Ned, who had climbed down from the wagonette. 'Do you think we could right the carriage together?'

'Not with the tree stuck in the middle of it, sir.' Bert rolled his eyes. 'It were an act of God, sir. Lucky the ladies was spared.'

'Their guardian angels must be working very hard.' Taverner tested the vehicle to see if he could move it at all. 'I see what you mean, Bert. This is going to take several men and more time than we have now.'

'What are you going to do?' Poppy asked anxiously. 'They're bruised and very cold. I'm afraid they will catch chills or worse if we leave them any longer.'

Taverner shrugged off his leather duster coat and handed it to Poppy. 'If you will be kind enough to hold that, Miss Robbins, I'll climb in through the roof. I'm sure I can lift the ladies out through the window and onto the side of the carriage.' He turned to Bert. 'You and Ned get ready to help them to the ground.' He turned to Arthur with a genuine smile. 'And you, young fellow, will assist me best by standing aside.'

'My name is Arthur and I want to help.' Arthur faced Taverner as if daring him to argue.

'Very well then, Arthur. If you will be kind enough to climb onto the carriage you can hold back the tree branches while I lift the ladies out one at a time.' Taverner patted Arthur on the back. 'Good chap. Talk to your mama and that will take her mind off things.' He waited until Arthur was safely ensconced, half-hidden by the leafy branch of the fallen tree, before joining him on the roof.

'Do take care,' Poppy said nervously.

Taverner ripped the leather, making the hole twice its original width. He lowered himself carefully and disappeared into the depths of the carriage. Poppy could hear his low voice talking to Arabella and Lottie, and although she could not hear his exact words she could tell by the tone of his voice that he was both comforting and encouraging them. She could only imagine how they must be feeling, having been trapped for so long. The first to emerge was Lottie, who burst into tears and clung to Arthur, endangering them both. However, Bert was immediately on hand. He lifted her as if she weighed less than a bag of feathers and passed her down to Ned, who set her on her feet beside Poppy.

'There you are, miss. No need to take on. You're safe now.'

Poppy wrapped her arms around Lottie and gave her a hug. 'You poor thing. It must have been dreadful in there.'

'We thought something must have happened to you and Arthur.' Lottie wiped her tears away on the back of her hand. 'I never have a hanky when I need one.'

Poppy was about to respond when Arabella struggled out of the jagged aperture and Bert helped her to the ground.

Arthur slid down to fling his arms around his mother. 'I thought you and Lottie were dead, Mama.'

'No, darling. We are very much alive, just wet, cramped and very cold.' Arabella turned to Taverner, who had leaped nimbly to the ground. 'Thank you for helping us, sir.'

Poppy could see that Arabella was still in a state of shock and she stepped forward. 'May I introduce you to Mr Edward Taverner, ma'am? His home is not far from here.'

Taverner inclined his head in a bow. 'We met once before Lady Dorrington, although I doubt if you will remember the occasion.'

Arabella stared at Taverner with a bemused expression. 'I do recall the event, sir. I believe your father is Baron Taverner.'

'He is, my lady. Might I give you both a lift to Domesday House? There is a back way onto the estate, which will be slightly quicker than travelling in the wagonette, and more comfortable.'

'Can you fit us all into your motor car, sir?' Arabella shot a worried glance in Poppy's direction.

'Don't worry about me,' Poppy said hastily. 'I should travel in the wagon so that I can keep an eye on Grundy. Not that I can do much for him.'

'That's settled then.' Taverner laid his hand on Arthur's shoulder. 'I'll show you how to start my motor car.' He nodded to Poppy. 'I'll send for the doctor as soon as I get home. Bert, I trust you to get the poor chap back to Domesday House as quickly as possible.' Without waiting for an answer Taverner escorted Arabella and Lottie in the direction of his motor car, with Arthur hurrying on ahead.

'Best be quick, miss,' Ned said urgently. 'I just checked on the coachman. He don't look too good.'

'I'm coming now.' Poppy followed him to the wagon and climbed in to sit beside Grundy. His face was ashen and the gash on his forehead was livid and seeping blood. 'Drive as fast as you can, or it might be too late for poor Grundy.'

Chapter Eleven

Poppy had only just arrived back at Domesday House when she was whisked into the drawing room by Mrs Whiddon without a by-your-leave. Arabella and Lottie had obviously suffered a similar fate and they were sitting side by side on a sofa set against the far wall. Poppy could see by the shocked expressions on their faces that they had met Lord Taverner before he'd succumbed to the rigours of drinking copious amounts of wine and had fallen asleep on another sofa. He lay with one arm dangling and a glass still clutched in his hand. A stream of red wine trickled like blood onto the rather threadbare Persian carpet. Mrs Whiddon marched forward and snatched the wine glass from her employer's limp hand.

'Darned old fool,' she said crossly. 'He often falls asleep with his cigar stuck in the corner of his mouth. One day he'll burn the rest of the house down.'

Poppy dared not comment for fear of aggravating Mrs Whiddon further. She sent a questioning look in Lottie's direction. 'Where is Arthur?'

'The boy is in the kitchen,' Mrs Whiddon said brusquely. 'Cook is preparing afternoon tea since we have visitors, although you'll be lucky to get a cucumber sandwich. Lady Taverner is the only one who keeps up the tradition, but she has a sweet tooth. Eats cake like there's no tomorrow.'

'A cup of tea and a biscuit would suffice, thank you,' Arabella said faintly.

'You look as though you need a tot of brandy in your tea, my lady.' Mrs Whiddon sniffed. 'I'll see what I can find. Only don't expect too much. We ain't much for entertaining these days.' She marched out of the drawing room without bothering to close the door.

Lord Taverner coughed and seemed to choke, but although his whole body jerked in a spasm he did not wake up and merely subsided with a snort.

'Is he Mr Taverner's papa?' Lottie asked in a whisper. 'He is rather shocking, don't you think, Mama?'

Arabella rolled her eyes. 'Eccentric is the word, Lottie. It happens in some of the best families.'

'He's very rude,' Poppy added in a low voice. 'But then this house is very strange. Arthur and I only knocked on the door here because the gatekeeper is even grumpier than his master. We had to get help to you quickly.'

'I was surprised to see Edward Taverner,' Arabella said, frowning. 'But he did help us out of a very difficult situation, and for that I'm grateful.'

'You did tell me that his family had an estate in Devonshire.' Poppy eyed her curiously. 'Have you been here before, Aunt Bella?'

'No, Poppy. I would certainly remember if I had ever visited this house.' Arabella glanced round the room and shuddered. 'It must have been a lovely home, a long time ago.'

'How are we to get home, Mama?' Lottie demanded tearfully.

'I don't know, my love. The carriage was badly damaged and I don't know if our horses have been caught. I just hope poor Grundy isn't too badly hurt.'

'We are rather stuck here at the moment.' Poppy sat down suddenly as her knees gave way beneath her. The full implications of their accident hit her with considerable force. They were miles from Dorrington Place, with no means of transport, and Grundy might be hovering between life and death.

'You don't think we will have to spend the night here, do you?' Lottie's eyes widened in horror. 'I would be afraid to sleep here. I dare say ghosts walk these floors after dark.'

'I suspect the beds are not properly aired,' Arabella added gloomily. 'And none too clean, if what I've seen so far is an example of Mrs Whiddon's housekeeping.'

'Perhaps there's an inn not too far from here,'

Poppy said hopefully. 'Mr Taverner might be persuaded to take us there in his motor car. Or perhaps he would drive us back to Dorrington Place.'

'I won't leave until I know that Grundy is properly cared for.' Arabella's eyes filled with tears. 'Oh dear, what started out as such a lovely day has turned into a nightmare.'

Lottie gave her mother a hug. 'Don't distress yourself, Mama. I'm sure Poppy will think of something. She's such a sensible person. She can always see her way around a problem. Isn't that so, Poppy?'

'You make me sound deadly dull, but I suppose I am quite practical most of the time.' Poppy smothered a sigh. Sometimes she wished that she was slightly dotty and helpless, like Lottie, but it was in her nature to sort out problems, whether her own or those of others. Poppy took a deep breath and rose to her feet. 'Perhaps I should have a word with Mr Taverner. He seems to be the only person here who lives in the real world.'

'Ask him to take us home, Poppy. It was your idea in the first place.' Lottie patted her mother's hand. 'We'll know more about Grundy's condition when the doctor has seen him.'

'But we can't desert Grundy, darling,' Arabella said miserably. 'We owe it to him to make sure he has the best possible treatment.'

Poppy could see that this conversation was going round in circles. Someone had to be practical and she seemed to have been chosen to find a solution to their problems. She left the room before either Lottie or her mama could raise an objection. However, the minute she stood outside the drawing-room door, she realised that in the maze of panelled corridors leading off the entrance hall she had no idea where to find Taverner. Mounted stags' heads gazed down at her, glassy-eyed, as she hesitated, trying to work out which way to go first. A faint smell of burnt toast assailed her nostrils and she decided to follow her nose. Mrs Whiddon had told them that Arthur was in the kitchen, so that seemed like a good place to start. The wainscoted passages were lined with oil paintings of dreary landscapes depicting ominous black clouds and icy-looking waterfalls. Then, as she neared the back of the building, Poppy was surprised to see much livelier works executed in charcoal and pastels. The nameplates revealed that the faces grinning at her were those of servants, probably retired or deceased now, who had once worked in the great Domesday House. There was even a painting of a sad-eyed black Labrador with a dead pheasant at its feet. Poppy shuddered and hurried on. Still life was one thing, but still death quite another, and not something she would want hanging on a wall in her home.

The kitchen was filled with acrid smoke from the burnt bread, which had apparently been left in the oven too long. Two charred, smoking loaves had been turned out onto the table with an elderly cook hacking off the crust in order to expose the soft white centre. Arthur sat on a high stool, swinging his legs while he munched a biscuit. He looked round and grinned at Poppy.

'You should hear Cook swear, Poppy. She could make Grundy blush.'

Cook's flushed face turned a shade deeper. 'That's not true, young master.'

'That's a lie, Cook. You would win a swearing competition if you went in for one.'

That's enough of your cheek, Master Arthur.' Mrs Whiddon nudged him in the ribs. She turned to Poppy with a smile etched on her lined face. 'What can I do for you, miss?'

'I was looking for Mr Taverner.' Poppy sensed that she was not going to get much help from either Cook or Mrs Whiddon. They seemed like a formidable pair, used to doing things their way.

'He went for the doctor, miss. The coachman is lying on the sofa in the morning parlour, if you wish to see him for yourself.'

'Is anyone with him, Mrs Whiddon?'

'He's unconscious, miss. There's not much point leaving a servant with him when he's in that state.'

'But he might come round and he won't know where he is. I'd like to see him, ma'am. I'll wait for the doctor to come.'

Mrs Whiddon pursed her lips. 'Very well, miss. Follow me.' She marched off with an irritated twitch of her shoulders.

Poppy turned to Arthur with an encouraging smile. 'Be a good chap and look after your mama, Arthur. She's in the drawing room with Lottie.'

He nodded, rendered speechless by another mouthful of ginger biscuit. Poppy gave him a gentle hug before hurrying after Mrs Whiddon.

Grundy lay on the sofa with a travel rug thrown over him. A cotton handkerchief had absorbed much of the blood from the gash on his forehead, but he was deeply unconscious. The right side of his body seemed to have borne the brunt of the impact when he was thrown from the driver's seat, and Poppy thought it likely he had broken bones, although no one had dared to take off his muddy garments.

'I'll leave you with him, then, miss.' Mrs Whiddon shook her head. 'He don't look too good. Let's hope Dr Standish gets here soon.'

'Yes, indeed.' Poppy waited until the door closed on Mrs Whiddon before pulling up a chair. She sat down, gazing at the injured man. She wanted to help him but she was afraid of doing him more harm than good with her efforts, and could only hope that Taverner had managed to find the doctor and would return with him shortly. Frustrated but determined to remain with Grundy, Poppy settled down to wait. The ticking of the grandmother clock on the far side of the room merged with the scrabbling sound of mice behind the skirting boards. The thorns of a neglected climbing rose scratched at the window panes as if begging to be admitted. The weather had deteriorated again and a strong wind slapped raindrops spitefully against the window, adding to the eerie atmosphere in the room. Poppy braced herself for a long and uncomfortable wait.

It was a relief when, only a short time later, the door burst open and Taverner entered, bringing with him the scent of rain on damp soil. He went straight to the sofa and leaned over, gently removing the temporary dressing from Grundy's head. He replaced it, turning to Poppy with a worried frown.

'That is going to need stitches. Unfortunately, the doctor was out on a case, but his wife promised to send him here as soon as he returns. I'd take Grundy to the hospital in my motor car, but moving him again is likely to make matters worse.'

Poppy rose to her feet and went to stand beside him. She gazed at Grundy with a feeling of acute helplessness. 'I agree, but there must be something we can do to help him while we wait for the doctor to arrive.'

'There's an old woman who lives on the edge of the village, who just might be able to help,' Taverner said slowly. 'They call her a witch, and there's talk about her turning people into frogs and such nonsense, totally without proof, of course. However, the people in the village are quick to use her services when illness or injuries occur.'

Poppy stared at him in disbelief. 'You are suggesting that we send for a witch?'

'She uses herbal remedies very successfully. She might even be able to sew up that nasty wound on Grundy's head. I think it's worth a try, but I want you to come with me. You would be more able to persuade her to come to the house.'

'Why would she be reluctant?' Poppy sensed even more trouble to come. If the villagers were scared of the witch, and the witch was reluctant to visit Domesday House, what did that say about the Taverners?

'Mother Hagerty fell out with my father many years ago. The feud continues, so I need you to persuade the old lady that she will be doing a favour for someone not in any way related to my family. Will you come with me, Poppy?'

'Of course. When you put it like that it would be impossible to refuse. In any case, I've never met a witch so I'm really curious.'

'I thought you might be.' Taverner reached for the bell pull. 'I'll have someone sit with Grundy while we're absent, but this shouldn't take long. Maybe Dr Standish will arrive in the meantime.'

'I hope so, but on the other hand I would love to see Mother Hagerty work her magic.'

Taverner seemed to get things done, despite the dilatory attitude of the servants. Ned was given the task of sitting with Grundy while Taverner drove Poppy the short distance to Mother Hagerty's home. Even in the pouring rain the thatched cottage looked surprisingly normal. Poppy had half expected to find it resembling the gingerbread house in *Hansel and Gretel*, or a cave in the deep dark woods. In reality the garden was surrounded by a neat wicket fence and the flowerbeds were well tended. Smoke rose in spirals from the chimney and chickens wandered about, pecking the ground for anything edible.

Taverner rang the bell and stood back. Poppy waited at his side, comforted by his commanding presence. The prospect of meeting a real witch was both exciting and nerve-racking, but when the door opened, the woman who stood in the narrow hallway was nothing like the bent old crone of Poppy's imagination. Mother Hagerty was dressed in serviceable black worsted, her hair tucked into a white mobcap, with the odd grey-streaked lock escaping around her temples. Her cotton-duck apron was covered in stains and her sleeves were rolled up to exposed bony arms and work-worn hands. The clinical smell of carbolic soap wafted around her person, quite different from the odour of brimstone that Poppy had anticipated.

'Good afternoon, Mrs Hagerty,' Taverner said politely. 'I have an injured man in desperate need of your excellent services. Would you be willing to oblige?'

Mother Hagerty looked him up and down, her lip curling in a scornful sneer. 'It's different when you need something, isn't it, sir? The last time I had anything to do with your family the old baron insulted me so that I vowed never to set foot inside Domesday House again.'

Taverner acknowledged her comment with a sympathetic smile. 'For that I apologise most sincerely, Mrs Hagerty. There is no excuse for that sort of behaviour.'

Poppy could see that he was not winning and she stepped forward, holding out her hand. 'Good afternoon, ma'am. You don't know me, but I was involved in an accident where the coachman was badly injured. Domesday House was the nearest place to ask for help.'

'That's your bad luck, miss. Fetch the doctor, that's all I have to say.' Mother Hagerty shot a suspicious glance at Taverner. 'But I suppose you've tried that already and the good doctor is unavailable, hence you've come to me in desperation.'

Poppy shot an anxious glance at Taverner but his urbane expression was unchanged. He acknowledged Mother Hagerty's comments with a nod.

'I quite understand your reluctance, ma'am. I believe that Dr Standish will make an effort to attend the patient when he is able, but your herbal remedies are legendary and your skill with a needle unchallenged.'

'You are soft-soaping me, sir,' Mother Hagerty said icily. 'But as the afflicted man has had the misfortune to end up in Domesday House, I won't hold that against him.'

'You are very kind, ma'am,' Poppy said hastily.

'Yes, I am.' Mother Hagerty backed further into the hallway. 'I'll fetch my bag and cape, but I am not doing this for nothing, Mr Taverner. I expect to be paid well for my services.' She disappeared into the depths of the cottage without waiting for an answer.

'You understand now why I brought you with me?' Taverner's fixed smile faded. 'My father has a way of alienating the local population second to none. This is why I choose to live in London.'

'But you came home now. May I ask why?'

'I received a letter from Miss Hayes, my mother's former maid, who was sacked by Mrs Whiddon for alleged misconduct. Miss Hayes was worried about Mama as she was barred from visiting the house.'

Poppy was not sure she believed him. It seemed unlikely that the notorious Eddie Taverner had left his businesses in London to visit his eccentric parents for anything other than something extremely pressing. However, she had to be content with his response as he had already walked back to his motor car.

Mother Hagerty had emerged from the cottage, locking the door behind her. 'You can't be too careful. Time was when you could leave your doors unlocked round here, but not nowadays. You can't trust anyone. Bear that in mind, maid.'

Poppy stood aside as Mother Hagerty marched past her and climbed into the vehicle as if this was something she did on a regular basis. Poppy hurried after her and squeezed into the dicky seat. The

202

Panhard was as impressive as Taverner had boasted, but it would have been even more exciting had Mother Hagerty produced a besom and flown off to Domesday House. Poppy stifled a giggle. It would not be politic at this moment to mention such a thing in front of the lady. A sense of humour did not seem to be one of her attributes and she had been unwilling enough to attend to Grundy in the first place. Poppy decided to save her joke to pass on to Lottie when they had a quiet moment together. Lottie, like her brother Adam, would always see the funny side of things. It was at times like this that Poppy missed Adam the most. She sat in silence during the drive back to Domesday House.

Mrs Whiddon backed away the moment she saw Mother Hagerty.

'What is that woman doing in my house, Mr Edward, sir?'

'Mrs Hagerty is going to help the injured man, Mrs Whiddon,' Taverner said firmly. 'Please see that she has everything she needs.'

Mrs Whiddon sniffed and tossed her head. 'I want nothing to do with black magic.' She stalked off in the direction of the kitchen.

Taverner's generous lips hardened into a thin line. 'I'm sorry, Mrs Hagerty. That was uncalled for.'

'I'll help you, ma'am,' Poppy said hastily. 'I can fetch what you need. You just have to tell me what it is you require.'

'Huh! I don't take no notice of Eliza Whiddon. I know too much about her past to make her comfortable in my presence. Take me to the afflicted person, miss. I'm not promising anything, but I'll do my best.'

Poppy glanced at Taverner.

'You know the way to the morning room, Miss Robbins,' Taverner said calmly. 'If there's anything you need, just ring the bell for a servant. I'll be in my study.'

'Yes, of course, Mr Taverner.' Poppy beckoned to Mother Hagerty. 'If you would be kind enough to come this way. I just hope we're not too late.'

Chapter Twelve

Mother Hagerty had just snipped the thread on the last stitch, closing the livid gash on Grundy's forehead, when the parlour door opened and Taverner entered. He was followed by a short gentleman wearing a black frock coat and a white shirt, the collar of which had such sharp points it seemed in danger of doing him a mischief if he bent his head.

'You're too late, Dr Standish,' Mother Hagerty said triumphantly. 'I've done your work for you.'

Poppy stepped aside as the doctor hurried over to the sofa to inspect Mother Hagerty's work.

'Hmm, not bad for a layman.' He peered at her over the top of his gold-rimmed spectacles. 'I hope you washed your hands first, lady.'

'I was tending the sick when you was in petticoats, Doctor.' Mother Hagerty snapped her bag shut. 'I've left a bottle of my special tonic for the poor chap,

Mr Taverner. That will be five shillings, if you please, sir.'

'That's my fee,' Dr Standish protested angrily. 'You aren't qualified, madam.'

Poppy was not about to stand by and witness such unfair treatment. She tapped Dr Standish on the shoulder.

'Excuse me, Doctor, but Mrs Hagerty has sewn up the wound and stopped the bleeding. I don't know how she did it, but she manipulated Grundy's arm so that it went back in its socket. I call that clever.'

'All in a day's work,' Mother Hagerty said smugly. 'He'll have a headache when he comes round, so I suggest a compress of brown paper soaked in a mixture of sage leaves and vinegar. It works every time. I haven't got round to setting the broken leg bones, Doctor. I leave that to you, as a professional, but I earned my five bob.'

'Just because you were lucky doesn't mean you should attempt to emulate a qualified physician, Mrs Hagerty. I, on the other hand, spent years at medical school.'

Poppy met Taverner's gaze with a silent plea for him to settle the matter. He put his hand in his pocket and took out five shilling pieces.

'Here you are, Mrs Hagerty. Thank you for coming and for attending to the patient. If you'd care to come with me I'll drive you home.'

Mother Hagerty tossed her head. 'There you are, Doctor. At least there's one gentleman in the room.'

She snatched up her cloak and bag. 'Good day to you, Miss Robbins. Ta for helping me. Mr Grundy will be fine when he's had a rest.'

Taverner held the door open for her but Dr Standish held up his hand. 'Wait a minute. What have you done to this man, you old fraud? He's too deeply asleep for it to be natural.'

'I gave him some of my special sleeping potion so that he didn't feel the pain when I sewed him up. I'll warrant you didn't learn how to make that in your years at medical school, you old quack.' Mother Hagerty swept from the room, leaving Poppy to face the irate doctor.

'That woman should be burned at the stake for being a witch,' Dr Standish said bitterly.

'I don't think they do that any more, Doctor.' Poppy glanced anxiously at Grundy, who was beginning to stir. 'Perhaps now would be a good time to set the bones in his leg?'

'Don't tell me what to do, young lady.' Dr Standish bent down to assess the injury to Grundy's leg. 'This is fairly straightforward, but I will need to make a splint. Find me some straight sticks and some cotton sheeting that can be torn up to make bandages. That will do until we can get the patient to hospital, where they will put a plaster cast on the afflicted limb. Hurry, if you please. I believe the herbal concoction is wearing off.'

* * *

An hour later Grundy was fully conscious and a strong dose of laudanum had deadened any pain he was feeling. Bert and Ned had lifted him into Dr Standish's chaise and the pair of them set off for the nearest hospital. Taverner had offered to drive them there in his Panhard, but Dr Standish refused politely but firmly.

Poppy stood beside Taverner on the carriage sweep as they watched Dr Standish flick the reins and his old horse faltered into an amble rather than a walk.

'It will take them twice as long to get to their destination,' Taverner said with a grim smile. 'I did offer.'

'Yes, I heard you. I think the good doctor prefers to do things his way. I get the feeling that he doesn't approve of the modern world.' Poppy wrapped her arms around her body with a shiver. 'It might be summer but it's a bit chilly.'

'Come inside. We've done all we can for Grundy, now we must decide what to do for you and the other ladies. I could drive you back to Dorrington Place, but it's getting rather late and the road is still blocked. I think you will have to stay here for the night, as was suggested earlier.'

Poppy followed him into the house. The fresh, damp earth smell outside was much pleasanter than the now all-too-familiar smell of burning that met her in the entrance hall. She wrinkled her nose and Taverner came to a halt, sniffing the air.

'That doesn't bode well for dinner tonight. Cook must have been at the sherry again.'

'Does this happen often?' Poppy made an effort to sound serious but once again she had the desire to giggle. Nothing was what it seemed in Domesday House. Perhaps she would wake up in her comfortable bed at Rainbow's End, and discover that all this had been a weird dream. She dragged herself back to the present and tried to concentrate on what Taverner was saying.

'Every so often. I keep telling Father to sack her, but he says she's been here too long for him to throw her out. I don't interfere with the running of this old mausoleum.'

'Perhaps I could help.' Poppy was hungry and she did not fancy eating what might be left of the disaster in the kitchen. The noxious smell suggested something more than just a burned saucepan.

'You?' Taverner had been about to walk away but he stopped and turned to give her a searching look. 'You are a guest, Poppy Robbins.'

'Yes, but not an invited one. I am quite competent in the kitchen. Perhaps I could help Cook to prepare something else?'

'I imagine she will be fast asleep in a rocking chair by the range, which is probably why whatever she was attempting to prepare was burned to a cinder.' Taverner met her enquiring gaze with a rueful smile. 'But if your offer is genuine, I would be very grateful indeed.'

'Lead on then. I'll see what I can do.' Poppy followed him to the kitchen where a haze of black smoke still lingered. Cook was slumped in a chair, snoring loudly with her head bent forward and her many chins resting on her large bosom. A young kitchen maid was attempting to lift a pan of charred food from the oven.

Taverner held up his hand. 'Stop that before you burn yourself, Jessie.'

The girl, who could not have been much more than thirteen years old, obeyed instantly, and stood back, gazing nervously at Taverner as he strode across the greasy flagstone floor. He snatched a cloth from Jessie's hands before lifting the heavy pan to the table.

Poppy gazed at the charred remains, screwing up her nose. 'I don't know what that was, but it's not even fit for the pigs now.'

'We don't have no pigs, miss,' Jessie said shyly. 'Us ate them all in the winter. Them was rabbits what Ned caught last night.'

'Is there anything else in the larder that I might cook?' Poppy asked gently. She could see that the child was nervous and expecting to take at least some of the blame for the fiasco. 'I'm sure Mrs Whiddon would want you to help me, otherwise everyone in the household will go hungry this evening.'

Taverner stared at her, eyebrows raised. 'You intend to cook for all of us, including the servants? That seems a lot to ask.'

'Yes, I do. Why not?' Poppy stood her ground. It was obvious that he thought her offer was an idle boast and she was determined to prove him wrong. 'I grew up helping in my parents' kitchen. I can assure you that you won't be disappointed.'

Taverner smiled. 'It's a most generous offer. How could I refuse?'

'Then that's settled. What time do you usually eat?' Poppy added hastily as he was about to leave the kitchen.

'I believe my parents dine at an unfashionably early hour, but don't worry too much about that. We will all wait upon your brave efforts.' Taverner left the room, closing the door behind him. Poppy found herself alone with a nervous Jessie and the drunken cook.

Poppy took an apron from a hook on the wall and tied it round her waist. She rolled up her sleeves. 'Lead on, Jessie. Show me what ingredients we have to work with.'

Grinning happily, Jessie sketched a curtsey. 'Yes, miss. Come this way.'

After a close inspection of the larder and the cold room, Poppy and Jessie emerged with their arms filled with vegetables, fruit and a large boiling fowl. Poppy set Jessie to work peeling carrots, parsnips and potatoes, while she dealt with the rather scraggy chicken. Her aim was to make a stew large enough to feed everyone, followed by an apple pie.

Working around the sleeping cook made things more difficult, but having grown up in a commercial kitchen, Poppy was not going to allow anything so trivial to put her off. She was in her element now and she worked tirelessly without interruption until Mrs Whiddon marched into the room and stood, arms akimbo, glaring at Poppy.

'What are you doing in here, miss? This isn't right.'

'Mr Taverner asked me to help out,' Poppy said calmly. 'There was a slight mishap with the rabbits.'

'They are burned to a crisp, Mrs Whiddon, ma'am,' Jessie added eagerly. 'Cook had several cups of that stuff she keeps in the special teapot and fell asleep.'

Mrs Whiddon picked up the teapot and took off the lid. She sniffed the contents. 'I see.'

'Everything is under control now. Dinner will be a little later than normal, I believe, but at least it will be edible.' Poppy laid the pastry top over the apples in the pie dish.

'This isn't how things are done,' Mrs Whiddon said, shaking her head so hard that her mobcap slipped over one eye. She pushed it back with an impatient hand. 'You're a guest, miss. You shouldn't be cooking for us.'

'My parents own a restaurant in Essex, Mrs Whiddon. I grew up assisting in the kitchen, so this is nothing new to me.'

'Well, thank you, I'm sure. I hope the master doesn't find out.'

'We won't speak about it.' Poppy trimmed the pastry before brushing it with egg wash. 'There, that's ready to go into the oven later. Everything is done now. The stew is simmering on the hob and I can't do anything more at the moment.'

'Her ladyship was asking for you, miss. I took her upstairs to her room, and the young lady as well. Your bedchamber is the next one along the landing. Shall I take you there now?'

Poppy took off the apron she had donned before she started cooking. 'It's all right, thank you, ma'am. I dare say I'll find it easily enough.' Poppy turned to Jessie, who was attempting to clear away the vegetable peelings. 'You were a good help, Jessie. I can see you making a fine cook when you're older.'

Jessie grinned. 'Ta, miss.'

Cook groaned, opened her eyes and sat upright, staring round the room as if trying to work out where she was. Mrs Whiddon marched up to her and slapped Cook's face. 'You're a disgrace, you old soak.'

'It was medicinal, for me aches and pains,' Cook protested, holding her hand to the afflicted cheek.

Mrs Whiddon turned to Jessie, who cowered and backed away. 'I'm not going to hit you, you stupid girl. Make a pot of coffee for Cook and clean up the mess. I expect to find the kitchen spotless when I come down.'

Poppy could not allow Jessie to suffer from Mrs Whiddon's wrath. 'Jessie has been a great help, ma'am. If Cook succumbed to exhaustion it would appear that she is overworked.'

Mrs Whiddon narrowed her eyes. 'Exhaustion is one thing – excess of sherry wine is another.'

'That's as may be, but speaking as an outsider it seems to me that Cook could do with an extra pair of hands in a kitchen of this size.' Poppy had a sudden vision of the kitchen at Rainbow's End and she remembered how her mother always managed to diffuse a difficult situation. She modified her tone. 'You seem to run the household as far as I can see, ma'am. Perhaps you could employ a couple of daily women to make things run more smoothly.'

'That may be your opinion, Miss Robbins. However, you're right in one thing. You don't belong here and I don't appreciate someone telling me how to do my job.'

Poppy realised that her attempt at mediation had failed. 'If you were doing it properly there would be no need to make any suggestions. I think Mr Edward Taverner would agree with me.' She turned on her heel and walked out of the kitchen. There was no point in arguing with a woman like Mrs Whiddon, who was a bully and a good example of someone who had allowed power to go to her head.

Poppy made her way to the main entrance hall and mounted the oak staircase, taking care to avoid treading on the carapaces of dead cockroaches. It would take more than a couple of cleaning women to bring the house up to scratch, but it was not her problem. Tomorrow, hopefully the road would be clear and they could take advantage of Taverner's offer to drive them back to Dorrington Place.

At the top of the stairs she met Lottie, who gave her a hug. 'I hate this old house, Poppy. It scares me in daylight, so what is it going to be like after dark? I think this place is haunted,' she added in a whisper.

Poppy glanced towards the staircase that led to the second floor. She could understand Lottie's fears, but agreeing with her would only serve to frighten her even more. 'It's just your imagination, Lottie. You know how it runs away with you sometimes.' Poppy tried to sound convincing but she also feared that there might be supernatural happenings in the small hours.

'I have a room with a big four-poster bed,' Lottie said urgently. 'I don't want to sleep alone. Will you share it with me?'

'Of course, if you want me to. Where's your mama?'

'Her room isn't too bad. I'm sure that horrid housekeeper was just trying to keep on Mama's good side because she's titled. I do hate snobs.'

'More than ghosts?' Poppy said, smiling.

'Now you're laughing at me.'

'No, not really. I do agree with you. Anyway, I want to see your mama before I do anything else. You've both had a terrible time being trapped in the carriage. I want to make sure she's all right.'

'Yes, she's fine. Arthur is with her. They put a truckle bed in Mama's room so that he can sleep in there with her. He's set himself up to be Mama's protector and he's obviously enjoying himself. He thinks he's the man of the house, with Papa and

Adam away from home.' Lottie rolled her eyes and laughed.

'We'll allow him to think that if it keeps him happy in this strange house.' Poppy stifled a sigh of relief. At least Lottie had not lost her sense of humour. 'Anyway, I'm hoping that tomorrow we can all go home to Dorrington Place. I've just spent the last hour in the kitchen preparing dinner tonight.'

Lottie's eyes widened. 'No! Really? I thought they had a cook.'

'Yes, they do, but she is rather partial to cooking sherry. I had to step in or there would have been nothing for anyone to eat.'

'You are so clever, Poppy. I wouldn't know where to start. That Mrs Whiddon scares me, too. She even tells Lord Taverner what to do. He ought to find another housekeeper who would do as he bids.'

'Well, that's his business, Lottie. I think Mrs Whiddon has been here for so long that she forgets her place, and Lord Taverner is . . .' Poppy sought for a suitable word. 'He's different.'

'I think he's a little mad,' Lottie said in a low voice. 'Don't make the meal tonight too delicious. I have a feeling we might not be allowed to leave if you do.'

Poppy laughed. 'Now that is ridiculous. I'm sure Cook is perfectly competent when she's sober, and I've only made chicken stew followed by an apple pie. Uncle Amos would say it's soup kitchen food.'

'Well, your uncle Amos is also a little off, if you

don't mind me saying so, Poppy. Although he is a brilliant chef.'

'I wonder how they're getting on at home,' Poppy said, sighing. 'I feel a little guilty spending so much time away from Rainbow's End when it's our busiest season.'

'I'm sure they will manage.' Lottie grasped Poppy's hand. 'Come and see my room. The four-poster is so huge that Mama and Arthur could sleep there with the two of us.'

'All right. I'll take a look, but I will have to return to the kitchen soon to check on the stew.' Poppy allowed Lottie to lead her to the room at the far end of the landing. The early evening sun filtered through the small window panes, casting a pattern of tiny squares on the bare boards. The room was simply furnished with a carved wooden chest, and a couple of chairs with seats padded in worn damask, which matched the tester and bed hangings. Lottie had been right about the four-poster, which dominated the room. Its ornately carved mahogany posts must have been the work of craftsmen a hundred years or more ago. Poppy sat on the edge of the bed to test the mattress.

'This feels a bit solid,' she said, pulling a face. 'I don't think we're going to have a very comfortable night.'

Lottie sat down beside her, glancing nervously around the wainscoted room. 'I can imagine secret panels opening in the early hours with ghostly figures emerging to scare us out of our wits.'

'Maybe we could appropriate some of Cook's supply of sherry. A couple of glasses of that and we would sleep like babies. The spirits would be wasting their time if they attempted to frighten us.'

Lottie's eyes widened and her lips trembled. 'So you don't think I'm imagining things?'

'Not necessarily, but everything is strange here.' Poppy slipped her arm around Lottie's shoulders. 'You're tired and hungry. You'll feel better when you've had some of my famous chicken stew, which reminds me – I need to go down to the kitchen and make sure it's simmering nicely.'

'You aren't going to leave me on my own in this haunted room?'

'Why don't you go and sit with your mama and Arthur until dinner is ready? After that I'll be with you until it's time to leave in the morning. Let's just hope that Taverner's men manage to clear the debris on the road.'

'I'll never grumble about my room at home ever again,' Lottie said with feeling. 'And please don't let me sit near the old man at dinner. I fear his table manners might leave a lot to be desired. If he slurps his stew I will have to eat in the kitchen with the drunken cook.'

Poppy went to open the door. 'Stop worrying, Lottie. We'll laugh about this experience in days to come.'

'I do wish Adam was here.' Lottie slid off the bed and crossed the room, glancing nervously behind her. 'I can't help feeling that someone is watching me in this room.'

'Nonsense, Lottie. It's just your imagination.' Poppy had not intended to speak so sharply but she was beginning to lose patience.

'I know I'm a coward, unlike Adam, who is so brave. He always knows exactly what to do.'

Poppy relented; she hated to see her friend so unhappy. 'Just think of all the stories you'll have to tell Adam on his next leave. Anyway, let's get you to your mama's room and I'll return to kitchen duties. It seems I can't get away from them for long.' Poppy opened the door. 'Which is your mama's room?'

Lottie hurried past her and knocked on the door to the adjacent room. She opened it, glancing over her shoulder. 'I'll see you at dinner then.'

'You most certainly will,' Poppy said cheerfully. She could see a long night ahead if Lottie could not control her nerves. A positive attitude seemed to be the only answer.

Poppy headed toward the stairs but came to a halt as one of the bedroom doors opened and a wraith-like figure emerged. The tiny woman was enveloped in a voluminous silk wrap that made her look like a child dressed up in a garment belonging to her mother. A white fluff of uncombed hair stood up around her head like a dandelion clock. Her pallid face was lined but her eyes were a startling shade of blue and child-like in their innocence.

'You must be the young lady my son told me

219

about,' she said in a soft voice, barely louder than a whisper. 'My name is Alice.'

'I'm Poppy Robbins. How do you do, Lady Taverner?' Poppy sketched a curtsey, which seemed the right thing to do in the circumstances.

'How do you do, Poppy Robbins? I thought I heard voices earlier. I don't normally venture far from my room. I am delicate, you see.'

'Perhaps you ought to sit down then, ma'am?' Poppy eyed her anxiously. Lady Taverner looked so frail that she might collapse at any moment.

'Come and talk to me, Poppy.' Lady Taverner retreated into her room, leaving Poppy little choice other than to follow her. The stew would have to simmer on its own for a little longer.

'I so rarely see people other than my maid, Hayes, but she has gone to visit her aged mama in Bristol, so I think she will be gone for a while.' Lady Taverner managed to get to her chair by the fireplace and sank down in a flurry of silk.

Poppy noticed that her ladyship's feet were bare and blue with cold, although it was reasonably warm in the room. She spotted a pair of well-worn slippers and bent down to pick them up.

'Would you be more comfortable with these on your feet, ma'am?'

'How kind. I thought I had lost them. My eyesight isn't what it used to be.' Lady Taverner held her feet up, allowing Poppy to put the slippers on for her. 'Thank you, my dear. Won't you pull up a stool and sit down?'

Poppy did as she asked and perched on a rather rickety stool. 'I cannot stay long, ma'am. There was an emergency in the kitchen and I am cooking dinner.'

'That doesn't sound right.' Lady Taverner shook her head, frowning. 'You are a guest. My son told me your carriage had come to grief during the storm.'

'Yes, ma'am. Your son has made us welcome and I am only too happy to help out.'

'I suppose Cook has been drinking again. They think I don't know what goes on downstairs, but I do. Hayes keeps me informed, or she did. I do miss her.'

'Can I get you anything, ma'am? I really need to go downstairs to the kitchen.'

'No, my dear. I am all right. The child brings me food every so often, or else I go downstairs to the kitchen when everyone else is in bed. I don't sleep much myself, and I rather like the old house when I have it to myself.'

'I see.' Poppy had a sudden vision of Lottie seeing the spectral figure of Lady Taverner wandering around after dark. She rose to her feet. 'Perhaps I could bring you a bowl of chicken stew when it's ready. I made it myself.'

'Thank you, my dear. That would be so very kind of you. I hope you are going to stay with us for a long time.'

Lady Taverner's smile was so sweet and innocent that Poppy leaned over to kiss her lined cheek.

'Of course, ma'am. Perhaps we could have a little chat after dinner?'

'That would be so nice.' Lady Taverner leaned back in her chair and closed her eyes, which seemed to be a cue for Poppy to leave the room. She went downstairs, wondering why Lady Taverner had been abandoned by the rest of the household.

The question was uppermost in her mind when she encountered Taverner in the entrance hall. He was dressed for outdoors.

'Ah, Miss Robbins, you see me about to inspect the work on your carriage. I found a local blacksmith and a wheelwright to assess the damage.'

'Do you think it will be shifted by morning? We would be out of your way then.'

He smiled and she was shocked to catch a glimpse of his mother's innate charm in his expression. Until this moment she had only noted a certain arrogance in his attitude. Perhaps he was not as unapproachable as she had first thought.

'I'm sure you cannot wait to return to civilisation. Domesday House is not the most welcoming place to be, and guests are not normally expected to earn their keep by working in a kitchen.'

'I told you I don't mind at all. I'm glad to do something in return for your assistance, especially with poor Grundy. I hope he is recovering in hospital.'

'I wasn't planning on staying for long, but I promise I will make sure that Grundy has the best possible treatment and is taken back to Dorrington Place as soon as he is well enough.'

'Thank you, sir.'

'If I'm not back in time for dinner I hope you will save me some.'

Poppy smiled. 'Of course.'

He hesitated in the doorway. 'Perhaps I was a little hard on you when we first met. I would like to talk to you about your particular problem with a certain Miss Flyte. Maybe after dinner, if you are not too tired?'

'Yes, that would be most welcome.' Poppy watched him walk away with mixed feelings. She had fully intended to broach the subject of his mother, who was seemingly abandoned to her room and left very much alone, but Taverner had a way of dominating the conversation to the extent that she had forgotten why she wanted to speak to him in the first place. At this moment it was the neglected Alice Taverner who was even more important than whatever Taverner had to say about Miranda Flyte. With everything that had happened in the last twenty-four hours Poppy had almost forgotten about Miranda and the blackmail she had attempted with Gervase Mulliner. She would need to have a very serious conversation with Taverner.

Chapter Thirteen

'What is it you wanted to tell me about Miranda Flyte?' Poppy poured the coffee that Jessie had left on a table in the drawing room. She handed a cup to Taverner.

He sat back in the armchair, eyeing her speculatively. 'As I told you when we first met, I've come across Gervase Mulliner in the past. He's a shady character, a gambler who lives off his wits. He bores anyone who will listen to the sad tale of how his uncle was cheated out of his inheritance, but Gervase would cheat his own mother if he thought he could get away with it.'

'Miranda has demanded a public apology from Lord and Lady Dorrington as well as from my mother. She and her cousin want money in reparation although she did not state an actual sum. My parents sent me away before I had a chance to challenge Miranda further.'

Taverner sipped his coffee. 'That was probably a wise move on their part. The Pettigrew family and their descendants are not averse to kidnapping, if it suits their purpose. You or Lottie might easily have been victims.'

'What can we do about it? I can't live at Dorrington Place for ever. My home is at Rainbow's End with my parents. A scandal could ruin them.'

'I understand. I can help, although I would need you to stay away from home until I tell you it is safe for you to return.'

'But what about my family? How will they manage without me?'

A wry smile curved Taverner's lips. 'According to Begg, they are doing quite well so far.' He put his cup and saucer down on the table. 'No, seriously, you must not think of going home yet. I will speak to your papa and I'm certain he'll agree with me. Begg is there to protect your family and I will deal with Mulliner. If he goes down, you won't have any trouble with Miranda. She is an opportunist and will move on to the next victim, who will be best advised to avoid her.'

'In the meantime, I am to do nothing? Is that what you're saying? I wasn't brought up to be a lady of leisure, Eddie. I need to do something useful. Don't misunderstand me, I love Aunt Bella and Lottie, but I couldn't live as they do.'

'You need a worthy cause to support?' Taverner's serious question was at odds with the teasing expression in his dark eyes.

'Now you're laughing at me,' Poppy said indignantly.

'Heaven forbid.' Taverner reached out to cover her hand with his. 'Not at all, my dear Poppy, I have too much respect for you, but I might have a suggestion that would suit us all.'

'What is it you have in mind, Eddie?' The warmth of his touch was oddly comforting, but she withdrew her hand, resisting the temptation to allow him to hold it any longer.

He inclined his head. 'We are equals in this – partners, you might say. My suggestion is that when the road is clear I drive Lady Dorrington, Lottie and Arthur back to their home, leaving you here for as long as it takes to put Mulliner out of the way.'

'You want me to stay here? Why?'

'Because, if I am being honest, I have neglected my family for years. I used to find myself at odds with my father when I was younger, but time has taken its toll on him and he isn't the man he was, as you may have observed.'

'I must admit he is a little eccentric.'

'That's being generous. But it's my mother who worries me most.'

'Exactly. That's the subject I was going to bring up next.' Poppy fixed him with a steady gaze. 'You must realise that your mama needs extra special care and attention.'

He acknowledged her comment with a nod. 'I agree entirely. I have been very remiss and I want to make up for it now.'

'How do you intend to do that, Eddie?'

'It's not going to be easy, I realise it now. Mrs Whiddon has taken control, which I should have seen sooner. She has not had anyone to account to for years, and Cook has resorted to drink. The entire household needs shaking up.'

'Yes, I did think that.' Poppy smiled despite the seriousness of the conversation. She sensed that the admission of failure on Eddie Taverner's part was costing him dear. 'You're right in saying all these things. Someone needs to take control.'

'And I think you are that person, Poppy. But only if you agree, of course. I don't want you to feel obliged or the need to humour me.'

'For me to stay on and help out is one thing, but to remain here indefinitely and take control of the household is another. Are you simply amusing yourself at my expense, Eddie?'

'I'm deadly serious. I cannot remain here because I have business to attend to in London. You, on the other hand, need something to keep you occupied until it's safe for you to go home.'

'You're asking too much of me. Besides which, your father might be a little lax when it comes to running this establishment, but he would never agree to someone like me taking over.'

'I can handle my father, and Mama is not in any condition to oversee the servants. You would have free rein with my backing.' Taverner held up his hand as Poppy opened her mouth to argue. 'You wanted to do something useful for humanity – well, this might not be as satisfying as feeding hungry children, but you would be rescuing a whole household, if not the entire estate.'

Poppy could see that he was serious, but she was still doubtful. 'It would be me against the servants who have been here for years. I'm not sure I could do it, Eddie.'

'Of course you could, if you put your mind to it. We haven't known each other for long but I have absolute faith in you.'

Poppy refilled her cup from the silver coffee pot and added a spoonful of sugar, stirring it vigorously while she tried to think of a valid excuse to refuse. On the other hand, it did make sense in a bizarre fashion. She could see the need for someone to take the running of the household from Mrs Whiddon's hands, as she had obviously exceeded her authority. It would certainly be a challenge.

'If I were to agree to this you would need to give me full control,' she said slowly. 'I would have to take on extra kitchen and cleaning staff. Bert and Ned seem to spend most of their time in the kitchen, drinking tea, I would expect them to take charge outside.'

'That is what they should be doing now. I know I'm to blame. I've lived in London for years and I've allowed everything here to slide.'

'I can't argue with that, but it would be difficult for me, as an outsider, to come in and start giving orders to the servants. They would look to your father for instructions.'

'He would not know where to start. Besides which, as you might have noticed at dinner, Pa has taken a liking to you, and my mother would be delighted to have you on her side. If you agree to help me you will have complete autonomy in all household matters. You won't find me niggardly when it comes to money, and I promise not to interfere.'

'Very well. But supposing I accept your offer, how would we explain my presence to your parents and staff?' Poppy pushed her cup away, untouched. She could see problems ahead and Taverner had an air of self-assurance that made her wary.

'You're right, of course. That could be a problem, but if this is to work, I suggest that we let it be known that you are my fiancée and the future mistress of Domesday House.'

'Your fiancée?' Poppy stared at him in a mixture of horror and amusement. 'Surely we don't need to go that far?'

'When I return to London, tomorrow or the next day, you will need to stand alone. If everyone believes that we are to be married, they will respect your wishes. I will make sure of that.'

'What would I tell Aunt Bella and Lottie? They won't believe it, for a start, and what would my parents think if they discover that I plan to marry without telling them?'

Taverner frowned thoughtfully. 'You could tell

Lady Dorrington that you wish to remain here to keep an eye on Grundy, and to oversee the repairs on her carriage.'

'It's really not my place to do either of those things. Aunt Bella is too intelligent to be taken in by such a story.'

'Then tell them the truth, if you think they can keep it to themselves, but it's best if everyone else accepts the fiction for now. You will be safe here from the scheming Miranda Flyte and Gervase Mulliner. Besides which, you will be doing me a tremendous favour that I will never be able to fully repay.' Taverner reached out to take her hand in his, holding it in a firm grasp. 'Believe it or not I love my parents and I hate to see them in this state. If you can at least get the house running as it should and the servants behaving properly, I will be eternally grateful. What do you say, Poppy?'

She met his earnest gaze and she could see that he was totally sincere. What he was suggesting was outrageous, of course, but it appealed to Poppy's sense of duty. She did not want to upset her parents, but perhaps the truth could be kept from them until she could go home and tell them everything. Pa would laugh, once he got over the shock. Mama might be angry at first, but her early life had been so filled with trauma that she would probably take it all in her stride. If there was one woman whom Poppy admired most in the world it was her mother.

'If it's too much for you I quite understand,'

Taverner said earnestly. 'It's asking a lot, I know but—'

Poppy held up her hand. 'I'll do it, Eddie. But to make it believable I ought to have a ring.'

He stared at her for a moment as if he could not quite believe that she had agreed, then a slow smile relaxed his taut facial muscles. He raised her hand to his lips.

'Poppy, I love you.'

'No, you don't. However, you might as well get used to saying it when anyone can hear.'

'Are you absolutely sure you want to go ahead with this?' Taverner frowned. 'I want you to be certain.'

Poppy could scarcely believe she had agreed to such a mad plan, but the idea was growing on her. 'Find me a suitable ring and we'll announce the culmination of our whirlwind romance. It might even be fun.'

Taverner rose to his feet as the door opened and Arabella bustled into the drawing room followed by Lottie.

Poppy realised that someone was missing. 'Where's Arthur? I thought he went out with you.'

'We've just had a lovely walk in the grounds,' Arabella said, smiling. 'They are a bit overgrown in parts, but the rose garden is still fragrant, if in need of a little weeding. We walked on and saw Ned fishing in the lake. Of course, Arthur wanted to stay and see if he could catch anything. Ned promised to bring him back before dark.'

'I wouldn't have minded staying there myself,' Lottie added. 'The lake is beautiful but you could do with a few sheep or a herd of deer to keep the grass down, Mr Taverner. That's how we do it at Dorrington Place.'

'I'll bear that in mind,' Taverner said seriously. 'If you'll excuse me, ladies, I have some paperwork to complete before I return to London.'

'Of course, but are you still able to take us home tomorrow?' Arabella eyed him anxiously. 'I don't want to put you out, Mr Taverner, but we are in desperate need of a change of clothing, and our absence will be causing concern.'

'I understand, my lady. Hopefully the road will be clear tomorrow morning. If so, I will drive you back to Dorrington Place first thing.' Taverner headed for the door, pausing to send a meaningful look to Poppy. 'I'll leave you to explain what we have just decided.' He left the room, closing the door firmly behind him.

'What was all that about, Poppy?' Arabella demanded as she took a seat. 'Is there any coffee left in the pot?'

'I expect it's cold by now.' Poppy reached for the bell pull. 'I'll send for more.'

'Anyone would think you were the lady of the house,' Lottie said, smiling.

'That's what I wanted to talk to you about.' Poppy glanced from one to the other. 'I think you'd better sit down, Lottie.'

Poppy explained as briefly as possible while Arabella and Lottie sat in stunned silence. She had just come to the end when Mrs Whiddon entered without knocking and set a tray of coffee on the table in front of Arabella.

'I thought you might need this after your walk in the grounds, my lady.' She shot a sideways glance at Poppy as she turned to leave. 'Mr Taverner has called a meeting in the servants' hall. Do you know why he wishes to speak to us, miss?'

'Perhaps you had better wait for him to address you, ma'am.' Poppy held Mrs Whiddon's gaze. It was obvious that she was suspicious and had sensed that something was afoot. She would not be pleased when she discovered her change in circumstances.

'Thank you, Mrs Whiddon,' Arabella said calmly. 'It is a beautiful evening. Such a pity the gardens are so overgrown.'

Mrs Whiddon sniffed and said nothing, but the tilt of her head and a twitch of her shoulders indicated that she resented the criticism. She closed the door with unnecessary force.

'I hope you realise what you are taking on, Poppy,' Arabella said, reaching for the coffee pot. 'That woman is not going to accept your authority without a fight.'

'I am ready for that. I know what I'm doing, Aunt Bella. Unfortunately, it's not in my nature to be idle, and I love a challenge.'

Lottie pulled a face. 'You've certainly got one on

233

your hands with that woman. Are you really sure you want to do this?'

'She won't win – I'll see to that – and it takes my mind off Miranda Flyte and her cousin. Eddie – I mean, Mr Taverner – is going to deal with them and we will all benefit from that, even you, Aunt Bella. I'm doing this in return.'

'I understand, my dear, and I appreciate everything you are doing, but I don't like leaving you here.' Arabella shook her head. 'And you haven't even got a change of clothes.' She filled two cups with coffee and handed one to Lottie.

'Perhaps you could pack a bag for me and give it to Taverner to bring here. I assume he will return here before he goes to London.'

'I'll do it,' Lottie said eagerly. 'I'd offer to stay here but I really don't feel comfortable in this creepy place.'

'I'm sure it won't be for long.' Poppy tried to sound convincing. Despite the fact that she had not known Taverner for long, she trusted his judgement even though she knew nothing about his business interests in London. Begg had trusted Taverner and Poppy trusted Begg.

'I must admit I will be glad to get home.' Arabella glanced out of the window at the darkening sky. 'I hope Ned brings Arthur home soon. I don't like him being out in the damp night air. You know how delicate he is.'

'He will have to toughen up when he goes to

boarding school, Mama,' Lottie said impatiently. 'You treat him like a baby.'

'I don't know how you can say such things, Lottie.' Arabella picked up her cup and saucer and took a sip of coffee. 'Arthur has always been sickly. I kept him at home for another year so that he might grow stronger before he endures the rigours of public school.'

'I'm sure he's much stronger now,' Poppy said firmly. 'He behaved amazingly well when you and Lottie were trapped in the carriage. He didn't panic or break down in tears. Arthur will go far, I'm sure.'

Arabella managed a weak smile. 'I just hope he doesn't go into the army like Adam. I live in dread of hearing that he has been posted to somewhere dangerous.'

Poppy suppressed a shudder. She felt much the same, if she were to be honest, but she had so far managed to put such fears to the back of her mind. Adam was brave and fearless; she could only hope that military discipline would save him from being too much of a hero if it came to a battle. She rose from her seat.

'Would you like me to go and find Arthur, ma'am? I'll bring him to you.'

'If you don't mind going out on your own, that would put my mind at rest, Poppy, dear. Thank you.'

Poppy made her escape, leaving Lottie and her mother to enjoy their coffee in the relative comfort of the shabby drawing room. Outside the evening air was sweet with the fragrance of damp earth, night-scented stocks and roses. The sky to the west was streaked with purple, orange and scarlet as the last rays of the sun plunged below the horizon. Bats circled overhead, but the robin's song was not dulled by the creeping darkness. Poppy made her way towards the lake, although the landscape changed subtly as the shadows deepened and she lost her way amongst a tangle of briars and overgrown shrubs. It would be easy to panic, but she followed her instincts and emerged onto the grassy slope leading down to the water's edge. There was no sign of Ned or Arthur and it seemed that they had returned to the house.

Duty done, Poppy retraced her steps as far as possible and once again took the wrong path. Darkness was swallowing up the land in great greedy gulps as she threaded her way along overgrown paths, hoping to emerge somewhere familiar. In the end it was the scent of cigar smoke that led her to the rose garden. As the moon emerged from behind a ridge of clouds, she could just make out the outline of Taverner, standing beneath a rose-covered pergola. He was smoking a cigar and seemed to be deep in thought. She went to join him, despite the thorns snagging her skirts from an overgrowing rambler.

Taverner turned to gaze at her in surprise. 'What are you doing out here after sunset, Poppy?'

'I went looking for Arthur. He was fishing in the lake with Ned and hasn't yet returned. His mother is worried about him.' Poppy was slightly out of breath as she reached him. 'What are you doing here, anyway? You were going to speak to the servants.'

He laughed. 'It didn't take long. I don't think they believed me, except young Jessie, who seemed to be enthralled by a vision of love at first sight and pure romance.'

'And you aren't?'

'I'm a practical man, Poppy. Our arrangement is a business matter, as you well know. But,' he added, taking something from his inside jacket pocket, 'I have found something you might care to put on.' He held up a gold ring and a solitaire diamond winked in the moonlight.

'You came across a ring? Just like that?'

'After I left you I went to see my mother. I thought you needed an ally in the house and I knew she would be on your side, or as much as is possible in her weakened condition.'

'I'm surprised you told her. Was she very upset?'

'You don't know my mother, Poppy. She is built of stern stuff and she approved of the scheme wholeheartedly. She even gave me my grandmother's engagement ring. I don't know what you said to Mama, but you made a lasting impression upon her.' Taverner held out his hand and somewhat reluctantly Poppy laid her left hand on his outstretched palm. He slipped the ring on her finger. 'There, that should convince the doubters that we are officially engaged.'

Poppy held her hand up so that the diamond winked and glittered in the moonlight.

'Are you sure you want me to wear this, Eddie? It must be very valuable.'

'If my mother thinks it right, then that is all I need to know. You and I have to trust each other, Poppy. At this point in time we need to work together.'

The moment of elation that Poppy had experienced dissipated into the night air as reality forced itself upon her. She was, after all, just a glorified housekeeper in return for Taverner dealing with two would-be blackmailers. It was simply business.

'Yes, you're right, of course. I will take great care of your family heirloom.'

Taverner leaned forward and kissed her gently on the lips. 'Sealed with a kiss, my dear Poppy.'

She swayed slightly on her feet. It would have been so easy to step into his embrace and make believe that they were really and truly engaged. The moonlight, together with the perfume of roses with just a hint of Havana cigar smoke, was as heady as a glass of wine. A warm breeze caressed Poppy's hot cheeks. She backed away hastily.

'I'll show the ring to Aunt Bella and Lottie. I don't think they really believed me when I told them of our plan.' Poppy said it more to remind herself that this was all play-acting than as a statement of fact.

Taverner nodded. 'Thank you, Poppy. This means a great deal to me. I won't let you down.'

'I believe you.' An involuntary shiver ran down Poppy's spine and she turned away. 'Good night, Eddie.'

She did not wait for an answer but walked quickly back to the house and entered through the servants' entrance. She was on her way past the kitchen when she heard Arthur's voice and she opened the door.

He was seated at the long pine table, eating a large slice of cake with a glass of milk to hand.

'Arthur, your mama is worried about you,' Poppy said firmly. 'You need to go to the drawing room and let her see that you're safe.'

'We was only fishing, miss.' Ned exhaled a stream of smoke from the rolled-up cigarette he was smoking. 'I brought the lad back and he was hungry.'

'That was a kind thought, but he should go to his mama,' Poppy said firmly. 'I believe you live in the stable block, Ned. It would be best if you did not smoke in the kitchen.'

Ned stared at her open-mouthed. 'Cook don't object, miss.'

'I'm sure she will agree with me. Tobacco and food do not go well together.'

'I'll speak to Mrs Whiddon then. She's in charge of us all, miss.'

'Not any longer. Mr Taverner has asked me to run the household while he is in London.'

'Miss Robbins is right, Ned.' Jessie emerged from the scullery, a dishcloth clutched in her small hand. 'Mr Taverner gave us all a talk earlier. He said Miss Robbins is in charge for now. Even Mrs Whiddon has to do as she says.'

239

'Well, I'll be jiggered. Who would have thought such a thing could happen in Domesday House?'

'It's true, Ned,' Poppy said firmly. 'So please go back to the stables and remember not to smoke in the house. Things will be a bit different from now on, but I'm sure we will all get on very well.'

Ned stubbed out his cigarette. 'If you say so, miss. I'll bid you good night then.' He stomped out of the kitchen and his footsteps echoed off the flagstone floor, getting fainter until the slamming of the outer door left an eerie silence.

Poppy glanced at Jessie, who was busy clearing the table. 'You should have finished for the evening, Jessie. Have you much more to do?'

'Just a little washing up, miss.'

'Right, well, do that and then make yourself a cup of cocoa and take it up to your room.'

'Thank you, miss. But I sleep in the broom cupboard.'

'That's appalling. It's too late now, but tomorrow I will find you a more suitable place to sleep. Good night, Jessie.'

Poppy turned to Arthur, who was staring at her wide-eyed. 'Come along, Arthur. You may bring your cake and milk to the drawing room. We'd better get there before your mama sends for the police.'

'You're in charge now?' Arthur said in a low voice. 'The old woman won't like it.' He paled visibly as he glanced over Poppy's shoulder. 'Oops!'

'No, the old woman doesn't like it.' Mrs Whiddon

stood in the doorway, bristling with anger. 'And she is not going to stand for it. You, Miss Robbins, may have persuaded Mr Taverner that you are going to run the household, but it's been my job for twenty years and I'm not giving up now. You've got a fight on your hands, lady.'

Chapter Fourteen

Next morning Poppy was up early. She washed, dressed and went downstairs to the kitchen where she found Jessie stoking the fire in the range.

'Good morning, Jessie.' Poppy glanced round the kitchen, and was pleased to see that it was clean and tidy. 'You must have worked hard to get everything spotless.'

'Good morning, miss.' Jessie straightened up, wiping a bead of sweat from her cheek. 'I got up a bit earlier than usual. I didn't want to give Mrs Whiddon cause to complain.'

'You've done well. Anyway, I suggest you put the kettle on and then you can show me where you sleep. We must do something about that.'

Jessie placed the kettle on the hob. 'If you'll follow me, please, miss.' She led the way from the main kitchen to a narrow passageway, where a little

242

further along she opened the door to the broom cupboard. Poppy peered over her shoulder and was horrified at the sight of a straw-filled palliasse pushed to the back of the dark space, half-hidden by mops, brooms, buckets and feather dusters. There was no ventilation in the cupboard and the smell of carbolic was so strong it made Poppy gasp for breath.

'This is where you sleep, Jessie?'

'Yes, miss. It's not too bad. I mean, it's quite warm.'

'It's not a suitable place for anyone to spend even one night,' Poppy said firmly. 'I will find you somewhere better, Jessie. Let's have that cup of tea and when Mrs Whiddon comes down I will tell her what is going to happen.'

'She won't like it, miss.' Jessie scuttled on ahead but she came to a sudden halt as she stepped into the kitchen.

'Where have you been, girl?' Mrs Whiddon demanded angrily. 'Where's my morning tea? You know I have it in my room first thing.'

'You must blame me for that, ma'am.' Poppy placed a protective hand on Jessie's shoulder. 'I discovered that this poor girl has been sleeping in a dark, musty cupboard. I wanted to see it for myself.'

'How I run this household has nothing to do with you, Miss Robbins. I don't care what Mr Taverner says. I work for his pa, and I take orders from him, not you.'

'That is how it was, Mrs Whiddon, but things

are different now. I have been given the somewhat onerous task of getting this house in order, but I'm sure that with a little effort we could work together harmoniously.'

Mrs Whiddon puffed out her cheeks and her lips worked soundlessly.

Poppy took advantage of the moment's silence. 'I am taking Jessie with me now. I will find her a more suitable room.'

'Twenty years or more I've run everything.' Mrs Whiddon's voice shook with emotion. 'I'm not handing it over to a slip of a girl from London who thinks she is cleverer than the rest of us.'

'I'm afraid you have no choice.' Poppy held her nerve, although for a moment she had wavered. Even on a good day Mrs Whiddon was slightly unnerving, but when annoyed it felt like taking a tiger by the tail. Poppy took a deep breath, reminding herself that she had Eddie Taverner and his delicate mother on her side. 'The kettle seems to have come to the boil, ma'am. I suggest you make tea for all of us while Jessie and I sort out her sleeping arrangements.' Poppy beckoned to Jessie. 'Come with me. We'll settle this for once and all.'

Jessie shot a wary glance at Mrs Whiddon, who by this time was purple in the face and breathing heavily.

'I'll be quick, Mrs Whiddon.' Jessie hurried after Poppy. 'She's ever so angry, Miss Poppy.'

'I dare say she is, but I'm doing this with Mr Taverner's blessing. Lord and Lady Taverner know all about it, so Mrs Whiddon will be wasting her time if she goes complaining to either of them.' Poppy headed upstairs to the second floor where the servants had their accommodation. She tried each door in turn until she found a small room at the back of the house that seemed to be unoccupied. It was furnished simply with a single bed, a washstand and a chest of drawers. A dormer window overlooked the gardens at the rear of the property, allowing sunlight to filter through panes of glass, which were in need of a clean.

'What do you think, Jessie? Is it too far from the kitchen?' Poppy turned to Jessie, but the rapt look on her face left little need for Jessie to answer.

She nodded vigorously. 'It's a room fit for a real lady, miss. Are you sure it's all right?'

'I most certainly am. I suggest you go about your kitchen duties first. You can make up the bed and bring your things upstairs when Cook can spare you. Don't worry about her. I will speak to that person very sternly. There is to be no drinking on duty.'

'Cook and Mrs Whiddon are very fierce when they get together, miss.'

'Not any more, Jessie. They have me to contend with.' Poppy ushered Jessie out of the room and closed the door. 'I think we've earned that cup of tea now. Let's see if Mrs Whiddon has followed my instructions.'

* * *

When Poppy and Jessie reached the kitchen it was obvious that Mrs Whiddon and Cook had been in a huddle, no doubt grumbling fiercely about their authority being challenged. Jessie disappeared into the scullery, but Poppy was not about to back down.

'I'm glad you are both here,' she said before either of them had a chance to speak. 'I know this must be difficult for you but I am merely carrying out Mr Taverner's wishes. I think you will find that a fresh outlook on running things might actually help both of you.'

'No one's complained about my cooking before,' Cook said angrily.

'But your weakness for cooking sherry has been a cause for concern.' Poppy was not about to be side-tracked. 'You have a drink problem, and that does affect everyone here.'

'So I enjoy a little tipple now and then.' Cook's jawline hardened. 'What of it?'

'Becoming incapable and falling asleep when preparing a meal is not only wrong but it is also dangerous. You might have a dreadful accident or harm one of your staff. It cannot go on.'

'I'll speak to Lord Taverner. He loves my food. He'll stand by me.'

Poppy shook her head. 'I don't think so, Cook. Perhaps you had better have a break and think about it. I don't know your age, but you might find it hard to get another position, especially if you do not have a character from your previous employer.'

Cook subsided into a chair with a heavy sigh. 'To think it has come to this. After all my years of devoted service.'

'And mine,' Mrs Whiddon added, her bottom lip quivering. 'To be humiliated by a person who knows nothing about the running of this old house.'

Poppy was about to answer when the door opened and Taverner strode into the kitchen.

'So there you are, my dear. You all look very serious. Is anything wrong?'

It took Poppy a moment or two to remember that they were supposed to be an engaged couple. She had been ready for a prolonged argument, but the atmosphere in the room had changed subtly the moment Taverner walked through the door. She eyed him speculatively. He was an imposing figure, but it was an underlying strength that gave him an air of authority.

She managed a smile, although the play-acting had made her feel uncomfortable. 'I am trying to explain to your staff that I am only attempting to make things run better. Any changes I make will benefit everyone.'

Taverner placed his arm around her shoulders. 'Absolutely, my love. Of course you must do what you think is best.' He turned to Mrs Whiddon, his smile fading. 'Miss Robbins is in charge of the household. There is no question of that. I should add that my father does not wish to be bothered by trivial matters. I hope that is understood.'

247

'Yes, sir.' Mrs Whiddon shot a malicious glance in Poppy's direction. 'If you say so, sir.'

Cook eyed him nervously. 'Does that include my kitchen, sir?'

'It most certainly does, Cook. I expect to find everything running smoothly when I return from London.' Taverner laid his hand on Poppy's shoulder. 'Can you spare me a few minutes, my love?'

'Of course.' Poppy followed him from the kitchen, closing the door firmly behind her. She would not put it past Mrs Whiddon to have her ear to the keyhole. 'What is it, Eddie? Don't you think you are overdoing the romantic nonsense?'

'Nonsense?' Taverner gave her a quizzical look. 'Really? Aren't we supposed to be engaged?'

'"Supposed" is the word, Eddie. We hardly know each other, so you can't blame people for being suspicious.'

'What if I said I had fallen for you the first moment I set eyes on you in Spitalfields Market? You were like a beautiful wildflower emerging from the dusty cobblestones and detritus in the gutter.'

Poppy laughed. 'Poppies are considered to be weeds by farmers.'

'You are determined to make light of this. I don't blame you, but the servants need to respect you and obey your instructions. I know I will be leaving my family home in good hands.'

'I'll do my best, Eddie.' Poppy was suddenly serious. She could see that he was in earnest and she realised that his concern for his home and his parents was genuine, as was his remorse for allowing his family home to sink into such a parlous state.

'I know you will. Come to my study and I'll give you the house keys.' Taverner turned to her with a smile that softened his stern features, making him appear almost boyish. 'I'm entrusting you with the secrets of Domesday House.'

'I'm not sure I like the sound of that,' Poppy said as she hurried after him. 'What horrors might I find hidden in the cellars?'

'Nothing, I imagine, other than a few spiders. Don't worry, there's unlikely to be anything here to disturb you, other than Mrs Whiddon. But I'm sure you can handle her.'

'I don't think it will be easy, but I'm used to difficult people.' Poppy experienced a sudden pang of homesickness. She had been referring to Uncle Amos, but really he was a dear compared to Mrs Whiddon, and the drink-addicted cook was going to be an ongoing problem. Poppy was beginning to realise the enormity of the problems she was facing. She quickened her pace in order to keep up with his long strides. 'Is the road clear now? Do you still plan to take Aunt Bella, Lottie and Arthur home to Dorrington Place?'

'Yes, to both questions. I had men out at first light and the carriage has been moved to the wheelwright's yard. I also checked on Grundy's condition with Dr Standish.'

'How is poor Grundy? He came off worst of all.'

'He's on the mend, but he'll stay in hospital for a while. I gave Standish instructions to have Grundy driven back to Dorrington Place when he is well enough. You don't have to worry about him.' Taverner stopped outside the study, opened the door and ushered her into the oak-panelled room. 'You'll find everything you need in here, Poppy.'

She gazed in alarm at the large kneehole desk, the top of which was barely visible beneath piles of documents, ledgers and household accounts.

'It looks a bit daunting,' Poppy said warily. 'I hope you don't expect me to sort out the paperwork.'

'No, not at all. It's the housekeeping accounts that are important. I think that Mrs Whiddon might have been supplementing her income by appropriating some of the monies set aside for household expenses. I would like you to check that, if you have a free moment.'

'I can find time, I'm sure. I don't trust that woman. She's had too much freedom over the years.'

'Which is my fault entirely. I admit that.' Taverner tapped a wall panel and a door opened to reveal an iron safe. 'There is enough cash to pay the tradesmen and any other expenses you might incur. The staff wages are paid quarterly, but I'll be back before then. Have you any questions?'

'No, I don't think so, at least not about organising the housekeeping. All I can say is that I will do my very best to keep everything running smoothly in your absence. But I would like to have some idea as to how long you expect this to go on. I want to return to my own home as soon as possible.'

'Of course. I understand that and I will endeavour to return as quickly as possible. I can't give you a date until I've settled matters with Gervase Mulliner. He's my main source of concern.'

'You are taking this very personally, Eddie,' Poppy said thoughtfully. 'You were keen to help me from the start, even though we were complete strangers. Is there something you aren't telling me?' A niggling suspicion had been bothering her since his sudden desire to keep her here at Domesday House, and she was determined to have an answer before he left for London.

'You're right, of course. I should have known I couldn't keep it from you, Poppy. You are far too astute.'

She smiled. 'It's no use flattering me, Eddie. You told me you knew all about Mulliner, but it's what you left out that is making me curious.'

He leaned against the desk, his brow furrowed and his hands thrust into his pockets. 'There was a young lady I was very fond of. It was some years ago and she came from a very strict family. They disapproved of me and the way in which I made my living. She was forbidden to have anything to do with me.'

It seemed to Poppy that each word brought back painful memories and her heart went out to him.

'That must have been so hard. Did you ever see her again?'

'Her father forced her to accept an offer of marriage from Mulliner, who had convinced him that he was about to inherit a fortune, including a title and a castle.'

Poppy sank down on a chair in front of the desk. 'That sounds oddly familiar.'

'He was lying, of course.'

'Why would he do that, Eddie?'

'She was an heiress and Gervase is a gambler. He is always in desperate need of funds.'

'Did he marry her?'

Taverner shook his head, his eyes darkening with anger. 'He persuaded her to elope. She died in childbirth after Mulliner abandoned her. He had set his sights on someone with a greater fortune and he simply walked away.'

'And you loved this poor unfortunate lady?'

'I was very young, but yes, I did love her. I never forgave Mulliner, but there was nothing I could do about the wretch – until you came to me with your problem. Now he is attempting to extract monies from Lord Dorrington and also your parents, I have a valid excuse for going after him. I believe him to be in considerable debt and growing desperate. He needs to be stopped once and for all.'

'Uncle Freddie and my parents were afraid that Mulliner might try to abduct Lottie or me, or even both of us. Is that the real reason you are keeping me here at Domesday House?' Poppy met his gaze with a searching look. 'Tell me the truth, Eddie.'

'I don't deny it, Poppy. But you are needed here, and now we are engaged I can protect you properly.'

'But that's just make-believe to keep the servants in line.'

'It's true as far as they are concerned, and that's what matters. I've taken on more ground staff so I know you will be safe here, even should Mulliner discover your whereabouts. Lottie will be secure at home, which is where I must go now.' Taverner walked round the desk. He took her hands in his, holding them in a firm but gentle grasp. 'Don't be afraid. I won't allow anyone to hurt you or your family.' He leaned over and kissed her lightly on the lips. 'I'll go straight on to London from Dorrington Place. I was planning to return here, but now you have taken charge I feel free to pursue Mulliner.'

'Really?' Poppy snatched her hands free and rose to her feet. Despite her attempts to keep him at arm's length and to remain objective, she was finding it more and more difficult. 'I thought you might be here for another few days at least, to help me settle in.' Poppy managed to control the tremble in her voice, but only just. It would not be good to let him see that she was suddenly afraid of being left alone to do battle with a determined housekeeper and the drunken cook.

'You'll manage well without me, and I plan to come back as soon as possible. *Au revoir*, Poppy.' Taverner kissed her again, this time lingering a little as their lips touched, but then he drew away and left the room without another word.

The sudden silence seemed to close in on Poppy. Taverner was gone, but the taste of him was on her lips and the warmth of his grasp remained on her fingers as if he was still holding her hands. Poppy sat down briefly but then she jumped to her feet. She was acting like a silly, love-struck girl. Taverner had already admitted that his heart belonged to the poor young woman who had been ruined by Mulliner, that being the reason for Taverner's desire for justice. Or was it revenge?

Poppy braced herself to face Aunt Bella and Lottie and bid them goodbye. As she hurried towards the great entrance hall she stopped briefly in front of a mirror and was shocked by her reflection. She pinched her cheeks to bring back some colour and forced her lips into a smile before following the sound of their voices as they prepared to leave.

Lottie was standing by her mother but she spotted Poppy and ran towards her, arms outstretched.

'I wish you were coming with us, Poppy. Are you sure you want to stay here?' She shot a wary glance in Taverner's direction. 'It's such a dreary place,' she added, lowering her voice.

'I have a mission now.' Poppy forced herself to smile and sound cheerful. 'It's me versus the Whiddon. I'm determined to win.'

Arthur grasped Poppy by the hand. 'It will be more fun if you come home with us.'

Poppy leaned down to give him a hug. 'I will visit you at Dorrington Place before I return to Rainbow's End, Arthur. That's a promise.'

'You must indeed.' Arabella turned to her, smiling. 'I don't like leaving you here, Poppy, but Eddie has explained everything to me. I understand.'

'What has he told you, Mama?' Lottie demanded peevishly. 'Why does everyone keep things from me and treat me like a child?'

'Because you can't keep a secret, Lottie.' Arthur grinned at her and backed away. 'Come on, I want to ride in the motor car. I'm going to ask Papa to buy one for us.'

'I hope your papa will be at home when we get there,' Arabella said wistfully. 'I hate it when he's away. If I had just taken you to Nine Oaks, Arthur, none of this would have happened. Next time you come down with a childish ailment I will not be quite so attentive to your needs.'

'Does that mean you will allow me to go to Papa's old school?' Arthur asked eagerly.

Arabella sighed. 'I suppose I must let you grow up.'

Taverner cleared his throat. 'I don't wish to hurry you, my lady, but I suggest we make a move now. I'm sure you are looking forward to going home.'

'I am, Mr Taverner, but I am extremely grateful for your hospitality, as well as your continuing care of Grundy.' Arabella beckoned to Lottie. 'We should be on our way.'

Lottie gave Poppy a hug. 'Goodbye. Please don't stay here any longer than necessary.'

'I'll see you soon,' Poppy returned the embrace. 'I'll miss you, Lottie. But please don't forget to send my things here. I'm longing for a change of clothes.'

'I promise.' Lottie turned away reluctantly and went to join her mother, Arthur hurrying on ahead.

Poppy followed them to the doorway and watched them climb into the motor car. She swallowed hard to prevent the tears from welling up in her eyes. It was all she could do to stand and wave as Taverner crank-started the engine and jumped into the driver's seat. Had there been room for one more in the motor Poppy would have squeezed in and said goodbye to Domesday House, but she steeled herself to smile and wave as they drove off. However, as the motor car disappeared into the distance she was overwhelmed with a feeling of loneliness. She felt small and insignificant, as if the old house was closing in on her with no way of escape. A sudden desire to run away was almost overpowering but then she realised she had nowhere to go. This time she could not prevent the tears from running down her cheeks and she choked on a sob as she closed the heavy oak door.

'What's up with you, maid?' Lord Taverner's voice close to her ear made Poppy turn with a start.

His lordship was still wearing the stained, slightly threadbare dressing gown with the design of a faded green dragon breathing fire on a black background,

'He looks like your son.'

'That's right, maid. Two peas in a pod, as they say. Of course, Eddie denies it, but he's got the same buccaneering spirit, which is why he's successful in his line of business.'

'What is his business exactly?' Poppy leaned forward, fixing him with an intense gaze. It was a question she had wanted to ask Taverner himself but had refrained from asking.

Lord Taverner heaved himself from his chair and went to refill his glass. 'Something in the City, maid. That's all I know and I don't enquire further. The money keeps this old ruin going and also keeps me in food and liquor.' He staggered back to his chair and slumped down. 'But a warning, maid. Don't upset old Whiddon too much. You'll be off home soon, no doubt, and then we'll revert to how things have been since Lady Taverner became an invalid. D'you take my meaning? There are things here best left buried in the ashes of the old east wing. And take my advice: don't venture down to the cellars, either. There are rats as big as cats and spiders that could eat a sparrow.'

Chapter Fifteen

When Lord Taverner's eyelids drooped and his empty glass slipped from his fingers, Poppy took the opportunity to escape from the Trophy Room. She had sipped her glass of Madeira but he had continued to drink steadily, regaling her with tales of his ancestors and their exploits at sea as well as on land. They seemed to have dabbled in everything from astrology to politics, although none of them had excelled in anything other than seafaring. He claimed to be the exception, but his claim to fame became rather hazy after four glasses of wine.

Poppy decided to go for a walk in the grounds rather than to take on Mrs Whiddon so soon after Taverner had left. She could hardly march into the kitchen exuding wine fumes in competition with Cook, especially at this early hour.

Poppy stepped outside and took a deep breath of

the sweet country air. She had no particular plan in mind, but Lord Taverner's warning about keeping away from the ruined east wing made it irresistible, and she found herself walking round the fire-damaged part of the old house. Three walls remained but the roof had fallen in long ago. The harsh outlines of the shattered masonry were overgrown and softened by wildflowers – valerian, campion and nettles – adding an air of romance to the scene. However, on looking up, she thought it odd to see exposed fireplaces clinging to the smoke-blackened walls, and there were gaping apertures that had once been bedroom windows. There did not seem to be any dangers lurking there, just a feeling of sadness and neglect. Poppy strolled on, heading for the lake. Perhaps Taverner would rebuild the east wing one day, if he ever chose to leave London and abandon the unspecified, doubtless nefarious business that occupied him at the moment.

As she threaded her way through the undergrowth, heading towards the glassy expanse of water, Poppy could smell tobacco smoke and she spotted Bert and Ned, sitting beneath a sturdy oak tree, smoking roll-up cigarettes. Bert jumped to his feet when he saw her.

'Good morning, miss.'

Ned scrambled to his feet and tipped his cap. 'Good morning, miss.'

'I'm sure you have work to do,' Poppy said calmly. 'But you won't get it done by sitting in the sun.'

'We're just having a break, miss.' Bert nudged his brother. 'Are we not, Ned?'

'Aye.' Ned nodded emphatically. 'A short break, miss.'

'Well earned, I'm sure.' Poppy glanced from one to the other. 'However, I think you might put a little more effort into clearing these paths. I'd like to see them neat and tidy before the day is out. You do know that Lord Taverner has put me in charge?'

'Aye, miss.' They spoke in unison.

'Excellent. I'll come and inspect your work this evening.' Poppy acknowledged them with a nod and walked on.

Having circled the lake, she decided to return to the house. She would have to face the Whiddon at some point in the day, and now was as good a time as any.

When Poppy entered the kitchen she found Mrs Whiddon seated at the table, drinking tea, while Cook was putting the finishing touches to a pie.

Poppy managed a smile. 'Good morning, Mrs Whiddon. Good morning, Cook. That pie looks tempting. Is it for luncheon?'

'Er, yes, miss. In a manner of speaking.' Cook shot a wary look at Mrs Whiddon, who remained stony-faced.

'It either is for luncheon or it is not,' Poppy said firmly. 'Which is it, Cook?'

'It's for the servants' hall.' Cook turned away

to open the oven door. 'The family have cold cuts today.'

Mrs Whiddon heaved herself from her seat. 'Can I help you, miss?'

Poppy held up her hand. 'Just a minute, have I got this right? The pie is for you, and the family have to make do with what is left from a previous roast joint.'

'It's a perfectly good cut of beef,' Cook said defensively. 'Lord Taverner's favourite.'

'I think Lord and Lady Taverner would infinitely prefer a delicious pie rather than leftovers.' Poppy kept calm, even though she was seething at the sheer dishonesty and lack of respect shown by the servants for their master and mistress. 'I suggest that you bake the pie and serve it hot with vegetables and creamed potatoes for the family luncheon. The cold meat will make a good meal for the servants' hall.'

Cook's face flushed and her lips folded into a thin line as she placed the pie in the oven. 'Jessie, peel more potatoes and carrots. Work faster, you lazy slut.'

'And less of that sort of talk, if you please, Cook.' Poppy managed to keep her tone level despite the temptation to raise her voice. She shot a warning glance at Mrs Whiddon. 'You need to keep a firm hand on your staff, Mrs Whiddon.'

'What do you know about dealing with servants, Miss Robbins?' Mrs Whiddon faced Poppy angrily. 'You are too young to have been mistress of a large establishment, so perhaps you should leave things to those with experience.'

'I have worked in a commercial kitchen since I was a child, Mrs Whiddon. My parents run a very successful restaurant in Essex. I know my way round a kitchen and I am used to dealing with staff, as well as ordering supplies and keeping accounts. We will leave it for today, but tomorrow morning I would like to go through the books with you. Is that understood?'

Mrs Whiddon exhaled loudly and her eyes flashed, but she nodded. 'Yes, miss.'

'Excellent. And to make things easier all round I have permission to take on extra staff. I will be interviewing applicants as soon as possible.' Poppy waited for a moment to see if either of them were to question her, but she was greeted by a stony silence. She thought she heard a faint sigh of relief emanating from the scullery, and she smiled to herself as she left the kitchen. She might have won the first battle, but even so, that did not mean she would win the war. It was obviously going to be a tussle for control between herself and the Whiddon, who was so entrenched in her position that it would be difficult to get the better of her.

However, her stand in the kitchen seemed to have paid off. Poppy had the satisfaction of seeing the chicken pie served for luncheon in the dining room. It seemed that Lord Taverner had grown used to having his food placed before him on a small table in the drawing room, which was obviously for the benefit of the servants as the dining room was rarely used. Poppy had insisted that all meals should be taken there from now on, and that had not gone down well. Grudgingly, the table had been laid and they were waited on by Jessie, who turned out to be inept and very clumsy. Lord Taverner growled at her when she spilled peas onto his lap, and when Jessie ran from the room in tears Poppy had to finish serving the food.

'I think I prefer eating from a tray in the drawing room,' Lord Taverner said crossly. 'That girl is an idiot.'

Poppy handed him the gravy boat. 'She is a scullery maid, my lord. The poor girl is not trained to wait on table.'

'Then find someone who is. They think I don't notice these things, but I do.'

'Of course you do, sir. I will make sure such a mishap doesn't occur again.'

'It was different when my wife was in good health. She kept everything running smoothly.' Lord Taverner reached for his wine glass. 'Poor Alice.' He took a mouthful, swallowed and slammed his glass on the mahogany table so that some of the contents spilled onto the polished table top.

Poppy eyed him thoughtfully. She had accepted the fact that Lady Taverner was an invalid and that her mind wandered, but she was beginning to have doubts. Perhaps her ladyship's condition was partly due to being kept to her room, and she had been made to think that she was suffering from a debilitating illness. Poppy decided to spend more time with Alice Taverner. After all, if she was persuaded to come downstairs and take up at least some of her former duties, perhaps it would be a more permanent solution to the problem of the housekeeper who thought she was in charge of the whole family.

In the middle of the afternoon, when a semblance of peace and tranquillity descended on the unhappy household, Poppy took a tray of tea and cake upstairs to Lady Taverner's room. She knocked, waited for an answer and, when there was none, she entered anyway.

'Good afternoon, my lady. I thought you might like a cup of Earl Grey and a slice of cake.'

Lady Taverner was lying on a chaise longue, still wearing her nightgown beneath the flowing organdie wrap she had worn yesterday. She stared at Poppy as if trying to place her.

'Do I know you, miss?'

Poppy placed the tray on a small table and moved it within Lady Taverner's reach before pulling up a chair. She sat down and extended her left hand, displaying the diamond ring.

'I'm Poppy. Do you remember giving this ring to your son, Eddie?'

Lady Taverner stared at it for a moment and then a smile transformed her face. 'I do. I want Eddie to be happy and it seems he loves you, Poppy.'

'Well, it isn't quite like that, but he did put the ring on my finger. I am here to help you, ma'am.'

'Help me?' Lady Taverner's brow creased into worried lines. 'But I am beyond help, my dear. I am very ill.'

Poppy leaned closer. 'Did the doctor tell you that, ma'am?'

'I can't remember, but my legs are weak. I find it very difficult to walk far. It's better if I lie down in a darkened room. I have to be kept very quiet.'

'How so, ma'am?' Poppy was intent on discovering the truth about Lady Taverner's condition. 'Who told you that?'

'Bright light is bad for my eyes. Mrs Whiddon takes care of me, Poppy. I am very fortunate to have someone to look after me in my sickly condition.'

'Have you seen the doctor recently, ma'am? He might disagree with Mrs Whiddon's ideas.'

'There is no need. I am past his help, Poppy. No one can do anything for me now. I have to rest and take my medicine.' Lady Taverner's gaze rested on a dark brown bottle standing next to a china cherub on the dressing table.

Poppy poured the tea and handed a cup to Lady Taverner. 'Would you like some cake, ma'am?'

'Just a tiny sliver, my dear. I have very little appetite.'

Poppy cut a small slice and laid it on a plate, which she placed on the table within Lady Taverner's reach. She was amused to see her ladyship's pale hand stabbing the cake with a pastry fork and raising it to her lips. Poppy took the opportunity of the distraction to get up and walk casually over to the dressing table. She picked up the bottle and read the label. As she had suspected, it was laudanum, and quite a significant amount. She replaced the bottle and returned to her seat. She sipped her tea, watching Lady Taverner demolish the cake before draining her teacup. So much for being unable to eat. Poppy was beginning to suspect that part, if not all, of Lady Taverner's condition was due to being bullied into submission by Mrs Whiddon. Although quite what a housekeeper hoped to gain by convincing her mistress that she was desperately ill was puzzling. Perhaps it had been easier for the Whiddon to exert control over the household without the presence of Lady Taverner. It seemed very far-fetched, but if true it was heinous. Poppy experienced a sudden rush of affection for the frail lady, together with a feeling of hostility towards Mrs Whiddon. Well, she would find she had met her match. Poppy was not about to allow this poor lady to be driven to an early grave, and as for Lord Taverner, he would probably drink himself to death under the rule of the termagant housekeeper.

Poppy put her cup and saucer back on the tray. 'Would you like another slice of cake, my lady?'

'Oh, no, thank you, dear.' Lady Taverner gave her a sweet smile. 'That was quite delicious, but I am only supposed to eat light meals. Mrs Whiddon has me on a strict diet, which will bring back my health and strength. Although it does seem to be taking rather a long time.'

Poppy rose to her feet. She could see that Lady Taverner was growing weary and she did not want to exhaust her.

'I'll take the tray away, ma'am. But I will return before dinner. Perhaps you might feel up to coming downstairs to join his lordship and me?'

'That's nice, my dear.' Lady Taverner lay back against the satin cushions and closed her eyes. 'So nice.'

Poppy took the tray downstairs and left it in the scullery. She now had a mission. She would go to the village and speak to Dr Standish, and while she was there she would ask around to see if there were any women willing to work at Domesday House. It was mid-afternoon and she had hoped that Lottie might have sent someone with her things, but there was still time. After all, Dorrington Place was less than two hours away now that the road was clear. Lottie would not let her down.

The old house creaked and sighed in the heat as Poppy left and walked briskly in the direction of the village. She found Dr Standish's house easily enough and introduced herself to his wife, who informed her that the doctor was out on a call. She looked surprised when Poppy requested a visit for Lady Taverner.

'My husband will come when he can, miss. But it's many months since he last saw her ladyship. Is she unwell?'

Poppy stared at her in surprise. 'You didn't know?'

'Well, the poor lady has suffered from megrims for many years, but that is all, as far as I know.'

'Lady Taverner is confined to her room and convinced that she has some incurable disease. I was wondering what your husband made of her condition.' Poppy could tell by Mrs Standish's expression that she was genuinely astonished.

'My husband's only visit to Domesday House recently was for that poor coachman, Mr Grundy. I don't think he's seen any of the family for many months, even a year or two.'

'Well, I would be grateful if he could call and see Lady Taverner. I'm new to the family but she is clearly in need of medical attention. I don't know when she last left her room.'

'That isn't like the Lady Taverner I knew,' Mrs Standish said stoutly. 'She was always doing things for the village. She used to attend church every Sunday and she gave the prizes at the village fête. She visited the sick and donated generously to the various charities. I really thought she might have gone away to visit relatives.'

'Hopefully your husband will be able to help her.' Poppy turned to leave but then changed her mind. 'There is one more thing. We are in desperate need of more help at Domesday House. Do you know of any women trained in service who are looking for employment?'

Mrs Standish thought for a moment. 'I might do,

Miss Robbins. Several women come to mind but I need to speak to them first.'

'We are quite desperate for help, Mrs Standish. If you could send anyone who might be interested to see me at Domesday House, I would be very grateful.'

'I will, of course, although there might be a problem.'

Poppy's heart sank. She could guess what that might be without asking, but she tried to appear unconcerned. 'I have Mr Edward Taverner's permission to deal with such matters. I would pay well.'

Mrs Standish did not look convinced. 'If Eliza Whiddon is still in charge, you might find it difficult to find anyone to work with her, Miss Robbins.'

'I am managing the household now, ma'am. Whoever comes to work at Domesday House will not have any trouble with the person in question.'

'In that case you may rest assured I will do my best to find women who are trustworthy and not afraid of hard work.'

'Thank you, ma'am. I am very grateful.' Poppy shook Mrs Standish's hand. She could do no more today, but at least she had made a start.

She set off in the direction of Domesday House at a brisk pace, but as she drew nearer she began to drag her feet. She might be on her way to solving one problem but that did not make the sight of the old house any more welcoming. As she trudged up the drive her thoughts went to her own home and her loving parents. She was supposed to be protecting them by hiding away in Taverner's country residence, but she was beginning to wonder if Taverner was simply using the threat posed by Gervase Mulliner and his cousin Miranda as a means of sorting out his own problems. She glanced at the diamond ring on her left hand and was tempted to take it off and toss it away, but she realised that it was simply her badge of office. She had agreed to remain at Domesday House and take on the redoubtable Mrs Whiddon, although as she approached the front entrance she wondered if she had been in her right mind. Eddie Taverner could be very persuasive. Her hand flew to cover her lips. The memory of his kiss was hard to eradicate and came back to haunt her when least expected. It obviously meant nothing to him, but the heat of his mouth on hers still lingered.

Then, as if someone had been waiting to let her in, the door opened and she was met by Bert, who was grinning from ear to ear.

'A messenger has delivered your things, miss. He left a small trunk for you. I just took it upstairs to your room.'

'My things! Thank you, Bert.'

Poppy rushed past him and raced upstairs. Just the sight of something from home that had been sent on from Dorrington Place was enough to lift her spirits. She opened the trunk and took out her clean clothes, rubbing her cheek against the cool cotton of a summer gown. A delightful scent of lavender took her back to her pretty bedroom at Rainbow's End, and she closed her eyes, wishing that she could transport herself there. Ever practical, she continued to unpack. She put her garments away in the clothes press, but she kept out her plainest and most practical dress and clean underwear so that she could change before dinner. It was only then that Poppy remembered her plan to check on Cook and ensure she was sober enough to do her work, otherwise everyone would be eating bread and cheese instead of a hot meal. She left her room and made her way downstairs.

When Poppy opened the kitchen door she was greeted by a savoury aroma emanating from a large black saucepan on the top of the range, but there was no sign of Cook. It was Jessie who greeted her with a wide smile.

'Cook isn't too well, miss. I thought I'd better start dinner or we won't have nothing to eat tonight.'

Poppy glanced round the immaculate kitchen, taking in all the details. The floor had been scrubbed, as had the pine table. The only items on it were a large mixing bowl containing what appeared to be the makings of a cake, and a basket of eggs.

'If Cook is out of action who did all this, Jessie?'

'It were me, miss. I'm one of ten at home and I learned to cook a long time ago. Ma needs all the help she can get.'

Poppy stared at her in amazement. 'You prepared a stew and, by the look of it, you're making a pudding, too?'

'My brothers and sisters love a good jam sponge. I hope Lord Taverner does, too.'

'I can't believe you did all this without being asked.' Poppy shook her head.

'Yes, miss. I'm sorry if I wasn't supposed to interfere.' Jessie's flushed cheeks deepened to scarlet and she averted her gaze, staring down at her feet in scuffed boots that looked several sizes too large for her.

Poppy was instantly ashamed. She had been feeling sorry for herself when there were others who were far worse off. Young Jessie had seen the need to step up and had done so with amazing results.

'I am more than grateful for your help, Jessie. You look too young to be so proficient in the kitchen.'

'I'm fourteen, going on fifteen, miss. I know I'm small, but we're not a tall family. People often think I'm younger than I really am.'

Poppy went to the range and picked up a spoon. She tasted the simmering stew and smiled, nodding emphatically. 'Rabbit stew. It's excellent, really tasty.'

'Thank you, miss.' Jessie reached for a cake tin and rubbed it with butter before spooning in the mixture. 'I love cooking, but I only get the chance to do it when Cook is having one of her funny turns.'

'You mean, when she is the worse for drink?' Poppy frowned. 'Tell the truth, Jessie.'

'Well, yes. I suppose that's what brings them on. She goes very odd and falls down a lot. Mrs Whiddon makes her go to her room.'

'Where is Mrs Whiddon?' Poppy was getting angrier by the minute. That woman had no right to call herself a housekeeper. She had left a young girl in charge of the kitchen and had turned a blind eye to Cook's addiction to drink.

'She has a lie-down in the afternoons, miss. She gets up in time for dinner.' Jessie scraped out the bowl and put it aside while she placed the cake mixture in the oven. 'I don't mind, though. I like having the kitchen all to meself.'

'I have to say that I'm impressed, Jessie. You obviously have a talent for cooking. It's a pity you don't live nearer to my home in Essex. I'm sure we could do with someone just like you to help in the kitchen.'

'That would be like a dream come true, miss.' Jessie brushed a dab of flour from her nose. 'Maybe one day it will happen.'

Poppy smiled. 'You never know. But in the meantime, I would be delighted for you to do more in the kitchen. I could teach you a lot and we wouldn't need Cook. She could retire to a nice little cottage in the village and drink sherry all day.'

'Don't tell Mrs Whiddon what I said, miss.' Jessie's smile faded. 'I'll feel the back of her hand and, I can tell you, she's got a really strong right arm.'

'No one is going to lay a finger on you. If you

get any trouble from Mrs Whiddon, come straight to me. I won't allow bullying. Anyway, I hope to interview some ladies from the village tomorrow morning. If we have more help there will be no need for Mrs Whiddon to play such an active role in the culinary department.'

Jessie put her head on one side. 'I don't want to speak out of turn, miss, but my sister Loveday is a good worker. She don't mind what she does, and she's particularly good at washing clothes. She beats the devil out of them in the tub with a dolly stick.'

'She sounds ideal. If she's interested you'd best fetch her in the morning. I'll be up early and I'll have a word with her.'

'But what will Mrs Whiddon say?'

'Leave her to me, Jessie.' Poppy looked up at the sound of a bell jangling. The drawing-room bell was being rung with some urgency.

'That'll be his lordship,' Jessie said nervously. 'I'm not a housemaid, miss. It's not my place to speak to the master.'

'I'll go and see what he wants.' Poppy headed for the doorway, but paused, turning to Jessie with a wry smile. 'I don't suppose you have another sister who might wish to wait upon the family, do you?'

Jessie laughed and shook her head. 'No, miss. I have six brothers and twin baby sisters, as well as Loveday.'

Poppy smiled. 'It was just a thought.' She left the kitchen and made her way to the drawing room.

Lord Taverner was pacing the floor. 'How long does it take for anyone to answer a summons, miss?'

'I'm sorry, my lord. We are short staffed at the moment.'

'Then hire some more bodies. I'm sure we can afford it. My son's illegal dealings in London ensure a comfortable life for us here in the country.'

Poppy did not like to pursue the matter, even though she was curious to know how exactly Eddie made his money. She faced the angry Lord Taverner with a straight look. 'How may I be of service, my lord?'

'My decanters are empty. I keep a well-stocked cellar and yet there isn't even a drop of sherry for me to drink. Fetch me a bottle of port and a couple of bottles of Château Lafite to have with my dinner, and a bottle of Amontillado, too, while you're about it.'

'I thought you told me not to venture down to the cellars,' Poppy said slowly.

'Only Mrs Whiddon is allowed down there. I have a small fortune in cases of vintage wines and I don't want servants helping themselves. You'll find the key in my study. It's in the tiger's mouth. No one dares look in there.'

Poppy acknowledged this with a nod as she left the drawing room and headed for the study. As his lordship had said, there was a large tiger-skin rug on the floor. She felt inside the gaping mouth, half afraid that the grisly beast would close its jaws on her fingers, but she found the key and tucked it into the pocket of her skirt. She patted the tiger's head.

'Sorry, old boy. Thank you for not biting me.' Poppy was half expecting the tiger to respond with a growl, and she closed the study door with a sigh of relief. Really, she should not be surprised, but nothing was as she might expect it to be in Domesday House.

It was the same in the cellar when she eventually found her way through the twisting narrow corridors and negotiated the steep stone steps. She lit the lantern that had been left at the entrance and unlocked the door. A blast of cold, musty air hit her as she went down yet more steps. The cellar was huge and the walls lined with wine racks. However, there did not seem to be the vast number of cases that Lord Taverner had mentioned. There were some empty wooden cases and also spaces in the wine racks. It seemed that Lord Taverner was under a misapprehension as to the size of his valuable collection of fine wines, or perhaps someone had been helping themselves unbeknownst to him. Poppy selected the bottles he had requested and was careful to lock up before she took them upstairs.

'Impressive, don't you think?' Lord Taverner puffed out his chest. 'I've got the finest selection of vintage wines in the county, maidy.'

Poppy set the bottles down on the table with the decanters. 'Do you ever check them yourself, my lord?'

'I don't go down there. That's what I pay the Whiddon woman for. She keeps a list, which I peruse once a month, and it makes compelling reading.'

'Do you keep these lists, my lord?'

'I never throw anything away. They're on my desk, somewhere. Maybe I'll get you to sort it all out for me, one day.'

Poppy nodded. 'I'll do that, sir. Is there anything else?'

'I don't suppose you know how to decant wine, do you? That's one thing that Whiddon can't do successfully.' Lord Taverner gave her a challenging look, his eyes twinkling mischievously.

'As a matter of fact I do, my lord. I was taught how to handle expensive wines so that I could do so in my parents' restaurant.'

'That's one up on old Whiddon,' Lord Taverner crowed. 'Eddie was quite right in taking you on, maid. You'll be an asset to the family. Now pour me a sherry, there's a good girl.'

Poppy stood her ground. 'I will, of course, but not until you have changed out of those filthy clothes and dressed appropriately for the lord and master of Domesday House.' Poppy knew she had crossed a line, but she could not bear the sight of him looking like a tramp any longer.

Lord Taverner stared at her in disbelief and then he roared with laughter. 'You cheeky little madam. No one speaks to me like that. At least not since my dear wife took sick.'

'She would be ashamed of you, my lord,' Poppy said firmly. 'Might I suggest you retire to your room and find some clean clothes?'

'I should send you packing, Poppy Robbins. Remember to whom you are speaking.'

'I'm fully aware of your position, sir. But you need to live up to it. I can help you to find a change of garments if it's beyond you. A beard trim would be a good idea, too.'

Lord Taverner rose from his seat with a roar. For a moment Poppy thought he was going to erupt like a volcano and she held her breath. She knew she had gone too far but she was not going to stand down. She met his fiery gaze evenly, although inside she was quaking.

Chapter Sixteen

To Poppy's surprise Lord Taverner exhaled loudly and then he seemed to collapse like a deflated balloon. He walked past her, moving crabwise towards the door.

'Decant the Lafite,' he said brusquely as he left the room.

Poppy breathed a sigh of relief. She had fully expected to be sent packing for insolence, but Lord Taverner had presumably gone to his room to shed his filthy garments and, she hoped, to dress in something more appropriate. She could hardly believe that her bold outburst had worked. Perhaps he simply needed a firm hand.

Poppy was convinced that someone, most likely Mrs Whiddon, had been taking his lordship's wine, either for her own use, or perhaps for Cook, although if many bottles had gone missing it was possible that she was selling them and keeping the money for herself. Poppy decided to take the opportunity to look for the lists Lord Taverner had mentioned, but she had barely left the room when someone rapped on the front door. She went to answer it and found Dr Standish standing on the step.

'You asked me to visit Lady Taverner?' Dr Standish took off his top hat as he stepped over the threshold.

'Yes, Doctor. I was very concerned to discover that you hadn't been called in to examine her, and yet she is confined to her room. She says she is mortally ill, but I'm not so sure.'

'I will best be the judge of that, young lady.'

'Of course, Doctor. Please come this way.' Poppy led him upstairs to Lady Taverner's room. She knocked and entered without waiting for an answer.

Lady Taverner was still recumbent on the chaise longue, but she opened her eyes and gazed blearily at Poppy. 'Is it time for my medicine?'

Dr Standish moved closer. 'What medicine is that, ma'am?'

Lady Taverner raised herself on her elbow. 'Is that you, Dr Standish? I haven't seen you for a very long time. Did you know that I am ill?'

'This is the first time I've been asked to visit you, my lady.' Dr Standish pulled up a chair and sat down. 'Perhaps you would like to tell me what ails you?'

A faint smile lit Lady Taverner's blue eyes. 'I thought that was your job, Doctor.'

'I see you haven't lost your sense of humour, ma'am. We have missed you in the village.'

'I am too weak most days to leave my room, Doctor. I get dizzy spells and I have little appetite.'

'Have you any pain, ma'am?'

'Oh no, Doctor. Nothing like that, although I do get headaches. Mrs Whiddon makes me up a tisane with herbs and that makes me sleep. She looks after me very well.'

Dr Standish glanced at Poppy, who said nothing, although it was on the tip of her tongue to tell him that she thought Mrs Whiddon was partly the cause of her ladyship's malaise.

'Do you mind if I listen to your heart, my lady?' Dr Whiddon opened his medical bag and took out a stethoscope.

Poppy looked away tactfully while the doctor examined Lady Taverner. When he had finished, he packed away the stethoscope, his brow furrowed.

'Am I dying, Doctor?' Lady Taverner asked feebly. 'Sometimes I think I am floating above my body and the angels are calling to me.'

'Pure fantasy, my lady. Your heart beats strongly and your lungs are clear.' Dr Standish stood up and reached for the bottle of laudanum. He shook his head. 'How much of this are you taking at a time, ma'am?'

Lady Taverner gave him a sweet smile. 'I don't know, Doctor. Mrs Whiddon measures out the dose, but I do feel better afterwards.'

Dr Standish turned to Poppy. 'I think she might be taking far too much of this for her own good. I need to speak to Mrs Whiddon. Better still, I will entrust her ladyship's care to you as you seem to be a sensible young woman.' He thrust the bottle into Poppy's hand. 'A couple of drops only when absolutely necessary. I think you ought to keep this bottle in a safe place.'

Poppy tucked it into her pocket. 'Yes, Doctor. I will.'

'I cannot sleep without it,' Lady Taverner said faintly. 'I will be awake all night.'

'I recommend good food and a little exercise, my lady. There is no reason for you to be confined to your bedchamber, as far as I can see.'

'But I am very weak, Dr Standish.' Lady Taverner sent a pleading glance to Poppy. 'You will attest to that, won't you, my dear?'

'I agree with the doctor, ma'am. If we build up your strength you will be able to walk without assistance. Maybe you could spend some time outside in the garden. Bert could carry you and sit you in a comfortable chair outside in the sunshine.'

'An excellent plan.' Dr Standish closed his medical bag with a snap. 'I will call again tomorrow, Lady Taverner. In the meantime, I suggest you do as Miss Robbins says. Now, if you'll excuse me, I have another patient to visit.'

'I'll see you out, Doctor.' Poppy followed him to the door. 'I'll be back soon with your supper, my lady.'

'I have very little appetite, Poppy.' Lady Taverner waved feebly. 'Don't worry about me. Just make sure that my poor husband has his dinner on time.'

'Yes, ma'am.' Poppy hurried after the doctor, but before she could catch up with him she was accosted by Lord Taverner. He rushed towards her waving a cravat, his shirt open to the waist. He was wearing trousers that looked as if they belonged to someone else and his stomach bulged over the waistband. His appearance was comical, but Poppy realised that he had at least made an effort to smarten himself.

'I can't work out how to tie this damned thing, Poppy. Do I have to wear it?'

She took pity on him. 'Perhaps we won't bother now, sir. Dinner will be ready in half an hour or so. Might I do up the buttons for you?'

'Buttons? Oh, yes, I suppose so, but this shirt is too small. That's why I don't bother to dress up. My trousers are too tight.'

'Have you thought about taking on a valet, sir?'

'We can't afford more servants, miss. Ask Whiddon – she'll tell you the state of our finances.'

Poppy stopped doing up his buttons, realising that the shirt would not stretch over his lordship's corpulent belly. 'Mrs Whiddon handles the money, my lord?'

'I can't be bothered with such details. I leave it to the Whiddon. She's run this place for centuries, it seems. Did you decant the Lafite?'

'I was about to do that when Dr Standish called, sir.'

'What did he want? Who's ill?'

'He came to see your wife, sir.' Poppy gave up her attempts to make him look smart. 'Apparently Lady Taverner has not been seen by him for quite some time.'

Lord Taverner shrugged. 'Whiddon looks after her. She would have told me had my wife needed to see Standish.'

Poppy nodded but she refrained from comment. It was no use arguing with his lordship, and it was becoming more and more obvious that Mrs Whiddon had been running the household with an iron hand for far too long. Her reign was about to come to an abrupt end, although Poppy needed more evidence before she could. This made her even more determined to expose the woman who had used the situation to her own advantage. It was obvious that she had encouraged Lord Taverner in his love of fine wines so that he drank to excess, while his lady was addicted to laudanum and whatever else was in the tisanes prepared by Mrs Whiddon. That woman must have a small fortune tucked away for her retirement, all of which rightfully belonged to the Taverners. Poppy could not wait to tell Eddie of her discovery.

Later that evening, Poppy and Lord Taverner ate a delicious dinner prepared mostly by Jessie, much to the disgust of Cook, who seized a bottle of sherry from the larder and stomped off to her room. Even Mrs Whiddon could find nothing to complain of and she also retired early, leaving Jessie to deal with the washing up and cleaning of the kitchen. Poppy saw to it that Lady Taverner had a bowlful of stew, and she stayed with her, making encouraging remarks while her ladyship ate. However, when Lady Taverner demanded a dose of laudanum, Poppy refused, insisting that it was only to be taken last thing before Lady Taverner lay down to sleep. There ensued a feeble argument but her ladyship was easily exhausted and soon she capitulated. It hurt Poppy to see the poor lady so weak and upset, but she knew she must follow the doctor's advice if she were to help Lady Taverner to get well again.

With Lord Taverner snoozing in his armchair, having drunk two bottles of the Lafite, Poppy went to his study and in the fading light of a summer's evening she set to work to retrieve and study the lists that Mrs Whiddon had kept concerning the wine cellar. They made interesting reading, but Poppy soon realised that they were pure fiction. If she had not seen the cellar for herself she might not have given the lists more than a cursory glance. However, the reality of what was in the cellar and Mrs Whiddon's bookkeeping was certainly creative. Poppy started on the household account books and it was obvious that these too bore no resemblance to the truth. Eventually the light faded and it was too dark to study the pages of spidery handwriting. Poppy put everything back in place and left the study, locking the door behind her.

*   *   *

Next morning Poppy had just finished her breakfast in the dining room when there was a knock on the door and she answered it to find a group of women standing on the carriage sweep. The most senior, a woman in her late thirties or early forties, introduced herself as Martha Hayes.

'Mrs Standish told us that you're in need of staff, Miss Robbins.' Martha stepped over the threshold. 'I was Lady Taverner's personal maid until five years ago when Mrs Whiddon found fault with my work and sacked me.'

'On what grounds, Miss Hayes?'

'She accused me of stealing a bottle of wine, which was untrue, but his lordship believed her. I haven't been able to get a job since. No one wants a servant who steals from them.'

At any other time Poppy might have been sceptical, but she had no difficulty in assessing Martha Hayes and she did not doubt her story. 'I do need someone to take care of her ladyship,' Poppy said slowly. 'If she agrees I will take you on for a trial period.'

'Then you believe me, miss?'

'Yes, I do. If you will kindly take a seat I will deal with the other ladies.' Poppy stood back to allow all the women to enter. There were six of them, including Martha Hayes. Each had worked at Domesday House and all of them told the same story. One way or another Mrs Whiddon had found an excuse to send them packing.

The last, and by far the youngest, was Jessie's sister.

'I'm Loveday Jarvis, miss. Jessie's older sister. She said you might give me a job in the laundry room.'

The resemblance between the sisters was very striking and Poppy took an instant liking to the young girl. 'Thank you for coming, Loveday. Jessie must have told you everything so if you are keen to start working here, I will be happy to take you on.'

'Thank you, miss. I can start today, if that suits.'

Poppy thought of the pile of unwashed garments there must be in Lord Taverner's room alone and she nodded. 'That will be excellent. Do you know your way to the kitchen?'

'Not really, miss.'

'I can show her,' Miss Hayes said firmly. 'May I go upstairs afterwards to see Lady Taverner?'

'Yes, indeed. She is in desperate need of your services, Miss Hayes. By the way, she seems convinced that you have been visiting family in Bristol. I don't think she knows that Mrs Whiddon sacked you.'

Miss Hayes took a deep breath. 'That sounds like Eliza Whiddon. Thank you for telling me, Miss Robbins.'

Poppy turned to the other four hopefuls. 'I am Poppy Robbins, and I am engaged to Mr Edward Taverner, as you probably know already.' She turned to the nearest applicant. 'What is your name and what is your speciality?'

'My name is Bessie Milner and I was a parlourmaid here until Lady Taverner took to her bed and then Mrs Whiddon gained control of everything.'

There was a murmur of assent from the remaining three hopefuls. In her short time at Domesday House, Poppy had learned so much about Mrs Whiddon's reign of terror that it was hard to believe, but here in front of her was the living proof.

'Is this true of you all? Have you worked here before?' Poppy looked from one to the other and they all nodded.

'I'm Mary Davey, miss. This is my sister, Nettie, and our cousin Maud. We was all cleaning women until Mrs Whiddon took against us.'

'I'm sure I can find work for everyone,' Poppy said firmly. 'We will settle pay and conditions later, if you are all keen to return.'

'We are.' Maud glanced at her cousins. 'I speak for all of us. But we don't want to work for Mrs Whiddon. She's still here, so we've been told.'

'She is no longer in charge. It's true that she is still in her position, but for how long I wouldn't like to say.' Poppy smiled. 'I don't suppose you know a gentleman's gentleman who is looking for employment, do you? His lordship is in desperate need of a manservant.'

Mary Davey nodded emphatically. 'Mr Frampton was Lord Taverner's valet, miss. He retired a while ago, but he would come back, I'm sure. Mrs Whiddon didn't like him, but he's a good man and very loyal to the family.'

'Mrs Whiddon didn't like him because he caught her stealing wine from the cellar,' Nettie added, grinning. 'It was all hushed up but we knew what was going on.'

'And that was the start of it.' Mary nodded vigorously. 'We all knew the truth of the matter so we had to go.'

'How very shocking.' Poppy was horrified but not surprised. She realised now that it was only the diamond ring on her finger that had kept her safe from Mrs Whiddon's machinations and, given time, she might even get round that. It was time someone put a stop to Mrs Whiddon's game.

'I could start right away,' Maud said eagerly. 'I can see cobwebs everywhere and the floor is filthy.'

'Me, too.' Mary pulled a face. 'I dare say there's parts of the house that haven't been touched since we left.'

'We are all able to begin work, miss.' Nettie peeled off her cotton gloves. 'If that's all right with you.'

'Of course. Please go to the kitchen and collect what you need to begin. If you see Mrs Whiddon, refer her to me. I'll be in the study, going over the accounts.' Poppy left them to find their own way. If Mrs Whiddon thought Poppy was going to go through the books it might scare her enough to admit defeat. There would be nothing more satisfactory than to tell the dishonest housekeeper that she no longer had a position at Domesday House. However, as she went to the study Poppy had a nasty feeling that it was not going to be so easy to get rid of the Whiddon woman. Somehow, she must persuade Lord Taverner that it was the only way. She found herself wishing that Eddie would return soon. When he was presented with the facts of the matter Poppy was certain he would have no hesitation in sacking Mrs Whiddon on the spot.

Poppy was immersed in the household accounts when, as she had expected, Mrs Whiddon burst into the study and stood, arms akimbo, glaring at her.

'How dare you usurp my authority, Miss Robbins?'

Poppy closed the ledger and leaned her elbows on the desk, meeting Mrs Whiddon's furious glare with a steady gaze. 'I beg your pardon? You are speaking to the future mistress of Domesday House, Mrs Whiddon. I expect a little courtesy from a servant.'

Mrs Whiddon bristled angrily. She was breathing as if she had just run a race, and her face was flushed scarlet. 'You don't fool me, miss. I know your supposed engagement was a ruse set up by Mr Edward. He's never liked me because I chastised him when he was a small boy. He was always in trouble and I doubt if he's changed. You are the imposter, Miss Robbins. I'll have none of your nonsense.'

Poppy rose to her feet so that they faced each other with only the desk to separate them.

'Don't threaten me, Mrs Whiddon. I have proof that you have been stealing wine from the cellar and you have been falsifying the accounts. I dare say you have made a pretty penny from that over the years.'

'That's a very serious accusation, miss.' Mrs Whiddon's eyes narrowed. 'I know things about Mr Edward that would not only discredit the family but would send him to prison for a very long time.'

Poppy was shaken by the sudden attack and alarmed by the threat against Taverner himself, but she was not going to allow the Whiddon to intimidate her.

'I don't believe you, ma'am. Do you think anyone in authority would take your word over that of Lord Taverner or his son? You have been systematically robbing his lordship, but it has to end now.'

'You can't prove anything, miss. All you have is a few lists that you could have altered yourself, and you don't understand the household accounts, so that means nothing.'

Poppy stared at her aghast. She had not expected the evidence she had uncovered to be flung back in her face as if it were a pack of lies, nor had she anticipated quite such an antagonistic reaction from the guilty party.

'I think Lord Taverner should be the judge of all this.' Poppy forced herself to remain calm although, if she were to be honest, she was a little scared. Mrs Whiddon was clenching and unclenching her fists and quite literally grinding her teeth. She was a big woman with muscular forearms and a thickset body that the severe black gown did little to disguise.

What might in another person be described as pleasantly plump was in her more reminiscent of a bare-knuckle fighter, and just as dangerous.

'I agree. His lordship will see my point of view.' Mrs Whiddon tossed her head and marched out of the room. Poppy had to hurry in order to catch up with her as she barged into the drawing room.

Lord Taverner glanced nervously at Mrs Whiddon. 'Is anything wrong, ladies?'

'This person has accused me of stealing your wine, my lord,' Mrs Whiddon said angrily. 'She thinks she can come here and cast aspersions on the person who has looked after you and Lady Taverner for all these years.'

Poppy stood her ground. 'Mrs Whiddon has been systematically emptying your wine cellar and reordering at considerable expense to you, my lord.'

'She's lying.' Mrs Whiddon tossed her head. 'She'll say anything to make me look bad, my lord.'

Poppy eyed Lord Taverner critically. He was wearing the stained dressing gown embroidered with a green dragon that she had earmarked for the laundry room. 'I thought I put that dressing gown ready to be laundered, sir.'

Lord Taverner wrapped the offending garment around his fat belly. 'I had to wrestle it from a strange young woman in my bedchamber. She said she works here but I don't know her.'

'That will be Jessie Jarvis's sister Loveday, your lordship. I've taken her on as laundry maid.'

'I am the person in charge of hiring servants,' Mrs Whiddon said through clenched teeth. 'I am the only one here with the expertise to know how to interview and choose the best candidate.'

'That position has been taken away from you, ma'am.' Poppy turned to Lord Taverner. 'Please back me up, sir. Tell Mrs Whiddon that I am running things here at Domesday House.'

Lord Taverner paled visibly and he blinked nervously. 'Well, it was suggested by Mr Edward, and I did think we would give it a try, Mrs Whiddon, if you don't mind.'

'What are you saying, sir?' Poppy demanded. 'You wanted me to take control. You said so yourself.'

'Well, I – er. You sort it out, Poppy, my dear. I'm sure Mrs Whiddon will be more helpful in the future. Isn't that so, Eliza?'

Mrs Whiddon bridled. 'I want it understood that I am still in charge. I'm sure there are things from the past that you wish to be forgotten.'

'That sounds like a threat,' Poppy said, aghast at Mrs Whiddon's brazenness.

'It's no threat, Miss Robbins.' Mrs Whiddon smiled triumphantly. 'Lord Taverner understands me. We have a long history, do we not, my lord?'

'Sort it out between you. I don't wish to be involved. You can fetch me a bottle of Madeira from the cellar, Eliza. I need sustenance.'

Mrs Whiddon shot Poppy a malicious look as she walked to the door. 'Of course, my lord. I might even indulge myself. My nerves are quite shattered by unfair accusations from some quarters.' She left the room, slamming the door behind her.

'What was she saying, sir?' Poppy fixed Lord Taverner with a frosty look. 'I can prove that Mrs Whiddon has been cheating you for years, and I suspect that she has been overdosing your wife on laudanum in order to keep her out of the way.'

'Eliza has been here for more than twenty years. She was a handsome woman in those days and an excellent housekeeper. I need more proof before I can be sure of any wrongdoing on her part.' Lord Taverner huddled in his chair, pulling the dressing gown up to his chin, although it still gaped open further down. 'Now leave me in peace, please.'

'I will,' Poppy said hastily. 'But I need your agreement to take on the extra staff we so badly need. They have all worked here before, except for Loveday, so they know what to do and will not get in the way.'

'I agree but please don't bother me with housekeeping problems. That's what I employ Eliza Whiddon for. Speak nicely to Eliza and she will do anything for you.'

Poppy smothered a sigh as she left the drawing room. It was becoming obvious that Mrs Whiddon had some sort of hold over Baron Taverner of Oakley. Perhaps there had been something between them twenty years ago when they were both younger, although it was hard to imagine the Whiddon as a *femme fatale*. Even so, she seemed to know how to handle his lordship to her best advantage. Poppy realised that, in the absence of Eddie Taverner, there was only one person who might stand up to Eliza Whiddon. However, it would take time to wean Lady Taverner off her addiction to laudanum and bring her back to her former self. Poppy had seen a glimpse of the spark that lay dormant in her ladyship's fuddled brain, and that had made her even more determined to make things right.

As she crossed the entrance hall the welcome smell of carbolic soap and lavender-scented furniture polish greeted her. Nettie was on her hands and knees, scrubbing the floor, while Mary attacked the cobwebs on the staircase with a long-handle brush. Maud was fully occupied with polishing the ornately carved oak chests, and hall chairs with barley-twist legs.

Poppy was about to praise them for their efforts when she saw Mrs Whiddon approaching from the direction of the cellars with two bottles clutched in her hands. She chose to ignore the cleaning women as she marched briskly towards the drawing room.

'I have here a bottle of Madeira for his lordship, and a bottle of cooking sherry, which I will take to the kitchen,' Mrs Whiddon said with a sarcastic smile. 'Do you wish to search me for evidence of thievery? After all, I might have a magnum of champagne concealed beneath my skirt.'

'You may think this is amusing, ma'am,' Poppy said icily, 'but I do not, and neither will Mr Edward when he comes home.'

'No one gets the better of Eliza Whiddon. There are things better left unsaid, but if you continue to challenge my authority you will be very sorry, Miss Robbins. Do you understand what I'm saying? I can make life very difficult for you.'

Chapter Seventeen

Poppy realised that Lord Taverner was unlikely to back her up, at least not if Mrs Whiddon was around. However, she had no intention of allowing Mrs Whiddon to resume her responsibilities as housekeeper, especially when it came to organising and directing the servants. That meant putting Jessie in charge of the kitchen, which oddly enough did not seem to bother Cook. She was kept happy with cheap sherry, which she decanted into a large Brown Betty teapot, enabling her to have a constant supply on hand. It was an open secret that the copious amounts of tea Cook drank was cheap Amontillado, but peace reigned while she was pleasantly tipsy. Poppy was aware of the situation but chose to ignore it while things ran smoothly. She now had many hands to help run domestic matters and she divided the household tasks equally between the

Davy sisters and Maud Sykes, with Bessie Milner acting as parlourmaid.

It was almost a week later that Ernest Frampton was finally persuaded to come out of retirement and he moved into Domesday House to act as Lord Taverner's valet. His lordship was reluctant at first, protesting that he had no need of a manservant these days, but Ernest was adept at handling him. Poppy was delighted to see a much cleaner, tidier version of Lord Taverner next morning at breakfast. To her relief there was no sign of the old dressing gown.

Martha Hayes settled in as Lady Taverner's personal maid as if she had never left, and Lady Taverner was obviously delighted to have her back. At the outstart Poppy explained the situation as regards the laudanum, and she warned Martha not to give her ladyship any of the tisanes that Mrs Whiddon might suggest. Martha understood without the need for further explanation, and almost immediately Lady Taverner's health began to improve. With Martha in charge, the sick room was transformed into a pleasant boudoir. The curtains were drawn back to let in the summer sunshine and the air was filled with the scent from bowls filled with roses and sweet peas from the garden. Lady Taverner was even persuaded to eat small meals, which Martha prepared for her in the kitchen.

Without backing from Lord Taverner, and with the other servants more than happy to take instructions from Poppy, Mrs Whiddon retreated into a morose, brooding state. She and Cook did not actively challenge Poppy's authority, but Mrs Whiddon made it plain that she was simply biding her time. This made Poppy nervous, but she was determined to restore order to the household. She made sure that Mrs Whiddon did not have access to the accounts, and she kept the keys to the safe in her possession at all times. However, Poppy was becoming restless and she was eager to return home. She was well aware that this state of affairs could not continue for much longer. She managed to keep a calm exterior but all she could think about was returning to her old life. With no news from Taverner, she was becoming impatient.

Her chance to change things came about one afternoon when Dr Standish called and found her ladyship seated in a chair on the lawn, shaded by a large umbrella. He congratulated Poppy on her ladyship's improvement, which she had to admit was mainly due to Martha's loving care.

'And how is Mr Grundy, Doctor?' Poppy asked as she saw Dr Standish to the door. 'I'm afraid I have been too busy here to visit him.'

'He is almost fully recovered. I think he is well enough to go home to Dorrington Place, although I would recommend that he does not take up his full responsibilities for a while.'

'That's excellent news. What about the carriage – is it roadworthy?'

'Yes, I saw the wheelwright this morning and

he gave me the bill, which I will forward to Lady Dorrington, of course, together with my account and that from the hospital.' Dr Standish shook his head. 'I'm afraid accidents cost a great deal of money.'

'There is no need to worry on that score, Doctor.' Poppy realised immediately that this was the opportunity she had been waiting for. 'Lady Dorrington will settle everything promptly, of that I am certain.'

Dr Standish pursed his lips. 'I hope so, Miss Robbins.'

'I could take care of Mr Grundy on the way back to Dorrington Place,' Poppy said hastily. 'Or Ned could drive the carriage and I will deliver the accounts personally. I would return next day.' She waited expectantly for an answer.

'That sounds eminently sensible, Miss Robbins. I can have Mr Grundy ready to depart as soon as you are available.' The relief on Dr Standish's stern features was obvious, and he even managed a tight little smile.

'Tomorrow, Doctor. I'll send one or both of the Hawke brothers to collect the carriage and I will accompany Mr Grundy back to Dorrington Place as suggested.'

'Excellent, Miss Robbins. I will personally ensure that Mr Grundy is prepared for the journey.' Dr Standish was out of the house and in his chaise before Poppy had a chance to draw breath. The prospect of spending even one night at Dorrington Place was quite intoxicating, although not strictly necessary.

If the horses were given a proper rest in between journeys it was possible to do the round trip in a day, but Poppy was determined to make the most of a break from the personal conflicts in Domesday House. She had not realised until this moment quite how stultifying it had been living under the cloud created by the Whiddon, and it had been made even more difficult as she had no one in whom she could confide. She felt quite light-headed with excitement as she began to make the necessary arrangements.

The first person she went to find was Ernest Frampton. Although she had only known him for a short time Poppy was convinced of his honesty and integrity. She found him in the laundry room, pressing a pair of Lord Taverner's trousers. Poppy hid a smile as she noticed a small, neatly sewn patch that repaired a tear in the material.

'Mr Frampton, I have agreed to accompany Mr Grundy, the injured coachman, back to his home at Dorrington Place. It means I will be away tomorrow night but I will return the next day. I will leave the keys with you. I know I can trust you not to allow Mrs Whiddon to have them.'

Ernest placed the flat iron back on the range. 'I understand, miss.'

'In particular I don't want her to have the key to the study or the wine cellar.'

'Yes, Miss Robbins. I'm not one to gossip, but Eliza Whiddon has had things her own way for far too long, in my opinion, anyway.'

'I couldn't agree more. I'm glad you understand.'
Poppy was about to leave the hot steamy room when
she had a sudden idea. 'Were you here when Mrs
Whiddon first came to Domesday House?'

'I started work here as a young man in the days of
the old Baron Oakley, Lord Taverner's father. That
was well before the arrival of Mrs Whiddon, which
made it so much worse when she accused me of
stealing a pair of gold cufflinks and had me sacked.
It was all untrue, of course, but I knew too much
and she was desperate to get rid of me.'

'What was it you knew, Mr Frampton? There is
some mystery attached to her longevity and her hold
over Lord Taverner that I don't understand.'

'It was the talk of the village at the time, but then
it was hushed up and no one was allowed to speak
of such things.'

'What things? Can you tell me?' Poppy glanced
over her shoulder to make sure there was no one
within earshot.

Mr Frampton lowered his voice. 'It was said that
she knew his lordship before she came here, and
that she had a child by him. Of course there was no
proof, miss. It might have been spiteful gossip.'

'What happened to the child, Mr Frampton?'

'I heard that the boy was raised by a couple
who were childless and he was treated as their
own. He would be a couple of years older than Mr
Edward.'

'Were they a local family, Mr Frampton?' Poppy

was mystified and yet she was sure there was a connection somewhere.

'I believe they came from north of the county, miss.'

'Do you recall their name?'

Mr Frampton frowned and scratched his bald pate. 'I used to be so good at names, but I fear they escape me sometimes these days. I think it was Mullins or something similar.'

Poppy caught her breath. 'Could it be Mulliner by any chance?'

'Yes, now you come to mention it I believe it was Mulliner, and the boy, although born out of wedlock, was named after a saint. I can't remember which one, not being very religious myself, but it was definitely a saint.'

'Does Gervase sound familiar?' Poppy held her breath. It was surely too much of a coincidence, and yet Mulliner had a nasty habit of turning up unexpectedly and uninvited.

'By George, that's the name. Gervase Mulliner.' Mr Frampton smiled triumphantly. 'You see, my memory is not so very bad. I remember the scandal at the time and then Eliza married Rob Whiddon. There was talk that the Baron Oakley greased his palm, as they say, but that's just gossip and I don't hold with that.'

The full impact of Mr Frampton's revelation hit Poppy with such force she felt quite faint and she clutched the back of the nearest chair. 'But if Lord Taverner is Gervase Mulliner's father, that mean that Gervase and Edward are half-brothers.'

'It could just be the gossipmongers at work again, miss. I met Mr Mulliner once and I can assure you he is nothing like Mr Edward, for whom I have the greatest respect.'

'I'm sure you must be right, Mr Frampton.' Poppy made an attempt at a smile, but she could only think of how Eddie would feel if he were to find out. From their previous conversation she had discovered that his dislike of Mulliner was because of a young woman, and had nothing to do with his birth. Unless Taverner had been lying to her, which put a new slant on matters. Poppy had a sudden need for fresh air.

'Are you all right, Miss Robbins?' Mr Frampton asked anxiously. 'You've gone very pale.'

'I'm fine, thank you. It must be the heat. Anyway, I need to make arrangements for Bert or Ned to drive the carriage tomorrow. I'll leave first thing in the morning.' She hurried from the laundry room without waiting for an answer.

Bert was the first person she came across in the stables and he was more than ready for a jaunt away from Domesday House, especially when Poppy told him they would be spending the night at Dorrington Place. His eyes lit up and he puffed out his chest.

'I've always wanted to see how the big houses go about their day-to-day business, miss. Wait till I tell Ned. He's going to be mad as fury, if you'll pardon the expression.'

'It will be his turn next time I need a coachman,'

Poppy said vaguely. 'We'll leave after breakfast in the morning, Bert.'

He tipped his cap. 'I'll be ready, miss.'

Poppy made her way back to the house and she went straight to Lady Taverner's room, where she found Martha tidying the dressing table while Lady Taverner took a nap on the chaise longue.

'Martha, I just wanted to tell you that I am accompanying Mr Grundy back to Dorrington Place tomorrow. Bert is going to drive the Dorringtons' carriage now that the wheelwright has finished his work.'

'Very well, Miss Robbins. Is there anything in particular you wanted me to do?'

'I'll stay the night at Dorrington Place but I'll be back next day. In the meantime, I want you to watch Lady Taverner very carefully. Don't allow Mrs Whiddon near her. If she insists, please don't leave her alone with Lady Taverner.'

'I understand, miss.'

'I knew you would. She's improved so much and you've only been taking care of her for a short while.'

'It's a pleasure to be back with her, Miss Robbins. I can't tell you how much it upset me to see her in such a state, but we're coming out of it slowly.'

'All thanks to you, Martha. It's such a relief to know she's in safe hands.' Poppy glanced at the frail figure of Lady Taverner as she slept, and she wondered if the poor lady knew about her husband's peccadilloes, especially the fact that he had a son with the housekeeper, born out of wedlock. Even now the scandal would be considerable, but that in itself gave Poppy an idea. Gervase Mulliner had threatened to expose a twenty-year-old scandal that could spell financial ruin for her parents, and embarrass the Ashton family. What, she wondered, would his reaction be if the tables were turned? How would the dapper socialite Gervase Mulliner feel if his ignominious birth was revealed to the world?

'Is there anything else I can do, miss?'

Poppy turned with a start to see Martha staring at her, openly curious. 'No. That's all. Just continue to do exactly as you have been doing. Take care of her ladyship until I return.' Poppy gave her an encouraging smile as she left the room.

In her mind Poppy was forming a plan, but it would depend upon what she discovered when she reached Dorrington Place. She could not wait to see Aunt Bella and Lottie again, but if all worked out as she hoped she might be able to return home to Rainbow's End sooner than she had anticipated. The mere thought made her happy and she felt better able to cope with Lord Taverner's odd ways and heavy drinking at dinner that evening.

Next morning, as Dr Standish had promised, Grundy was ready to travel back to Dorrington Place. Bert had to help him into the newly refurbished carriage, and Poppy climbed in after him. She laid a rug over Grundy's knees and Bert closed the door. Minutes later they were off at a brisk pace and Poppy leaned back against the squabs, revelling in the fact that she had left Domesday House behind, at least for the time being. She gazed out of the window, taking in the glorious view of verdant fields and hedgerows studded with red and white campion, green ferns and the frothy pink flowers of hemp agrimony growing in the damp roadsides. Shortly after they left, Grundy's eyes closed and his head lolled to one side as he slept. He hardly awakened at all during the two-hour drive, except for the half an hour when they stopped to allow the horses to rest at a wayside inn. Poppy gave Bert some money to purchase tea and buns for them all, but Grundy opted to remain in the carriage and Poppy stayed with him.

It was almost midday when they finally drove through the impressive iron gates of Dorrington Place. Poppy could have cried with delight. Even though it was not her own home it felt comfortingly familiar. It was a relief to get out of the carriage and stretch her legs. She was greeted by Lottie, who pushed past the butler and raced across the forecourt to fling her arms around Poppy.

Laughing and handing her overnight case to the head footman, Poppy returned Lottie's embrace.

'Come inside and tell me everything,' Lottie said eagerly. 'Mama is in the morning room, waiting to see you.'

Poppy turned to Bert, who was waiting for instructions. 'I think Mr Grundy lives in the coach house, Bert. If you drive him to the stables they'll direct you.'

Bert was staring round, open-mouthed. 'This really is a big house, miss. I'm afraid I'll get lost.'

Poppy laughed. 'Don't worry, Bert. There are plenty of people here who will come looking for you. Just tell them you've brought Grundy home and they'll fall over themselves to take care of you.'

Bert mumbled something unintelligible and climbed back onto the box. He flicked the whip and the horses set off at a pace that suggested they knew they were going home.

'It's so good to see you, Poppy.' Lottie grabbed her by the hand and dragged her into the entrance hall. 'Don't worry about your case, Poppy. Anderson will have it taken to your room. How long can you stay?'

Breathless and laughing, Poppy almost bumped into Lottie as she came to a sudden halt and thrust open the door facing them. Arabella Ashton rose from the sofa and came towards Poppy, arms outstretched.

'My dear girl. How are you? I really felt for you, being left on your own in the awful house.'

'I'm very glad to be here,' Poppy said earnestly. 'You won't believe all that I have to tell you.'

Arabella guided her to the sofa and sat down beside her. 'You must tell us everything. You are just in time for luncheon so we can have a nice leisurely chat. How long can you stay?'

'Don't tell us you have to return immediately?' Lottie added anxiously.

'I said I would return in the morning. Bert drove your carriage so perhaps I could hire a vehicle in the village to take us back?'

'I won't hear of it.' Arabella shook her head. 'That's nonsense. I will get one of our coachmen to drive you back to Domesday House. I won't call it "home" because it is hardly that.'

'I'm sure Poppy has made improvements, Mama.' Lottie squeezed in beside Poppy. 'I expect you have that dreadful Whiddon woman eating out of your hand.'

'Is Lord Taverner still wearing that hideous dressing gown?' Arabella laughed. 'I wish Freddie had been there to see it all.'

'Is he not home?' Poppy was glad to change the subject. She did not want to talk about Domesday House.

'No, it's a terrible nuisance, but he had to go into London for some reason. He's at the house in Piccadilly and we are going to join him, although Arthur hates London and wants to stay in the country.' Arabella rose to her feet and went over to a side table. 'Would you like a glass of sherry before luncheon, Poppy? You look a little pale. It might do you good.'

Poppy nodded eagerly. 'That would be lovely, Aunt Bella. It has been a strain staying on in that house with no one to talk to. I have so much to tell you both that I don't quite know where to start.'

Arabella filled three small glasses from a cut-crystal decanter. She handed one to Poppy and another to

Lottie before resuming her seat in between them on the sofa.

'We have time before luncheon is served. Come on, Poppy dear, do tell all. Lottie and I are agog with curiosity.'

Poppy took a sip of the sherry and felt its effect immediately on an empty stomach. It gave her the courage to embark on her account of what had occurred during her time at Domesday House. Arabella and Lottie listened avidly.

'Oh, my goodness!' Arabella's hands flew to cover her scarlet cheeks when Poppy repeated what Mr Frampton had told her. 'I can't believe it, Poppy. How that man Mulliner keeps popping up around you like a bad penny, I will never understand.'

'Or that he might be Eddie Taverner's half-brother, Mama.' Lottie stared at Poppy wide-eyed. 'Do you think it's true?'

'I honestly don't know,' Poppy said, sighing. 'Mr Frampton certainly seemed to believe it, and Eddie spoke very harshly when he mentioned Mulliner's name. Although his version of why they are at loggerheads is rather different. He told me that Mulliner had taken advantage of a young woman whom Eddie loved, and she died tragically.'

'No! How dreadful.' Lottie clasped her hands together. 'Isn't that awful, Mama?'

'It is indeed.' Arabella shuddered. 'Incomprehensible. Do you know who the unfortunate young woman was, Poppy?'

'No names were mentioned, but he seemed quite upset just talking about her. It must have been true love.'

Arabella glanced at the diamond ring on Poppy's left hand. 'Well, even so, he seems to have recovered now, if that's anything to go by.'

'It's only temporary.' Poppy covered the ring with her right hand. 'It was a ruse to make the servants do as I requested. Mrs Whiddon in particular.'

'Are you sure about that?' Lottie demanded mischievously. 'I mean, it seems a bit extreme, if you ask me. Maybe he hopes you will actually fall in love with him.'

Poppy opened her mouth to deny it but a tap on the door preceded a parlourmaid, who came in to announce that luncheon was served.

Luncheon was an informal affair. The food was excellent and the surroundings were a testament to good taste and unostentatious luxury. Poppy began to relax and even saw the funny side of things as she recounted what had occurred at Domesday House after Arabella and Lottie had left. Even so, the conversation kept returning to Gervase Mulliner and his relationship to Eddie Taverner.

'We must remember that Mulliner and his cousin Miranda are the reason that you and Lottie had to come here in the first place,' Arabella said thoughtfully. 'No matter what his lineage, Mulliner still poses a threat to both of you. I'm of the opinion that he intends to demand money at some stage. I can think of no other reason for his behaviour.'

'He knows that Uncle Freddie is wealthy.' Poppy frowned. 'But I wonder if he's aware of his relationship to Eddie?'

'Do you think that Mrs Whiddon has kept in touch with her son?' Lottie toyed with a peach on her dessert plate, prodding it with the silver blade of a fruit knife.

'Don't do that, Lottie,' Arabella said impatiently. 'You're setting my nerves on edge. I wish your papa were here. I'm going to insist that he comes home immediately. Never mind business matters. This is more important.'

'Do you really think that Mulliner is such a danger, Aunt Bella? Surely you and Lottie are safe here with an army of servants to look after you?' Poppy looked from one to the other. 'You aren't afraid, are you, Lottie?'

'I don't know, but I wish Adam was here instead of playing at soldiers somewhere.' Lottie sighed and pushed her plate away. 'Gideon would protect me, if he knew what was going on, but he's miles away on the other side of London.'

'We don't want to involve anyone else in this horrid situation.' Arabella shook her head. 'I'm going to send a telegram to your papa, Lottie. I'll insist that he comes home immediately.' She rose from her seat. 'In fact, I'll write it now. One of the footmen can take it to the village post office. That should bring Freddie home.' She hurried from the dining room, leaving Poppy and Lottie still seated at the table.

'I don't know what Papa can do,' Lottie said crossly. 'I just want everything to go back the way it was.'

'I'm afraid it's gone too far. Because of the accident, we are involved with the Taverners at Domesday House as well as Eddie. At least I am. You can walk away, Lottie,' Poppy added with an encouraging smile. 'In fact, I'd advise you to do so, but I need to speak to Eddie. I must see him before I return to Domesday House. He needs to know the full extent of the Whiddon's treachery and dishonesty. He is the only one who could send the wretched woman packing.'

'But you can't go to London on your own, Poppy. We're supposed to stay out of the way.'

'Obviously you can't go with me – that would be a bit silly – but I have to speak to Eddie.'

'You're not going to tell him that Mulliner is his half-brother?'

'I'm not sure he has been completely honest with me. I want to know why he left me at Domesday House to face the Whiddon.'

Lottie pulled a face. 'Look how much you've done for that family in such a short time. Edward Taverner has gone back to his business in London, whatever that might be, and you have taken charge of his household in Devonshire. In my opinion he's taken advantage of you.'

'You could be right, Lottie. Anyway, my mind is made up. I am going to London and no one is going to stop me.'

Lottie pushed her chair back and jumped to her feet. 'You are so brave. I would come with you but I don't want to upset Mama.'

'You must stay here, but you can help by lending me some money. I'll pay you back when I get home.'

'That's all right. I have my pin money and I'll give you that, but how will you manage on your own?'

Poppy stood up slowly. 'I'm not like you, Lottie. I've been raised differently and that makes me more independent. I'll leave here tomorrow with Bert, but I'll get him to drop me off at the railway station. When I get to London I'll go straight to Spitalfields Market where Eddie has his office.'

Lottie stared at her in a mixture of awe and dismay. 'But what if he's not there? You can't go home to Rainbow's End, so where will you stay?'

'I'll worry about that when I get there,' Poppy said firmly. 'I just need you to cover for me. You must tell your mama that I have returned to Domesday House and I will swear Bert to secrecy, so that the Taverners think I am simply spending a couple of days here with you. I don't want anyone to know that I've gone to London. Can you do that, Lottie?'

Chapter Eighteen

When Poppy left Dorrington Place next morning she had received an emotional hug from Arabella, who wished her well at Domesday House, but had made it clear that she was welcome at any time should matters there become too difficult. Poppy felt awful deceiving someone who had always been so kind and generous to her, but Lottie did not appear to have any qualms and actually seemed to be enjoying the drama. Bert had been sworn to secrecy, as had the junior coachman who had been given the task of taking them back to Domesday House. Poppy had not told Bert the real reason for her trip to London, but had allowed him to think she was going home to visit her parents for a day or two before returning to Devonshire. Poppy had said goodbye to him at the railway station with real regret. Even in a short time she had grown fond of Bert and his lazy brother, as she had the rest of the servants, with the exception of Cook and the Whiddon. She boarded the train with a sense of anticipation and excitement. She was taking a huge chance by travelling to London on her own, but she was determined not to allow nerves to get the better of her.

Her journey was uneventful and she took a hansom cab from the station, using some of the money that Lottie had given her.

Spitalfields Market was busy as usual. Poppy felt small and insignificant as she threaded her way around the stalls in the crowded market place, and now she was really nervous. She edged towards Taverner's office, hoping against hope that her journey had not been in vain, but there was no sign of him and the door was locked. She stood there, undecided as to what to do next.

A small child tugged at her skirt. 'He ain't there, miss.'

Poppy looked down to see a boy of five or six, gazing up at her with big brown eyes and a very dirty face. His clothes were ragged and none too clean, and to her dismay she saw that he was barefoot. He was just the sort of child she had once hoped to help.

'Do you know where I might find Mr Taverner?' Poppy asked gently.

'It's Thursday, miss. Don't you know nothing? He'll be at the orphanage, of course.'

'The orphanage?' Poppy thought for a minute that the child might be teasing her but it was obvious from his expression that he was deadly serious. 'Where is that?'

'I dunno the name of the street, miss. I'm only five and a half. I can't read as yet, but Mr Taverner says all of us nippers must learn our letters.'

'Does he now? Well, that's good. I should like to go there, if you could take me.' Poppy opened her reticule and took out a farthing. The boy's eyes lit up and he grabbed the money.

'Follow me, miss.' He raced off and Poppy had to run to keep up with him as he weaved in and out between the pedestrians on the narrow pavements. It was difficult for Poppy, but somehow she managed to keep up with him and found herself in King Street. The terraces of tall red-brick houses were interspersed with small shops and the odd warehouse, some of them with broken and boarded-up windows. The boy stopped in front of a double-fronted five-storey building with stone steps leading up to the front door. He reached the top step and came to a halt, grinning at her.

'I can't reach the knocker, miss.'

Poppy caught up with him at last and she rapped on the door. 'Do you have a name, boy?'

'Of course I do, miss. What d'you think I am?'

'No offence meant,' Poppy said hastily. 'I have to call you something.'

'"Oi, you" is what I gets normally, but me name's Davy.'

Before Poppy had a chance to ask for his full

name the door opened and a stern-looking woman wearing a grey dress and a voluminous white apron glared at her with an uncompromising frown.

'I think you've come to the wrong place, miss.'

Poppy was momentarily taken aback by this overt rudeness. 'I was told I might find Mr Taverner here,' she said brusquely.

'I said it's Thursday so he is bound to be here, Miss Potts. I come for me reading lesson.' Davy slipped past the woman and disappeared into the gloomy depths of the house.

Poppy could hear young children screaming and babies crying. It was not a very auspicious introduction to the King Street Orphanage.

'Mr Taverner is fully occupied, Miss er . . .' Miss Potts eyed Poppy suspiciously. 'You ought to make an appointment to see him at his office.'

Poppy did not waste time in explaining that the office was locked. She stood her ground. 'My name is Poppy Robbins, ma'am. Perhaps you would be kind enough to tell him that I am here and would value a few minutes of his time.'

Miss Potts sniffed and stepped back into the narrow hallway. 'You'd best come inside and wait, but I can't promise anything. Close the door behind you. The orphans are as slippery as eels when it comes to sneaking out of the building.' She turned away and marched off towards the back of the building.

The smell of boiling cabbage with a hint of

onions did not quite overcome the odour of carbolic and Jeyes Fluid. Poppy glanced round at the drab surroundings and her heart sank. She could only imagine how the poor orphans must feel when they stepped over the threshold for the first time. The walls were painted dark brown halfway up and the rest was a rather drab shade of cream. The bare boards on the floor and stairs were scrubbed clean but there were no pictures on the walls to relieve the dullness and not a single rug or runner on the floor. Poppy was tempted to open the door and escape out into the steamy heat on the narrow pavement, but almost immediately the sound of footsteps echoed off the high ceiling and Eddie Taverner strode towards her. She could tell by his astonished expression that her arrival had taken him by surprise.

'Poppy, what on earth are you doing here?'

'I need to talk to you, Eddie. Your little friend Davy took pity on me as I stood outside your locked office and he brought me here.'

'That boy will go far,' Taverner said with a rueful smile.

'What are you doing here is more the question,' Poppy countered boldly. 'I thought you had business interests in London. I'm sure you don't make money from exploiting poor little orphans.'

'No, that's true. This is a charity I support wholeheartedly and I visit whenever I can. I suppose this is my way of paying back a little to society. But you're right, it isn't how I make my money.'

'I suspect you are involved in some sort of jiggery-pokery, but that isn't why I'm here.' Poppy met his smile with a steady gaze. 'Do you find that amusing?'

He shook his head. 'I feel like one of the orphans being scolded by Miss Potts.'

The twinkle in his dark eyes was almost irresistible, but Poppy was not going to allow herself to fall for his undeniable charm. 'I hope you aren't comparing me with that person,' she said stiffly.

'Of course not.' Taverner glanced over his shoulder. 'We can't talk here. I'll be free in half an hour or so. Why don't you come to the classroom and wait while I finish what I'm doing?'

It was an invitation that Poppy could not resist and she followed him into the depths of the building. He ushered her into a room filled with small children seated behind wooden desks. The girls wore grey dresses and white pinafores, and the boys were also in grey uniform. Poppy was struck by the pallor of their skin and their lank, wispy hair, but even more disturbing was the lack of expression on their young faces. Miss Potts was seated behind a desk on a dais but she rose to her feet when Taverner entered the room.

'I will leave it to you, Mr Taverner. Don't allow them to take advantage of you or the young lady.' She marched out of the classroom.

The children did not move but Poppy sensed their feeling of relief when the woman in charge was no longer present. She waited eagerly to see what exactly it was that Taverner brought to the orphanage, but instead of taking his seat behind the desk he merely leaned against it in a casual manner.

'Well, now, where were we?' Taverner said lightly. 'Who remembers the story so far?'

Dozens of hands shot up and he pointed to one little girl with golden plaits. 'You first, Hannah.'

She stood up, clasping her hands behind her back. 'You was climbing the tree, mister. And you disturbed a wasps' nest.' Hannah giggled and covered her mouth with her hand as she collapsed back onto her seat.

'You got stung on the nose, mister.' A small boy stood up, pointing at Taverner and the whole class erupted into laughter.

'That's right. I did get badly stung and my nose swelled up to twice its normal size.' Taverner smiled and waited for the laughter to die down. 'Why did that happen?'

'You was stung by a wasp,' another boy volunteered.

'You was told not to climb the tree,' Hannah added seriously.

'Exactly so. The moral of that story is that I should have listened to my pa, but also that I should have made sure there was no wasps' nest in the tree. It's all right to have adventures, but you have to learn to think for yourselves. Now, we're supposed to be learning the alphabet. Who can start us off?'

Poppy covered her ears as the whole class shouted in response. The previously subdued children began competing with each other to repeat the alphabet. Taverner folded his arms and nodded his approval. When they came to the end he stepped off the dais and took a paper bag from his pocket.

'Very well done, all of you. Now come up one by one and you can have a boiled sweet, but you must go back to your seats quietly or we will all be in trouble.' Taverner held the bag out and one by one the children marched solemnly to the front to take a sweet.

Poppy's eyes filled with tears as she heard each of them say, 'Thank you, sir,' before returning to his or her desks. The eldest could have been no older than six or seven and her heart went out to them. It was true they were clean and clothed, with shoes on their feet – except for Davy who seemed to have joined in on a temporary basis – but they were all children in need of love and attention.

'You've done well, all of you. I have to leave you now, but I will be back at the same time next week,' Taverner said firmly. 'Be good and look after each other.' He ushered Poppy out of the room just as Miss Potts appeared and the class subsided into total silence.

'Thank you, Mr Taverner,' Miss Potts said stiffly. 'May we expect to see you next week as usual?'

'Of course. You know I rarely miss the opportunity to spend time with the children.'

'The funds you donate help feed and clothe them, sir.' Miss Potts shot a sideways glance at Poppy.

'I hope this continues, even should you marry and have children of your own.'

Poppy looked away, wishing she had had the forethought to take off the dazzling diamond ring and put it away somewhere safe. She had the feeling that Miss Potts assumed that Taverner was her intended and there was a warning in her words.

'Good day to you, Miss Potts.' Taverner reached the front door and opened it, allowing Poppy to go first. 'I'll see you next week, ma'am.' He followed Poppy out into the stifling heat of midday.

'What will happen to Davy?' Poppy asked urgently. 'He is still in there.'

'Davy is a law unto himself. He will have found his way to the kitchen and used his charm to persuade one of the cooks to give him food. Then he will evade all attempts to keep him in and he'll be roaming the streets by mid-afternoon.'

'But he's so little to be all on his own in the city.'

'He's one of thousands, Poppy. Sadly we cannot help them all.'

Poppy fell into step beside him. 'But there must be more that could be done. Those poor children looked so sad.'

'They are fed and clothed and they have beds to sleep in at night, otherwise they might be living on the streets and begging for food. We do what we can. Anyway, I don't know about you but I'm hungry. I suggest we go to my house in Fournier Street. My housekeeper will have luncheon ready for me and she always makes far too much.'

'You have a house in London?' Poppy stared at him in surprise.

'Did you think I slept under one of the railways bridges?' Taverner laughed. 'What odd ideas you have about me, Poppy. I am quite respectable, really.'

She had to quicken her pace in order to keep up with him. There was little opportunity to talk as Taverner seemed to know just about everyone in the area and had to respond to greetings from almost every passer-by.

When they reached the house in Fournier Street she was impressed by the imposing frontage. A maid wearing a neat black uniform opened the door to admit them and Taverner's housekeeper emerged from somewhere at the back of the house. She advanced on them, smiling.

'Luncheon is ready, sir. I see you've brought a guest. I'll just lay another place at the table.'

'Thank you, Mrs Kent. This is Miss Robbins, my fiancée. Poppy, may I introduce my much-valued housekeeper, Mrs Kent.'

Poppy shot him a withering look. 'Eddie, you promised not to say anything.'

'Don't worry, my dear,' Mrs Kent said affably. 'Mr Edward never could keep a secret, even when he was a boy.'

'You've known him that long?' Poppy stared at her in surprise.

'Yes, of course. This was Lord Taverner's town house before he retired to the country. He chose to live in the East End rather than in a smarter area of London. He said he felt more comfortable amongst the dead silk weavers and the market traders than with the rich and famous.'

'Pa is a man of the people,' Taverner said, smiling. 'Poppy is well acquainted with my father, Mrs Kent. We'll be in the parlour if you could let us know when luncheon is served.'

'Of course, sir.' Mrs Kent nodded and hurried off in the direction of the kitchen.

Taverner entered a room on the left-hand side of the hallway and beckoned to Poppy.

'Come and sit down. I think you have some explaining to do.'

Poppy entered the parlour and was suitably impressed by the elegant décor and furnishings. The subtle shades of blue and green were restful and the sofa was comfortable. She sank down amongst the satin cushions and felt instantly at home, which was ridiculous considering she had only just walked into the house.

'I am not the only one. You are even more of a mystery now than you were when I first met you. Then I believed you were a small-time criminal with a penchant for helping the poor and needy. Now I am totally confused. Who are you, Eddie? And what are you?'

Taverner went to a side table and filled two glasses

327

with sherry. He handed one to Poppy and he stood with his back to the fireplace, holding his glass in his hand.

'I am what you see. This was my childhood home in London and you now know Domesday House. It was a strange coincidence that took you there.' He raised his glass in a toast. 'Here's to strange coincidences.'

She sipped the sherry, eyeing him suspiciously. 'Why did you tell your housekeeper that we are engaged? You know it's a farce.'

'Mrs Kent is a stickler for propriety. She is the keeper of my morals and I would not offend her for anything. She would be horrified if I brought just any beautiful young lady into my home without a chaperone.'

'And yet you are a self-confessed crook. How do you make your money, Eddie?'

'I wouldn't call myself a crook. Sometimes I might bend the law a little but I make my money on the stock market.'

'That sounds very respectable.' Poppy sipped her drink. 'Why haven't you got an office in the City with clerks to do most of the work for you? Begg led me to think you were some kind of market trader.'

'I am a lot of things to many people,' Taverner said with a wry smile. 'But I like to work closely with the business heart of the city. I mix with the merchants who make the money in the first place, and I get valuable information first-hand. I'm not one to sit in an office all day.'

'Davy, the child who took me to the orphanage in King Street, told me that you go there every Thursday. Is that true?'

'I try to be there for the little ones. I help them to learn their letters and I talk to them. I tell them stories that I think might amuse and interest them. They seem to get something from my visits.'

'What inspired you to help the orphans? Surely you could just donate money and that would salve your conscience.'

Taverner shrugged and put his glass back on the tray. 'Perhaps, like you, I feel the need to help those who have not been so fortunate in life. Children are helpless and need protection, but above all they need education to get themselves out of poverty.'

The door opened and Mrs Kent entered the room. 'Luncheon is served, sir.'

'Thank you, Mrs Kent. We'll be in directly.' Taverner waited for her to leave before turning to Poppy. 'I'm sure you must be starving after travelling all the way from Devonshire, but you haven't told me why you've come all this way on your own. It must have been something very pressing.'

Poppy rose to her feet. 'Yes, that is something I wish to talk about. It's the reason I left your home and went to Dorrington Place.' Poppy followed him to the dining room and he pulled out a chair for her. She sat down, gazing appreciatively at the table laid with a white cloth and matching linen table napkins. A bowl of roses in the centre gave out a sweet scent that reminded her of Rainbow's End and she was suddenly homesick. Until now she had managed to put all thoughts of her family to the back of her mind, but now she was so much closer to home the pain of missing them was real and physical.

Taverner sat down opposite her. 'Are you all right, Poppy? You look sad.'

'It's nothing really. I was just thinking of my parents. The bowl of beautiful roses reminded me of the gardens at Rainbow's End.'

At that moment the young parlourmaid entered the room and placed a basket of hot bread rolls on the table and a plate of butter. She left the room, passing Mrs Kent, who brought in a bowl of salad and a platter of cold roast chicken, which she placed on the table.

'Thank you, Mrs Kent,' Taverner said, smiling. 'That looks delicious.'

'I'll leave you to serve yourselves, sir.' Mrs Kent nodded to Poppy and scuttled from the room, closing the door behind her.

Poppy did not need a second bidding. She had not realised quite how hungry she was until the aroma of hot bread wafted around her. She concentrated on helping herself before passing the platter and salad bowl to Taverner.

'Well, Poppy. Is this a good time for you to tell me why you felt it necessary to see me so urgently?' Taverner reached for a bread roll and broke it into small pieces.

Poppy stabbed a slice of chicken with her fork. 'You left me to deal with the Whiddon, but I hadn't heard from you. Did you intend to abandon me there permanently?'

'No, of course not. I've been attending to business matters while attempting to track down Mulliner and Miss Flyte – with no success so far, I should add.'

Poppy hesitated, trying desperately to broach a difficult subject in the most tactful way. She took a deep breath. 'You told me why you dislike Gervase Mulliner, but was that the only reason?'

A look of genuine surprise crossed Taverner's handsome features. 'What else could there be?'

Poppy toyed with the chicken, her appetite deserting her. 'I learned some disturbing news from Mr Frampton, your papa's former valet. Do you remember him?'

'Yes, of course. I thought he had retired years ago.'

'Your pa was in a terrible state and so I asked Mr Frampton to come out of retirement and look after him. I had to take on more servants. You told me I might.'

'Yes, of course. Go on, please.'

'Well, I've had a terrible time with Mrs Whiddon. She resisted all my attempts to sort out the problems created by her incompetence.'

Taverner nodded. 'That sounds like her. She's a difficult woman.'

'Not only that, but I think she's been encouraging

331

your papa to drink more heavily than he normally would, and she's part of the reason for your mama's so-called illness. Mrs Whiddon has been giving her tisanes that make her sleep and large doses of laudanum.'

'I know Whiddon has got used to running everything,' Taverner said, frowning, 'but I had no idea to what extent.'

'There's worse to come.' Poppy bit her lip. There was no way to sugar-coat the awful truth. She lowered her voice. 'It might just be gossip, Eddie, but Mr Frampton said that your papa and Mrs Whiddon knew each other before she came to work at Domesday House. It seems that they had a child, who was given up for adoption as a newborn.'

'What are you saying, Poppy?'

His bleak expression went straight to Poppy's heart, but there was no holding back now. 'The baby boy was adopted by a family called Mulliner and he was named after a saint. Do I have to go into more details?'

Taverner rose to his feet and went to stand by the window, staring out into the walled garden. 'So if I understand what you're saying, the rumour is that Gervase Mulliner is my half-brother. Is that right?'

'I'm so sorry, Eddie. That's what Mr Frampton told me, and he doesn't seem the type to spread stories that he doesn't believe are true. I realise that you already have reason to dislike Mulliner and this news must make it infinitely worse.'

Taverner returned to the table and sat down. 'I thought I had seen the last of Mulliner until I met you and learned your story, but I had no idea that he might be my half-brother. I know my father was no saint, but somehow I can't believe that he would ever have been intimate with Eliza Whiddon, even in his youth.'

'What do you think Mulliner wants of us now? Is it just money he's after?'

'That seems to be the only logical answer, Poppy. He obviously knows that blackmailing my father would be pointless. Pa relies on me for money these days, and I doubt if Mulliner would dare approach me. I would say that Lady Charlotte is his prime target, although he knows that you two are close, hence the fact that you are both at risk. It all depends upon how desperate he is for money. He used that woman Miranda Flyte to get to you as well as Lottie. I haven't been able to trace her, which is odd.'

'Perhaps she has another name, Eddie.'

'Anything is possible. But one thing of which I am absolutely sure. Gervase Mulliner is not my half-brother. I think Mrs Whiddon put that story about to suit herself. Perhaps she has been holding it over my father all these years. She certainly has got away with appalling behaviour. Had I spent more time at home I might have prevented all the misery she has caused.'

'Do you think that Mulliner is her son?'

'It makes sense, Poppy. It explains a great deal,

although his desire for revenge against your parents and the Ashton family is a separate matter, which happens to have brought us together.'

'What will you do now?' Poppy reached out to lay her hand on his as it rested on the table. It hurt her to see the pain of guilt in his eyes. The diamond ring on her finger flashed in the sunlight and she knew what she had to do. 'I want to go home. Will you take me there now, please?'

Taverner shook his head. 'You know that's not a good idea.'

She held up her left hand, pointing to the ring. 'We have to draw him out. If we announce our engagement officially it makes me a prime target for kidnap and a demand for ransom. I'm not afraid of Mulliner, but I am frightened of what all this is doing not only to you, but to my parents and the Ashton family. Mrs Whiddon will have taken over again in my absence and your parents are also at risk. We have to stop Mulliner and his awful mother before they do any more harm. What do you say, Eddie?'

Chapter Nineteen

The sight of Rainbow's End basking in the afternoon sunshine brought tears to Poppy's eyes. She climbed out of Taverner's Panhard motor car without waiting for him to assist her and she ran to the front door. She let herself in and came to a halt in the entrance hall. The dining room was empty and laid up for dining that evening.

'Mama,' she called excitedly. 'I'm home.'

The inner door opened and Flora Robbins emerged from the kitchen, her arms outstretched.

'Darling Poppy. I thought I must be dreaming.' She hugged her daughter. 'I've missed you so much. We've all missed you terribly.'

'I know, Mama. It's been horrible being so far away, but I'm here now.'

Flora glanced over Poppy's shoulder. 'Mr Taverner. You brought my girl home. Thank you so much.'

'This will be a short visit, Mrs Robbins. Poppy will explain.'

Flora looked from one to the other, frowning. 'I don't understand. Is it safe for you to come home or not, Poppy?'

'It's a little complicated, Mama.' Poppy turned to Taverner. 'I can't lie to my parents, Eddie.'

'Who's lying?' Daniel Robbins stood in the kitchen doorway. 'What's going on, Taverner?'

'I think we all need to sit down,' Taverner said firmly. 'Poppy and I have something to tell you that mustn't go any further than these four walls if we're to put a stop to Mulliner's games.'

Daniel stepped forward to embrace Poppy. 'It's good to have you back where you belong, my dear.' His smile faded as he glanced at Taverner. 'But I want to know how you fit into this, Taverner.'

'I think it's obvious, Daniel, my love.' Flora seized Poppy's left hand. 'You're engaged?'

Poppy sent a desperate look in Taverner's direction. 'Yes and no. It's complicated, Mama.'

'If we could go somewhere quiet where we won't be disturbed I'll do my best to explain,' Taverner said firmly. 'I can assure you both that I have Poppy's best interests at heart and the wellbeing of your whole family.'

'We'd better go into the parlour. We won't be disturbed for a while yet.' Daniel moved quickly to open the door. 'Your mama and I deserve a full explanation, Poppy.'

'Yes, of course, Pa.' Poppy managed a smile but she was suddenly nervous. Her parents were wonderful, but they were clearly anxious and might even forbid her to continue helping Taverner. She shot a sideways glance at Taverner and was relieved to see that he looked supremely confident. She relaxed just a little as she took a seat next to her mother.

Flora and Daniel listened intently while Taverner explained the situation. Their astonishment was obvious and Poppy had difficulty in suppressing the desire to give each of her parents a comforting hug. It was unfair to bring all this back to her own home, but there seemed to be no other way. When Taverner came to an end, he waited politely for someone to speak.

Daniel reached out to hold Flora's hand. 'I appreciate your candour, Mr Taverner. But you must understand that my wife and I do not wish our daughter to be involved in this hare-brained scheme.'

'But, Papa, I am involved already,' Poppy protested. 'Mulliner includes you and Mama in his desire to get even.'

'I don't understand,' Flora said, frowning. 'We don't know anyone called Mulliner. Who is this person?'

Poppy exchanged looks with Taverner and he gave her a barely perceptible nod.

'His mother was Mary Pettigrew, the elder sister of Ralph Pettigrew. You must remember him, Mama.'

Poppy watched her mother's reaction carefully. 'You and Uncle Freddie travelled to Pettigrew Castle to rescue Aunt Bella.'

'Of course,' Flora said, sighing. 'It isn't something I would easily forget. We did save her, thank goodness, but it was more than twenty years ago. How does Mulliner fit in?'

Poppy turned to Taverner. 'You're the best person to explain, Eddie.'

'Mary Pettigrew married Sir Charles Mulliner,' Taverner said slowly. 'It turned out that they were childless and they adopted the illegitimate son of my parents' housekeeper, Eliza Whiddon. I think Mulliner is trying to prove something, but I suspect his main motive is greed. He wants money – it's as simple as that – and he doesn't care how he gets it.'

'I understand that,' Daniel said patiently. 'However, we aren't wealthy like the Ashtons. Why would Mulliner involve us in his scheme to extort money?'

'Only Mulliner could answer that, sir.'

'What do you intend to do next, Mr Taverner?' Flora asked anxiously. 'Is Poppy in any danger?'

'I am going to hunt Mulliner down and if I can't find him I will go looking for Miranda Flyte. I can't help thinking that she holds the key to this mystery.' Taverner rose to his feet. 'I'm afraid I must leave you now, but I will keep in touch. I hope to get this matter resolved very quickly. In the meantime, I know Poppy will be safe at home with you.'

'I will make sure of that,' Daniel said firmly. 'No one threatens my daughter and gets away with it. Just say if you need help, Taverner. I want to meet this man Mulliner who threatens my family.'

'You may depend on me, sir.' Taverner shook Daniel's hand and bowed to Flora. 'Good afternoon, ma'am.'

Poppy jumped to her feet. 'I'll see you out, Eddie.' She hurried to the front door and opened it. 'What do you want me to do?' She tried to sound casual but he was standing so close to her that she could feel the warmth of his body. The heady aroma of his expensive cologne and his own personal scent drew her even closer.

'Just stay at home, Poppy. Don't take any risks. I'm going to sort this business out once and for all.'

'I know I am not important to Mulliner personally, but we are open to the public. It would be easy enough for him to find out where I am. I told you, I could draw him out. Then he'd have to declare his hand.'

'No, I don't want you to be any part of this, Poppy.'

Poppy met his intense gaze and she knew he was speaking the truth. She was lost in the depths of his dark eyes and his words wrapped around her like a warm blanket. It would be so easy to give way to the feelings that he evoked in her, but there were still answers needed. She forced herself to look away.

'We have to be practical, Eddie. What about Domesday House and your parents? I've left them to the mercies of the Whiddon. That doesn't sit well with me. I grew fond of them in the short time I spent in their company.'

'I have matters to attend to in London and then I will go and see my parents. Don't worry about them, Poppy. You've put good people in charge and I will deal personally with Mrs Whiddon. I don't want you to be involved.'

'But I am involved, Eddie. I really do care about your parents and I was just getting somewhere with Domesday House. Given time I would have brought it back to its former glory.'

Taverner raised his hand and caressed her cheek. 'I believe you, Poppy.' He bent his head and kissed her gently on the lips, but as she responded in a way that seemed only natural, he drew her into his arms and kissed her deeply until she was light-headed and trembling with desire. When he released her, just as suddenly she was left standing in the doorway, shocked by her reaction to his embrace. It was only the sound of the motor car engine that brought her back to reality. She was engulfed in a maelstrom of emotions as she watched him drive away. The last rays from the setting sun reflected in the diamond ring, turning it into a flame. Poppy raised her hand to her lips and closed her eyes. Eddie Taverner might think he could place her anywhere he chose and she would stay there like an obedient child, but he was wrong. Her personal safety meant nothing when the people she loved were in danger. Then she held her hand to her heart. He might also think he was battling on alone, but he would be mistaken in that, too. She would be with him all the way. She just had to decide upon a plan.

Next day, after a surprisingly good night's sleep, Poppy was up early and found herself automatically slipping into the normal daily routine. Daniel, as usual, had gone to give the gardeners their instructions before collecting a list of the produce needed for the kitchen that day. Flora was in the kitchen going over the bookings with Mrs Burden, Ivy Morris and Meg. The staff greeted Poppy eagerly and listened avidly to her brief account of her time in Devonshire. She could have made it even more exciting, but they needed to start work and she did not want to hold them up any longer than was necessary. It amused Poppy to find herself some sort of heroine to the kitchen staff at Rainbow's End.

She left them and went to join her mother for breakfast in the dining room.

Flora sipped her tea, eyeing Poppy curiously. 'So you are engaged, but you are not engaged. I didn't want to press the point last evening because I could see that you were tired and a little overwrought. But, darling, I don't quite understand how that works in practice.'

341

'Eddie did try to explain yesterday, Mama.' Poppy avoided meeting her mother's gaze by concentrating on buttering a slice of toast.

'It seems a very circuitous way to go about things. I mean, if you are supposedly engaged to Mr Taverner, what difference would that make to Mulliner?'

'It wasn't meant for him, Mama. Eddie had to leave me at Domesday House for my own safety while he went looking for Mulliner, but the staff had to accept me as part of the family and an engagement seemed like the best plan.'

'What did Lady Taverner say to that?'

Poppy laughed. 'I believe it was her idea. This ring belonged to her mama and she offered it to Eddie.'

'She must think a lot of you, Poppy.'

'I don't know about that, but I did try to help her. The horrid housekeeper had managed to convince Lady Taverner that she was an invalid. Whiddon dosed the poor lady with herb tisanes that made her sleepy and confused, together with large doses of laudanum.'

'That's awful, darling. Did you put a stop to it?'

'I asked the doctor to call and he was horrified by her ladyship's condition. He took over her treatment and I reinstated Lady Taverner's personal maid, whom the Whiddon had sacked. I think Eliza Whiddon had been planning to take over the whole household for years.'

'How dreadful. I have to say, I am glad you are at home, my dear. I thought you would be safer at

Dorrington Place, but then that accident placed you in jeopardy again. Who would have thought it?'

'Who indeed, Mama? It seems that Eddie and I were destined to be together.'

Flora gave her a searching look. 'Are you sure the engagement is just a ploy? It seems to me there is something going on between the two of you, even if you don't realise it.'

'It is just make-believe, Mama. I think perhaps I ought to take the ring off now and put it somewhere safe. After all, I will have to give it back to Lady Taverner when all this business with Mulliner is settled.'

'Yes, dear,' Flora said doubtfully.

'Eddie will find Mulliner and he'll make sure that he is no longer a threat to us or to the Ashtons.'

Flora sighed. 'I just hope you will be able to settle down again after all that turmoil, Poppy. It sounds very upsetting.'

'Everything will be fine, Mama. Just wait and see. In the meantime, what would you like me to do today? How many bookings have we? I'm eager to start work again.'

'Well, dear, first of all you can do the flower arrangements. I'm afraid I didn't have too much time to do them when you were away. Take a trug and pick whatever you like, only make sure it's all right with your father first. He treats the flowers and plants as if they were part of the family.'

Poppy laughed. 'Well, I suppose they are, to

him. Don't worry. I'll be very careful. I know what to avoid and the blooms I am allowed to pick. I'm really looking forward to having a nice quiet time in the flower room.'

As always, the flower room was an oasis of peace. The sweet scent of roses and lilies filled the air and sunlight streamed in through the open windows. Poppy was just about to finish the last and most complicated arrangement when the sound of male voices and laughter broke in on her peaceful solitude. The door opened and Adam rushed in, followed by Gideon.

Adam wrapped his arms around Poppy and twirled her round until she was dizzy. 'I've missed you, Poppy, my girl.' He released her and she had to clutch the worktop until the room stopped spinning.

Gideon gave her a peck on the cheek. 'It's good to see you again, Poppy. I'm sorry not to have called sooner, but I've been so busy with Pa's practice and studying for my final examinations that everything else passed me by.'

'I've been away, Gideon. I went to Dorrington Place with Lottie.' Poppy had the satisfaction of seeing a rosy blush spread across Gideon's cheeks.

'How is she? I had hoped she might still be here.'

'You really have had your head stuck in your dreary old medical tomes,' Adam said, laughing. 'The girls had to run away to Devonshire for fear of being kidnapped and held to ransom. Isn't that right, Poppy?'

'Well, yes, I suppose so. But you mustn't worry, Gideon. Lottie is safe and well at home, and probably a little bored, if the truth were told.' Poppy turned to Adam, who was leaning nonchalantly against the worktop, twirling a daisy between his fingers. 'I thought the army were going to send you to foreign parts, Adam.'

He grinned. 'I got as far as Wellington Barracks. In fact, I came round to see you and that's when your mama told me you had gone to Dorrington Place with Lottie. What's going on, Poppy? What has that fellow Mulliner to do with all this?'

'Yes, tell us, Poppy,' Gideon added. 'Why were you and Lottie in danger?'

Poppy placed the last sprig of sea holly into the arrangement and stood back, gazing at it with a critical eye. 'That's good. I haven't lost my touch.' She glanced at Gideon and she could see that he was genuinely worried about Lottie. 'Don't worry, Gideon. Nothing is going to happen to Lottie. Her papa is due to return to Dorrington Place today or tomorrow, and anyway they have a small army of ground staff as well as house servants. I doubt if a mole could get into the ground without being spotted.'

'Moles tunnel underground,' Gideon said gloomily.

'That's my point exactly.' Poppy turned to Adam and snatched the drooping daisy from his fingers.

'Leave my flowers alone, Adam Ashton. Aren't you supposed to practise marching or something when you're off duty?'

'I thought you might be pleased to see me, Poppy dear.' Adam clutched his hands to his heart, rolling his eyes dramatically. 'I've missed you. Have you been lonely without me?'

Poppy laughed. 'If only you knew what I've been through during the past few weeks since you went off to play soldiers.' She placed the daisy in a jar filled with water. 'That's enough about me. What are you two up to today?'

'Actually, I came bearing an invitation for you and your mama to attend my mother's autumn fashion show at Marsh House,' Gideon replied. 'She said to tell you and your mama it's a preview of the show she will put on in London.'

'I know I would love to come,' Poppy said eagerly. 'I'm sure that Ma would be really delighted to accept, depending on what bookings we have for that evening. Why don't you go and wait for me in the garden and I'll find out if Mama can get away from here for a few hours.'

'You do that, Poppy.' Adam opened the door for her as she picked up the large floral display. 'We'll meet you by the brook. Don't be too long.'

Poppy brushed his cheek with a kiss as she walked past. It was so good to see both her old friends again. It almost felt like days gone by, and yet not quite. Something had changed, but it was difficult to explain exactly what it was. She took the flowers to the torchère in the entrance hall and arranged them to their best advantage before going off in search of her mother.

Flora was in the wine cellar checking the stock with Beasley. She looked up, frowning.

'Is anything the matter, Poppy? I thought you were busy in the flower room?'

'I've finished the arrangements, Mama. I came to pass on an invitation from Aunt Amelia. Gideon just brought it. She's asked us if we would like to attend the preview of her London fashion show at Marsh House.'

'Oh, Poppy. You know how much I would love to, but we are so busy here. I really can't get away.'

'As a matter of fact you can, Mama. I've checked the bookings and so far that evening there are only two parties of four. I'm sure that Uncle Amos and Mrs Burden can manage that easily, and you need some time away from Rainbow's End. Do say yes.'

Flora laughed. 'I can see that you will not leave me alone until I do agree to accompany you, but it would be lovely. I'll just finish off here and then I'll write a note to Amelia, accepting for both of us.' Flora hesitated, her brow creased into deep lines. 'I'd almost forgotten that you aren't supposed to go anywhere, Poppy. Didn't you promise Eddie Taverner that you wouldn't leave here until he says you may?'

'I had my fingers crossed behind my back when I said that,' Poppy said, smiling. 'We're going, and I don't care what Eddie Taverner says. What harm could possibly come to me at a fashion show in Marsh House? Write the note and Gideon can take it to his mama.'

'Oh, all right. You win, Poppy. Anyway, it will be nice to do something together, and as you say, Marsh House is so out of the way. Who on earth could harm you there?'

'Wonderful. I'm looking forward to it already.'

'As your friends are here, why don't you spend some time with them?' Flora handed the check list to Beasley. 'I think that's enough for today. We'll finish this off tomorrow, Beasley.'

'Thank you, ma'am.' Beasley tucked the list away in a dusty ledger. 'I'll bring up the wine for luncheon.'

'I don't know what I'd do without you, Beasley.' Flora picked up her skirts and followed Poppy up the steps to the ground floor. 'I'll write the note, Poppy, and you can enjoy some time with Adam and Gideon. You'll be safe enough with an army officer and a doctor. Even Eddie Taverner could not find fault with that.' She hurried to the entrance hall where she found paper and a pen on the desk.

'Thank you, Mama. It would be nice to spend a little time with them.' Poppy waited for her mother to scribble a note of acceptance before going to find Adam and Gideon. As she had suspected, they had followed the river bank to the clearing beneath the trees, and were pelting each other with last autumn's beech mast.

Poppy waved the note. 'Mama says yes. We would love to accept.'

Gideon smiled. 'That's good, Poppy. Why don't you come back with us to Marsh House and give the letter to my mother in person in case I forget or mislay it?'

'I'm supposed to stay close to home,' Poppy said, half to herself. But then she remembered her mother's words. What harm could come to her with two old friends, both of them young and strong and unlikely to allow any harm to come to her?

Marsh House had changed little since Poppy had been going there as a child. The grounds were better cared for now, but the old dead tree still stood in the middle of a neatly clipped lawn, its bare branches a lookout post for crows and squirrels. The only real change was the fact that the barns had been converted to workshops. The noise of the sewing machines was such a constant thrumming sound that it seemed almost as natural as that of a beehive or the babbling of the brook that ran alongside the outer wall. Part of the rambling old farmhouse was used as a surgery for Dr Todd Taylor and Gideon, although Todd also had consulting rooms in Harley Street, where sick children were brought for his expert opinion. The long gallery at the top of the house was where the fashion shows were held. Poppy had grown up with stories from her mother of how both she and Amelia had struggled when they were young, but now they were both successful wives, mothers and businesswomen. They filled Poppy with admiration as well as enduring love and devotion.

Amelia had premises in the West End, but she preferred to work from home and her office was set up in the former dairy. It was there that Poppy headed, hoping to give Amelia the acceptance note in person. As luck would have it, Amelia was seated behind her desk, frowning over a pile of leaflets. She looked up and a smile transformed her face. Her blue eyes shone with pleasure at the sight of Poppy.

'This is a lovely surprise, Poppy. I haven't seen you for ages.'

'It's good to see you, too, Aunt Amelia. I've been in Devonshire, staying with Aunt Bella and Lottie, and I've only just returned home.'

Amelia gave her a quizzical look. 'I sense there is more to that story but, as I said, it's lovely to see you. Did Gideon give you the invitation?'

'Yes, and I've brought the acceptance note from Mama. I wanted to give it to you in person in case Gideon mislaid it.'

Amelia laughed. 'You know my son so well. I think he was hoping that Lottie might be at Nine Oaks.'

'It's a long and complicated story,' Poppy said

wearily. 'Lottie had to return to Dorrington Place for her own safety.'

'You can't leave it there, Poppy.' Amelia set the leaflets aside. 'I want to hear the full story. My head is so full of details about gowns and accessories, and everything that goes with putting on a fashion show, that it will be a blissful relief to listen to someone else's problems.' She leaned back in her chair and folded her hands in her lap. 'Sit down, Poppy, and start at the beginning. Tell me everything.'

Amelia was a good listener and she sat quietly taking in everything Poppy said until she came to the end of the complicated story.

'My goodness. Who would have believed it? Of course, I remember hearing about poor Bella's experiences with the Pettigrew family, but it's hard to believe that someone who is not related to them by blood has taken it upon himself to avenge the family name.'

'I think Gervase Mulliner is interested only in what he can make from the situation,' Poppy said grimly. 'If he is Eliza Whiddon's son I wouldn't expect him to have any feeling for others. He is just out for himself.'

'You've mentioned Eddie Taverner, but I think I detect something more than a casual acquaintanceship, on your part at least.' Amelia smiled. 'I can't say I blame you, dear. He's a handsome devil, quite ruthless in business, but tireless in fund raising for the various children's homes.'

'You know him?'

'I've met him a couple of times at charity events. He can be very charming, but I wouldn't care to get on the wrong side of him.'

'He's been very fair with me,' Poppy said defensively. 'It was Begg, Uncle Amos's right-hand man, who told me to get in touch with Eddie. I wanted to do something for poor children, but I didn't know how to go about it.'

'And you became involved with someone who, on one hand is a benefactor to orphans, and on the other is a ruthless businessman.' Amelia leaned forward, picking up the bundle of leaflets. 'You have given me an idea, Poppy. I've been studying these fliers and there was something missing. I couldn't put my finger on it, but you've solved the problem.'

'I have?' Poppy stared at her in surprise. 'How so?'

'I haven't always been well off, Poppy. My father, God rest his soul, was a dedicated doctor in the East End who rarely took money from the sick and needy. We were reduced to living in poverty until my grandfather left me a mourning garment manufactory. I was fortunate and I've worked hard, as have your parents.'

Poppy nodded in agreement. 'Yes, I realise that, Aunt Amelia. I can't tell you how much I admire both you and my mama.'

'We try to give back to society, Poppy. I will allot time for you in the middle of the show, when you can put your case for the orphans in King Street and ask for donations to the charity. You will be responsible for collecting the money and keeping a record of the donors. You could even set up a raffle and I will give one of my millinery creations as a prize.'

Poppy was breathless with excitement. 'That is so kind of you. It's a wonderful idea. I'll put everything I can into organising it. My parents might be persuaded to add a meal for two at Rainbow's End as another prize.'

Amelia smiled. 'I love your enthusiasm, but it will entail some effort on your part. Are you sure you want to do this, because I need to get the amendment to the leaflets to the printers today.'

Poppy had a sudden vision of Taverner's face if he discovered that she had broken cover in such a way. She knew instinctively what he would say and it would not be in the affirmative. But Taverner did not rule her life. Then she remembered young Davy, starving, dirty and yet eager to learn his letters. That decided her. She was not going to pass up this golden opportunity to raise money for the orphanage.

'I'll do it, Aunt Amelia. Thank you for giving me a chance to actually do something good. I've seen so much that is horrible recently that it will be wonderful to put it all to one side and help at least a few poor children.' Poppy rose to her feet and was about to leave when the door opened and Gideon burst into the office, followed by Adam.

'Mama, there's a telegram for you. It's just arrived.'

Amelia opened it and her face paled to ashen.

'What is it, Aunt Amelia?' Poppy asked urgently. 'Are you all right?'

'It's from Freddie. I can hardly bear to read it out.' Amelia handed the document to Gideon.

'What does it say?' Poppy demanded.

Gideon swallowed hard. 'Arthur kidnapped. Ransom demanded. Bringing family to Nine Oaks today. Frederick Ashton.'

Chapter Twenty

Poppy was so shocked that even when Adam drove her back to Rainbow's End she had difficulty in putting her feelings into words. Adam said nothing during the journey, but Poppy could tell by the set of his jaw that he was fuming. It was only when he drew up outside her home that Poppy had the courage to speak.

'What will you do now, Adam?'

'I haven't any choice other than to return to the barracks, but I'll request compassionate leave. My parents and Lottie need me.'

'Yes, of course. I wonder why they are coming to Nine Oaks, especially since your papa has only just returned to Devonshire.'

'I don't know, Poppy. I'll find out later.'

'Try not to worry, Adam. The police will find Arthur and I'll do what I can to comfort Lottie. I really thought it would be one of us girls who was taken hostage. It never crossed my mind that they would take a ten-year-old boy.'

Adam's knuckles whitened as he clutched the steering wheel. 'They'll regret laying their hands on him if I get hold of them. Arthur can be a pest, but he's my brother and no one harms my family and gets away with it.'

Poppy climbed out of the motor car. 'Don't do anything stupid, Adam. Leave it to your papa and the police.' She moved away quickly as Adam put his foot down on the accelerator and the car shot forward, careering out into the lane at a speed that sent clouds of dust into the air. Poppy entered the house wondering how she was going to break the news to her parents. They had always been fond of Arthur, and while Mulliner's threats had been vague, this time he had gone one step further and they were all involved.

All was quiet at Rainbow's End. It seemed that Mrs Burden and the kitchen staff were having their afternoon break, but Flora and Daniel were in the kitchen. They greeted Poppy with obvious relief.

'It could have been you, Poppy.' Flora took a seat at the table, but Daniel remained standing at her side.

'Why did you go to Marsh House, anyway?' he demanded angrily. 'I thought you had promised Mr Taverner that you would stay at home until Mulliner was apprehended.'

'I was with Adam and Gideon so I knew I'd be safe.'

There was a stony silence and Poppy looked from one to the other. 'The whole family will be at Nine Oaks later today. Perhaps you could call on them, Pa? I doubt if we can help, but at least they will know we are all thinking of them.'

'I think you should, darling,' Flora added, giving Daniel the special smile she reserved for him. 'You know that Freddie thinks the world of you.'

Daniel shrugged. 'I don't know that, Flora. But I do know how I would feel if it were Poppy who had been abducted. This business has gone on for long enough. We all need to stand up to Mulliner and bullies like him.'

'Where would they take a boy of Arthur's age?' Flora said, frowning. 'Arthur wouldn't go quietly. He would kick up a terrible fuss.'

Poppy had a sudden idea that almost took her breath away. However, it was not something she could share with her parents. It was just a theory, but if the Whiddon really was Mulliner's mother, and if he had become reconciled with her after having been raised by adoptive parents, then the logical place to take a small boy would be Domesday House. It was not too far from Dorrington Place, and it was not high on anyone's visiting list. The Whiddon had seen to that over the years.

'What do you think, Poppy?' Daniel asked eagerly. 'You seem to know more about this than any of us. What did Taverner tell you about Gervase Mulliner?'

'I don't think he knows any more than you and I,

Pa. Mulliner's adoptive mother was Miss Pettigrew before she married Sir Charles. Maybe Mulliner has only just learned the history of the Pettigrew family, or perhaps he always knew and he is simply desperate for money. Either way that doesn't help us to find Arthur. Poor boy, he must be very scared.'

'Go to Nine Oaks, Daniel,' Flora said firmly. 'You can make sure the servants have everything ready for the family when they arrive. They'll be exhausted and worried sick, so they need a hot meal and beds that are aired and ready for them.'

Daniel dropped a kiss on the top of Flora's copper curls. 'You are always so practical, my love. I'll go now and I'll let you know if I learn any more from them.' He left the room.

Poppy heard the back door open and close. She could imagine her father striding out through the gardens that belonged to Rainbow's End, and across the ha-ha that separated Ashton land from theirs. She had complete faith in her father. Pa would make sure that everything was being done properly at Nine Oaks, and Mama would no doubt start baking pies or something that she could send round to the great house, just in case the cooks there had not had time to prepare a proper meal for the travellers. Poppy went to her room and closed the door. If she was right about Mulliner taking Arthur to Domesday House there was only one person who could help.

*　*　*

Next morning Poppy was up while everyone else was fast asleep. She washed, dressed and put on her best bonnet before leaving the house, taking care not to disturb her parents or the live-in staff. It was a fine morning with a promise of a hot day to come. The grass was pearled with dew as she made her way to Nine Oaks and she was accompanied by birdsong from the trees and hedgerows. As she had expected, there was already activity in the great house. Poppy knew that Ivy's sister, Betsy, was one of the scullery maids, and she found her outside in the yard filling a hod with fuel for the range.

'Heavens above, miss. You gave me a start.' Betsy straightened up. 'What are you doing here so early?'

'I need to see Mr Adam,' Poppy said urgently. 'It's very important. Will you go upstairs to his room and ask him to come down immediately.'

Betsy's mouth drooped at the corners. 'I daren't, miss. It would be more than me life was worth to go above stairs.'

'It really is important, Betsy. Tell him it's to do with Master Arthur.'

Betsy's eyes filled with tears. 'I can't bear to think of it, miss. He used to play bat and ball with us kids in the village. Who could do such a wicked thing?'

'Who indeed! So please fetch Mr Adam, Betsy.'

'I'll do it for Master Arthur, but if I lose me job it will be your fault, miss.' Betsy lifted the hod and carried it into the scullery.

Poppy waited anxiously and was beginning to

359

think that Betsy had failed in her mission when the back door flew open and Adam stepped out into the yard. He stared at her bleary-eyed.

'What on earth is going on, Poppy? Why are you here at this ungodly hour?'

'I think I know where Arthur might be.'

'Tell me. I'll go there and bring him home.'

'It's not as easy as that, Adam. I may be wrong but I have a feeling that Mulliner might have called on his birth mother to help him. If so, then Arthur is probably hidden away at Domesday House.'

'Then that's where I'll go. Gideon will come with me and we'll force the truth out of that woman.'

'That won't work. You haven't met the Whiddon. She's an extremely difficult person to deal with, as I know to my cost. I can easily believe that Mulliner is her son, but this needs to be done by stealth if we're to rescue Arthur.' Poppy laid her hand on Adam's sleeve. She could feel his distress and she knew how fond he was of the Afterthought. 'I don't think they'll hurt Arthur. They're both greedy and self-serving, but I don't imagine they would stoop to violence, especially to a child.'

Adam shook his head. 'Well then, General Robbins, what do you suggest?'

The title made Poppy smile in spite of everything. 'I don't think I can do this on my own, but if you would drive us to the railway station we can catch a train and then hire a vehicle of some sort at the other end. I was running the household for a while so all the servants

know me. They think I am engaged to Eddie Taverner.'
Poppy held up her hand to show off the diamond ring.

'A fine stone.' Adam eyed the ring suspiciously.
'Is it true?'

'Of course not. I'll tell you everything on the way
to the station. You may leave me there if you don't
wish to go to Devonshire, but I am going anyway.'

'Try to stop me. I'd do anything for Arthur. I
might make jokes about the young pest, but I love
him really.' Adam gave her a searching look. 'Did
you leave a note for your parents?'

'I just scribbled something to the effect that they
were not to worry.'

Adam frowned. 'Which will probably make them
even more anxious. However, if I do something
similar, both sets of parents will realise we've gone
together, and they'll know I will look after you.'

'Really? Like the time you pushed me into the
lake at Nine Oaks when I could barely swim?'

'When we were children? I pulled you out, didn't I?'

'If I remember rightly it was Gideon who saved
me from drowning. But it doesn't matter now. Let's
go before your parents wake up.'

'Give me a few minutes to throw some things in a
bag.' Adam hesitated. 'You're travelling light. How
long do you expect to stay at Domesday House?'

'As long as it takes. I left some clothes there.
Please hurry, Adam.'

*　*　*

It was mid-morning by the time they arrived at Paddington Station. Adam had changed his mind about driving there as he did not want to leave his motor car parked in a side street for days. Poppy understood, but she was frustrated at having to wait for one of the grooms to bring a carriage round to the side entrance, and by this time the traffic in London was building up so that it took much longer than she had hoped to reach their destination. They had just missed one train and would have to wait for an hour before the next one. Adam made light of the delay, but Poppy's fears were justified when she spotted Taverner striding along the platform towards them.

'What the hell did you think you were doing, Poppy?' he demanded angrily. 'If you're planning to go to Devonshire you'd better think again.'

'You can't stop her, if that's what she wants.' Adam stepped forward, placing himself between Poppy and Taverner.

'You don't understand, Eddie,' Poppy said hastily. 'I think that's where Mulliner has taken Arthur.'

'Then it's just as well I came to stop you from making a grave mistake.'

'What do you know?' Poppy demanded, edging between them. She turned to Adam, frowning. 'For goodness' sake stop acting as if you're going to start a fight. Let's talk about this sensibly.'

Adam took a step backwards. 'I don't like the way he talks to you, Poppy.'

'This isn't about me. We're all trying to find Arthur.' Poppy eyed Taverner curiously. 'Well? How did you know I was here, for a start?'

'I went to Rainbow's End earlier to tell you what I know, but you'd gone and your parents were frantic. I had a feeling you'd head for Domesday House and it appears I was right.'

'I hope you aren't just saying that?' Poppy faced him angrily. 'What news of Arthur?'

'I know that Arthur isn't at Domesday House because Mrs Whiddon called on me in Fournier Street yesterday.'

'She's in London?' Poppy's hand flew to cover her mouth. 'Why would she leave Domesday House?'

'She came to demand money from me in return for information as to Arthur's whereabouts.'

'Why would she come to you and not my father?' Adam demanded impatiently. 'This sounds like a hoax to me.'

'It doesn't ring true, Eddie,' Poppy added slowly. 'Arthur isn't part of your family.'

'No, of course not, but Eliza Whiddon knows she's finished at Domesday House. I was going to give her the sack and she pre-empted me. She and Mulliner are working together to get as much money from me and from your family, Adam, as they can. The only thing that prevents us from going to the police is the fact that we still don't know where they are keeping Arthur.'

'What did you say to her, Eddie?' Poppy clenched her hands at her sides. She could only imagine how a child held captive by unscrupulous blackmailers must be feeling. It made her physically ill to think of poor little Arthur alone and frightened.

'I told her I wanted proof that Arthur was safe and unharmed.'

'What did she say to that?' Adam slipped his arm around Poppy's shoulders and gave her a comforting hug. 'I would have wanted to strangle the woman.'

'A natural reaction.' Taverner nodded in agreement. 'But that wouldn't solve anything. I sent her away, but I know she'll be back with an increased demand. I needed to speak to your parents, Ashton, and to Poppy's mother and father. But you two put a stop to that by running away.'

'We didn't run away,' Poppy said crossly. 'We were trying to save Arthur.'

'You won't do it by travelling to Devonshire. You'd best come with me and I'll drive you home, Poppy. You, too, Ashton.'

'All right,' Poppy said slowly. 'But where do you think Arthur is being held? You must have some idea or you wouldn't be so sure of yourself.' Poppy fell into step beside Taverner with Adam close behind them.

'Mrs Whiddon came to London, which makes me think that Mulliner and Arthur can't be too far away. I've been trying to find Miranda Flyte, with no luck so far, but I'm sure she knows something. They were working closely together in the beginning but she seems to have faded into the mist.'

'I agree.' Poppy clutched Taverner's arm in an attempt to keep up with him. 'At one time I couldn't seem to move but I'd find her at my side.'

'I have contacts,' Taverner said vaguely. 'I'll find her soon, don't worry on that score. The best thing you can do, Poppy, is to stay at home with your parents and allow me to do the rest.'

'Yes, Eddie,' Poppy said meekly. She avoided meeting Adam's gaze as he caught up with them. He always knew when she was not telling the whole truth.

There was little that Poppy could do during the next few days other than to obey Taverner's instruction and stay at home. The restaurant was very busy and there was plenty to occupy her, but she was desperate to help in any way she could. Freddie and Arabella allowed Lottie to visit nearly every day but only if she was accompanied by Adam or Gideon. This amused Poppy because she knew that spending more time together was exactly what Lottie and Gideon wanted. They would have been perfectly happy, except for the fact that Arthur was missing. Adam had returned to the barracks as the police were now involved. Even so, he was not happy about leaving his parents and Lottie, but Freddie had promised to let him know the moment there was any news.

When she was not working in the kitchen or the restaurant, Poppy spent time preparing the raffle for the upcoming fashion show at Marsh House. Amelia was very sympathetic and had visited the Ashtons at Nine Oaks, arriving in a brand-new motor car she had recently purchased, with Gideon at the wheel. She had even managed to persuade a distraught Arabella to attend the show at Marsh House together with Lottie, Poppy and Flora.

On the evening of the fashion show Gideon drove to Nine Oaks to pick up Arabella and Lottie, and then on to Rainbow's End to collect Flora and Poppy. It was a bit of a squash in the back seat, but that made them all giggle and it set the tone for the evening. Arabella looked pale and tired, but after a glass of champagne when they arrived at Marsh House, and the sympathetic greetings from friends and acquaintances alike, she seemed to revive a little. Poppy was thrilled to see so many well-dressed, well-heeled ladies taking their seats in the long gallery. It boded well for the raffle and contributions to the King Street Orphanage. She had not had an opportunity to tell Taverner of her plan to raise funds for the institution. In fact, she had not seen him since he had brought her home from Paddington Station. It was frustrating, but there was nothing she could do other than to wait for him to contact her, or at least to pass on to the family any information he might have regarding Arthur's whereabouts. Poppy tried resolutely to put Taverner out of her mind.

Amelia had suggested that Poppy should give her speech at the interval when the ladies were served with wine and tasty canapés that Amelia had ordered from Rainbow's End. This would be the best time to offer the raffle tickets and the guests would be more likely to purchase them when in a happy mood. As the first half progressed it was obvious that the gowns, travelling outfits, evening dresses and millinery were going down very well indeed. Amelia's assistants were busy noting down orders and the names of ladies who wished to book a private appointment with Amelia herself. Poppy had just reached the back row when she saw a familiar face and she froze, her heartbeat racing. At first she thought it was her imagination, and then she realised from the look on the young woman's face that the person seated at the far end of the row was none other than Miranda Flyte.

For a moment both of them stared at each other as if frozen with shock, but then the woman next to Miranda stood up and asked for some raffle tickets. Miranda seized the opportunity to slip past them and she had left the long gallery before Poppy had completed the transaction. She bundled up the remaining tickets and the pouch containing the money and thrust them into Lottie's hands.

'That was Miranda Flyte. Take over from me, Lottie. I'm going after her.' Without waiting for an answer Poppy hurried past the surprised ladies and broke into a run. When she reached the top landing she caught sight of Miranda's elegant feathered hat disappearing round the curve in the staircase. There was nothing for it but to descend as fast as she could and give chase. What she had not bargained for was that Miranda had a motor car at her disposal and she drove off just as Poppy stepped out of the front entrance. In the twilight Poppy could just see Gideon's motor car, which happened to be the same model as Adam's. She did not think twice as she cranked the engine and climbed into the driver's seat. She had only driven a motor car once, but she had watched carefully when Adam was at the wheel and she had no intention of allowing Miranda to get away. Poppy put her foot on the accelerator. The car shot forward in a series of bunny hops, but she was not going to be put off. She managed to get control of the vehicle and sped after Miranda's motor car, which was getting further and further ahead. It was almost dusk, but the roads were quiet and Miranda's motor was light coloured and impossible to miss. Poppy pressed down on the accelerator regardless of the speed limit. The local constabulary would almost definitely be having supper in the police station and the only living thing Poppy saw was a fox as it hurled itself over a hedge to safety.

They were miles from the nearest village when Miranda's car juddered to a halt. Poppy had to slam on the brakes or she might have crashed into the stricken vehicle. She leaped out and marched up to the driver's side of the motor to prevent Miranda from getting out.

'Where were you going in such a hurry, Miss Flyte?'

'None of your business,' Miranda said crossly. 'I think this wretched thing needs filling up with motor spirit. I should have stolen a horse.'

'Where is Arthur Ashton?' Poppy folded her arms and leaned against the door. 'You're not going anywhere until you tell me what I want to know.'

'I don't know what you're talking about, Poppy.'

'Then why did you run away the moment you saw me?'

'I remembered a previous engagement,' Miranda said vaguely. 'Where is the nearest place to buy motor spirit?'

'I'll take you to one, but only if you tell me where to find Arthur.'

'I told you I don't know anything about the boy.'

'But you do know that Arthur is just a child, so you must have some idea of his whereabouts. You are related to Mulliner in some way, so please don't feign ignorance.'

Miranda clasped the steering wheel with both hands. She sat very still, staring ahead and avoiding meeting Poppy's eyes.

'You can sit there all night or you can come with me.' Poppy turned and started walking back to Gideon's car. She resisted the temptation to glance over her shoulder when she heard the car door open and close, followed by the sound of quick footsteps.

'You can't leave me here, in the middle of nowhere. It will be completely dark soon.'

'It's not my fault you ran out of motor spirit.' Poppy climbed into the driver's seat. She was confident that Miranda would not try to walk on her own in the dark. 'Tell me what you know or I'll leave you here. You'll be unlikely to be found before dawn, unless of course the foxes or badgers fancy a taste of human flesh.'

Miranda shuddered dramatically. 'They don't harm people, do they?'

'Only those who kidnap innocent children and keep them away from their loved ones. I'm losing patience, Miranda. Tell me where Arthur is and I promise I will drive you to wherever you were heading.'

Miranda shifted from one foot to the other. She wrapped her arms around herself and shivered visibly. 'I knew it was a mistake to go to that wretched fashion show. Why venture into the sticks when you can view the fashions in the comfort of a London salon?'

Poppy drummed her fingers on the steering wheel. 'I'm not waiting much longer.'

'Grimstone Hall. It's about three miles from here.'

'I know it,' Poppy said as she opened the door and picked up the cranking handle. 'It was empty for years. I heard that someone had bought it.' She went round to the front of the car and cranked the engine. It was sheer luck that it started at the first swing and she resumed her seat. It was fortunate that Poppy was well acquainted with the area and she drove off, heading for the hamlet where Grimstone Hall was situated. They did not speak during the three-mile drive, although Poppy shot a sideways glance at Miranda from time to time. The anger she had felt at first had melted away, leaving her even more curious. Miranda had not admitted anything, although Poppy was certain she knew exactly what had happened to Arthur. She drew up in front of the mansion, which looked as grim as its name in the pale moonlight. The once-white stucco was now discoloured and chunks had fallen off to reveal patches of the original brickwork. The unlit windows stared blindly into the darkness and the only sound was the hoots of two owls calling to each other.

Miranda's breathing was ragged. 'He'll kill me when he finds out I've made a mess of things,' she said anxiously. 'And if he doesn't, that mother of his will.'

'All I care about is Arthur. Is he here, Miranda? You'd better not be lying.'

Miranda climbed stiffly from the passenger seat and walked over to the front door. She tugged at the bell pull and the sound of it echoed eerily throughout the ground floor of the seemingly deserted house.

'Are you sure this is the right place?' Poppy was suddenly nervous. There was something odd going on with Miranda. She was visibly distressed and trembling. But before Poppy could question her there was the sound of heavy footsteps advancing towards the main door, and it opened with hinges grating metal on metal.

'What's going on?' Mulliner held a lantern in his hand, his lips twisted in anger. 'Why have you brought her here, you stupid woman?'

'It wasn't my fault, dearest,' Miranda said feebly.

Poppy stared at them in disbelief. 'What is going on between you two?' When neither of them answered, she raised her voice. 'Where is Arthur? I've come to take him home.'

Chapter Twenty-One

Mulliner grabbed Poppy by the arm and dragged her over the threshold. 'You don't come here demanding things, Miss Robbins.' He glowered at Miranda. 'Come inside, woman, and close the door.'

The entrance hall was in deep shadow, making it difficult to pick out any details, but the smell of must and damp was almost overpowering.

'Let me go, Mulliner,' Poppy cried angrily. 'I brought Miranda here because her motor car ran out of fuel. I had no idea that you were here.'

'Why wouldn't I be? She's my wife.'

'For my sins,' Miranda said in a low voice.

'What did you say, wife?' Mulliner struck her a blow, sending her reeling and she collapsed on the floor. 'You'll behave with respect in front of our guest, Miranda.'

Poppy helped Miranda to her feet. 'You're cousins,

but you still married this brute. You must be even more stupid than I thought, Miranda.'

'Leave me alone.' Miranda pulled away from her and staggered unsteadily towards a door on the far side of the hall.

'Go with her,' Mulliner said abruptly. 'Unless you too want to feel the back of my hand.'

'I would walk out of here but I think you're holding the child, so I'll do as you say.' Holding her head high, Poppy hurried after Miranda and found herself in a dimly lit room with a fire burning in the hearth. Seated in one of the only two chairs in the otherwise empty room, was none other than Eliza Whiddon. She cackled with laughter.

'The boot is on the other foot now, then, Miss Robbins. Does your supposed fiancé know that you're gallivanting around the countryside at night?'

'I heard that you were in town, Mrs Whiddon.' Poppy managed to keep her voice steady with difficulty. 'So it's true, this man is your love child.'

Mulliner threw back his head and laughed. 'That woman doesn't know the meaning of the word love. She sold me when I was an infant.'

'You had a decent upbringing with the Mulliners, Gervase. Which is more than you would have had, had I tried to raise you myself.' Eliza shot a cursory glance in Miranda's direction. 'What's the matter with her? Why is she snivelling?'

'Your bullying son just clouted me round the

head,' Miranda sobbed. 'He's a brute. I don't know why I married him.'

'You married me because you wanted to get away from your bullying father.' Mulliner placed the lantern on the mantelshelf. 'I've fed and clothed you for the last five years, haven't I? And what do I get? Nothing but whining and complaints.'

'Where were you this evening, Miranda?' Mrs Whiddon demanded. 'You took the motor car that my son bought with his hard-earned money. Did he say you could drive it?'

'I sent her on a mission, Ma.' Mulliner sprawled in the chair opposite his mother. 'We can't keep the brat much longer. I sent Miranda to the fashion show where she would mix with wealthy, overdressed women showing off their jewels. Miranda is a talented dip, with a gift for lifting expensive gems from the unwary.'

Despite the difficulties in which she found herself, Poppy was fascinated by the insight into Miranda's criminal activities. 'Why did you insinuate yourself into my family, Miranda? We aren't wealthy. We work hard for our living.'

Miranda shuddered. 'It was fun at first. Gervase knew that you are friendly with the Ashtons. They are disgustingly rich.'

'So we were there to provide you with an excuse to mix with the aristocracy? Did you intend to kidnap Arthur all along?'

'Who says we kidnapped him?' Mrs Whiddon lit

a small black cheroot with a spill from the fire. She puffed smoke into the still air.

'Oh, for heaven's sake, give the boy back to his family,' Miranda said, wiping her eyes on a scrap of a handkerchief. 'He's more trouble than he's worth. Anyway, I reckon I did you proud tonight, Gervase. I didn't deserve a clip round the lughole.'

Mulliner jumped to his feet. 'Show us what you got then.'

Miranda backed away from him. 'No. Not unless you let the boy go. I'm sick of looking after him. I don't like kids and he's a grumpy little devil. He tried to bite me this morning when I took him his bread and water.'

Poppy faced Mulliner. 'Let him go. I'll take him home and I won't tell anyone where I found him.'

Mulliner laughed. 'You must think I'm a fool, Poppy Robbins.' He turned to Miranda. 'Take her to the boy and lock her in with him. I'll deal with Miss Robbins in the morning.'

'You can't do that,' Poppy protested, backing away. 'They'll come looking for me. I left a room filled with dozens of people, all of whom witnessed my sudden departure.'

'They won't think about looking here,' Mulliner said casually. 'I'll send you home with a message in the morning, but the boy stays here.'

'What about the jewellery I stole this evening?' Miranda held up a gold chain with a diamond-encrusted cross, a gold watch and a pearl necklace. 'There's a few quids' worth here, Gervase.'

'The motor car she drove up in is worth more than those gewgaws. You're a fool, Miranda. It's not just the money I want, it's the public humiliation of the Ashtons and the Robbinses. But for them I might have grown up in a castle with a noble lord to sponsor me.'

'No, you wouldn't,' Mrs Whiddon said firmly. 'Mary Pettigrew was Ralph's sister. Even if he had inherited the title and the castle, it wouldn't have made any difference to her. She would still have married Charles Mulliner, and you were adopted. You haven't an ounce of Pettigrew blood in your veins.'

'You say that, Ma, but they did choose to have me as their son. If my uncle had not been cheated out of his inheritance I would have been officially related to the nobility, and that would have opened doors to me. As it is I've had to resort to abducting a spoiled brat in order to boost my income.'

'You spend money like a fool, Gervase. It wouldn't matter how much you were given, it would be gone in a flash.' Mrs Whiddon tapped ash from her cheroot into the fireplace. 'I have no patience for you.'

'According to what you say, Ma, my real father is a peer of the realm, even if I was born on the wrong side of the blanket.'

'Oh dearie me, such a sad story.' Mrs Whiddon puffed on the cheroot. 'Your pa was a blacksmith,

Gervase. I made up the story about Lord Taverner being your father because it suited me to have a hold over him.'

Poppy could see that Mulliner was shaken by this admission. His mouth worked silently and he clenched his fists. 'That's not true, but I paid him back for denying me my birthright. I set fire to Domesday House. It's a pity the whole place did not go up in the conflagration.'

'Don't say any more, Gervase. Don't incriminate yourself.' Miranda hurried to his side. 'She's just saying that to irk you, Gervase.'

'I'm telling the truth,' Mrs Whiddon said, curling her lip. 'You're no aristocrat. Your father was a drunk and a bully. I dare say you take after him more than you know. You were lucky to have been adopted by a well-respected family.'

'I don't believe you.' Mulliner stared at her, shaking his head. 'You're an evil old woman and you're lying for some reason best known to yourself.'

Mrs Whiddon shrugged. 'Believe what you like, son. From now on I think I'd better take charge of matters here.' She pointed to Miranda. 'You, do something useful. Take Miss High-and-Mighty to the boy's room and leave her there.'

Poppy was about to refuse, but she wanted to make sure that Arthur was unharmed. Miranda picked up a candlestick and lit the candle with a spill.

'Come on then, Poppy. Don't try to escape because Mulliner will catch you and bring you back.

You don't want to get on his wrong side, as I know to my cost.' She left the room with Poppy following.

It was a relief to get away from the poisonous atmosphere that Mrs Whiddon and her son created around them. Miranda led the way to the first floor, which if anything was even more dilapidated. Poppy was glad that she could not see into the depths of the shadows, but the cobwebs hanging from the ceiling tickled her neck and stuck to her hair. She could imagine great hairy spiders crawling all over her, which made her flesh creep. When she reached the landing she hesitated in order to pluck a cobweb from her hair and shake out her skirts.

'He's in here.' Miranda took a key from the chain hanging from her waist and unlocked the nearest door. 'Go inside, Poppy. Don't try anything.'

Poppy stepped into the room. A single candle flickered in the draught when Miranda closed the door. An iron bedstead was pushed up against the far wall and Poppy could see a small shape curled up on the bare mattress. She picked up the candlestick and crossed the floor to make sure that the child was Arthur. He looked as though he had cried himself to sleep as the tears had dried on his dirty cheeks. He was fully dressed although his shoes were nowhere to be seen. Poppy resisted the impulse to wrap her arms around him and give him a hug; she did not want to wake him. She could only hope his dreams were pleasant. It was a relief to know he was alive and reasonably well, but now she was faced with the problem of how to get him away from this awful place and back to the safety of his loving family.

There was a worn armchair by the fireplace. Poppy sat down gingerly, half expecting the springs to burst through the threadbare material, but to her surprise it was reasonably comfortable. She did not doubt that a search party would have been sent looking for her, but Grimstone Hall was in a secluded spot at the end of a narrow lane and they would have difficulty in finding it in the darkness. Poppy sank back in the chair and closed her eyes. She did not expect to sleep but she knew she must get some rest. She needed to be alert at daybreak when she would try to find a way to get Arthur to freedom.

It was not quite light when Poppy awakened to find Arthur tugging at her sleeve.

'Poppy, you came for me.'

She sat up straight, gazing at him dazedly for a moment and then she put her arms around him. She held him close and there were tears of relief in her eyes.

'We've all been searching for you, Arthur. I was fortunate that someone led me to you, although it was quite unintentional on their part.'

Arthur drew away, meeting her anxious gaze with a smile. 'I wasn't scared, Poppy. I was just angry with them for bringing me here. Is my mama very upset?'

'Yes, of course she is, and so is your pa.' Poppy stood up and stretched. Her limbs ached from the cramped position in the old chair, but she was now wide-awake and alert.

'I tried to pick the lock,' Arthur said ruefully. 'But it didn't work. That Miranda person brings me food every so often but it's worse than the pigswill they feed to the porkers on the home farm.'

Poppy was momentarily distracted. She gave him a searching look. 'Are you interested in farming, Arthur?'

He grinned. 'I should say I am. I spend most of my spare time with Matthews, the farm manager. I'd rather work on the farm than go to boarding school, Poppy.'

'We'll worry about getting you home safe and sound before we start thinking about school.' Poppy went over to the window and looked out, but it was a sheer drop, with nothing that might help them climb down to the paved yard below.

'I thought about that,' Arthur said smugly. 'I'd have had a go, but I didn't think I would make it.'

'You were right.' Poppy went to the door and turned the handle, but as she had expected, it was locked. She bent down and peered through the keyhole. 'The key is still in the lock.' Poppy went back to the window and threw up the sash. She leaned out, looking to left and then to the right. 'There's a small chance that I could reach the room next to this one.' She straightened up and turned to Arthur, smiling. 'There's a reasonably wide windowsill here and a similar one outside the next room. They're connected by a narrow ledge, but I think I could make it.'

Arthur ran to her side, clutching her arm with both hands. 'I don't want you to fall and kill yourself, Poppy.'

'Neither do I, Arthur. But I've got to try it or we'll have to wait for Miranda to bring us some breakfast. Even if I could get past her there is always Mulliner to contend with, and that awful mother of his, too.'

'Let me go, Poppy. I'm smaller and lighter than you.' Arthur peered out of the window. 'I could do it, I think.'

'No, Arthur. Thank you for offering, but I can reach further than you can. I'm going to have a go and just hope the other window isn't locked.'

'But what if that's Mulliner's room, or Miranda's?'

Poppy pulled a face. 'There's only one way to find out. We need to get away from here quickly.'

'All right,' Arthur said doubtfully, 'if you're sure, but please be careful.'

'I most certainly will.' Poppy pulled up a hard wooden chair and climbed on it. She stepped out onto the windowsill, taking care not to look down. She faced the wall and took a deep breath. It was foolhardy and dangerous, but anything was better than being at the mercy of the Whiddon and her wretched son. Miranda seemed to be more of a pawn in the unhinged game they had chosen to play. Poppy concentrated hard on the task in hand. She managed to get a finger hold in an exposed patch of brickwork, and she felt for the narrow ledge with her right foot, moving a few inches at a time. It was sunrise and she could feel the welcome warmth on her back as she edged carefully towards the next windowsill. She could only hope and pray that the window was unlocked and that the room was empty.

At last she had both feet on the sill, and she peered into the room, hardly daring to breathe. Thankfully it appeared to be empty and unfurnished. She put her hands flat on the glass and she could have cried with relief when it moved upwards. She practically fell into the room but there was no time to waste in congratulating herself and she jumped to her feet. Within seconds she was out on the landing and had unlocked the door to Arthur's room.

Poppy laid her finger on her lips and Arthur acknowledged her with a grateful smile. Together they crept downstairs and tiptoed across the hall to the front door. Its hinges groaned as Poppy flung it open and they raced down the steps to the waiting car. With Arthur in the passenger seat, Poppy cranked the engine and it started at the second attempt. Poppy leaped into the driver's seat and they were off down the twisting, weed-covered drive, heading towards the lane.

Arthur kneeled in the seat, facing backwards. 'I think Mulliner has seen us, Poppy. He's shaking his fist. What a lark. You should see his face.'

Poppy put her foot down on the accelerator. 'We'll go straight to Marsh House, Arthur. Your parents might have returned to Nine Oaks, but this motor car belongs to Gideon Taylor. I need to return it to him. I'm sure he will take us home.'

'That's all I want,' Arthur said earnestly. 'I was beginning to think I'd never see Mama and Papa again. I even missed Adam and Lottie, although they both tease me all the time.'

'They were so worried about you, Arthur. They only tease you because you're their little brother, but you've been so very brave throughout this ordeal. Maybe they'll treat you more like a grown-up now.'

Arthur yawned. 'I should hope so. I'm blooming hungry, Poppy. Do you think they'll have had breakfast at Marsh House?'

Poppy laughed. 'I'm sure they will give you the top brick off the chimney should you ask for it.'

'But you can't eat a brick, Poppy.'

'It's just a saying. You'll get anything you want, within reason, and breakfast seems like a good place to start.'

Arthur leaned forward, pointing at the vehicle Miranda had been forced to abandon earlier. 'Whose motor car is that? Why have they left it in the middle of the road?'

'It belongs to Mulliner, or at least he says it does. It wouldn't surprise me if he stole it, but I was pursuing Miranda last night and she came to a halt because the vehicle needed motor spirit. I'll report it to the police when we get to Marsh House. It's not too far now.'

'I expect they all have gone home,' Arthur said sulkily. 'Nobody knows that I was with Mulliner and that horrible woman.'

'That doesn't mean the search for you has stopped, Arthur.' Poppy shot him a sideways glance and saw that he was crying silently. It was harder to witness than any temper tantrum and she reached out with her left hand to pat him on the shoulder. 'Your parents are desolate without you, Arthur. You haven't been forgotten.'

He sniffed and wiped his nose on his sleeve. 'I really fancy bacon and eggs. Do you think the cook at Marsh House would do some for me?'

Poppy answered with a nod and a smile. 'Definitely. We're almost there.'

Poppy had expected to find everything quiet after the hectic activity of the previous evening, and she was surprised to see another motor car parked by one of the barns, and several uniformed police standing round in a group. Gideon and his father were talking to the more senior officer. Heads turned as Poppy drew up a short way from them.

Arthur jumped out of the car and ran over to Gideon, throwing his arms around his old friend.

'I'm safe, Gideon. Poppy rescued me.'

Poppy climbed more slowly from the vehicle and was immediately surrounded by people. Amelia had come running from the house together with her long-time friend and business partner, Mariah, and her daughter, Betsy. The police officer strode over to speak to Poppy and everyone stood back politely.

'The boy says you rescued him, miss. I understand that you have suffered an ordeal, but if you feel able to give me some details I would be grateful.'

'Of course,' Poppy said tiredly. 'I'll tell you everything I know, but would it be possible to send someone to inform his parents that he is safe?'

'I will see to that right away.' The officer glanced at Amelia. 'Might we go inside, Mrs Taylor? I'm sure Miss Robbins would like to sit down, and perhaps one of you ladies might like to put the kettle on. A nice cup of tea would be very welcome.'

'Never mind tea,' Arthur said eagerly. 'I am starving. Could somebody cook breakfast for me, please? I've been living on bread and water and scraps of horrid stuff for days.'

There was a rush towards the house and Poppy found herself being escorted into the music room. She sat down to give a statement to one of the constables while the other officers headed off in the direction of Grimstone Hall. Arthur had been led away to the kitchen with promises of bacon, eggs and as much toast and strawberry jam as he could eat.

Poppy was suddenly overcome with fatigue after the traumatic experiences of the previous night, but she revived a little after having drunk a most welcome cup of tea. The constable thanked her for her time and he hesitated in the doorway as he was about to leave.

'Congratulations, Miss Robbins. It was a brave thing you did. I hope the family are properly appreciative.'

Poppy stared after him, frowning. She might not move in the same circles as the Ashton family, but Uncle Freddie and Aunt Bella had always made her feel like part of the family. It was just a relief to have Arthur safe and unharmed. Perhaps the young policeman thought she wanted some sort of reward, which was the last thing on her mind. She thought of young Davy, the orphan child with the freckled nose and impudent grin. Arthur was being returned to his adoring parents and luxurious home, while Davy and others like him slept on the streets. Life was so unfair, especially if you were born poor. It was then that Poppy remembered the raffle and the money raised for the orphanage in King Street. She left the music room and went to the kitchen in the hope of finding Amelia.

Arthur was seated at the large table surrounded by admiring women as he ate his bacon and eggs, while also managing to give a very colourful account of his time as Mulliner's prisoner. Poppy stood in the doorway and listened. She did not try to correct any of his more flowery descriptions. The poor boy had suffered enough and this was his moment of glory. She could only be thankful that he had come through the ordeal virtually unharmed. She smiled as Betsy broke away from the group and came to stand at her side.

'He seems none the worse for his adventures.'

'He's a brave little boy,' Poppy said, nodding. 'Some children would have been terrified but I think he was more angry than scared.'

'He was lucky you found him when you did. Things could have turned out very differently,' Betsy said seriously. 'His parents will be overjoyed when they get the news that he's safe.'

The reason for Poppy's attendance at the fashion show last evening had been overshadowed by Arthur's rescue, but it was important to recover the money. 'Do you know what happened to the raffle money, Betsy?'

'Don't worry, I put it in the safe in Mrs Taylor's office. There was a bit of a to-do after you left last evening. Some jewellery was stolen, and a gold watch. Of course, everyone knew it must be that dreadful Miranda Flyte. She's been trying to insinuate herself into society for some time. I'm not sure how she managed to get an invitation for the show last night, but she most certainly won't be allowed anywhere near Marsh House again.'

'I've told the police where to find her and the man she married. I hope the law catches them before they have a chance to escape.' Poppy glanced at Arthur, who was having a slice of toast buttered for him while one of the other women hovered with the jam spoon at the ready.

'He was so brave. His parents will be very proud of him.'

'Gideon has driven over to Nine Oaks to fetch Lord and Lady Dorrington,' Betsy said excitedly. 'We've never had such goings-on at Marsh House. It will seem quite dull when it's all over.'

'I'll leave Arthur with you, Betsy. I've given my statement to the police and I'm not really needed here now.'

'I understand,' Betsy said gently. 'You must be very tired. You should go home and rest.'

'I will, but first I need to collect the raffle money from Mrs Taylor's office.' Poppy left the kitchen and made her way to the old dairy where she found Amelia in conversation with the police sergeant.

Amelia looked up and smiled. 'Poppy, my dear. You are the heroine of the hour. Sergeant Smith was just telling me how brave you were to rescue Arthur in those circumstances. You must have been terrified.'

Sergeant Smith's severe expression lightened into a half-smile. 'You are a very brave young lady, Miss Robbins.'

'Anyone would have done the same,' Poppy said, blushing. 'I'm just glad that Arthur is safe and well. He's enjoying a lovely breakfast and being waited on hand and foot by an admiring audience.'

'I have your address, Miss Robbins.' Sergeant Smith strolled over to the doorway. 'If we need any more information, someone will contact you at home. In the meantime, I suggest you get some rest.

Good day, ladies.' He stepped outside, putting on his peaked cap.

'You did do well, Poppy.' Amelia rose to her feet and walked over to a steel safe. 'I expect you've come for the raffle money.'

Poppy nodded. 'It was unfortunate that I couldn't stay to raise more, but any contribution is welcome.'

Amelia opened the safe and took out a bulging leather pouch. 'You'll be surprised. After the fuss died down and the ladies were leaving, many of them added a contribution to the fund without wanting anything in return. It seems that your brave action touched their wealthy hearts.' She handed the money bag to Poppy. 'Well done, is all I can say.'

'Thank you, Aunt Amelia.' Poppy was impressed by the weight of the bag and the jingle of the coins. 'I'm amazed by their generosity.'

Amelia resumed her seat behind the desk. 'It's a worthy cause, and one I would like to support. As I told you, I know what it's like to be very poor. I wasn't an orphan but I saw much poverty and hardship on the occasions when I accompanied my father on his rounds. He had patients who were living hand to mouth.'

'Anything you can do to help would be very much appreciated.' Poppy untied the leather string and as she opened the money bag she saw the glint of a few gold sovereigns amongst the copper and silver.

'My actual show is in the West End next week. Perhaps you would like to speak to the audience at the interval and put the case for the orphans? I am more than happy to have my name associated with such a worthy cause.'

Poppy could hardly believe her ears. 'That's wonderful, Auntie. Thank you.' She left the office with the pouch in her hand. It was only then that she realised she had no means of getting home. She could wait for the Ashtons to arrive, but that would take time and she was eager to get home. She could only hope that Gideon would have stopped at Rainbow's End to tell her parents what had happened and that she was safe, as was Arthur. They would have been desperately worried when they discovered that she had not returned home the previous evening. Their lives had been turned upside down since that first fateful day at the fair on Wanstead Flats when Miranda Flyte had erupted onto the scene. Poppy could only hope that the police had caught up with Miranda and Mulliner, as well as his despicable mother. If so, the occupants of Grimstone House would be facing very long prison sentences for abduction, kidnap and more.

This thought made Poppy smile as she turned the corner into the stable yard and careered into a tall man, who lifted her off her feet.

'Poppy Robbins, what the hell did you think you were doing?' Taverner set her back on the ground, glaring at her. 'You took a motor car when you can't drive and you put your life at risk by dashing off into the night in chase of a criminal. What were you thinking?'

Stung by the unfairness of his remarks, Poppy glared at him. 'I borrowed a vehicle, and I can drive. Anyway, Eddie, I don't see what it has to do with you.' She met his angry gaze with a toss of her head and he set her back on her feet.

'You might have been killed!'

Poppy dangled the money bag in front of his face. 'I raised all this money for the orphanage. I don't deserve to be scolded like a naughty child.'

Taverner snatched the pouch from her and tossed it into a gardener's wagon filled with cut grass. He swept her into an embrace and a kiss that was fierce in its intensity and yet achingly tender. She struggled at first, but she could not help herself and she gave in to the heart-stopping emotions that threatened to overcome her. However, the moment was shattered by an angry voice.

'Let her go, sir. You can see she wants nothing to do with you.' Adam's fist shot out and he caught Taverner a blow on the side of the head that made him release Poppy instantly. She staggered and would have fallen if she had not grasped the side of the wooden wagon. She looked up into Adam's furious face.

'Did he molest you, Poppy? I came out of the house and I saw you struggling.'

Taverner grabbed Adam by the scruff of the neck. 'Army officer or not, you don't get away with that.' He fisted his hand and was about to strike Adam, when Poppy made a grab for Taverner's arm.

'Stop it, both of you. I've got nothing to say to either of you.'

'I've come from Nine Oaks to take you home, Poppy,' Adam said indignantly. 'He was assaulting you.'

'Mind your own business, Lieutenant,' Taverner said angrily.

'I've had enough of this.' Poppy leaned over to rescue the money bag. 'I'm tired and I'm hungry, and you two are big boobies. I am not a toy to be fought over. I'd rather walk home than be beholden to either of you.' She marched off with her head held high.

Chapter Twenty-Two

'Poppy, wait!' Taverner's voice rang out across the cobbled yard.

Reluctantly Poppy came to a halt. She turned to face him. 'Haven't you scolded me enough, Eddie?'

His dark expression lightened and his lips twitched. 'I wasn't telling you off. I was merely pointing out the dangerous situation you faced last evening.'

'And yet here I am, safe and sound, with Arthur rescued from his kidnappers and soon to be reunited with his family. Have you got anything else to say?'

Taverner inclined his head. 'All right. I'm sorry, Poppy. I shouldn't have ranted at you like that, but you were supposed to stay close to home, for your own safety. Instead of listening to common sense you came here.'

Poppy held up the pouch. 'And this is the money

I raised for the orphanage in King Street, Eddie. I haven't had a chance to count it, but the ladies were very generous. Not only that, but Mrs Taylor has invited me to speak at her show in the West End next week, where I should be able to double this amount, or even more.' She thrust the bag into his hands. 'Take it.'

'I'm sorry, again. What more can I say? But you should not have put yourself at risk.'

'Why not? What is it to you anyway?' Poppy took off the diamond ring and pressed it into his free hand. 'We were never engaged. I don't know why I allowed myself to take part in such a stupid charade. Now you are free of me.' She turned her back on him and walked away.

'Wait. Maybe I don't wish to be free from you.'

Poppy spun round to face him. 'I believe you, but it's only because you like to control me, for some unknown reason. I'm sorry I ever set eyes on you.'

'Is he bothering you again, Poppy?' Adam had been standing back, but now he hurried to her side. 'I apologise for behaving badly just now, but I won't allow anyone to take advantage of you.'

'Keep out of this, Lieutenant,' Taverner said with ominous calm. 'This is between Poppy and me.'

'I've said all I have to say.' Poppy linked her hand through the crook of Adam's arm. 'Take me home, please, Adam. My parents will be frantic with worry.'

'They know you're safe,' Adam said firmly. 'I

visited Rainbow's End with the good news earlier, and I promised your family I would bring you home.'

'Then what are we waiting for?' Poppy shot a sideways glance at Taverner and his baffled expression was oddly satisfying. She knew that at least one of her remarks had hit home. Eddie Taverner was too used to getting his own way, and it would do him good to experience a rebuff occasionally. She allowed Adam to guide her to where he had left his motor car, but as she settled herself in the passenger seat she could not help glancing at her left hand, which felt surprisingly bare without the heavy gold and diamond ring on her fourth finger.

Adam cranked the engine and leaped into the driver's seat. 'You should be more careful about the company you keep, Poppy. That fellow is a hustler, and I don't like the way he treats you.'

Poppy leaned back in her seat and sighed. 'I doubt if I'll be seeing him again, Adam. From now on I'm going to stay at home and concentrate on helping my parents.'

He turned his head to give her a wide grin. 'Or you could marry me. I'm a very good catch, so Lottie tells me. I think you'd make an excellent soldier's wife.'

'I think your parents might have something to say about that,' Poppy said, smiling. 'You need to marry someone from your own class, not a commoner like me.'

'There's nothing common about you, my girl.

And you know me better than anyone in the world, apart from Lottie, of course.'

'It's not a joking matter, Adam. You have to consider the title and everything that goes with it. My parents own a restaurant. We might have grown up together, more or less, but that doesn't put us on an equal footing socially.'

Adam concentrated on the road ahead, narrowly avoiding a farm cart. 'The woman I marry will have to adapt to the life I have to lead as a soldier of the Queen. I believe that things are getting very difficult with the Boers. As I said before, another war is likely and I would like to have someone at home waiting for my return or, if the worst happens, someone who will grieve for me as only a wife can.'

'You are serious, aren't you?' Poppy stared at his profile, willing him to look at her, but he kept his gaze fixed on the road ahead.

'I love you, Poppy. I always have and I know you care for me. You are Lottie's best friend and you will look after her when I am away. She needs someone like you, as do I.'

Poppy was suddenly breathless. She had thought at first that Adam was joking, as he often did, but she could see now that he was deadly serious.

'I don't know what to say, Adam. You've taken me by surprise.'

'You need to think about it, of course. I doubt if you can give me an answer right away, but I am expecting to be posted fairly soon. You will consider it seriously, won't you, Poppy? I think we would do very well together.'

His undeniable sincerity left Poppy feeling confused. She had always been very fond of Adam, but marriage was another matter. She was not afraid of army life, but one day Adam would have to take up his duties as Earl of Dorrington, and if she married him that would make her a countess. If she were being honest Poppy was more afraid of censorship from society than any dangers she might face as an army wife.

'You're very quiet, Poppy,' Adam said anxiously. 'I hope I haven't upset you.'

'No, of course not.' Poppy managed a weary smile. 'You've taken me by surprise and I'm a bit tired after everything that's happened in the last twenty-four hours.'

'You must be totally exhausted after your ordeal. I won't utter another word, at least not yet. I have to return to the barracks later today, but I will call on you next week. Do you think you will have your decision by then?'

'I promise I will give you my answer when I see you next.' Poppy closed her eyes and drifted off into a dreamless sleep despite the noise of the engine and the wind in her face.

Flora burst into tears at the sight of Poppy as she climbed out of Adam's car. She rushed over and flung her arms around her daughter.

'Darling girl, we were so worried. You gave us such a fright.'

Daniel emerged from the house. 'Your mother tells me you drove Gideon's motor car, Poppy. What were you thinking of? You might have been killed.'

'I had driven Adam's motor, so I knew what to do.' Poppy sent a look for help to Adam, who nodded in agreement.

'It's true. Poppy has mastered the rudiments of driving.'

'You don't agree with what she did, do you?' Flora faced him anxiously. 'I mean, driving off into the night after a woman who turned out to be married to a criminal. I don't call that sensible.'

Daniel placed his arm around Flora's shoulders. 'I think we all agree on that, my love. But Poppy is home safe and sound. Let's be grateful for that.'

'Yes, of course. But we have been very worried, Poppy. Please don't do anything like that again.' Flora clutched her husband's hand as they retraced their steps into the house with a subdued Poppy following them and Adam not far behind.

Adam caught Poppy by the hand as she was about to enter the house.

'I really should return to Nine Oaks. I'd like to spend some time with Arthur before I leave for the barracks, but I'll stay here for a while if you wish.'

'Go home, please, Adam. I need to give my parents a full account of last night's happenings, and I don't think I'm going to get off easily. Tell Lottie I'll see her soon. She's not to worry about me.'

Adam kissed her on the cheek. 'I will do that, Poppy. I wish I could stay at Nine Oaks for longer, but I have to return to duty.'

She caught hold of his hand and gave it a gentle squeeze. 'I understand.' She waited on the step, watching Adam crank the engine before driving off with a final wave. She turned slowly and went indoors, following the sound of her parents' voices. She knew she had some explaining to do, but as she entered the parlour she had a feeling that this was not all about her escapades. She sat down opposite Flora and Daniel, who had occupied the sofa, sitting very close together.

'You aren't wearing your engagement ring, Poppy.' Flora gazed speculatively at Poppy's left hand.

'You haven't given me time to explain.' Poppy folded her hands neatly in her lap. She felt as if she were a child again, caught out in some misdemeanour. 'You know it was only a sham to make the servants at Domesday House obey my instructions. I gave it back to Eddie this morning.'

'Thank goodness for that,' Flora said earnestly. 'He is not a suitable match for you, Poppy dear. You deserve better.'

Daniel cleared his throat. 'Adam spoke to me earlier today. He asked for my permission to propose to you, and I gave it willingly.' He glanced anxiously at Flora. 'We both agree.'

'He did ask you to marry him, didn't he, Poppy?' Flora frowned. 'Perhaps you shouldn't have mentioned it so soon, Daniel.'

'It's all right,' Poppy said hastily. 'Yes, he did ask me to be his wife and I said I needed time to think it over.'

'Why would you hesitate, Poppy? You and Adam were childhood sweethearts.' Daniel shook his head. 'You would become a countess in the fullness of time. You would never want for anything again in your whole life.'

'Yes, darling,' Flora added enthusiastically. 'Just think about it. You would live in grand houses and have servants at your beck and call.'

'We would all benefit.' Daniel raised Flora's hand to his lips. 'Your mother and I could retire and live in comfort for the rest of our lives. Freddie has already said he will give us the house and land.'

Poppy stood up abruptly. 'Doesn't it matter how I feel? You haven't once asked me if I love Adam enough to want to be his wife. All you are thinking of is yourselves.'

'That's not true,' Flora protested tearfully. 'We are thinking about your best interests. You do care for Adam, don't you?'

'Yes, Mama, of course I do. But he's more like a brother to me. You know very well the society in which his family moves would never accept me.'

'You are as good as anyone else.' Daniel rose to his feet, towering over Poppy. 'You come from a very respectable family.'

'I know that, Pa, but we are not aristocrats. I grew up working in our kitchen and helping out wherever I was needed. What do I know about etiquette and society manners?'

'You would soon learn, but it's up to you, my girl. You must do as you see fit.' Daniel headed for the doorway. 'I have work to do. You know where you'll find me if I'm needed.' He left the room.

'I'm sorry if I've offended Pa,' Poppy said anxiously. 'But I haven't given Adam an answer, and I really don't know what I will say to him.'

Flora smiled wearily. 'You must follow your heart, Poppy. We've told you what we think would be best for you, but it's entirely your choice. Marrying into the Ashton family would seem to be most young women's dreams come true, but if it's not for you then we must accept that.'

Poppy leaned over to give her mother a hug. 'Thank you, Ma. I don't want to disappoint you and Pa.'

'You would never do that. I understand what you're saying, but your father thinks a little differently. He wants the best for you and nothing less will do. Now I suggest you go to your room and relax. Everything is running smoothly so you must take some time off.'

Poppy did as her mother suggested, but when she lay down on the bed she found she could not rest. She sat up, staring out of the window onto the parterre garden and the back of the house, but her mind was not on the neatly weeded beds filled with roses, nor the clematis clambering in purple and pink profusion over the pergola. Her thoughts were a colourful kaleidoscope with snatches of memory. Adam's proposal had startled and confused her, but not nearly as much as the sweet intensity of Eddie Taverner's kisses. Their engagement had been a total sham, and yet she missed the comfort of his grandmother's ring on her left hand. It had felt like a talisman against the troubles that had beset everyone around her since Miranda Flyte hurtled into their lives. But Adam was an old friend and she could trust him with her life, while Eddie might be exciting but had brought nothing but chaos and disorder to her door. She subsided against the pillows and closed her eyes. She did not need either of them. That would be the safest, most comfortable course to take. Her life was here in Rainbow's End, helping her parents to maintain the high standards they had set in the catering business. In years to come she would take over and run things her way, and in her spare time she would raise money to help waifs and orphans. She turned onto her side and curled up in a ball.

Next day Poppy tried to resume her normal duties but she found it hard to concentrate. She was in the cellar, checking the wine bins and crates of ale with Beasley, when Lottie appeared at the top of the steps.

'Poppy, can you spare a minute?'

Poppy handed the list to Beasley. 'We've almost finished. May I leave this with you, Mr Beasley?'

He smiled and nodded. 'Yes, of course, Miss Poppy. I know what to do.'

'Thank you.' Poppy climbed the steep stone steps. Lottie was waiting for her in the narrow passageway.

'I don't know how you can go down there. It's so dark and full of spiders.'

'You get used to it,' Poppy said airily. 'Is this a social call, Lottie?'

'You might say so. Actually, because of what you did for the Afterthought, Mama and Papa want to do something for you, Poppy.'

'I didn't do it with any idea of a reward.'

'Of course not, but this will be fun for both of us. Come to the parlour and they will explain.'

Lottie's obvious excitement was infectious. Poppy led the way to the parlour where she found her parents chatting to Arabella and Freddie. They stopped talking and turned to greet her with wide smiles. Arabella stepped forward to take Poppy's hand in hers.

'Dear Poppy, you know we can never thank you enough for saving Arthur from those awful people. It felt like history repeating itself when I heard he had been kidnapped. It was your mama who saved me.'

'With a little help from me, my love,' Freddie said, laughing. He placed his arm around Poppy's shoulders and brushed her cheek with a kiss. 'Arthur has told us in the minutest of details how you climbed out of the window and clung on for dear life until you reached the next bedroom. We can never repay the debt, Poppy.'

'But what Freddie is saying,' Arabella added eagerly, 'is that we would like you to be our guest in the London house. We thought you might enjoy visits to the theatre and museums or Madame Tussaud's. In fact, anywhere you would like to choose.'

'Do say you'll accept, Poppy.' Lottie gave her an encouraging smile. 'We'll have fun together.'

'But what about Arthur?' Poppy protested faintly. 'It sounds as if you're leaving him out of this.'

'Not at all.' Freddie went to stand beside Daniel. 'Arthur doesn't care for London and its entertainments. He is like me in that respect, so I have arranged for him to spend a few days with my home farm manager, Matthews, and his family. Arthur is as excited as if I had booked a trip to the moon for him.'

'Well, what do you say, Poppy?' Flora leaned forward in her chair. 'Don't worry about us. We will manage, just for a week.'

Poppy thought quickly. 'Would it be possible to include Mrs Taylor's fashion show in the outings? She said I could raise some more money for the orphans if I attended.'

'That sounds wonderful.' Flora nodded eagerly. 'I will accompany you and I'm sure Lottie would enjoy it, too.'

'Perhaps I might bow out of that one.' Freddie winked at Daniel. 'Much as I love to see my beautiful wife in fashionable garments, I draw the line at sitting for hours watching an interminable procession of gowns and accessories pass before my eyes.'

'What do you say, Poppy?' Lottie eyed her expectantly.

'If it's all right with Ma and Pa, how could I refuse?' Poppy hardly had time to finish the sentence as Lottie hugged her enthusiastically.

'We'll have a wonderful time. Maybe Adam can join us for an outing or two.'

Poppy's pleasure dimmed slightly. She realised then that this was not the reaction of a young woman in love. She would have to refuse Adam gently but firmly. Both families would be disappointed but she would rather live the life of a spinster than give herself to a man she could not wholeheartedly love. Adam would recover once he got over the shock of being rejected, and there must be dozens of eligible and charming young débutantes who would make him a wonderful wife.

'You look tired, Poppy dear,' Arabella said gently. 'I think you need to rest today and we will call for you in the morning.' She turned to Flora with a smile. 'Is that convenient for you, Flora?'

'Of course it is. Poppy deserves to have some fun. She's spent far too much time working hard when she should have been enjoying herself.'

Daniel shook Freddie's hand. 'Thank you,' he said simply.

'No thanks needed. It's our pleasure.' Freddie

beckoned to Arabella and Lottie. 'We'd better go home and leave Poppy to relax. I'm sure she won't have much time to stand still with all the outings and shopping you two have planned.'

Poppy smiled. 'I can't wait.'

'I have work to do in the grounds so I'll see you out.' Daniel led the way with the Ashtons following.

'Why don't you go to your room and rest?' Flora suggested gently. 'Bella was right. You do look a little pale.'

'But I've done nothing today, Ma. I don't like leaving you with everything to do.'

'Don't worry about us. I have Amos and Mrs Burden in the kitchen as well as the maids and, of course, dear old Beasley. I don't know what I would do without him.'

Poppy was conscious of an overwhelming need to be on her own for a while and she nodded. 'All right. I'll rest now, but I'll help you in the restaurant tonight, and then I won't feel too bad about spending a few days away.'

'You must not even think about us when you're staying with Freddie and Bella. But,' Flora added cautiously, 'I hope you will consider Adam's proposal seriously. You could do so much worse, my love.'

'I will give it some thought,' Poppy said reluctantly. She could not bring herself to disappoint her mother, at least not just yet. She did not want to go to her room and she wished people would stop treating her as if she was recuperating from a serious illness. If the truth were told she had quite enjoyed the excitement of chasing Miranda Flyte in Gideon's motor car, and she had risen to the challenge of climbing out of the window and onto the narrow ledge with a feeling close to enjoyment. Now she was being treated like a fragile flower and she was finding it irksome. However, not wanting to cause a fuss she went to her room and lay down on the bed, but she could not relax.

Poppy tried to concentrate on the exciting outings that Lottie and her mother had planned. They would spend hours going round the department stores in Oxford Street, trying on hats and possibly a few gowns. They would buy new gloves, shawls and bottles of expensive perfume that they fancied but did not need, all of which would be handed to the maid who followed them dutifully, carrying the parcels and bandboxes. Then there would be luncheon in smart restaurants, followed perhaps by a visit to Madame Tussaud's or another place of entertainment, and then tea and ice cream at Gunter's. There was so much to do in London, if you had the money, and of course the Ashtons had almost unlimited resources. Perhaps the only thing that really excited Poppy was the prospect of speaking at the fashion show and attempting to convince the rich matrons to donate money to the orphanage. She wondered if Taverner had yet had the chance to pass the collection on to Miss Potts, the matron at King Street, although she did not doubt his intentions in that respect. Eddie

Taverner might not be above the practices in business that made him money, but she was certain he would not cheat the orphanage out of desperately needed funds. She was still angry with him, but conversely she felt the need to speak to him. In particular she was anxious about young Davy, who had left an indelible impression upon her. He was just one child out of the many who were in desperate need of care and protection.

In the end she gave up all attempts to rest and she went downstairs to the kitchen, but the luncheon session had finished and there was nothing she could do. Still feeling unsettled and restless, she decided to go for a walk by the brook, which always had a calming effect on her spirits, but even that familiar place failed to address the disquiet she was experiencing. She sat down on a tree stump and stared into the shallow, fast-flowing water. A week spent with the Ashtons was going to make it even harder to refuse Adam's proposal of marriage, as she knew she must. She loved Adam and his whole family, although not in the way she might give herself to him body and soul. He was a dear friend and he held a special place in her heart, but marriage was out of the question.

That night Poppy dreamed about Davy and she awakened in a cold sweat. She could not recall the details, but she had a feeling that he was in even more danger than might be expected for a child of the streets. She dressed hastily and hurried downstairs. The grandfather clock in the hallway struck six. It was early morning but she could hear voices coming from the kitchen. She recognised the strident tones of Mrs Burden and the high-pitched voice of Meg, who seemed to be getting into trouble yet again. The day had already begun badly and the bad dream had unsettled her. She realised that she was not yet ready to answer the inevitable questions she must face when she told her parents that she had changed her mind about staying with the Ashtons. She would have to explain the reason for her change of mind, but neither of them was likely to believe anything other than the plain truth. She could imagine their disappointment and dismay when she told them she had no intention of accepting Adam's offer of marriage. She smiled to herself. People had been put away in Colney Hatch for less, but it was no laughing matter.

She was about to go to the kitchen when the doorbell jangled on its spring.

Poppy opened the front door. 'Eddie!' She stared at him in astonishment. Eddie Taverner was the last person she had expected to see, especially at this hour in the morning.

'I know it's ridiculously early, and I apologise, but I need to speak to you, Poppy.'

She stepped back into the hall, holding the door open. 'Come in. What's happened? I can tell that something is wrong.'

'I received a telegram late last night informing me that my father has passed away.'

Poppy reached out to clasp his hand. 'Oh, Eddie. I am so sorry.'

He curled his fingers around hers. 'You know that he and I were never close, but even so, he was my father.'

'How can I help?' Instinctively Poppy knew that there was more.

'I have to travel to Devonshire immediately to sort everything out, but my mother contacted me separately. She is asking for you, Poppy.'

'I don't understand. Why would she need to see me?' Poppy eyed him suspiciously.

'Apparently you helped her a great deal when she was suffering at Whiddon's hands. She hasn't forgotten, and I think perhaps she needs the company of another woman, one to whom she can speak freely.'

'Is there no one else?'

'I can understand your reluctance, Poppy. You don't owe me or my family anything, but if you have any affection at all for Mama I would be most grateful if you would come to Devonshire with me, today.'

'Today? I don't know, Eddie. I am supposed to be spending a week in London with the Ashtons.'

Taverner took a deep breath. 'Ah, yes. Lord Ashton and his family. Does that mean you are seriously considering the redoubtable lieutenant's proposal of marriage?'

'How did you know that Adam had asked me to marry him?'

'It was obvious from the way he was carrying on after your heroic escapade.' Taverner held up his hands. 'Don't look at me like that, Poppy. I was just as impressed by your bravery as anyone, but you would be making a big mistake if you agreed to marry him.'

'I think that is my business,' Poppy said stiffly.

'So you didn't accept his offer?'

'Why would it matter to you, Eddie? You and I only pretended that we were a couple to confound the Whiddon. She is probably languishing in a police cell as we speak, so she is no longer a threat to your family.'

'You don't wish to come with me. I quite understand. I'm sorry for bothering you, Poppy.' Taverner turned to open the door, but Poppy laid her hand on his sleeve.

'I haven't said I wouldn't accompany you, Eddie. I just needed a moment to think.'

'If you're coming we need to leave right away. I'm sorry to press you, Poppy, but I have a train to catch.'

Poppy met his intense gaze and she knew then what she must do. Suddenly all the doubts and fears she had experienced recently melted away into nothing.

Chapter Twenty-Three

'Just give me time to pack a valise.' Poppy was about to mount the stairs but she hesitated. 'There's something bothering me, Eddie. I'm worried about Davy. I had a bad dream last night. I think he might be in trouble.'

Taverner smiled. 'I'm sure you have a genuine connection with that child. As a matter of fact, he turned up on my doorstep last evening. He was in a very agitated state, dirty and very hungry. Mrs Kent took him in and fed him.'

'Is he all right?'

'He had been badly bullied by older boys, but he's safe now.'

'You aren't going to put him in the orphanage, are you? I mean, I know he will be looked after physically, but he needs a real family.'

'I haven't made any decisions as yet. The telegram from home put everything else out of my mind.'

'I understand, but Davy is a special boy. I don't like to think of his spirit being crushed by living in an institution, even one that is as well run as the orphanage in King Street.'

'We'll talk about Davy *en route*, if you don't mind, Poppy. Mrs Kent will take care of him until we return from Domesday House.'

Poppy nodded. 'Give me five minutes and I'll be with you. I'll write a note for my parents and one for the Ashtons. I'm not going to be a very popular person after this.'

'You will be more than popular with me and my mother. Consider it an act of mercy,' Taverner said with a wry smile. 'I'll wait outside.'

Domesday House appeared to be slumbering in the late afternoon sunshine. A heat haze hovered over the gravelled carriage sweep and the trees that lined the drive were bowed down beneath a cloak of dusty green leaves.

Ned drew the tired old horse to a halt in front of the main entrance. He leaped from the driver's seat to help Poppy alight.

'Welcome home, Miss Poppy, and you, too, my lord.' Ned carried their luggage to the front entrance and knocked on the door. It was opened by Bessie Milner, the parlourmaid Poppy had hired. She dropped a deep curtsey and stood aside.

'Of course, you are Baron Taverner of Oakley now,' Poppy said, smiling. 'Do I have to call you my lord or Eddie?'

'I think I prefer Eddie.' Taverner turned to Ned. 'Thank you, that'll be all for today. I'll speak to you and the rest of the servants later. In the meantime everything will carry on as usual.'

'It's good to have you home again, my lord.' Ned took the cases inside before returning to the carriage. He climbed onto the driver's seat and drove off in the direction of the stables.

Poppy paused on the top step, gazing at the grounds, which were not as overgrown and neglected as they had been before she arrived the first time.

'This could be so beautiful with a bit more work. I was quite sorry to leave, Eddie.' Poppy followed him into the cool interior, gazing round with approval at the recently scrubbed floor and dust-free surfaces.

Taverner turned to Bessie, who was standing by at a respectful distance. 'Is my mother up and about?'

'No, my lord. According to Miss Hayes, Lady Taverner is feeling a little under the weather.'

'I'd better go to her room,' Poppy said, frowning. 'Miss Hayes will tell me everything I need to know.'

'Thank you, Poppy. I'm sure that Mama will be all the better for seeing you.' Taverner put his hand in his pocket. 'It might help if you put this on, just for now. I don't want to upset her even more than need be.' He held his hand out and the diamond ring rested in his palm.

Poppy hesitated and then she took the ring and slipped it onto her finger. 'Just for now, then, Eddie.' She turned away and walked slowly towards the staircase. It was not something she would willingly admit, but the weight of the ring on her fourth finger was oddly comforting. It might be her imagination, but the atmosphere in the house felt quite welcoming. During her brief stay in Domesday House, Poppy had formed an attachment to Lady Taverner and she would do anything in her power to help her ladyship get through a period of bereavement. Poppy mounted the stairs and made her way to Lady Taverner's bedroom.

Miss Hayes opened the door and her taut expression melted into a welcoming smile.

'You came, miss. I am so pleased to see you.'

'How is her ladyship?' Poppy asked anxiously.

'She is naturally very upset. She was married to the late Lord Taverner for many years. We are all aware that he could be a trifle difficult at times, but even so, they were husband and wife.'

'Of course.' Poppy glanced round the room and was agreeably surprised by the tidiness and the general cleanliness that Miss Hayes had brought about. 'You've made such a difference, Miss Hayes. Everything looks absolutely pristine.'

'Thank you, miss.' A dull flush spread from Miss Hayes's neck to her thin cheeks. 'It's nice of you to say so.' She backed towards the doorway. 'Do you mind if I have a short break, miss? I've been up since dawn and I could do with some fresh air.'

'No, of course not. You may take as long as you like. I'll sit with Lady Taverner.' Poppy crossed the floor to stand beside the chaise longue.

Lady Taverner lay quite still with her eyes closed, but she opened them when Poppy pulled up a chair.

'Poppy, is that you?'

'Yes, ma'am. I'm sorry for your loss.'

Lady Taverner's blue eyes narrowed, and she raised herself to a sitting position. 'I loved him once, Poppy, but he was a weak man. He had a fondness for drink and he wasn't always faithful.'

Poppy sat down and took one of Lady Taverner's thin hands in a warm clasp. 'I'm sure that's just gossip, ma'am.'

'Eliza Whiddon told me what went on between her and my husband. It happened before we were married, but she bore him a son.' Lady Taverner's fingers closed over Poppy's hand with surprising strength for someone so frail.

'Are you sure she wasn't making it up, ma'am?' Poppy said gently. 'I mean she could have told you anything.'

'Her son came to the house,' Lady Taverner said faintly. 'A hateful man called Gervase Mulliner. He demanded money from my husband. Of course, George would have none of it and threw the fellow out, but that night a fire started in the east wing.

You've seen what little is left of it. It's a mercy we were not all burned in our beds.'

'Don't distress yourself, ma'am. The people who attempted to ruin your family, including Mrs Whiddon, are locked up in prison, facing charges that will put them away for a very long time.' Poppy could see that Lady Taverner was working herself up into a highly emotional state. 'Edward is here. He won't allow anyone to harm you.'

'Eddie is a good son.' Lady Taverner sighed. 'Whatever people say of him he is a fine man and I am proud of him. He has a kind heart. You know that, don't you, Poppy?'

'Yes, of course I do,' Poppy said, smiling. 'You must try not to upset yourself, ma'am.'

'But Whiddon's son might descend upon us again, demanding his rights. He is older than Edward, and he could claim the estate as his.'

'No, ma'am. The late Lord Taverner was not his father. He has no valid claim on the estate,' Poppy said hastily. 'Eliza Whiddon lied about everything, but I heard from her own lips that Gervase Mulliner's father was a common blacksmith. She has been arrested, as I said before, and you are free from both of them, ma'am.'

Lady Taverner collapsed against the cushions with a sigh. 'After all these years.'

'You won't be troubled by either of them again. Eddie will see to that, anyway.'

'You won't desert my son, will you, Poppy?

Edward needs you more than you can imagine.' Lady Taverner fixed Poppy with an appealing gaze that made it hard to look away.

'I will stay for as long as he needs me, ma'am.'

'You are still wearing the family ring. Never take it off, Poppy. It's yours whether or not you decide to marry my son.'

'You do know that our engagement was simply a ruse to keep Mrs Whiddon in order?' Poppy said gently.

'I hadn't forgotten.' Lady Taverner closed her eyes. 'I would dearly love a cup of tea. Ordinary tea, mind you. Not that dreadful tisane that Whiddon used to make me drink.'

'If you promise to rest I'll go downstairs to the kitchen and make myself known to the servants. I'll order a tray of tea to be sent up to you directly.'

'Thank you, dear.' Lady Taverner sighed happily. 'I feel so much better now you and Edward are here.'

There was no sign of Cook when Poppy entered the kitchen. Jessie was up to her elbows in flour, kneading a ball of bread dough. She looked up and smiled with pleasure when she saw Poppy.

'I knew you'd come, miss. I told them all that you wouldn't let us down.'

'I'm not back permanently, Jessie. I came because Mr Edward told me that Lady Taverner wanted to see me.'

'She has her ups and downs, poor lady.' Jessie placed

the dough in a mixing bowl and covered it with a damp cloth. 'Can I get you anything, miss? A nice cup of tea and a slice of saffron cake, perhaps?'

'That sounds too tempting to refuse, but I really came to ask for a tray of tea to be sent up to her ladyship. Is Cook about?'

'She left, miss. Or rather Mr Frampton sent her packing. He found her dead drunk when she should have been preparing dinner. It was my half-day off, so I wasn't here. Anyway, he told her to pack her bags and leave, so I'm the cook now. Loveday helps me if I get too busy.'

'You are very capable,' Poppy said seriously. 'But if you find it's too much for you I will advertise for an experienced cook.'

'I can manage, miss. I don't know all the fancy recipes that they usually enjoy in big houses, but I can make good plain meals.'

'Just keep doing as you are now, Jessie. I'm sure we are all very grateful.'

'Yes, miss. Thank you.' Jessie bustled about making a large pot of tea and cutting slices off a delicious-smelling saffron cake. 'Her ladyship is rather partial to my cakes,' she added proudly. 'Shall I take tea to Mr Edward? I believe he's in the old master's study, or he was when Nettie went in to dust.'

'No, it's all right. Send someone up to Lady Taverner's room. I'll take a tray to the study. I need to speak to Mr Edward anyway.'

Jessie opened the door that led to the servants'

hall. 'Bessie, if you've finished your tea will you take a tray up to her ladyship, please? Miss Poppy ordered it.'

'Good afternoon, miss.' Bessie hurried into the kitchen, smoothing her apron. 'It's lovely to have you back with us.'

'It's only temporary,' Jessie said in a hushed tone. 'Not permanent, so to speak.'

'Please stay with us, miss.' Bessie took the tea tray from the table. 'Things run so much better when you're here.'

Poppy smiled. She was flattered but also slightly apprehensive; she needed to speak to Taverner. She took the tray to the study and went in without bothering to knock.

Taverner was seated at the desk with piles of documents spread out and others spilling from filing baskets. He looked up, his brow furrowed in a frown.

'I've never seen such a mess, Poppy. My father was not a businessman by any manner of means.'

'I've brought you some tea and cake.' Poppy looked round for a space on which to put the tray, but as there was none she had to place it rather precariously on the seat of a wooden chair. She poured the tea and handed a cup to Taverner, who placed it unceremoniously on a pile of what looked like unpaid bills.

'You did your best while you were in charge here,' Taverner said slowly. 'But I found a sheaf of bills and final demands hidden in a box under the desk.'

'Can I help?' Poppy eyed the piles warily, but at least she had had some experience in sorting out the late Lord Taverner's shocking account-keeping. For once she felt quite sorry for Eddie Taverner. He was obviously at a loss.

'Would you? I didn't bring you here to settle my family finances, but I have enough to do without sorting this out.'

'I've had a chat with your mama. She's resting now but I'll spend longer with her later. She needs to take things easy, especially after bereavement. Have you organised your father's funeral?'

Taverner sipped his tea. 'I need to pay a call on the vicar this afternoon.'

'You do that, Eddie. I'll go through the papers. I have had some experience, as you rightly pointed out. Then I'll try to persuade your mama to come downstairs for a while, maybe even for dinner.'

'Goodness knows what we'll have to eat,' Taverner said gloomily. 'Apparently Mr Frampton sacked the cook.'

'Don't worry, it's all under control. Young Jessie has taken over in the kitchen and she's doing very well. You won't get exotic or fancy meals, but she's a good plain cook and none of us will starve.'

Taverner put his cup down and reached out to take Poppy's left hand in his. 'Are you sure you don't want to marry me, Poppy? I need a wife like you.'

She snatched her hand free. 'That's not funny, although it's the second proposal I've had in the past few days.' Poppy picked up the nearest pile of bills. 'I'll make a start here if you want to visit the vicar when you've finished your tea.'

Taverner took a bite of saffron cake. 'You'll be telling me next not to spoil my appetite for luncheon.'

'Do you want a wife, Eddie, or a nanny?' Poppy said, laughing. 'I am not applying for either position.'

Taverner finished the slice of cake. 'Perhaps I should marry Jessie. I love her cooking.' He strolled out of the study, allowing the door to swing shut behind him.

Poppy picked up a ledger and tossed it at the closed door. Men, she decided, were the most irritating of creatures.

She set about going through the mass of paperwork and once she had sorted it into neat piles she realised it was not as bad as it had first appeared. In fact, the system she had instituted in her short time at Domesday House seemed to have worked reasonably well, and it was not difficult to set things straight.

Taverner was nowhere to be found when Bessie announced that dinner was served and Poppy ate alone at the vast mahogany dining table. After she had finished her meal she went upstairs to sit with Lady Taverner for an hour, which enabled Miss Hayes to go to the servants' hall and enjoy her meal in peace. Lady Taverner chatted for a while, but it was obvious that she tired easily and she fell asleep mid-sentence. Poppy waited for Miss Hayes to return before leaving the room with a promise to return later.

It was early evening but Taverner had not yet returned. Poppy could only assume that he was still with the vicar, arranging his father's funeral, and there was nothing she could do until he returned. She decided to go for a walk in the grounds and enjoy the evening sunshine and fresh country air. As she walked slowly towards the lake, she was pleased to see that Bert and Ned had taken her advice and had cleared the pathways of weeds and brambles. The view was breath-taking and the fiery sunset turned the water into molten gold. Poppy's thoughts strayed to young Davy, who no doubt was being spoiled by Mrs Kent, but she wished that they could have brought him here to run wild in the grounds and experience a way of life that a child of the slums could hardly imagine. Poppy continued on, lulled into a dreamlike state by the hum of bees as they went from one wildflower to another. She did a circle of the lake and was on her way back to the house when she caught a glimpse of Taverner riding horseback along the tree-lined drive. She quickened her pace so that she caught up with him as he dismounted outside the stable block.

'Is everything all right, Eddie?'

Taverner handed the reins to a stable lad. 'It's all in hand. The funeral will take place on Friday.' He gave her a searching look. 'I know you would prefer to be at home in Rainbow's End, helping your parents, but could you stay until it's over? It would be a great help to my mother. I think she will need you even more after my father is laid to rest. Just for a few days, unless you feel otherwise.'

'Are you actually asking me for help, Eddie?'

He smiled. 'Yes, Poppy. I am asking for your most valuable assistance.'

'Then I will stay on, if only for your mother's sake.'

'But not for mine?' Taverner asked wistfully.

Poppy laughed. 'No, Eddie. You've already told me you need a meek little wife, a housekeeper and a nanny. I am none of those things, but I have an inexplicable affection for this old house and I am fond of your mama. I won't let her down.'

'Thank you, Poppy.' Taverner hesitated. 'I do appreciate everything you've done for my family. I'll be glad of your support.'

'I had almost forgotten the fashion show in London. It's tomorrow evening, Eddie. I have been allocated time in which to ask for donations to the orphanage. I really should be there.'

'That can be arranged. I have some business to transact in London, too. We can stay overnight in Fournier Street, if that suits you.'

Poppy smiled delightedly. 'I'll be able to see Davy.'

'You really have taken that child to heart, haven't you?'

She nodded. 'Yes, I don't know why, but he is so independent, even though he's so young. His spirit is irrepressible. I don't know why, but he touches something in me.'

Taverner nodded. 'I've set everything in motion here. We'll leave first thing in the morning.'

It was late afternoon on the following day when they arrived in Fournier Street. Mrs Kent opened the door, her thin face flushed and a worried frown creasing her brow.

'Thank goodness you've come home, sir. I've been driven mad by that young limb of Satan. He's escaped three times and I've had to go running round the streets, chasing after him. I'm not as young as I was, sir.'

Taverner stepped inside and placed his arm around his housekeeper's shoulders.

'You've done well to put up with the little imp, Mrs Kent. Did he say why he wanted to get away? I should have thought he would be delighted to be looked after by a kind lady like yourself?'

'He has the manners of an urchin, sir. That's all you can expect from a wild child from the slums. I have been going out of my mind.'

Poppy wanted to laugh but she managed to maintain a straight face. 'I am so sorry, Mrs Kent. Where is the boy now?'

'I locked him in his room, miss. I had to do something. The police brought him back last time and they threatened to lock him up, but the little demon just laughed.'

Taverner gave her a gentle hug before releasing her. 'I'll have something to say to young Davy, Mrs Kent.'

'Maybe it would be better if I spoke to him first?' Poppy suggested hastily. She could envisage the scene if Taverner scolded the boy without first hearing him out. Davy was very young, and small for his age, but he was used to surviving on the streets. Poppy could imagine how the child must have felt being confined to a house with someone he did not know, and rules with which he was not familiar.

'Very well. I need to go to my office anyway.' Taverner hesitated in the doorway. 'I'll be back in time to take you to the fashion show, Poppy. Do what you can with the boy. If he won't behave I'll take him to the orphanage and let Miss Potts deal with him.'

Poppy's heart sank at the thought. Davy would inevitably run away time and time again, and in the end he would fall foul of the law. If nothing was done he would end up in prison, his life ruined.

She went upstairs to his room, turned the key in the lock and entered slowly.

'Davy, it's me, Poppy.' She closed the door behind her, looking round at an apparently empty room. 'Davy?' For a moment she thought he must have climbed out of the window, but it was firmly closed. It was only a slight flutter of the overhanging bedspread that made her step forward and whisk it off the bed.

Peering up at her, Davy grinned. 'I thought you was the old woman come to scold me again.'

'Mrs Kent means well, but you ran away. That wasn't very nice, was it?'

'I ain't nice and I don't like being shut in.' Davy lowered his voice. 'She wanted to take me clothes off and put me in a tub of water. I ain't having nothing like that.'

Poppy perched on the edge of the bed. 'I understand how you feel, Davy. How would you like to come with me to the country for a few days? Mr Eddie lives in a big house with lots of land around it. You could help in the gardens or the stables, and have all you can eat at mealtimes.'

Davy eyed her suspiciously. 'It ain't a school?'

'No, it's Mr Eddie's family home. His pa died recently and we are helping to put matters straight for Mr Eddie's ma.'

'What if I says no?'

'In that case you can go back on the streets and take your chances, or you can go into the orphanage in King Street with all the other children.'

Davy frowned. 'What do I have to do to earn me supper? I'm a good dip.'

'There'll be no need for you to pick pockets or do anything illegal. You are a child, Davy. I will make sure you are taken care of. The choice is yours. What do you want to do?'

Chapter Twenty-Four

Davy was tucked up in bed, having been persuaded to take a bath, although he made a great fuss and it took both Mrs Kent and Poppy to convince him that hot water and soap were not actually harmful. In the end he had quite enjoyed the experience and had allowed Mrs Kent to take his clothes to be washed. Poppy dressed him in one of Taverner's old shirts, and Davy had gone to bed quite willingly.

Poppy had changed into her best silk gown in a shade of green that matched her eyes and complimented her fiery hair. She knew she was looking her best, and it was flattering that Taverner had also made an extra effort with his appearance. His white dress shirt was starched to a glossy sheen, and he wore a maroon brocade waistcoat and a black tailcoat with matching trousers. They arrived at the fashion show just as the last guests were being welcomed. Amelia saw them and greeted Poppy with open arms. She acknowledged Taverner politely and Betsy showed them to their seats next to Arabella and Lottie.

'Mama isn't here?' Poppy glanced round at the audience, disappointed at not seeing her mother.

'They are very busy tonight, my dear,' Arabella said in a low voice. 'But she sends her love and hopes you will be home soon.'

'I feel guilty for taking time off.' Poppy smiled ruefully. 'I love working at Rainbow's End, but it's all I've ever done. It's actually nice to get away, although that makes me feel even worse.'

Lottie grasped her hand. 'I've missed you, Poppy. So has Adam.' She said no more as the gaslights dimmed and Amelia walked on to the stage to introduce her collection. After that there was little time to chat as the models glided up and down the catwalk.

Amelia was as good as her word and, at the start of the interval, she announced that Miss Poppy Robbins was going to give a brief talk on the subject of the King Street Orphanage.

With the audience already in a good mood, due to the success of the show, Poppy went on to the stage and spoke up for the many deprived children on the city streets. When she finished speaking there was a flutter of white handkerchiefs as many of the ladies present wiped their eyes, and when the collection was taken Poppy was agreeably surprised by the generosity of the patrons.

'Well done, Poppy,' Taverner said softly. 'That obviously came from the heart and the audience responded.'

'Thank you, Eddie. That's praise indeed, coming from you.'

'Am I so hard on you, Poppy?'

'You can be,' Poppy said in a whisper. She looked round as Betsy came hurrying down the aisle between the rows of seats.

'Excuse me, my lord,' Betsy said in a low voice. 'There's a messenger outside. He says it's urgent.'

Taverner rose to his feet. 'I'm sorry, Poppy. I have to go. It's a business matter.'

Arabella leaned forward. 'At this time of night, sir?'

'I apologise, Lady Dorrington. If I don't return by the end of the show would you take Poppy home with you?'

'Eddie, I am not a child,' Poppy protested. 'I can get a cab to Fournier Street.'

'Nonsense, my dear,' Arabella said sharply. 'We're staying at the house in Piccadilly. You will come with us. I understand why you felt the need to go to Domesday House, but you did promise to stay with us for a while. Lottie was very disappointed, weren't you, darling?'

'Yes, I really was. Please stay tonight,' Lottie added eagerly. 'We can share my room and chat into the early hours, as we did when we were girls.'

'Hush!' An irritated voice from the row behind

them made Lottie subside into her seat, and when Poppy looked round she was just in time to see Taverner leaving the hall.

The second half of the show was even more glamorous and exciting than the first, and Poppy enjoyed looking at the lovely creations, but every now and then she glanced over her shoulder, hoping that Taverner had returned safely. She knew so little about his business, but she suspected it was not entirely legal and might occasionally be dangerous. When the show ended and he had still not returned, she had convinced herself that this was possibly one of those times.

'You must come with us, Poppy dear,' Arabella said firmly as they filed out of the hall.

'I can't put you to all that bother.' Poppy stepped out into the street, looking around hopefully for a cab, but in vain.

'I sent a boy to tell my coachman that we're ready to depart,' Arabella said firmly. 'I can't leave you here on your own, Poppy.'

Lottie grabbed Poppy by the arm. 'You are coming home with us. I won't have any arguments.'

'I didn't mean quite like that,' Arabella said, laughing. 'But, please agree, Poppy. I won't rest if you take a cab on your own into such a rough part of town. For once I agree with Lord Taverner.'

Poppy turned to her with a questioning gaze. 'When did you ever disagree with Eddie? I thought you barely knew him.'

'I've met him a few times, that's all, but he has a reputation for jiggery-pokery, whatever that might be. You will have to ask your papa, Poppy. I'm sure he will understand.'

'Don't let that upset you,' Lottie said hastily. 'It's probably just gossip. Do come with us now. I've made a note of the gowns that I think will suit me. You can advise me over a cup of hot chocolate.'

It had started to rain and Poppy had not brought anything other than a flimsy lace shawl. She recognised the Ashtons' carriage as the coachman drew it to a halt at the kerb and a footman jumped down to open the door.

Arabella hesitated with one foot on the step. 'Do come with us, Poppy. Your mama will never forgive me if I leave you on your own. You'll be soaked in a matter of minutes.'

Lottie gave Poppy a gentle push. 'You're coming with us. Chop chop.'

With one last glance in the hope of seeing Taverner emerge from the crowd, Poppy climbed into the carriage and sat down next to Lottie.

It was a short drive to Piccadilly and the Ashtons' elegant mansion was as warm and welcoming as ever. Poppy gave herself up to the luxury of being waited on by an army of servants, and she did her best to put Davy and Taverner out of her mind, at least for one night. Lottie's maid produced a lace-trimmed lawn nightgown and wrap for Poppy, together with a pair of velvet slippers. Another servant brought them a pot of hot chocolate, which they drank from dainty cups by the fire in Lottie's bedroom. To Poppy, who was used to a certain measure of economy at home, it was sheer indulgence to have a fire in the middle of summer. However, it was a chilly evening and Lottie's pretty room was bathed in firelight as they sat on the hearth rug, sipping their drinks.

Lottie would not allow Poppy to waste time fretting about matters over which she had no control and so the conversation revolved around the garments they had seen at the show. Lottie had a good eye for what suited her and almost unlimited money when it came to purchasing a wardrobe. Poppy was only too happy to indulge her friend and they slipped comfortably into their old ways when, as children, they had shared a room, swapping secrets beneath the bedclothes and giggling about things that in retrospect barely warranted a smile.

Next morning Lottie's maid selected and laid out a simple but very stylish blue cotton gown with a white lace collar for Poppy, which Lottie told her to keep.

'It makes me look sallow,' Lottie said firmly when Poppy protested. 'You have such lovely peaches and cream skin. That shade of blue really suits you.'

There was no arguing with Lottie once she had made up her mind, and Poppy did not try very hard. She seldom bought new clothes and always had to be mindful of the cost. It was a pleasure to go down to breakfast knowing that she was as well dressed as any fashionable young lady. To her surprise the only other person in the dining room was Adam. He leaped to his feet.

'Poppy, this is a lovely surprise. I was out for an early morning ride so I thought I'd come home for breakfast.' He hurried round the table to pull up a chair for her. 'Where's my sister?'

'She's coming. She had difficulty deciding which ribbon to put in her hair.' Poppy sat down, smiling.

Adam resumed his seat. 'That sounds like Lottie. But why are you here? Have you come to stay? And why wasn't I informed?'

'It was just last night. I have to leave after breakfast, Adam. Anyway, how is it that the army can spare you so much? You seem to spend more time at home than in the barracks.'

He took a sip of coffee. 'That won't last. We're sailing for the Cape next week. I don't know when or even if I will get home again.'

'Don't say that,' Poppy said, horrified.

The door opened at that moment and Lottie breezed into the room. She came to a halt staring at Poppy. 'What have you said to upset her, Adam? I can't leave you for a moment without you doing or saying something untoward.'

Adam reached for the silver coffee pot and refilled his cup. 'I was being realistic, that's all.'

'He said he might not return from the battlefield.' Poppy glared at him. 'You mustn't even think like that, Adam.'

'He just does it for attention.' Lottie went straight to the sideboard and began helping herself from the serving dishes. 'Come and get some food, Poppy. We need to be quick or Lieutenant Guzzle-guts will have eaten everything in sight.'

'I say, Lottie. That's below the belt, even for you.'

Adam's pained expression made Poppy laugh. 'I don't think you two will ever grow up.' She stood up and walked over to the groaning sideboard to choose from the array of breakfast dishes. However, the sight and smell of the food made her think of Davy, and the other poor orphans who would never have seen, let alone eaten, such a feast, and her appetite deserted her.

'What's the matter, Poppy?' Lottie demanded as she saw the small portion of buttered eggs that was all Poppy had on her plate. 'Are you feeling unwell?'

'I'm not very hungry, that's all.' Poppy went back to her chair and sat down. 'I really should leave as soon as I've eaten. I need to get a cab back to Fournier Street.'

'You don't have to do that,' Adam said hastily. 'I'll take you. I am not due back at the barracks until midday.'

Poppy was going to refuse and then she realised that she had the pouch filled with donations for the orphanage to take with her. Perhaps it was not a good idea to travel on her own with a lot of money in her possession. 'Thank you, Adam. That would be very helpful.'

'I thought you might stay for a while,' Lottie said, pouting. 'We could have spent the day together.'

'I have something important to do today, but maybe if we're still in town tomorrow you and I could go shopping together,' Poppy suggested tactfully although, if the truth were told, she enjoyed such outings to start with, but found spending hours and hours wandering round department stores rather tiresome.

'I was looking forward to spending today with you, Poppy.' Lottie slumped down on her seat and began toying with the food on her plate. 'I don't see enough of you these days.'

'I am a working woman. I have to earn my keep.' Poppy could see that Lottie was about to go into one of her sulks, but she herself was eager to get back to Fournier Street. It was not that she thought anything might have happened to Taverner, who seemed to live a charmed life, but Davy would be anxious and Mrs Kent would be worried.

'What is it that you have to do so urgently?' Adam sat back in his chair. 'As I said, I will take you anywhere you wish to go.'

'It's that wretched orphan child you told me about, isn't it?' Lottie stabbed a piece of devilled kidney with her fork. 'It's not fair.'

Adam laughed. 'Marry me, Poppy. We'll have a string of little Ashtons for you to worry about.'

'That's a shocking thing to say.' Lottie rolled her

eyes. 'You don't talk about things like that to young ladies, Adam.'

'It's all right,' Poppy said hastily. 'I know he's joking.'

'Am I?' Adam shrugged. 'What do you think, Poppy?'

She pushed her plate away. 'If you are serious about taking me to Fournier Street I would like to go now.' Poppy turned to Lottie with an apologetic smile. 'We will have our shopping day soon, I promise.'

Adam jumped to his feet. 'I'll have the chaise brought round, Poppy. I'll drive you myself.'

'Where's the motor car?' Lottie demanded suspiciously. 'You haven't broken it already, have you?'

Adam pulled a face. 'It wasn't my fault. Anyway, the other fellow's motor car came off worst. Dulcinea is being treated by a qualified mechanic.'

'You gave your motor car a name?' Poppy stared at him in amazement.

'Dulcinea was Don Quixote's ideal woman, if I remember rightly, but she only existed in his mind.' Lottie laughed. 'You see, Adam. I do recall some things my governess tried to drum into my head.'

'Be quiet, Lottie. You're not funny,' Adam said crossly. 'I can give my motor a name if I want. Dulcinea just came to mind.'

Poppy could see an argument about to erupt into a full-blown quarrel. 'It's a very pretty name. I don't see why a motor car shouldn't have a name. It moves along and it breathes out fumes – it's almost human.'

'I'll order the chaise.' Adam left the room before Lottie had a chance to respond.

'I didn't offend you, did I, Poppy?' Adam asked urgently as he helped her into the chaise. 'I do say things without thinking occasionally.'

Poppy settled down on the seat and waited while he climbed in and took the reins. 'I wasn't offended. I know you were teasing me.'

He encouraged the horse to walk on. 'I do want to marry you, Poppy. I've always thought we would end up together. At least, I hoped you might come to love me.'

'I do love you, Adam. I always have, but perhaps not in the way you want. I'm not the bride for you.'

He shot her a sideways glance. 'Isn't that for me to decide?'

'Perhaps, but I don't see myself as an army wife, staying at home with the children while my husband risks his life for Queen and Country.' Poppy reached out to lay her hand on his as he grasped the reins. 'I'm sorry, Adam. I care for you too much to risk making your life miserable.'

'And yet you're willing to break my heart now.'

'I think,' Poppy said slowly, 'in fact, I am sure that you love army life more than anything or anyone. I couldn't compete, nor would I want to.'

'But it's my career now.'

'That is what I am trying to say, Adam.'

'It's Taverner, isn't it? You're in love with him, but you won't admit it.'

Poppy clasped her hands, instinctively protecting the Taverner ring. 'That's not true.'

'Then why are you still wearing that diamond ring? You can't wait to get back to him, and that's the truth.' Adam flicked the whip over the horse's head and the startled animal broke into a trot, sending pedestrians scurrying out of their path.

'Now you're being childish,' Poppy said crossly. 'You can drop me off here and I'll walk the rest of the way.'

'I'm not leaving you on your own in this part of London,' Adam said through gritted teeth. 'You've made your feelings very clear, Poppy.'

'No, Adam, I haven't made you understand at all. I do care for you very much, and I want you to be happy, but if you married me it would be a disaster for both of us.'

'I don't agree.' Adam stared straight ahead and Poppy knew better than to argue with him.

They drove on in silence until Adam drew the horse to a halt outside the house in Fournier Street. Poppy had barely alighted when the front door opened and Mrs Kent hurried to meet them.

'I'm glad you're home, miss. I have a message for you from his lordship.'

'What is it, Mrs Kent? What's happened? Is Davy all right?'

'The boy was driving me mad, so his lordship took Davy with him.'

'Where have they gone? What happened, Mrs Kent?' Poppy clutched the side of the chaise for support, all her senses alert. Something really bad must have occurred. 'Tell me, please.'

'There's been trouble at your home, miss. A police constable came with a message from his lordship. He couldn't tell me much but his lordship said you need to go to Rainbow's End right away.'

Adam leaped down from the driver's seat. He put his arm around Poppy. 'It's all right. Don't worry, I'll take you there now.'

'But what sort of trouble?' Poppy asked dazedly. 'Are my parents all right?'

Mrs Kent wrung her hands and her lips trembled. 'There was a fire, miss. I'm sorry I don't know anything more.'

Adam lifted Poppy off her feet and practically threw her into the chaise. He jumped up to take the reins. He tipped his cap to Mrs Kent. 'Thank you, ma'am. We'll get there as quickly as possible.'

'What can have happened, Adam?' Poppy asked anxiously. 'Can't you make that animal go any faster?'

The traffic grew lighter when they left the city and the roads were relatively clear on the way to Rainbow's End. Adam was a considerate driver and he tried to spare the poor horse as much as he could, despite Poppy's obvious agitation.

A pall of black smoke met them when they drove past Nine Oaks. The lane onwards was blocked by a horse-drawn fire engine and a crowd of smoke-blackened estate workers and villagers who had, according to the fireman in charge, formed a human chain to fetch water from the river.

'My parents. Where are they?' Poppy fought down a feeling of hysteria as she looked in vain for her mother and father. She was about to push past the fire officer, but he restrained her.

'You can't go in there, miss. It's too dangerous. The roof has fallen in and the fire could break out again. We have to keep damping everything down.'

'But my parents – are they safe? Is Taverner here?' Poppy struggled to control the urge to scream their names.

'Miss Poppy.' A childish voice cut through the low babble of voices and Davy charged between the firemen, keeping his head down and butting anyone who got in his way.

Poppy ran towards him and scooped him up in her arms. 'Are you hurt, Davy?'

His face was streaked with soot but his grin was wide and as cheeky as ever. 'Mr Eddie sent me to fetch you.' He grabbed Poppy by the hand. 'Come with me.'

'You can't go that way, miss.' The chief fireman barred their way.

'Let them through, Officer.' Adam came up behind Poppy and Davy. 'The boy seems to know a safe path.'

The fire chief saluted reluctantly. 'Very well, sir. But you must take responsibility for their safety.'

'Lead on, young man,' Adam said, patting Davy on the back.

Davy darted off and Poppy had to run in order to keep up with him, but he seemed confident that the way was safe and he led them round the side of the smouldering building to the stable block. There were even more weary volunteers sitting or standing around, and all of them looked exhausted. There was a murmur of acknowledgement from them as Poppy rushed past but all she could think about was her parents and Taverner.

Davy disappeared into the coach house, followed by Poppy and Adam. The acrid smell of smoke had reached even this far, but Poppy uttered a cry of relief when she saw her parents seated side by side on a wooden bench. She barely recognised Taverner, who was leaning against the wall. His face and arms were blackened by smoke, as were his clothes. A tear in his shirt revealed a raw-looking burn on the back of his left shoulder, and his hands were bleeding.

Poppy looked round in desperation. 'Has anyone sent for the doctor?' She laid her hand on Taverner's arm. 'Your poor hands, Eddie.'

He managed a tired smile. 'They'll heal. At least we are all safe.'

'You risked your life for my family.' Poppy stroked his cheek with the tip of her finger. 'Thank you, Eddie.'

'Take care of your parents. They need you.' Taverner raised her hand to his lips and brushed it with a kiss. 'I'm all right, Poppy. Don't worry about me.'

'Poppy, my dear girl.' Daniel rose from the bench and moved towards her. He too was covered in soot but he seemed to be unhurt. He wrapped Poppy in an emotional hug.

'Pa. I'm so glad you aren't injured.' Poppy reached up to kiss his cheek, leaving a clean mark on his dirty face. She broke away to hurry to her mother's side and sat down beside her.

'Are you all right, Ma? Are you hurt?' Poppy put an arm gently around her mother's shoulders.

'I don't think so, darling. I twisted my ankle, but your father carried me to safety. It all happened so quickly.'

Adam had been standing quietly in the doorway but he moved forward to shake Daniel's hand.

'I'm so glad you're safe, sir. You must bring Aunt Flora to Nine Oaks. Our home is at your disposal for as long as it suits you.'

'Thank you, sir. That's very kind.' Daniel dashed his hand across his eyes. 'Everyone rallied to help us. I'll never forget it.'

'What about you, Taverner?' Adam demanded stiffly. 'You look as though you've been doing your bit.'

'He's a hero, that's what he is.' Davy hurried to Taverner's side. 'He saved everyone from the fire.'

'Where is Mrs Burden?' Poppy glanced at her father. 'And Ivy and Meg. Were they in the house, and how did the fire start?'

'I think Mrs Burden's daughter has taken her in,' Flora said wearily. 'The others had already gone home when that madman burst into the house.'

'What madman?' Poppy looked to her father for an answer, but he closed his eyes, and shook his head.

'It was Mulliner.' Taverner's voice shook with anger. 'I came here to let your parents know that you would be staying at Domesday House until after the funeral. I happened to be in the kitchen with Davy when he entered the house.'

'I thought he was in prison,' Poppy said faintly. 'Why did he come here?'

'He was granted bail.' Daniel wiped a grimy hand across his forehead. 'He came looking for trouble. He started with us and was going on to wreck Nine Oaks, apparently in revenge for being caught out in his crimes.'

'The fellow knew he would go to prison,' Taverner added tersely. 'He decided to make you all suffer.'

'But did he get to Nine Oaks?' Poppy looked from one to the other.

'I arrived just in time to stop him.' Taverner shook his head. 'But he had already set fire to your home, Poppy. I am so sorry.'

'No need to be sorry, sir,' Daniel said quickly. 'You caught the rat and handed him to the constable, and you saved Flora and me, as well as Mrs Burden. You don't need to apologise for anything.'

'That's right,' Flora added tiredly. 'Things would have ended quite differently had you not turned up when you did.'

'Don't forget me, missis.' Davy wagged his small finger at Flora. 'I run to the village to get help.'

'You did, so.' Taverner ruffled Davy's curly hair. 'You did well, boy.'

'You were very brave.' Poppy leaned over to kiss Davy on the cheek, which he instantly rubbed away, leaving a comical smear on his face.

'What will we do now?' Flora reached out to her husband. 'Daniel, we've lost everything. I doubt if there's anything to be saved from the embers. We're ruined.'

Chapter Twenty-Five

Daniel sank down on the hard wooden bench and wrapped his arms around Flora.

'We will rebuild eventually, my love.'

'We only have the clothes we're wearing now,' Flora said on a sob. 'And look at the state of us.'

Poppy moved closer to Adam, who was watching with a concerned look on his handsome features. 'Did you mean that about my parents staying at Nine Oaks?'

'Of course I did. I'll take them now in the chaise. I'll come back for you.'

'That won't be necessary, but thank you, anyway. I could walk if needs must, but are you quite sure that your mother and father won't mind?'

Adam gave her a pitying look. 'Come on, now, Poppy. You know my family better than that. My pa will take care of them until they get back on their feet. Maybe there's a cottage on the estate they can have, but in the meantime you will be our guests.'

'You're such a good friend, Adam.'

He pulled a face. 'That's not what I want to be, but I suppose it will have to do. You're not going to change your mind, are you?'

Poppy shook her head. It hurt her to dash his hopes yet again, but she could not lie. 'I'm so sorry, Adam.'

'I could tell by the way you looked at Taverner just now that he is the one you really care for.'

There was no bitterness in Adam's voice but the truth of what he had said hit Poppy like a physical blow, leaving her momentarily lost for words.

'I'll always have a special place in my heart for you, Poppy. I'm not saying it's easy to let you go, but all I want is for you to be happy.' Adam kissed her on the cheek before turning away. He walked over to where Daniel and Flora were sitting. 'Would you care to come with me now? I'll take you to Nine Oaks, but I'll have to leave straight away.'

He was being so magnanimous that Poppy had to fight back tears. 'Won't it make you late back at the barracks?' she asked anxiously.

'Don't worry about me, Poppy. You know I get away with everything. Anyway, I have someone who will cover for me if I'm not too late.' Adam helped Flora to her feet. 'You'll feel better after a warm bath and a change of clothes, ma'am. My mama and sister have wardrobes filled with garments and I know they would tell you to take your choice.'

Flora managed a watery smile. 'Thank you, Adam. You always were a dear boy.'

'It's very good of you, sir.' Daniel smiled wearily. 'I knew that we were dealing with a madman when it came to Mulliner, but I never thought it would end like this.'

Poppy flung her arms around her father's neck. 'Don't give up, Pa. We'll rebuild Rainbow's End.'

Daniel held her at arm's length, his eyes filled with tears. 'We've worked so hard to make the restaurant and gardens a success, love. Maybe the old name for the house was a warning we shouldn't have ignored.'

'I thought it has always been called Rainbow's End, Pa.'

'It was known as Hope's End.' Daniel brushed his torn shirtsleeve across his eyes. 'It was an omen.'

'Come now, sir,' Taverner said brusquely. 'You don't believe in that mumbo-jumbo. You own the land and the beautiful gardens. I know you will think of this as a mere set-back when you have recovered from the shock of what has happened.'

'Of course you will, Pa.' Poppy gave her father's hand a squeeze. 'Take Ma and go with Adam. There's nothing you can do here.'

Flora leaned heavily on Adam's arm. 'Poppy is right, Dan. We should go to Nine Oaks.'

Poppy stood aside while her parents followed Adam towards the chaise, and she waited until they were safely ensconced in the vehicle. They had always

449

been so strong and resolute, even in hard times, but now they looked overwhelmed and exhausted. She turned to Taverner and was shocked by the pallor that a coating of soot could not quite disguise.

'You really need medical attention, Eddie. Shall I take you and Davy to Nine Oaks? I can drive your motor car.'

'I've given a statement to the police,' Taverner said tiredly. 'We'll go back to Fournier Street. Mrs Kent is terrifyingly efficient when it comes to dressing wounds of all types.'

'I'm not sure I like the sound of that.' Poppy beckoned to Davy. 'You won't try to run away again if we return to Fournier Street?'

'Nah,' Davy said stoutly. 'I'm hungry and the old lady is a good cook.' He put his head on one side. 'Are you really going to drive, miss?'

Poppy smiled. 'I most certainly am.'

'I have sore fingers. That doesn't mean I can't handle the steering wheel.' Taverner walked slowly towards his motor car, which was parked a little way from the barn, but Poppy ran ahead. She had cranked the engine and jumped into the driver's seat before he reached the vehicle. Davy jumped into the back seat, urging her to drive off at speed.

'Get in, please, Eddie.' Poppy met his stern gaze with a bright smile. 'I promise you will be safe in my hands. I am a very competent driver.'

Reluctantly Taverner lowered himself into the passenger seat. Poppy was quick to notice the spasm

of pain he suffered as the burn on his back touched
the leather, but he said nothing. She drove off and
was determined to prove to him that she was at
least as good behind the wheel as he, although she
did not expect him to acknowledge the fact. Davy
fell asleep almost immediately, and Taverner sat in
silence. Poppy was so busy concentrating on the
road ahead that she was grateful that he refrained
from commenting on her progress.

When they finally arrived at the house in Fournier
Street she turned to him with a smile.

'At least I didn't mow anyone down, Eddie.'

'You are a very good driver. Thank you, Poppy.'
Taverner opened the door with difficulty. 'You were
right. I couldn't have driven this far.' He climbed
out with a muffled groan. 'It seems a pity to wake
the boy,' he added, staring down at Davy, who was
curled up on the back seat.

Poppy stepped out of the car and leaned over to
lift Davy into her arms. He was so sound asleep that
he did not wake up, even when she laid him on the
sofa in the front parlour. Mrs Kent was hovering
in the background making distressed noises like an
agitated mother hen.

'Mr Eddie, I don't like the look of those burns.
What have you done to yourself, sir?'

'He rescued my parents and our cook from the
flames,' Poppy said proudly. 'Unfortunately the
building was razed to the ground, but it can be
rebuilt. Thanks to Eddie, everyone was saved.'

Mrs Kent gazed at Davy, who was snoring loudly. 'The boy is unharmed?'

'He's just exhausted,' Poppy said, trying not to smile. Perhaps Mrs Kent did have a soft spot for the naughty child.

'If you take care of him I will look after the master.' Mrs Kent stood, arms akimbo, glaring at Taverner as if daring him to refuse.

'I would be grateful, Mrs Kent,' Taverner said meekly. 'The burns sting like the devil.'

'Into the back room with you, sir. We'll have that shirt off first and then I'll fetch warm water, liniment and bandages.' She hustled Taverner from the room, closing the door firmly behind her. Poppy took the hint, realising that her presence during Taverner's treatment would not be welcome. She sat in a chair by the window, overcome by a sudden feeling of exhaustion. So much had happened in the last twenty-four hours that it was hard to know what was uppermost in her mind. She had turned down an offer of marriage from Adam, who had been the love of her young life, and the home in which she had been born and raised had burned to the ground. Almost without knowing it she had taken on responsibility for a small child and she was about to give the Taverner ring back to the man who had placed it on her finger. She could not in all conscience return to Domesday House now that her parents needed her, and her efforts to help the destitute children would have to be put aside until such time as she was free to concentrate on fund raising. And to make everything even more complicated, she would have to part from the man she had come to love more than life itself.

The drive back to London had been a distraction, but now, sitting in the quiet front parlour, she found herself overwhelmed with the disaster that had befallen her parents. A lifetime of hard work had quite literally gone up in smoke, leaving them homeless if not actually penniless. Poppy barely noticed the time passing as she struggled to come to terms with the day's events, but she came back to the present with a start as the door opened and Taverner walked into the room. The tell-tale traces of soot had been washed from his face and he had changed his clothes. Apart from his bandaged hands there was no outward sign of the damage from his dramatic dash into the burning building.

'Are you all right, Poppy?' Taverner gave her a searching look. 'You've had a terrible shock, but at least everyone escaped unhurt.'

Poppy nodded. 'Yes, I'm grateful for that. I'm just concerned for my parents. I don't know how to help them.'

'They can rebuild Rainbow's End if they have insurance. Do you know if that's the case?'

'I don't know, but I hope they have made provision for such a disastrous occurrence.' Poppy jumped to her feet. 'I forgot the funds I raised at the fashion show. I had a leather pouch filled with money for the orphanage, Eddie. I must have dropped it somewhere.'

He smiled. 'Mrs Kent found it on a chair in the entrance hall. She put it in the laundry basket for safety.'

'The laundry basket?' Poppy said dazedly. 'Why did she do that?'

'Her reasoning is that it's the last place a robber would look, and I think she might have something there.' Taverner laid his hands gently on Poppy's shoulders. 'Don't distress yourself, my love. We will work out something for your parents. I have many contacts in the city and with various trades. If they want to start again, I can help.'

Poppy felt herself melting in the warmth of his gaze. 'Thank you, Eddie. That means a lot to me, especially right now. I've lost the only home I've ever known and my parents are shocked beyond measure.'

'You will never be homeless if I have anything to do with it, Poppy. You're still wearing my ring and I want to keep it that way for the rest of our lives.'

'I don't understand. What are you saying?' Poppy lowered her head and closed her eyes, as a wave of dizziness swept over her. 'It's all too much for me to deal with right now.'

'Look at me, Poppy.' Taverner raised her chin with the tip of his index finger. 'That's the only reason I'm not going down on one knee and begging you to be my wife. But when the time is right and you are fully yourself, I will do it properly and that is a solemn promise.'

'I'm hungry.' A small voice from the sofa brought Poppy back to earth.

'It's all right, Davy. Mr Edward and I were just talking.' With great reluctance she moved away from Taverner's warm grasp.

'You was cuddling,' Davy said judicially. 'But that's all right. I like both of you. I wouldn't mind if you was me ma and pa.'

The tender mood was broken, but Poppy noted the twinkle in Taverner's expressive eyes and she laughed. 'Stay there, you cheeky boy. I'll go and see if Mrs Kent has some food for you.' She left the parlour but Taverner followed her.

'Davy has a good point,' he said softly. 'However, I'm afraid I will have to leave you here for a while, Poppy. I need to return to Domesday House.'

'I'm sorry, Eddie. I'd forgotten that it's your papa's funeral on Friday. Of course you must go. I should be there too, if only for your mama's sake.'

'But don't you want to be with your parents?'

'I do, most certainly, but they will be well cared for at Nine Oaks. Ma grew up there with Aunt Bella. They are more like sisters than just friends, and Pa's father was the head gardener. They are as much at home at Nine Oaks as they were at Rainbow's End.'

'Of course I want you with me, Poppy. But what about the boy?'

Poppy thought quickly. 'We can't leave him here.

455

That wouldn't be fair on Mrs Kent or Davy. We can take him with us. He will be able to run free with plenty of people to keep an eye on him so that he doesn't get into trouble.'

Taverner eyed her warily. 'Poppy, darling, you aren't thinking of turning Domesday House into an orphanage, are you?'

'The thought never occurred to me, Eddie.'

'Can I really go to your house in the country, guvnor?' Davy sidled out of the parlour.

Taverner ruffled Davy's curls. 'Do you promise to be good? You won't run away like you did when Mrs Kent tried to look after you?'

'Cross me heart and hope to die, guvnor.' Davy tugged at Poppy's arm. 'I can smell sausages frying, miss. I'm bloomin' starving.'

'We'll eat and then we must leave for Devonshire,' Taverner said firmly. 'I would drive but my hands are too painful.' He glanced at Poppy, shaking his head with a smile. 'I know you would love to take the wheel, but it's too far, and driving in the dark is hazardous. We'll take the train.'

Poppy would have liked to take the wheel again, but what Taverner said made sense so she nodded. 'All right, Eddie. I'd better write a note to my parents. They have enough problems without me adding to them by going to Devonshire without letting them know.' Poppy ushered Davy into the dining room.

* * *

Lord Taverner of Oakley's funeral was a quiet affair. Poppy realised then that he might have been well known, but it was obvious that he had not been a popular member of the community. Lady Taverner, on the other hand, attracted much sympathy and the ladies who organised local fêtes, festivals and made the flower arrangements to adorn the church outdid themselves. The cool interior of the Norman building was redolent with the scent of garden flowers, and the pews filled with those closest to the remaining family. Lady Taverner managed to greet her old friends and received such a warm welcome that Poppy felt tears stinging the backs of her eyes.

When the ceremony ended the house servants and outside workers filed out of the church into the late summer sunshine. There were no arrangements for any kind of reception at Domesday House and, having said the goodbyes in hushed voices, the mourners dispersed. Poppy and Taverner walked back to the house, while Ned drove Lady Taverner and Miss Hayes in the family carriage. The servants followed on at a respectful distance. The only lively person was Davy, who skipped on ahead, darting off now and then to chase a bold squirrel or a cheeky blackbird.

Dinner that evening was served in the dining room with Taverner at the head of the table. Lady Taverner chose to sit on his right and Poppy sat opposite. It was a simple meal of onion soup followed by roast chicken and all the accompaniments, with an apple pie for dessert. Jessie might not be a fancy cook, but everything she sent to the table was well-seasoned and delicious.

Taverner put his plate aside as he leaned closer to his mother. 'You are being very brave, Mama. You must say if all this is too much for you.'

'No, dear. I won't say I've enjoyed today, but it was good to be out and about again. I allowed Whiddon to dominate me for too long. I see that now.'

'It was not your fault, ma'am,' Poppy said hastily. 'She was keeping you sedated so that you had little choice in the matter. Now you are free.'

'Thanks to you, Poppy.' Lady Taverner smiled and patted Poppy's hand. 'I would not dream of interfering,' she added, looking pointedly at her son, 'but I see the Taverner ring is still being worn. Am I to take that as a good sign, Eddie?'

'I'm optimistic, Mama,' Taverner said with a hint of a smile. 'But I want Poppy to be free to make up her own mind without any pressure from anyone, least of all me.'

Poppy laughed. 'I am here listening to you both.' She squeezed Lady Taverner's hand. 'More important than that, how are you feeling, ma'am? How will you cope when Eddie has to return to London?'

'I will manage, Poppy. It won't be easy, but thanks to you I have most of my old servants restored to me. I rely on them for everything.'

Taverner frowned. 'That puts me in a bad light. I am your only son and I should be taking care of you now that Papa is no longer with us. I won't leave you to the mercy of the servants again, Mama, good though they may be.'

'Does that mean you will spend more time here?' Poppy asked cautiously.

Taverner rose to his feet. 'I suppose it does. If you'll excuse me, Mama, I need to think and I'd like to go for a walk and smoke a cigar.'

'Of course, my dear. Your papa loved a good cigar after dinner.' Lady Taverner raised herself from her chair. 'Shall we adjourn to the drawing room for coffee, just like we used to in the old days before Whiddon spread her poison throughout the house?'

Taverner proffered his arm. 'Allow me, Mama. I'll see you to the drawing room before I go for a walk with my Punch Clasico cigar. You will have nothing to worry about from now on, I promise you that.'

It was not yet dark when Lady Taverner wearied and Miss Hayes took her upstairs to her room, leaving Poppy free to do as she pleased. Davy had been put to bed earlier, having worn himself out, and a quick check on him proved that he was sound asleep in the room adjacent to her own. Poppy decided to go for a walk and she took a shawl from the cupboard, wrapping it around her shoulders. It was a fine night, but a chilly wind rustled the leaves in the trees. She caught a waft of Havana cigar smoke and as she walked towards the lake she could see Taverner's tall figure outlined against the darkening sky. Her heart did a little skip of sheer pleasure at the sight of him and she quickened her pace.

He looked round and with a final puff of fragrant smoke he tossed the butt into the water.

'Is everything all right, Poppy?'

'Your mama has gone to bed. She's exhausted after everything that's happened, and so is Davy. He is sound asleep.'

'And how are you? After everything you've been through recently you have a right to feel a little tired.'

The tender concern in his voice was not lost on Poppy and she swallowed hard. 'I am fine, thank you, Eddie. It's odd, but I feel calmer here at Domesday House than anywhere else. I would never have believed it after my first impressions of the old place.'

He slipped his arm around her shoulders and drew her to him. 'This could all be yours, my darling. I've always thought of Domesday House as a burden rather than a blessing, but you've changed all that. I don't know how you've achieved it, but it seems that just your presence here has had an amazing effect. I'm beginning to see everything differently.'

'I don't know why that is,' Poppy said breathlessly. 'I've done nothing.'

'You've shown me where I belong, Poppy. Before I met you I looked at my heritage as something to be avoided at all costs. I went to great lengths to make money, even if it was not strictly legal or even moral.'

'I can't believe that, Eddie. You spent time with the orphans and you raised money to make their lives better. Don't tell me you are a bad man because I won't believe you.' Poppy laid her hands on his chest and she could feel his heartbeat racing. 'You are a good man.'

He shook his head. 'No, I am flawed, but you make me into the best person I can be. I don't want to lose you, Poppy.' Taverner clutched her left hand and raised it to his lips. 'For some odd reason you have not discarded my ring. I know I've said all this but now I am ready to accept my title and the responsibility for the land and the lives of those who depend on me. I love you, Poppy. I can't do all this without you.' He held her at arm's length before sinking down onto one knee. His face was pale in the dying rays of the sun but his eyes were alight with tenderness.

'I love you more than anything else in the world, Poppy. Will you marry me?'

She sank to her knees and wrapped her arms around his neck. Their lips met in a pledge of love and burning desire. When at last she could breathe again, Poppy managed a smile.

'Yes, Eddie. With all my heart.'

He lifted her to her feet and they walked very slowly through the darkening shadows to the house.

* * *

Next day Taverner announced their engagement first to his mother, then Davy, who jumped around almost bouncing off the walls for sheer joy. Then Taverner addressed the assembled household and gave them the good news. There was clapping, even a few cheers from Ned and Bert, and congratulations all round. When the excitement died down Taverner explained that he had to return to London to finish off important business, but he would return the next day or as soon as humanly possible. Poppy had agreed to remain at Domesday House in order to look after Lady Taverner and Davy.

Poppy made Eddie promise to visit her parents at Nine Oaks to explain why she had remained in Devonshire. It was hard to part with Eddie now that they had admitted their love for each other, but she knew he must have something important to do in London and for that she was not needed. It would be hard to wait, but it was only for a short time.

Three days later Davy was outside playing with a ball that Ned had given him. Poppy was watching from the drawing-room window and she smiled to see him so happy. Then the smile on her lips turned into a gasp of astonishment. She ran to the front door and flung it open. She stepped outside to see what looked like a procession of vehicles. Eddie was at the front, driving his motor car with Mrs Kent in the passenger seat. Behind him was Adam, driving his car, with Lottie at his side and Gideon Taylor in the back seat. Several carriages came behind, one of which had a lozenge bearing the Dorrington coat of arms on the door. Just when Poppy thought she had seen the last in the procession, there were three large carters' vans pulled by handsome dray horses.

Eddie drew the motor car to a halt in front of the house. Davy was the first to reach him. He hugged Mrs Kent as she climbed out of the car, almost knocking off her hat. Poppy went down the steps more slowly and walked into a fierce embrace.

'I can't believe how much I've missed you, Poppy,' Eddie said a low voice.

She looked into his eyes and smiled mistily. 'Me, too. Let's stay together from now on.'

'That's all been arranged.' With his arm still around her waist, Eddie turned and encompassed the visitors with a gesture. 'We are going to hold a grand wedding here at Domesday House. I've brought everyone who matters to us both.'

Poppy uttered a cry of delight as her parents alighted from one of the carriages. She ran to them and hugged each of them in turn. 'I'm so happy to see you and you're looking so much better.'

Daniel kissed Poppy on the cheek. 'I had to come to give my only daughter away.'

'I couldn't be happier for you, darling,' Flora said, hugging Poppy. 'We're all here. Your uncle Amos is in one of the carriages with Begg. Bella and Freddie are here, too, as are Amelia and Todd. Amelia has given you one of her model wedding gowns complete with a veil and shoes.'

'Are you still at Nine Oaks, Mama?' Poppy asked anxiously. 'There is plenty of room here if you do not wish to remain so close to what was Rainbow's End.'

'We have the cottage where your pa was born and raised. It is rather lovely and so very peaceful. I am quite content at the moment, and Edward has been wonderful.'

'I know that, but what has he done, Mama?'

Eddie had been directing the flow of carriages but he came towards them in long strides. 'That was to be a secret, Flora. However, it's my wedding present to you, Poppy.'

'What have you done, Eddie?' Poppy stared at him dazedly. Suddenly Domesday House had come alive with visitors clamouring for attention and workmen unloading what appeared to be marquees onto the grassy sward in front of the house.

Daniel slapped Eddie on the back. 'He's only gone and bought Rainbow's End, what's left of it. You tell her, old boy.'

'I am using my ill-gotten gains to build a home for destitute children, Poppy, my love. It won't be an orphanage as such, it will take the slightly older orphans like Davy and give them a good home, but they will be taught a trade. Your father is going to organise horticultural lessons, your mother and your uncle Amos are going to teach cooking, and we will involve other tradesmen, too.'

464

'But it's your home, Ma,' Poppy said anxiously. 'Are you sure you agree to this?'

Daniel placed his arm around Flora's shoulders. 'We're not getting any younger, Poppy love. Freddie has given us the lease on the cottage where I was born.'

'We have a place of our own now, Poppy, and enough money to keep us in comfort,' Flora added, smiling. 'We can work shorter hours but still be part of Rainbow's End.'

'You're not putting me in a home, are you, guvnor?' Davy as usual had somehow managed to overhear the conversation.

Eddie ruffled his hair. 'You'd best ask the future Lady Taverner.'

Davy's eyes widened. 'Who?'

'It's me, Davy.' Poppy gave him a hug. 'Of course you will stay here and live with us. You will always be my boy.' She turned to Eddie with a happy smile. 'You did all that for me?'

'This is just the start, my love. I've got a Special Licence so that we can get married tomorrow. The vicar has agreed and all our guests are here.'

Poppy looked to her mother. 'But we need food for all these people, and wine.'

'Of course,' Flora said smugly. 'We have brought it all with us. Eddie spared no expense. Now may we come inside? Your guests are queuing almost as far as the gates.'

* * *

The next morning Flora and Amelia helped Poppy into her wedding gown and veil. Daniel had brought flowers from the gardens at Rainbow's End for her bouquet and one for Lottie, who had also been dressed by Amelia. Davy was persuaded to be the page boy, which he did with great solemnity. The church, which only a few days previously had been the site of a solemn funeral, was filled with flowers. The ladies of the village had been called upon with only a few hours' notice, but they had responded magnificently.

Poppy walked down the aisle on her father's arm to meet Eddie at the altar. She was surprised and delighted to see Adam acting as his best man. It meant he had forgiven her for refusing his proposal. Losing one of her dearest friends would have been a high price to pay for the happiness she was certain she would have with the man she loved and trusted with her life.

The ceremony over, they signed the register before processing down the aisle to emerge into bright sunshine and cheering crowds. It seemed that the whole village had turned out to welcome the happy couple. Eddie invited them all back to Domesday House to celebrate in the three huge marquees that had been erected overnight.

The party began the moment they arrived back in the grounds decorated by Chinese lanterns and bunting. A small orchestra played beneath the trees, and the servants, all in their Sunday best, served champagne to the guests, after which Eddie told them they could join in the party and everyone would help themselves from the buffet set out in the largest marquee.

The Dowager Lady Taverner, having already added her heartfelt congratulations, was settled in a comfortable chair in the shade, waited on by the faithful Miss Hayes.

Poppy was surrounded by her friends and family, and Eddie practically had to fight his way to get to her side. Finally he did so as the orchestra struck up a lively country dance and couples began to whirl around to the music.

Eddie held out his hand. 'May I have this dance, Lady Taverner?'

'It would be my pleasure, sir.' Poppy slipped into his arms and she knew now she had come home at last.

Dilly Court

Discover more from the nation's favourite author of historical drama.

Sign up to Dilly Court's email newsletter or follow her on Facebook to hear about new books, exclusive competitions and special offers

Join the community:
https://smarturl.it/DillyCourt

🌐 www.dillycourt.com   👤 dillycourtauthor

The Rockwood Chronicles

High upon the beautiful cliffs of the Devonshire coast, the once proud
Rockwood Castle is crumbling into ruin. Can the Carey family save
their home and their family before it's too late?

In this spellbinding six-book series, Dilly Court opens a door into Rockwood Castle –
chronicling the changing fortunes of the Carey family...

Book One: Fortune's Daughter

Abandoned by her parents, headstrong Rosalind must take
charge of the family. Until the appearance of dashing
Piers Blanchard threatens to ruin everything...

Book Two: Winter Wedding

Christmas is coming and Rockwood Castle has once again been thrown into
turmoil. As snowflakes fall, can Rosalind protect her beloved home?

Book Three: Runaway Widow

It is time for the youngest Carey sister, Patricia, to seek out her own
future. But without her family around her, will she lose her way?

Book Four: Sunday's Child

Taken in by the Carey family when she was a young girl,
Nancy Sunday has never known her true parentage.
Now eighteen years old, can she find out where she truly belongs?

Book Five: Snow Bride

The course of true love does not run straight for Nancy. Her life is filled with difficult
choices – but with Christmas around the corner, which path will she choose?

Book Six: Dolly's Dream

The eldest daughter at Rockwood, Dolly, dreams of a bigger life
beyond the castle walls. But with the family's future under threat,
will Dolly's heart lead her astray – or bring her home?

Don't miss another exciting instalment of
The Rockwood Chronicles, Book Seven:

The Lucky Penny

Flora is forever grateful for the day the Stewart family
rescued her from her life of poverty on London's streets.
Adopted as one of their own, she shed her rags and was
finally given a place to call home.

When a twist of fate calls her back to the cobbles,
Flora's new life is torn apart.

**Flora must make her own way if
she is ever to find where she truly belongs . . .**

If you love Dilly's books and haven't discovered
The Rockwood Chronicles yet, read on for an
extract of Fortune's Daughter

Chapter One

Rockwood Castle, Devonshire, May 1839

'Wait for me, Bertie.' Eight-year-old Rosalind Carey stumbled over the rocks in the cove as she tried in vain to keep up with her elder brother. The moon had vanished behind a bank of clouds, throwing the beach into a sea of shadows, and a south-westerly had blown in from the Atlantic, hurling waves onto the shore. All Rosalind could see were the white soles of Bertie's bare feet as he scampered towards the cliffs, leaping across pools of salt water like a mountain goat. Suddenly he was gone and she was alone in the darkness with the waves crashing on the foreshore as the incoming tide swallowed up the strand. She could hear the shouts of men riding the waves in a small boat as they prepared to leap out and drag it onto the shore. There were flashes of light from oil lamps in the mouth of the cave that had been carved into the red sandstone by centuries of high tides, where local men prepared to receive the bounty from the sea. It had been her brother's idea to catch the smugglers red-handed, but she realised now that it had been the foolhardy boast of a twelve-year-old boy who should have known better.

The voices were getting closer and she could hear the keel of the boat grinding on the pebbles as it reached land. She glanced over her shoulder and the clouds parted, allowing a shaft of moonlight to reveal the men dragging kegs and tubs onto the beach.

'Bertie,' she cried on a sob, 'where are you?' But her brother had disappeared into the scrubby foliage that grew at the base of the cliff and she knew that she was on her own. With a last burst of energy, but hampered by her wet skirts, she tried to follow him. If she could reach the cliff path that led to Rockwood land she would be safe. Then the sudden staccato report of a gun being fired from the cliff top was followed by the barked orders of the preventive men. Rosalind made a grab for the branch of a thorn bush, but it snapped, sending her tumbling backwards onto the hard-packed sand and stones. Stunned and winded, she lay there gasping for breath.

'Don't make a sound.' A hand clamped over her mouth and she was pinned to the ground by a warm body. His face was close to hers and he smelled of the sea. 'I'll take my hand off your mouth if you promise not to scream.'

She nodded vigorously.

'Are you hurt?'

'I don't know.'

'Keep very still or they'll see us.'

Rosalind had little option but to nod again, sensing that she was not in any danger from the boy, who had appeared as if from nowhere. She could feel a trickle of warm blood running down her cheek from a cut on her head. Her rescuer edged further into the shadows, dragging her with him, and she looked up, following his gaze as he watched the men push the boat back into the foaming waves and leap on board. More shots were fired, but they missed their mark, and Rosalind found herself hoping that the smugglers would get away. The lights had been extinguished in the cave and no doubt those who had been waiting to collect the contraband would be well on their way to safety. Rosalind knew all the cliff paths, and the exploits of the smugglers were legendary. Tales of their brushes with the law circulated from below stairs to the Carey family, who had owned Rockwood Castle since the eleventh century. Hester, the housekeeper, who had been part of the household ever since Rosalind could remember, had regaled them with tales of the derring-do of the free traders, and their brushes with the preventive men. Bertie and Walter had listened avidly, as had Rosalind, although Patricia, being four years her junior, had usually been tucked up in bed with Raggy, her beloved rag doll.

'Are you sure you're all right?' the boy sounded anxious.

Rosalind blinked and rubbed her eyes. She had drifted off into a daydream and her head ached, but now she was back to reality. 'Yes, I think so.' She moved away from him so that she could study his face. The moon had come out from hiding and although they were still in the protective shadow of the cliffs, she could make out his features and she was not afraid. 'Who are you? Why did they row away and leave you here?'